The Driftwood Tree

by
John E
an
Catherine Edmunds

Illustrated with original line drawings and poetry

Circaidy Gregory Press

Copyright Information

Paperback ISBN 978-1-910841-36-5
Also available in .pdf and ebook formats

Printed in the UK
by Catford Print

Published by
Circaidy Gregory Press
Creative Media Centre
45 Robertson Street
Hastings
Sussex TN34 1HL

www.circaidygregory.co.uk

Chapters

Chapter One

The Pigman of Rossdore

It was a good day to be collecting driftwood. Peder walked bare-foot across the coral sand, dragging a bleached silver birch behind him while the wind whistled round his sheepskin gilet and rattled his dun trousers. Across the estuary, villagers were working the fields, harvesting a meagre crop of oats. Living was never easy on the Kenmare banks, despite its sheltered location, but driftwood, regardless of its condition, would at least guarantee warmth during the Kerry winter.

Peder had inherited his strength and stature from someone unknown. As a lad, when he had asked who his father might be, his mother had burst into tears, remembering being raped by a gang of drunken men in Garrah. He never asked again, but one day when he was fully grown she spoke, just once, of a huge man, a fisherman, no name, no details, and simply ended the painful conversation with a throwaway, "Maybe it was him, bein' you's growin' to be a big man yourself, Peder O'Brien."

At the foot of the cliff, hidden by windswept buckthorn, Peder chopped the small tree into manageable pieces, tied the bundle with tarred rope and shouldered his lumber. His wolfhound led the way up the cliff path as the wind pelted them with stinging sand. They rested at the top to get their breath back, listening to the raucous cries of terns and kittiwakes.

"Poor ole Tam," said Peder. "You's panting like an old man. Would ye like me to carry you up to the bothy?"

gathering driftwood

Peder walks the white strand,
sand between toes, kittiwakes calling,
bleached-wood gatherer working with waves.

seas shift with the swoosh of currents, he strides
through the shallows, shakes his head
water drops, drops everywhere, skin hot-cold-wet

the hound licks the salt, tastes the sea,
wind plays, glints silver, swirls black-angry,
the hound reaches out, nuzzles his master's hand

The bothy had been constructed of the same weathered boulders that formed a dividing line between an absentee landowner's land and Kerry County's poorer acres. The building had no windows, just a rough stable-door and a hole in the roof to let the worst of the smoke out. Peder had lime-washed the walls and attempted to build a fireplace with smooth stones culled from the stream.

The ancient black-bouldered wall had been constructed countless generations ago. Peder had made a ramp of river stones, but crossing the

2

wall still took some ingenuity. Each time an animal needed to be taken to market, the beast had to be bound, placed in a net and manually lowered to the far side. Getting back was easier, requiring just rope and muscle. The wolfhound had his own route – a hole no one else could find, hidden behind the gorse.

Above the bothy, peat bog stretched endlessly as far as the eye could see, punctuated by swathes of gorse and hazel, always leaning to the east. The peaty soil, grey-green lichenous boulders, bleached grass and rushes which danced in the wind had been the backdrop to Peder's life for seventeen years, and aside from rare visits to Garrah village was the only world he had ever known.

Millicent O'Brien had borne a son despite the best efforts of the Carmelite nuns of Garrah's convent, and as was the way in Kerry, had suffered the pains of a solitary birth without even a sip of water. She had lain on filthy rags on a heather bed, hoping the child would die quickly, as the memory of rape filled her with dread, yet when that first stark cry filled the bothy she realised she desperately needed him to survive. She worried about her ability to feed him, as she was so malnourished herself, but was determined to find victuals somehow. It was springtime. There were tiny eggs in nests, feral goats full of milk, and roots and rhizomes to be grubbed from beneath moorland plants. Silken mud from the stream's bed served as soap. Twice she seized a sickly lamb and dispatched it, carefully preserving the carcass behind a cataract close to the bothy.

For years, Milly had lived a solitary existence, the black-bouldered wall marking the boundary of life itself. Occasionally, while the child slept, she would clamber over the wall in the darkness and plunder what she could from the cottars of Garrah. With time she became highly proficient in taking things that would prove useful, not that Garrah's people had much worth taking.

When Peder reached the age of six, he contracted a raging fever that would not abate. Milly sought help in Garrah, only to discover that all the children there had contracted identical symptoms – scarlet fever. The convent had closed its doors on them. The priest, Father Latchford, was nowhere to be seen, and the only physician resided in Killarney, over Mangerton Mountain, far too busy to deal with insufferable villagers. All the fishing boats had been tied up as the villagers strived to contain the deadly outbreak. Doors remained tightly closed, livestock roamed the village unattended and vermin scuttled out of drains to help themselves.

Milly hadn't seen Garrah in daylight for years, but when she walked the cobbled street, a shuttered window was flung open and a voice

3

screamed, "Scarlet woman! Damn you, Milly O'Brien, get back in your grave; you have no right to be coming here. You're dead! Leave us be!"

There would be no help in Garrah. She hurried back uphill and resolved to fight the fever in her own way, leaving the village to its own devices.

bothy

the bothy nestles in mists and mizzle, silver
cascades between wild grasses, gentian and bilberry

lower cloaked valleys rise through bent blackthorn
clouds drape the hillside, the rain smells sweet

wind-hewn rock heather-scent, pathways feeding
the heat in the heart of the peat, honeyed hills

and here sits the bothy, red-brackened
among the wind-worn bones of Kerry

One day, when he was aged thirteen, Peder's mother persuaded him to walk two dozen of their geese to market. Christmas was approaching, though it meant little to Peder. Milly worked hard to get the geese clean, well fed and looking healthy.

"There's good money in geese," she said, "but not in Kenmare. Best you tar their feet and walk 'em over the hill to Rossdore where you'll get a better price. Follow the boundary wall down to the river and cross the bridge there. It's about ten miles to Rossdore so you'll need to set off in darkness to reach it in time for the Christmas buyers."

She gave Peder some copper coins, the first he had ever handled.

"You sell 'em at three florins. No arguin'. If they bitch at the price, you tell 'em, no sale and walk away. They'll soon know you're a fair man to deal with and will come back. Florins are shiny, like oyster shells but otherwise they look like pennies. You keep these coins in your belt in case you need things to eat. I'll walk over the hill as far as the bridge and see you safely across."

"Will it be tonight?" said Peder.

"Yes – market is held on the Monday afore Christmas. I'll be waiting in the dark at Kenmare Bridge for your return, but don't take chances, mind. I'm trustin' you, Peder O'Brien. God love us and keep you safe."

They rose at midnight to the sound of the wind whispering and geese murmuring. The geese followed Peder beside the wall with Milly behind clucking softly. By the time they had crossed the river, the sky was just beginning to lighten on the horizon. A proud Milly waved to her adventurous offspring and returned to the bothy.

By ten o'clock Peder had reached the market where a helpful man, who introduced himself as Conor Connolly, penned the geese inside a wattle enclosure beside the town clock. He organised a crowd of exuberant buyers and announced the price.

"Three florins, first come, first served! Best birds in Kerry, I'll be bound."

By midday, Peder had become a successful market trader with seventy-two florins burning a hole in the pouch strung to his belt.

"You buyin'?" said Conor.

"What's to buy?" said Peder, full of enthusiasm.

"Sheep, cattle, goats, horses, poultry, pigs."

"Pigs?" said Peder, "There's pigs for sale?"

"Follow me Mister O'Brien sir."

5

At the far side of market, where the square joined the metalled road to Killarney, and Bantry, four sows and a snoring boar were resting beneath a four-wheeled dray

"God love us," said the vendor, "S'all I've got left sir, young 'uns were sold on the hoof by seven this very morning but them hogs are still unsold, so, what way are you?"

Peder watched the man's face closely.

"How much, sir?"

"Guinea each."

"Too much," said Peder. "Besides, I don't have that kind of money, I'm but a boy."

The vendor took his cap off and scratched his head.

"What do you have then?"

Ignoring him, just as Milly had advised, Peder turned on his heel. There was a busy café adjoining the square, but as he headed inside the pig vendor tapped his shoulder and said, "Four guineas and I'll gi' ye the boar for free, all found."

Peder looked the man straight in the eye.

"And how will I manage 'em?" he said.

"Turnips. I've half a sack. Jus' keep givin' 'em a few snippets an' they'll follow you anywhere. Trust me lad, an' if you're comin' again, I'll be lookin' out for you."

To Market

white geese and grey in the whispering fields:
Peder lifts his eyes to the mountain beyond,
sombre beneath the weight of clouds.

The way is clear: two stunted rowans
frame a passage to new light
across the black boulders where the blackthorn stoops.

The flock moves on among flowering grasses,
hawkweed and bracken
shivering in the early morning breeze

then wait, nervous,
wondering what lurks ahead in the shuffling gorse-drift
far from home.

6

When Peder was seventeen, Milly was caught red-handed stealing a pail from a terraced house in Herring Lane. The catcher was Ronny Dunn, a hurley player for Kenmare Town who was very much the worse for drink. He wrestled Milly to the ground and kicked her repeatedly until she lay still, bleeding profusely from the head. Within minutes, she had been drenched in the culvert that flowed down the lane and dragged to the lock-up on the quay.

Later that morning, a Catholic priest, Father Latchford addressed a seething crowd brandishing sticks and *sleans*. "So, what are we to do with her?"

The lawless mob, incited by a priest irritated at having his morning quiet hour interrupted, let it be known they would settle for nothing less than a lynching.

"The scourge! The scourge! She's the scarlet woman!"

"What say you?" said the priest, egging them on.

"Shave her head, shave the Jezebel's scarlet tresses!"

Milly was forced to her knees and systematically shorn of every trace of her heritage by a rabble of incensed women who tore her dress to ribbons and dragged her naked to the punishment post.

Fisherman Paddy Killeen tied her to the post with hemp-rope, his cap pulled down over his eyes so that he couldn't look into hers. Killeen had been one of the rapists all those years ago when Milly had been scarcely sixteen. Taking up the scourge and counting aloud, he inflicted forty strokes with the lash.

She was dead before the first twenty.

The mob took turns to spit on the lifeless naked form hanging from the punishment-post, before slinking up alleys to their cottages, some already feeling guilty at the terrible deed. A shocked and weeping nun remained to whisper a few Latin verses. The priest had hurried away, refusing to administer the last rites as it had begun to rain. By midday a storm was moving across the peninsular.

Milly

The leaden sky gives out hints of malice
as clouds sweep in, mountains in flux (a nun
looks away, and then, after the deed is done
she weeps). The mob taunts with jeers, embraces
the pain of torn flesh, the screams of gulls.

7

Milly hangs shackled and bloodied, flesh
striped and torn, dying eyes pierce the ground her feet
cannot reach. Smudges of birds fly past,
dead hope floats by on a trickle of blood.
Milly darkens into shadow, stares now with blind eyes

The priest takes a drag of his cigarette,
lifts his collar against the weather, strides away.

Peder returned from market in Rossdore after dark having sold twelve
gilts and bought his first Connemara stallion – a grey, fifteen hands high
and a bit of an oddity.

"Never look a gift horse in the gob," the seller had said. "An' if
there's any truck wi' him, I'll take him back, Peder O'Brien, no messin',
God love us."

There was no light showing in the bothy, which was unusual, as Milly
should have been at home on such a wild night, but before going to
investigate, Peder bedded the pony down under a tarpaulin for shelter
from the storm. He went indoors and lit the fire in an effort to warm the
place and sat there, restless and worried. There was no way to tell the
time, but as the storm rattled overhead, he came to a decision to find his
mother. He donned a waterproof against the furies, and accompanied by
his hounds, Dar and Kee, climbed the black wall and walked down the
winding hill to Garrah.

Peaty gullies ran beside the road and down to the troubled sea. The
storm was starting to ease, though the wind persisted under black clouds.
Garrah remained hidden behind curtains and hostile doors, afraid to reveal
itself, while Peder strode down its cobbles, now streaming with water. At
last he reached the quayside of the guilt-ridden village and came face to
face with its awful truth.

In deep shock he struggled to loosen the waterlogged ties that bound
Millie to the stake. The ropes were blooded and didn't cut easily with his
small knife. He couldn't stop crying and in his distress, the rain and
darkness, nothing made sense. It took a long time to recover her saturated
body. Her clothes were a sodden mess. After shedding his sheepskin gilet,
he took off his shirt and tried to cover her nakedness, all the while
screaming abuse at those villagers who were responsible.

Eventually, alone on the blasted quayside, he knelt beside the lifeless body and lifted Millie off the ground. She never was a great weight. Holding her close, he carried her through Herring Lane, passing closed doors and shuttered windows, all the way to the bothy, the wolfhounds following in silence.

Discovery

Peder brushes past bracken,
head bowed, close enough to Garrah
to smell its guilt.

The harbour wall stretches,
defined by a line of lobster pots,
boats and buildings merged

and so the day begins

an earthquake:
shuddering ground, splinter of timbers
masonry shivering with pain –
under the weight of water

Few knew that Milly and Peder had been mother and son. They had never gone anywhere together and on the rare occasions that Peder had been in Garrah, most considered him an itinerant tinker and avoided him. Peder had found friendship in Rossdore, and established a reputation there as an honest trader. He became known as a gentle giant, and anyone there would have befriended him, but he felt he must deal with those who had slain his mother on his own. He knew she had been a petty thief, but her butchering could never be justified as a punishment for her crimes.

The bothy remained battened down against the November gales. The eye of the storm passed over in an eerie silence. Peder donned his sheepskin gilet and sniffed the air. It was time.

"We're goin' to Garrah to deal with the devil," he told the dogs. He opened a gap in the black-bouldered wall, having rounded up two hundred sows and boars, leaving only the piglets behind in a walled enclosure. Now he strode at the head of his army like some legendary Irish chieftain. Despite the stillness, the windows of Garrah remained blinded and doors stood defiantly closed as the culvert stream hurried brown and angry, down the road. Harried by the dogs, the grunting swine now started to charge. Fences fell as they roared like a vandal army, snouting under the surface, rooting out turnips, parsnips, beets and carefully prepared potato clamps, trampling all vegetation underfoot, borne along by some unholy spirit. As they entered Herring Lane, anything and everything scattered: dogs and cats ran for cover, rats sought safety, gulls screamed overhead. Down, down, the grunting, pillaging, squealing army scavenged.

Along the quay, creels, fish-boxes, ropes and nets were scattered. Paddy Killeen saw the approaching herd, and tried in vain to defend *Skellig Maid* moored to the harbour wall. He tripped over his own feet, scattering the embers of his clay pipe, and a whoosh erupted as refined fish oil caught alight. The nine *curragh* fishing boats of Garrah lying in tandem inside the tiny harbour had no chance of surviving the inferno.

The swine swerved away from the quayside and headed for the sheltered side of Garrah with its Convent, manse, church and the landowner's house. As the fire took hold along the quay, people panicked and scrambled for safety, Father Latchford among them. Another horde of hogs burst out of Sea Lane, cutting off his means of escape, and in the mêlée that followed, the priest was bundled off the quay and into the deep water where the Garrah burn flowed into the harbour. Moments later all that remained of him was a black Connemara hat, bobbing on the water.

Peder whistled the dogs in. With flames sweeping along the quay, the pigs followed noisily uphill, passing through the gap in the wall.

10

The next day, Peder buried his mother and sealed the wall with boulders. He was never seen in Garrah again.

Garrah was abandoned. As years passed, the track became overgrown and hard to trace and the ancient black stone wall suffered irreparable damage from the weather. The few buildings that still stood were roofless and broken. The quay became unsafe and no longer functioned. Bracken, broom and heather took over. Peder's bothy lay hidden a mile away through the foothills.

Millicent O'Brien's last resting place was marked by a huge boulder with no inscription. Some things were best left unsaid.

Garrah

Blackened boulders sob rain and sleet –
ruination lies beneath the thrum of insistent water
remembering the drowning of evil; a priest's hat
that bobbed in the harbour, lit by flames of retribution.

Snuffles and grunts fade away, the trampling
of trotters in mud long gone, wrecked lives.
Westerlies howl across the hillside as winter slips in.
Garrah is no more. Creels, fish boxes, ropes and nets,
nine curraghs, now burnt ash – flotsam, all gone.

Through sheets of rain you think you see
bright bracken, flame coloured, lit by a lightning strike
in memory of Millie. Heather ripples like hordes of swine
bearing down on the village; hawthorn bends
against the weather; a man, hounds close by,
strides forth seeking vengeance –

then lightning forks and blinds your eyes. A gull screams,
the seventh wave crashes, shocks your eyes open.
Fires extinguished, old hurts forgotten,
Garrah lies broken, abandoned.

Chapter Two

Beyond the Extra Mile

The morning tide had ebbed, leaving the beach quiet, though further out to sea the waves harried the weathered promontories of Bolus, Sheep's and Mizen Head, the Skelligs and a score of inhospitable islands. Peder was gleaning seaweed, filling wicker pannier-baskets with bladderwrack, thongweed and carragheen while Paddy, his pony, helped itself to sweet-tasting crunchy fronds along the high-water mark. Peder's tanned back glistened with sweat, his shirt hung round his waist and his black boots were tied to the pony's halter. He worked alone from choice, the dogs and pony, seals on the shoreline and seabirds his only companions. Having this vast strand to himself with the sun blazing overhead was a delight. A religious man might have given thanks. Sitting down beside a weathered boulder, he searched for a crust and a piece of cheese in his knapsack while Paddy the pony enjoyed a crisp green apple.

"Don't get too comfortable," said Peder as the wolfhounds growled a warning. "We're not the only pebbles on the strand. We have company, I'm thinking."

He stood in the rock's shadow and watched a distant pair of strangers on the shore splashing along the Atlantic's edge.

"No business of mine," he said to Paddy. "There's enough space for all in Kerry and likely for Cork as well."

Peder had never actually seen Cork or Killarney, though he had visited Skibbereen and Kenmare Town and seen the Auxiliaries Militia. He'd taken an instant dislike to them and returned to Rossdore deeply concerned.

The seaweed-filled panniers were heavy and overflowing and there was still a good two-mile walk uphill to where he had built a walled enclosure to protect his vegetable patch.

"You poor ol' fellah." he said to the pony. "Will I be takin' it easy 'cos it's a terrible climb an' there's no wind to be had."

He slapped the pony's flank and shoved hard to show at least he was willing to lend a hand.

The strangers on the strand had disappeared, but when Peder stopped for Paddy to drink from the brook in the willow grove, a brazen female voice came out of nowhere and wished him a good day.

12

"God love us!" said Peder. "And where's did you come from?"

He turned to discover a pair of smiling barefoot colleens wearing dresses made from jute-sacks.

"Will you allow us to get past as you're blocking the way with that old donkey of yours?"

Peder had scarcely room to manoeuvre under the whispering willows. Stunned into silence, he stumbled into the brook and collapsed at the feet of the first colleen.

"I didn't ask you to scrub the donkey," she said, laughing.

"Iss no donkey," said Peder. "He's a pony, a Connemara from Skibbereen. I fetched him myself, paid good money. I'm no squatter or tinker, I'm a pig farmer, and I'm collecting seaweed for the goodness it gives back to the land and..."

He scrambled back to his feet, still struggling with the fast flowing brook.

"I've seen you before," said the colleen, "at Rossdore market. I didn't mean to be contemptible when I called him a donkey."

"What's a contemp-bull?" said Peder, unable to keep pace.

"It's me being rude. I'm very sorry. Can you forgive me?"

"No hard feelings," said Peder.

The girl turned to her companion, a slightly smaller version of herself.

"This is my kid sister, Jo. She's deaf and dumb after the measles so our Mam taught her everything."

Peder felt awkward. He had never met anyone without the hearing before.

"Our Da was a fisherman, lost at sea," said the colleen, "We had to move house then and take a charity place at Kilgarvan, home to river rats, brambles and a forest of bracken, but we survived by the grace of Saint Brigid."

Peder hauled himself up the bank and found a safe place to stand while the girl continued talking.

"I'm Mary Anne Flynn. I've been promised to a house near Kenmare starting next Monday as housekeeper. He's a military man, an officer in the King's Dragoons. Mam lent me a dress for the interview together with a pair of shoes. Don't know why I'm telling you all this but there, we're only tryin' to be friendly."

Tongue-tied and blushing, Peder smacked the pony's flank but only succeeded in showering both colleens with river-water as the dappled-grey struggled to climb the bank. Mary Anne slipped off the path as the trembling beast, weighed down by loaded baskets, bucked and snorted. Peder ran to help Mary Anne while Jo seized the breeching-strap. The pony calmed instantly as Jo stroked its muzzle and made friends, earning Peder's silent respect.

"Get away, hup-hup-hup! Get on you mad beast – get up there!" he said, adding, "Sorry Paddy, I'm only tryin' to help."

The Connemara refused to move, just as stubborn as its taskmaster.

"Aw, let him alone," said Mary Anne. "Why don't you carry the baskets instead?"

Peder burst out laughing and sat on the path beside the stream.

"Everybody's against me!"

"You poor ol' sod," said Mary Anne. "Will I be feelin' sorry for you?"

She joined in his laughter whilst her sister took hold of the reins and led Paddy through the willows and up the bank. By the time they reached open pasture they were friends.

bladderwrack burdened,
beachcombing pony crunches
briny sea-feast

There had already been trouble in Crookstown and Ennishean with the fledging IRA, and the following market day, auxiliaries marched into Rossdore. They arrived in trucks and surrounded the small town in the hope of discovering armed rebels. It was the first time the militia had been seen in Kenmare District. Kerry folk were remote from Cork City, and even further from Dublin, and locals had little interest in politics and government. Even when Cork burned, no news reached them. A newspaper was something you wrapped a bit of meat in. Though plenty were capable of reading official notices, they tended to ignore the information contained.

At first, no one took much notice, thinking the soldiers must be travelling performers. Nobody in Rossdore had seen a uniform in town before, let alone a rifle. Folk at market had no idea what was happening as they were surrounded by men in khaki uniforms bearing fixed bayonets, wearing steel helmets, with a few sporting tam o'shanters. Without warning, an officer grasped an auxiliaries' rifle and fired it at the Catholic Church's bell.

The crowd fell silent.

The officer took aim again and fired, shattering the bell.

"Everybody line up facing the walls. Nobody move. Stand still and keep quiet!"

The order was repeated and no one dared disobey.

Another officer drew his revolver and emptied the entire chamber into the air. Pairs of auxiliaries frog-marched people against the walls around the market square. Women sobbed and men remained mute. Father O'Halloran tried to usher fearful children into the Catholic church, but was stopped by another soldier.

"All out!" yelled an auxiliary. "Ev'ry one of ye, get back to the wall, an' stop that snivellin' or you'll get what's comin' to yer – bloody papists!" He spat at the priest, and shoved the butt of his rifle into his back.

Peder O'Brien had heard stories of a great war, far away in a land he never wanted to visit. He had seen broken and blinded men in Bantry and Skibbereen scarcely as old as himself begging on the streets for coins, bearing terrible wounds. He had given generously as he was a successful stockman, and though he lived on the edge of a virtual no-man's land, nobody had ever questioned his right to earn an honest shilling. Yet war had found him. He could smell it; catch a whiff of a culture so alien it stifled everything he believed in. It was here, in Rossdore's market square, and he didn't like it.

At six-feet five, under an unkempt mop of hair, there was no place for him to hide, and neither did he try. Peder had sold six boars that morning before the sun had touched the church roof, and had just enjoyed his weekly shave at the hands of Willy Toomey. Business complete, he had bought a loaf, a slab of butter and a Kerry cheese off Katy Robins from her dairy stall, and was headed for the café across the square when the auxiliaries surrounded the market.

A cluster of elderly folk were lined up against Dooley's Hardware Store next to the Sunshine Café. Peder stood with them facing the windows, his mind racing. He had heard about such things, but never expected to be experiencing them, not here. Market shoppers grasped willow baskets and paper-wrapped purchases and held them close with trembling hands. Apart from the weeping children, no one made a sound. A platoon of soldiers began searching every basket and package, tipping the contents onto the cobbles.

Peder kept tight hold of his purchases. The notion that strangers would pillage his victuals was unthinkable.

"Drop it!" said a voice from behind. "That man – drop it, on the deck, now!"

The clunk of the bolt of a Lee-Enfield rifle echoed off the glass window of Dooley's Store.

"Won't tell you ag'in," said the man, only now the voice was accompanied by the rancid smell of onion breath over Peder's shoulder.

Peder turned round. The man barely reached his chin.

"You lookin' fer a bullet?" sneered the auxiliary.

Peder tried to hand him his paper bag but it was refused. The rifle was levelled at his chest.

A female voice screamed, "Don't you dare!" from the Bantry road. As the soldier turned to see where the voice was coming from, Peder grabbed his rifle and tossed it over the shop-front, out of sight.

"Just you'n me now," said Peder, into the silence of the square. "Who's afeared this time?"

Instantly rifles cocked right across the market. Peder felt sweat on his brow.

The auxiliary backed away, never losing sight of his adversary, but looking pale in his ill-fitting khaki tunic.

Authority in the form of a sergeant as big as Peder arrived in the market square. The only other NCO started barking orders to his minions, not wanting to get involved in this insignificant incident. The sergeant faced the rebel.

16

CE

"So you fancy your chances then, big fellah?" he said. "But not ag'in him." He indicated the embarrassed soldier. "He's but a shrimp, no stripe, no medals and no brains. Cannon fodder left over from Flanders. But me, I got medals, three stripes and a brain. So, where were you when England needed you – not one o' they Cath'lic conchies, scared to fight for your country?"

Peder remained mute. No sense arguing with a full company of militia. At least he was still standing, and he believed he had the support of Rossdore's citizens.

The burly sergeant unbuttoned his tunic, dropped his holstered belt and handed it to the infantryman who had already been damned as being lily-livered.

"Last man standing," said the sergeant. "No messin'. Queensbury rules, though I'm right out of proper boxin' gloves so it'll 'ave to be bare-knuckles." Turning to his men, he added, "Fair's fair. If he wins, I don't want no reprisals, but some of us 'as to teach these papists respect."

Within minutes all thoughts of searching through belongings were put on hold as the soldiers created a crude boxing ring by linking arms – real arms, rifles held horizontally.

Peder had little idea of what he had let himself in for though he knew, from the crude obscenities of the soldiers, that he was supposed to be the fall guy. He kept his sheepskin gilet on and faced up to the inevitable against the man the conscripts were calling 'Jacko'.

respect for terror:
cow down, bow down, look sharp now –
the bell tolls no more

17

Neither man had a chance to indulge in the niceties of pugilism. A swift double jab to the cheek was followed by a swingeing right hook between the eyes, temporarily blinding Peder. After a barrage of left jabs, Jacko's right fist smacked into Peder's cheek.

Peder spat unfamiliar blood out of his mouth. Knowing nothing about bare-knuckle fighting, he felt a wave of nausea and stumbled into Jacko, grappling with him simply to stay on his feet.

"No 'olding!" shouted a soldier. "Are you a man or a pig?"

Others began squealing and grunting in mockery.

By this time every man and woman in Rossdore had crowded round the makeshift ring, with children peeping through the legs of adults, youngsters shouting for Peder, hoping against hope for a miracle as the pigman clung onto Jacko's arms.

"Fight you papist coward!" screamed the soldiers. "Got no guts! Irish fairy!"

Jacko stepped back. Peder felt sick as the proverbial pig. Blood ran down his chin and his eyes were already closing from the effects of Jacko's bombardment. Again the sergeant began taunting his adversary, planting merciless blows under the heart and delivering a stinging blow on Peder's ear as he tried to defend himself. Peder began to wilt and felt his legs collapsing. He knew the only way to end the punishment was to fall down at Jacko's feet.

The NCO had both arms wide open and was manoeuvring for the final curtain. With his fists level with Peder's elbows, he threatened the ultimate blow. Jacko reigned supreme, unbeaten in untold bouts. An honourable survivor of the Great War, he always led from the front. A tumult filled the market square, soldiers chanting, "Kill, kill, kill!" Maybe it was all over, if only the officer would deliver the *coup de grâce* – yet Peder still stood defiant. Inside his head all he could hear was the word 'coward'. It offended his principles, left him outraged.

He wiped his forearm across his brow, tried to focus on his opponent's face, and hung on. The beefy sergeant looked to his left, grinned and then looked to his right just as Peder's massive fist buried itself in his face. It was a blow so fierce, so powerful, so filled with all the hatred Peder could muster and delivered with such force that Sergeant Jackson gasped out loud and sat down on the road seeing stars.

"Ouch!" squealed Peder, cradling his injured fist.

The shouts of the auxiliaries went out like a candle. The crowd started to murmur, still nervous of reprisals. Half a dozen soldiers helped the groggy sergeant to his feet.

"Bloody hell," spluttered Jacko. "One punch. Can you believe that? Congratulations Irish – here, let me shake the hand of a real gentleman."

He grasped the hand that had delivered the most telling blow struck in all Kerry and raised Peder's left arm high.

"You's a good 'un, Irish, you beat me fair and square. Honest to God, you pack a punch good enough to be a champion."

And with that, under orders of the lieutenant, the company formed ranks and marched back to the convoy of trucks waiting at the crossroads of Bantry Road.

outraged innocence
begets bare-knuckled fury:
fate turns on the blow

The citizens of Rossdore led Peder in triumph to Willy Toomey's barbershop where he had a good wash in hot water and a twenty-ounce steak applied – somewhat gingerly – to a pair of black eyes. Several well-wishers popped in and of course every boy in town began shadowboxing. The town had acquired a home-grown hero.

Gradually the market wound down, with traders still talking about the day's events. Citizens went home and the few vehicles and carts brave enough to risk the grim roads of Kerry were loaded for tomorrow's market over the hill in Macroom.

Josephine Flynn had gasped and even shed tears at the events that had confronted her while trying to stay out of harm's way. Peeping through the bull's-eye windows of the barber's shop, she watched entranced as Willy dowsed candles, and wondered if she dared make a cheeky suggestion.

Jo had never seen Peder's holding. The massive-bouldered wall kept everyone at bay and if they dared climb the wall, the hounds were always on watch looking after the pig herd. She had heard Peder O'Brien was not given to making friends readily. Stories were still doing the rounds about how his mother had been murdered by men from Garrah, but this morning, Peder O'Brien had fought his own bloody and brutal fight with all Rossdore watching in fear and dread. She could not help but feel for this brave and unyielding man who had shown such courage in the face of the callous auxiliaries. It struck her that hero worship might be considered unseemly for a girl of twenty, and with the sun lowering itself over the hills of Kenmare she knew her mother would be fretting. Nevertheless, she wrapped herself inside her lambs-wool shawl and pushed open the door.

"We is closed," said Willy. "Don't you have a home to go to?"

Jo indicated she was deaf and dumb by pointing to her ears and her mouth and making a cross with her fingers.

"Ah missy, I'm reading you just fine," said Willy, "but my missus'll be here soon for the trimmings and if she sees me chatting to you, it could be curtains for Willy Toomey, I'm thinking."

Jo took hold of Peder's hand and picked up his parcel of shopping, which was still holding together despite everything. She dropped it into her wicker basket, and before anyone could say a word, wrote I TAKE YOU HOME in shaving cream on the big mirror over the sink.

Peder couldn't see too well, despite the good intentions of the butcher next door. The black eyes looked fearsome together with the nose plugs but there was no denying Jo. She had waited and walked past Willy's window so many times she had lost count and with the sun lowering, please God, it was now or never.

She led Peder through town, along Kenmare Road, up West Road, and across the river through hazel and alder thickets on a path that only pigs, hounds and Mister O'Brien himself used. It was a silent trek. The colleen could see perfectly well, but was incapable of speaking. She had her own language, could lip-read brilliantly and besides, everyone knew that love couldn't be hurried. It had its own tempo and likely, girls only got the one chance.

one river to cross
one path to follow homeward
one foe defeated

Chapter Three

Calum the Fisherman

Jo had never been so far west along the Beara peninsula before, and was full of wonder at being almost surrounded by the sea. These emerald hills were gentler than the winded heath of the mountains. Even in autumn there were green tufts showing in the bracken where feral goats had failed to find them. Michaelmas daisies, cotton grass and celandines grew profusely, along with a score of less familiar species – so many Jo couldn't contain herself, and fell to gleaning and sniffing every new plant that revealed itself. Peder waited patiently. Girls – especially southern colleens – were forever inquisitive.

Jo took to accompanying Peder to Rossdore when he walked the pigs to market. Once there, she would disappear inside Dooley's Store with a few pennies, and emerge later with a cheese, a loaf and a jar of honey. She always wanted to be off home again, careful to call it 'home' as if she were to remain at the bothy, it would be her home as much as his.

Pig farming was a precarious business. Peder had been warned that he risked everything trying to wrest a living out of land that didn't belong to him, and with several hundred acres now scarred and barren, the time had come to comply with the authorities by becoming a legal tenant. The question was, where? The terrible potato famine, mass emigration and warmongering patriots had left Ireland in a bad way. Peder believed he and Jo had a future, but life would be hard.

No one had ever heard Jo's voice. Left deaf and dumb by the measles, she could only make guttural sounds or whistle with her fingers. She and Peder had their own way of communicating and made conversation by using facial expressions and a blend of hand and finger signs. At market, everyone made a special effort to speak to her simply, taking delight in knowing Josephine Flynn had become Peder O'Brien's lady. There hadn't been a wedding. Such events were out of the question due to the cost. It was understood that a couple who were wholly unrelated made the best basis for a family, and in Rossdore, Father O'Halloran asked searching questions before allowing a pairing. Weddings were only for the privileged few, and most couples simply moved into whichever dwelling had space.

21

Nothing would be the same again after the Great War and Easter Uprising. The country had finally broken the shackles of English rule, and though it wasn't ratified as yet, everyone clung to the hope of a peaceful settlement. Hundreds of thousands of acres changed hands as big landowners sought to abandon the sinking ship of Eire. Men who were used to being left out of politics were now up in arms, banging imaginary drums, thumping non-existent pulpits and laying down petty laws in the hope of a sympathetic audience.

"I'm hearin' nothin'," said Peder. "Long as people need food, we shouldn't be frettin' some."

Despite his words, he was still troubled that honest working men couldn't see where the next meal was coming from.

One morning he took Jo's hand and they went for an exploratory walk, away from Rossdore, past the derelict holdings of Garrah, and westward against the prevailing wind, searching for a better place. Eventually they found a well-used track running between the bay and the estuary. Over another bank, they discovered a path that looked as if it had been in use for centuries. An abandoned dwelling stood in the lee of a small bluff, looking eastwards across the sea to Sheep's Head five miles away.

"Who'd've believed!" said Peder. He turned to Jo, arms outstretched, and shrugged his massive shoulders as if to say, *Yes?*

Jo knew the reasons for seeking a better place, but she could be argumentative, a problem not made easier by the difficulties of communicating. In no way did Peder O'Brien overawe pint-sized Josephine Flynn.

"Something wrong?" said Peder, spreading his hands wide to sign the question.

Jo touched her jaw with the right hand signalling a problem, then repeated the sign for emphasis. Peder loved this intimate communication, not least because it only worked when they could see each other.

How far are we from Rossdore? Where is the nearest neighbour? Will there be running water?

She didn't want to end up a recluse, friendless, an outcast – and what about winter?

How will we take pigs to market and will the ceaseless wind be in our faces? Tell me!

Jo's song

We cross tufted grasses
seek shelter and home
close by the sound of the sea.

Follow me through bracken,
counting the daisies,
in sight of the sea, the sea.

Further on, further on – there –
do you see? A dwelling,
protected, facing the sea.

we climb the hills
and the ceaseless wind blows –
must we leave so soon?

Oh, let us remain by the sea
with the meadow flowers;
let us remain by the sea.

Jo stood in the entrance of the abandoned cottage, a stone's throw from the sea as the sun broke through the clouds. Today was unusually mellow. It would be different when sheeting rain kept the headlands hidden from view and wind made work impossible, but today was for dreaming.

You want us to live here? she signed. *No roof, no floor, no windows, no door, no table, no seats, no fireplace, no nothin'?*

She demonstrated everything with fluttering fingers.

"You like it?" said Peder. He spoke directly to her at all times as if she had the hearing, feeling it was the right thing to do. She had another talent: a sixth sense, an ability to feel vibration. Through it she could sense the cry of a gull, the chuckle of a stream and the crash of breaking waves. Jo never thought of herself as handicapped.

They followed another goat path down to the rocky beach, wondering why the place had been abandoned. Someone long ago had laboured hard to drag those huge boulders from the shore and build the place. They would have needed powerful hands to lift such massive stones.

"Must've been Vikings," said Peder. "Even I could walk through that doorway without havin' to stoop down an' the capstone lintel has to weigh as much as a donkey."

Jo had spotted a pitch-black boat with its foresail loose and its mainsail furled against the mast. Its occupant was too busy to notice the couple on the shore. There were several boats fishing in the bay, it being a quieter day; mainly curraghs but also the occasional fat-bellied *púcán* working the shallows. She clicked her fingers to get Peder's attention. He was surveying potential pasture. This was good land, far better than the higher ground of the moors. It was heathery with bracken, gorse and a few hardy saplings. He would have spoken but Jo had her forefinger on her lips, the sign for him to keep quiet. She pointed to the shoreline.

"Issa *púcán*," said Peder. There was no such word in Jo's vocabulary, so he smiled to indicate that everything was just fine and continued along the path, dodging weathered boulders.

Out on the boat, the fisherman stood up and stretched an aching back after resetting a lobsterpot. Seeing the couple on the shoreline, he gave the usual Kerry greeting – a sort of half-wave, enough to acknowledge their presence.

"Hello!" called Peder in response.

The fisherman picked up a small anchor, twirled it from the side across the bow and over the water. Having secured a meaningful bight, he hauled the boat closer to shore. As the craft passed over the anchor, he heaved the anchor off the bottom and expertly repeated the action. In

24

barely a minute, the fisherman was clambering over the boat's side into knee-deep water.

the fisherman's craft

pitch-black púcán
sits in the shallows
brown sail furled
steady as she goes

anchor twirls
drops, pulls, hauls
shore approaches
steady, steady

slap of wavelets
salt tang, shingle grit
lobsterpot re-set
steady as she goes

"Cal – Calum Dunn; son of John Henry Dunn of Portleán, only me da went down on a schooner chasing the cod off the Newfoundland Banks when I wuz a nipper. Glad to see you."

The firm handshake was accompanied by the smell of fish. Calum didn't clasp Jo's hand, she being a colleen, but bowed courteously instead.

"Haven't seen ye afore," said the fisherman, "but that's nothin'. I ain't seen lots of people to speak of, only folks in Portleán an' a few from Bantry. I got me boat an' me Mam an' a few neighbours, I'm happy. I

25

took over the púcán when I realised me da wasn't comin' back." He paused. "Sorry. S'good that I don't have too many people to talk to, begob, I'd be rabbitin' on all day."

Peder finally got a word in. "Peder O'Brien, an' this is Jo Flynn – or was – we're settin' up home together so from now on," he placed an arm round her shoulder, "she'll be Jo O'Brien."

"I'm all ears now. Tell me more."

Calum returned to the púcán, picked up half-a-dozen mackerel and brought them back to the shore, where he lit a fire with heather and gorse branches.

"I'm thievin' your supper," said Peder. "What will your Mam say to that?"

"Tch, tch – isn't it enough that she'll be dinin' on lobster tonight? She allus gets the best of the sea anyways. Besides, by the time I get back to Portleán I'll have another crock of fish ready for the stove. Am I not the best fisher in the bay?"

Peder asked who owned the abandoned holding. Calum said it had been empty since long before he was born.

"Aside from a few feral goats and stray sheep, I'm thinkin' it don't belong to anyone at all."

"So you wouldn't mind much if we stayed a night here, just to get the feel of the place?"

"Holy Mother, will you believe this – are we not friends already. Portleán is hardly any distance. You'll do me the greatest kindness by stayin' with us tonight. We've got space enough and beddin', God love us, I'd be hurt if you stayed anyplace else."

Peder raised his arms in surrender.

Calum burst out laughing. "Will ye get that," he said. "The big man knows when he's beat."

He picked up the anchor warp and dragged the púcán closer to the shore.

Peder lifted Jo up and carried her through the shallows to the vessel before clambering over the side himself. It was the first time either of them had been in a boat. The púcán was a beefy vessel, wooden built and tough.

A nearby small island had been joined to the mainland earlier, but was now marooned as the flood tide poured through the channel.

"*Oileán Muc*, Island of Pigs," said Calum. "Dunno how it got its name as there's nothin' but rats livin' in the burrows of birds now. There used to be puffins and petrels when Da was alive."

26

He looked across to the island, seeing desolation in the loss of so many notable seabirds.

"How come?" asked Peder. "Why the rats?"

Calum pointed to the island shore.

"See those timbers? Them's old boats. They've been deliberately left to rot and every time we get a storm they sink lower in the sand. It's a wicked waste after all that effort, but rats were allus there, livin' under the decks, thievin' food under the noses of sailors, and of course, rats breed thousands more. I s'pose they're on the mainland as well but I'm thinking they know the tides and at first light, scuttle back to Oileán Muc."

Jo sat in the bow, enjoying herself with so much to see, to smell, to taste. The setting sun promised a good day tomorrow. Her silent world was being transformed.

Peder sat amidships, careful to keep out of the way of the boom thing that threatened to decapitate him. Fortunately the soft breeze meant the púcán moved slowly through the narrows. She was buxom but perfectly stable with brown sails that creaked and muttered with each breath of wind. When the sun sank behind the headland and the breeze increased, the old boat began to canter.

"Nearly home," said Calum. "I can smell the smoke. Me Mam is a great cook an' loves showin' off with the stove. Now sit still mountain man, the breeze is from behind an' this boat is in a terrible hurry to be back."

dinner

she sits back and watches:
fish stew simmers, the smell
floats over the water
calling the fisherman home
to peat-glowing hearth

saffron suffuses the stew with gold
sweet and wild
the wind from the island
brings scents of crushed thyme

she stirs the pot: the wooden spoon
pushes shells around

meeting chunks of potato, salted
dried herring, pink shrimps,
a handful of herbs, a sip, a decision,
a pinch of black pepper –
dinner.

Ireland's famine was long gone, but the country still bore the wounds, and survivors in rural areas relied on a cautious resourcefulness. The lack of roads had seen too many people move to Cork and Waterford, leaving the peninsulas devastated. Fifty years on, the people of Munster were still struggling. Roman Catholicism had failed to fill the vacuum, doctors and professional men were conspicuously absent. Distribution of basic foodstuffs depended on whether or not you could walk to market, and education rested on home-grown talents and hand-me-down stories.

Calum's mother, Hannah, was delighted to have unexpected guests and set about preparing her cottage to entertain 'a lovely couple of whelps'. She was never happier than when 'doing' for visitors, and the smells now filling her home could most likely be sniffed right across the small community of Portleán. The loss of so many due to the Great War and emigration to the colonies had left Munster reeling from a skills shortage, and Hannah knew the future lay on the shoulders of the next generation. Therefore fish stew – first time for the O'Briens – needed due homage.

"Get that inside ye. Let it stick to yer bones my *páistes* (children). There's plenty more where that came from."

Hannah sang as she served them, songs that hadn't been heard in the Dunn home for many a year. Life could only get better with the O'Briens' arrival.

28

Calum took the next day's change in wind direction as a sign that he ought to visit Bantry Town, fifteen miles distant, to find out who owned the abandoned holding. Peder and Jo watched the púcán's stately progress as they walked back along the peninsular. Hannah had supplied a wicker basket filled with tasty things to eat. As soon as they reached the holding, Peder's wolfhounds bounded up joyfully, having lost the trail yesterday when the O'Briens had embarked in the púcán. This was the third generation of wolfhounds Peder had owned. He had recently bought another dog, the runt of the litter, and called it Chip, a name Jo had grasped with a simple click.

On the other side of the Beara over two hundred swine ran free, unfenced. If Peder's pigs followed, it would create mayhem. Peder told Jo that if they were to move to the Cork side of the peninsular, it would need to be before the November gales. The couple munched noisily, anxiety fading as they discussed becoming legal tenants. No longer squatters or trespassers, they would be in possession of a proper title. There would be hurdles; an uneducated man would always be at a disadvantage.

"Peder O'Brien?" folks would say. "Well aye, the pigman, you'll find him in Rossdore on most Tuesdays – as honest as the day is long. Peder's a fair man."

Peder might have been trusted, but his problem was the lack of an influential voice to speak for him. Rossdore and even Kenmare were both small when you needed someone 'in the know'.

in the spring

ragwort tethers hewn rocks
peeks around corners
springs from chimney tops, creeps under eaves
while birch saplings twist through empty windows,
find light and spread leaves in the sunshine

a garden of grasses surrounds the front door,
sends spikes of foxgloves to welcome the guests

this is where they will make their home
and sit by the glow of the soft burning peat;
this is where they will build their nest
this is where it begins

Jo's mother, Martha, and her sister, Mary Anne, had moved out of their hovel into a superior residence owned by the Dragoon Officer in Kenmare. Martha was now the Major's cook and Mary Anne acted as housekeeper. The officer had received a pension and been given the house as part settlement. The Dragoons had been decimated in the first months of the Great War and Major Thomas Alan Redmond, having commanded an artillery company at Passchendaele, had been awarded the silver Military Cross and bar. He still suffered terribly from the effects of mustard gas poisoning and had retired at the age of forty, a shadow of the fine officer he had once been.

Jo had arranged to meet her mother and sister at market in Rossdore while Peder traded a large herd of pigs. Things were moving now that Calum Dunn had discovered the current owner of the abandoned *shieling* simply wanted to lease it at a fair rent. Peder's problem was his inability to prove his entitlement.

The Sunshine Café was buzzing that morning. Mary Anne had been granted leave by her employer. The Major always spoke in military terms and calling it 'leave' was second nature to him. Mary Anne had her own pony and trap, a Connemara towing a four-wheeled gig, and was proud to be able to drive her mother into town in style.

Peder shook hands on several local deals while Mary Anne, Martha and Jo sat outside with cheese scones and a pot of tea, deep in discussion. Major Redmond had offered to underwrite the landowner's covenant.

There would be no need for Peder to attend the offices in Bantry; the Major would sign the agreement in perpetuity, which meant Peder would become the Major's factor. Peder didn't understand the legalities, but faced by a trio of Flynns, he surrendered and settled for a pork pie, a cheese scone and a cup of tea.

Calum had walked over the hills to assist with escorting the fifty gilts to Rossdore, just ahead of winter. The fisherman and pigman were now firm friends, though sitting in the unseasonable sunshine outside the café, neither man had much idea of what Peder's new responsibilities might be.

"You mean," said Calum, "this crazy pickle-herring will hand over ten per cent of every guinea he'll be earning for the rest of his life?"

"That's the bargain," said Mary Anne, "and an excellent one, too. The Major has taken Peder's word on trust. The war is over, Calum. We're creating the new Ireland. Consider ten percent as a donation for our country. That's a small price to pay for freedom and food on the table."

Peder didn't answer. Jo could be tetchy, but had nothing on Mary Anne.

Martha handed Peder the last piece of scone.

"You've put your hands to the plough," she said. "It'll be hard going at times but you'll carry the day, both of you."

Martha rarely spoke, so everyone at the trestle table gave her their full attention.

"Life lived in fear is a life not lived," she said. "Peder, you have the world at your feet and despite the handicap of the hearing, Josey is the perfect partner. I'm thrilled you've begun so well."

She stifled a sob.

"We must be movin'," said Peder. "There's not much light to be had at the end of October and Jo's bought the biggest cheese in town which means I'll be havin' to carry it home."

"Poor thing," said Mary Anne. "It'll be you that gets to eat it, doubtless."

Jo remained seated for a time. Martha gave her an enquiring look.

I'm fine, Jo signed, rolling her eyes while patting her tummy. *Too much to eat.*

"You're lookin' a bit flushed," said Martha. "Not like you to be arguin' with a scone."

Then without warning Jo vomited. Not much, just enough to cause her mother to say quietly, "Tch, tch. Now there's a thing! I'm guessing I could be a grandmother in the New Year."

the last piece of scone

a crumb too far
in her delicate state
she'd sooner have kippers
or coal on her plate

Peder, make ready –
prepare for confusion
prepare for a glimpse
in the world of a woman

all the old certainties
turned on their head
your wife can't eat scones –
craves seaweed instead

Chapter Four

Portleán Allies

Dawn was a distant glow beyond the Maughanaclea Hills, though Rossdore still lay hidden. Across the bay, Sheep's Head and the Mizen could just be seen in the early light. Chip, the youngest of Peder's hounds, kept close to his master as they dropped down to the rough and ready quayside at Portleán. Calum was already there, waiting to ferry them across to the Royal Naval base at Bere Island, eight miles away.

Chip spied a dopey hare and brought it down, despatching it in one high-spirited dash, then sat on the bank, the trophy dangling from a bloodied mouth.

"You's a good 'un," said Peder. "Hannah will have that in the pot by the time we get back this evening."

The púcán's sails were flapping in the breeze as if the black boat wanted to be off.

"An' there's me thinkin' you wuz wantin' to be away before dawn," said Calum. "Did you enjoy your lie in?"

Peder grinned, whistled the wolfhound onto the boat and walked over to Hannah's doorway to present the still warm hare for the cooking pot.

"Now that's a fine catch to be having first thing of a mornin'," said Hannah. "That's real meat. All we get in this house," she winked at Peder, "is fish, fish and yet more fish. No wonder me teeth are failin'."

She handed Peder a wicker basket filled with *boxties* (potato pancakes).

the chase – too swift to forfeit
the catch – crunching jaws, pumping blood
the dinner – jugged hare and dumplings

The steady breeze filled the brown sails and pushed the boat across the water at a good speed. Chip stood in the bow sniffing hard, the first time at sea for the hound. Calum and Peder sat on the gunwale, backs to the wind, and watched the departure of a huge warship. Peder had never seen a vessel so vast. Calum was lost in thought, worried about Peder's proposal and the reason for this trip. Several warships were moored to huge iron buoys between Bere Island and the peninsular. Calum steered well clear and aimed for the pier at the eastern end of the island.

"I hope that you know what you's doin'," he said. "These are British ships. They don't take kindly to visitors. All *iascaire* (fishermen) are up to no good as far as they're concerned."

"I'm only wishing to trade," said Peder. "There's hundreds of sailors here, so there must be a need for meat. Bacon, ham, pork, gammon, trotters, lard – ain't no waste with pigs. If we can deliver 'em on the hoof, we might do some business."

The púcán gained the lea of the island and fetched up beside a forbidding pier. Peder tied a rope to a stanchion while Calum lowered the sails.

"If they don't like the look of us, we can leave quick enough, but Chip must stay in the boat," said Peder. "If anythin' spooks him, he could end up bein' trouble."

All Hannah's food had been devoured on the way across, so on the command: "Sit – stay – wait," the hound settled in the bow contentedly.

A political agreement obtained by successive British governments had allowed three ports to remain in the Irish Free State before further negotiation finally secured freedom from British rule. Bere Island was always going to be a bone of contention but, for now, Peder had spotted a viable market for pigs. The only problem was, who to ask? Initial enquiries were met with blank stares from rank and file sailors. Unsure as

34

to identifying uniforms, Peder made for the only man wearing a white shirt and tie, though remembering his manners, he waited until the man took notice of him.

"What are you after?" was the first question, swiftly followed by an admonition to several men who were manhandling laden barrels up a ramp.

"Good morning," said Peder, "I would like to see the officer responsible for buying meat, sir. I'm a pig farmer from Portleán and wondered –"

"Quartermaster's office. This is munitions. Wait here – don't move. This is a restricted area. No civilians. I'll get someone to take you. Is he with you?" He nodded at Calum.

"Yes sir, he's my ferryman: Calum Dunn of Portleán."

The officer called over a rating who led them to a huge complex of grey-painted buildings. He opened a door marked VICTUALS and ushered them into a vast warehouse, the biggest building either man had ever seen, filled with hundreds of drums of unidentifiable substances: jute sacks, cans, tins, boxes, bins, all neatly sorted in line, stacked and separated by sheets of timber. They stared wide-eyed at the electric lighting, ladders, trolleys, sweating lascars and unintelligible notices; the towering pillars and concrete floors painted in a maze of coloured lines. Union Jacks were draped over iron girders and railings, all under the cover of a towering roof on an island in Bantry Bay, barely ten miles from Portleán.

The rating guided them through the warehouse to an office and knocked at a door, which was opened by another shirted officer. The rating saluted and words were exchanged, but the vast shed and its contents absorbed the sound.

The officer beckoned.

"Mother of God," said Calum. "Too late now, he wants to talk to you."

"You'n me, both," said Peder.

"Listen Ped, if it comes to trouble, get back through that door an' run like hell."

"Shush will ye, there won't be no trouble, and for God's sake try to look pleased."

Peder bent down to get under the lintel.

"I can only offer you a bench to sit on," said the officer, "but you're welcome. I'm a Derry man myself, from the Bogside – joined the navy at fourteen to see the world and this is as far as I got. So, what way are you?"

The firm handshake inspired confidence.

"Well aye, we're doin' just fine – sir." Peder remembered just in time to respect the uniform. "This is the biggest building I've ever seen – sir. I had no idea such things existed on the Beara, or so many ships at anchor."

"Protocol. Defence of the realm and all that. Looking after Europe's welfare. If the Kaiser had got his way, I doubt any of us would still be here. War's a terrifying leveller. A million men sacrificed, and for what?"

Peder was too young to have experienced the Great War, and living in such a remote community, knew little of other men's conflicts. For Calum, the after effects of hostilities meant simply he turned left on leaving Porteán quay and fished out of sight of the flotilla of British warships. His mam had warned him not to get involved, but you can't keep turning left forever. Maybe that was why Hannah hadn't objected to him ferrying Peder to the island.

"Tch, tch," she had said. "Will I allus have you tied to my apron strings?"

Quartermaster Bill Barry used the wall-mounted telephone to summon tea and biscuits. He seemed remarkably hospitable to a pair of strangers who had wandered into his domain, but most likely the Irish tongue had made the difference. They didn't know it, but they were already considered trustworthy.

"So – you're into pigs are ye?" said Bill. "Are you sellin' on the hoof or butchered?"

"On the hoof, sir. I'm a tenant-farmer looking fer regular customers – if I knew how many to fatten, I could plan ahead. They're all grazers, runnin' free, and won't have far to travel as Calum here is volunteerin' to tote 'em. I have three hundred at the moment, barrows and gilts. I keep the sows and boars as my breeding stock."

"Used to keep a pig in the back garden when I was a nipper," said Bill. "Gave it everything for the cause. Me da butchered it at Christmas and shared it amongst neighbours. By New Year's Eve everyone had partaken of an honest meal."

Bill's reminiscences spilled out over tea and hard-tack biscuits.

"Listen lads," he said, "I know the value of having a ready supply of pigs on the doorstep. Anyone delivering fresh produce in the meat department will be appreciated by my superiors. It's a fine proposal. We get fish by the ton from Castletown, but meat, real meat..." He licked his lips. "I'll be talking to himself by the end of the day and have no doubts

36

that Commander Urry will give me the nod. He'll need to interview you and obtain a signature together with a contract – standard practice – but he's a fair man. How am I to stay in touch with you? Granted we're close, hardly a dozen miles, but –?"

"We can return any time sir, weather permitting. Tomorrow if you wish, well aye."

The quartermaster held out his hand.

"Make it the day after. Tell any man on the quay that you have an appointment with Officer Barry in the quartermaster's section and he'll escort you. If the weather turns, don't take chances. Wait for the next fair day."

They shook hands, scarcely believing their good fortune.

"What did I tell yeh?" said Calum, as they sailed back to Portleán. "You go where angels fear to tread. That officer wuz cryin' into 'is mug. Divil a one Ped, you wuz leadin' 'im like an ol' bull with a ring through his nose."

Peder grinned. He'd had a feeling about today and now the day had delivered.

> barrows and gilts – full-fattened and ready
> the Bogside to Bantry Bay – hungry for meat
> an Irish brogue seals the bargain

Peder walked home with a freshening wind at his back. Fisherman and farmer, "mackerel and bacon," as Calum had said.

"More like pig ignorant, I'd say," had been Peder's response, "but survivors."

As he tramped along the track in the dark he mused on his good fortune. For ten weeks he and Jo had been struggling to make their home in this abandoned holding. Now, at last, any thought of quitting had been banished. He hadn't been able to keep still in the weeks before it was all due to happen.

Stop fretting, said Jo. *We're going to be fine. Our baby will be born safely in Hannah's house. 'Tis all arranged. By then we'll have a roof over our head and a fire in the grate. I'm not due for several weeks. My sister has been granted leave by the Major and Hannah has attended several births in her time, so don't you worry. This place is right for us.*

It's beautiful. I can look through windows at the sea and the hills. Who could ask for anything more?

"Am I not allowed to dream? I wuz just imaginin', you know. *Leanai* (children), our *leanai* – five or six, maybe more, runnin' through the house, climbin' stairs, listenin' to stories and singing."

Nursery rhymes! She wrote the words on her slate and held it up in front of his face.

"What's that?" he said.

She mouthed the words and danced round the bare room, seizing Peder and trying to make him join in.

"Tch, tch," he said. "No wonder you's pregnant. Behave yourself, or it'll be twins you'll be bearing."

The O'Briens' house may have lacked a roof, it may have lacked most everything, but not for much longer. The entire community of Portleán had decided that if this was to become a home, then the village would see to it.

They started arriving at dawn: a dozen carts and traps, packhorses, donkeys, and a pair of coal black shires with nodding massive heads, drawing a covered wagon along the track. They brought baulks of timber, long stored under canvas and tarpaulin, along with planks and posts, reeds and willow, thatching spars, boxes and packing cases, carefully salvaged spikes, nails, tacks, dowels, cramps, bolts, screws, latches and glass wrapped in sheepskins. The women had saved precious remnants of cloth to make mats, curtains and cushions. Some of the men had rescued a door, complete with hinges and lintels, from the Atlantic Ocean.

The early-morning procession consisted of men, women, children, dogs and even an owl, rescued after being savaged by a feral cat. The bird was proudly borne by Griff Sullivan, who despite being barely five feet tall, joked that he would be just fine doing a bit of thatching on the roof.

"The owl will discourage the gulls," he said. "He owes us a favour."

Nineteen labourers and a dozen youngsters hoisted and pushed, dug and pulled, clearing a hill of detritus into manageable piles and spreading the debris along the track. Together they watched the first lighting of the stove in Jo's newly decorated kitchen, and the first purlins fixed after the ridgepole had been lifted into place. A new iron pump gushed into a Belfast sink, much to the delight of children who had never seen anything like it before. All had been salvaged from a wrecked trawler that had gone down off Shott Head the previous winter. The Sullivan brothers constructed a new porch, facing south across Bantry Bay, while others laid a stone path to the track.

It took all day, but volunteer hands made it a labour of love. Even Jo's stove had come from the wreck. Newly blackened, it stood against the east wall, making use of the original chimney.

As the sky darkened outside, the volunteers melted into shadows, now lit by candle-lanterns. Calum, Ronny, Griff and a tall fellah called Tad Milligan bedded down in the kitchen, ready to start again in the morning. They could still see stars between the rafters but it didn't matter. The night lay soft as a whisper.

The next day the laths were laid and the thatchers took over. Each sheaf was tied to its neighbour and malletted hard down before being fixed with willow branches and held down under tarred fishing nets, hung with stones from Portleán's small quarry.

It took another day to complete, but the weather stayed kind, and when Portleán's women and children arrived with baskets of freshly-baked treats, Josephine O'Brien, eight months pregnant, stood in her own doorway and burst into tears.

Ron and Griff produced a set of uillean pipes and a squeezebox and young Rees Hogan a *feadan* (tin-whistle*).* They were joined by Bridey Sullivan on fiddle and Frank O'Connor with a bodhran. Unable to hear, Jo could still sense the rhythms of the dancing. The tears were dried as music filled the house. Of course there would be a ceilidh, such events were traditional; and the whole community joined together to hear and sing *sean-nós* (old-style) tunes and enjoy the *craic*.

> one man's wreck is another man's fortune
> sea-cleaned, recycled, lived in and loved
> home, hearth and harbour reclaimed

"The only headache," said Peder the next morning, "is keeping the herd in one place. As soon as I plant hedging the pigs devour it in a flash. Even posts get trashed before I can hang barbed wire on them and besides, who can afford barbed wire?"

"Why not lead 'em over the causeway to Muc Island?" said Calum. "'Tis due a low tide this week according to Lennie Hogan, and he knows. He fishes t'other side of Bere Island at night, right under the noses of the navy. I can help and likely others will too. Young Rees and the Sullivans are allus glad to get out of the boatshed for a day and me mam will come over and keep Jo company."

"Which day and what hour?" said Peder.

"I'll check the tides and let you know," said Calum.

"The dogs can round up the herd," said Peder. "We'll need a few tasty treats, some of them fish-heads and giblets, pigs like that sort of thing, even if they're not supposed to."

"I'll come over later," said Calum. "The moon's fillin' an' that's a sign of a big tide, trust me. I'll be put the word round the village."

The next morning, thunder rattled behind the Caha Mountains and delivered a sodden day, but so long as the meadow-grass stayed upright, it would dry out eventually. Now that the O'Briens had settled into the Portleán community, Peder fully understood that no matter that he kept pigs, he would be enlisted for haymaking like everyone else. Cattle, sheep, horses, goats and geese could only survive the rigours of winter if they had access to fodder. From first light till sundown, you laboured to bring the harvest home and if meadows were strewn with flowers it would be a bonus for grazing stock.

Peder worried that pigs left nothing but barren ground, but by moving the herd to virgin land, he was actually doing the community a great favour. All that bracken, heather, wind-blown thistles and gorse was being removed, leaving clean fields, perfect for planting. The villagers had fish from the sea, milk and *im* (butter), berries and honey, corn and *práta* (potatoes), eggs and meat of their own fattening. Life was good and pigs were the best of the bunch for rooting. Peder O'Brien was a godsend.

Calum called that evening to confirm that the lowest tide this month would be six o'clock the following evening.

"A fine thing that," said Peder. "How are we goin' to know when it's six? I only know the days 'cos Jo keeps count, but there's no clock to be seen anywhere in Portleán. How long will it take the herd to reach the island?"

"Ah sure, if we move 'em across tomorrow, likely we can pen 'em in on a dry beach during the day then lead 'em over the causeway at slack water. We don't want to be wrestlin' with pigs in the middle of the night now, do we? They should be on the bank, sniffin' the island's green grass soon enough."

"More like bracken and gorse," said Peder. "Muc Island is end to end infested with it. Big as houses, though that's good for pigs 'cos they'll scratch and grub all day and like it."

40

"And there's a good set on the weather right now," said Cal. "Griff, Tad, Rees, Frank and Matt are giving us a hand. It should be dryin' out come five o'clock. We'll have a couple of hours to cross. The boys will be with us soon as they've done their chores."

Calum took the lead when things needed a firm decision. The first visit to the Navy had worked wonders. Quartermaster Barry's superior officer had embraced the idea. Peder and Calum had returned to Bere Island to follow up the contract, accompanied this time by Tad and Frank who had behaved impeccably. Peder had signed the contract, having practised his signature under the diligent eye of Jo. No more crosses – this was a legal document. Bill had witnessed, Commander Urry had shaken hands with everyone involved, and beginning on the first of June, Mister Peder O'Brien had contracted to supply the British Royal Navy with twelve gilts every month, on the first day of the month – or as close to that date as possible bearing in mind the fickle weather.

No one in Portleán could believe it.

"Holy mother, Peder, if yer fell in a ditch you'd come out smellin' of roses. What's it with you?" said Tad as they embarked in Frank's bigger púcán. "All I get from pigs are grunts and here's Peder laughin' fit to burst makin' money out of the British Navy. Mind you, all Portleán will benefit from toting animals across the sound and we're grateful to Peder for offerin' us the job o' shippin' 'em."

The early morning round-up across unfenced pasture passed off without drama. The hardest task was the piglets as they were excited as kids at market and wholly uncontrollable, trying the patience of the most placid stockman. Matt had the answer.

41

"Leave 'em be. I'll sort 'em," he said, whistling his black and white sheepdog out of his buggy. No sooner had the dog hit the ground, the entire circus of piglets froze. More whistles from Matt were followed by soft Gaelic words, as the dog approached his quarry: *fanacht* (stay), *ar shiúl* (away), *teach tag* (come by), *siar* (back), *ceart* (right), *d'fhág* (left). Every piglet stood mesmerized. The sheepdog fixed his eye on the biggest gilt and lay on the ground, wholly in command.

"Well who'd 'ave believed," said Calum. "Matt's dog is worth its weight in silver. I wonder if it can swim. It'd be fine roundin' up the herring, sure enough."

Peder kept the rest of the herd placid with shredded turnips. The house had been enclosed by stout walls, as otherwise the pigs would have devoured everything within reach. Jo still complained about the smell by holding her nose and wafting noxious odours with the other hand. Tonight she would have to put up with the additional reek of three hundred pigs congregated around the place.

The men bedded down wherever there was room. The wolfhounds growled under their breath for a time but eventually, as darkness fell, the only discernable sound was snoring.

bracken, gorse, heather and windblown thistledown:
a feast for the taking with snuffle and grunt
when time and tide coincide

Jo woke feeling flushed, but refused to wilt under the heat. She was relieved when Calum's mother, Hannah, arrived and whooshed the men outside.

"Have ye nothin' better to do with yerselves than to get in the way of an honest woman?" she said. "Damnty, an' did I not have to climb through half the pigs in Cork to reach this house an' I'll be cleanin' me *bróga* fer a week afore they're fit to use ag'in."

She said several more choice words as the men grabbed boxties and sausages and cleared the oaken table in one fell swoop.

Hannah had brought goat's milk along from a neighbour, knowing it to be ideal for an expectant miss.

"We'll be takin' it easy," she said. "Men's work is all about gettin' plastered in filth from top to toe, usually accompanied by swearin' and blasphemin'. By the time they get back, pigs will feel far more homely than men and dogs, mark my words."

The holding lay barely two hundred yards from the sea, but to reach Muc Oileán meant a trek of half a mile inland then back along the strand in order to cross. Most of it would still be in flood, save for a small dry level, which was usually covered with seaweed. Several half-submerged wrecks lay in the gap between the island and the mainland, deliberately scuttled. Their creaking bones, which served only to remind of the horrors of war and the futility of conflict, would be eventually swept away. Not surprisingly, they were home to untold numbers of brown Norway rats.

"I once fancied livin' on this island," said Calum, "but 'tis a graveyard 'cos of the currents and winds. It's allus suckin' an' groanin' as if them old sailors are cryin' an' dyin'."

"Sounds of the sea," said Griff. "At least on this side of the Beara it's well sheltered, but why didn't they dump them old boats on t'other side? They'd a broken up in no time at all."

"They tried," said Calum, "but they don't 'ave engines and 'ad to be towed by a naval tug. Me da used to work at Bearhaven during winter an' they wuz roundin' up volunteers to help. It had to be done in a big hurry 'cos of the riots in Dublin ag'in the British government. After that, Da went back on the Newfoundland Banks. I never saw 'im ag'in."

"Fine man 'e was," said Tad. "When I see you fishin' out there on the water, I see your father in you. You should be proud of 'im, Cal, 'e was the best."

Peder strapped the biggest boar in a harness and whistled the wolfhounds round the herd. The volunteer helpers lined up in strategic positions on the pathway along the cliff top.

Initially there were scraps and tussles as the boars tried to seize the best places in the pecking order, but the dogs darted into minor frays and sorted out the culprits. Eventually the herd got the idea and followed King Boar. The squeals and grunts descended to sea level by midday then settled into a contented hubbub of grubbing everything edible off the tidemark: bladderwrack, kelp, sea lettuce, thongweed, ragworm, starfish, cuttlebone, mussels and razor shells. That kept them fully occupied. Some even went for a paddle in the sea.

By five o'clock, a clear pathway could be seen leading to the island. It was time to reel in King Boar. Peder took hold of the rein and marched at the head of his army. The well-fed herd were weary after climbing the bank and it took much noise from dogs and men to force a way through the tidal debris. The emerging path was strewn with boulders, pebbles, sand and mud, and overhung with willows, gorse and rotting timbers. The bigger pigs managed but the piglets were being trampled underfoot and needed swift action if they were not to be lost. Helpers lined up to pass individual gilts higher up the bank. Men shed jackets and shirts, trying to keep their balance. It took an hour to rescue the fallen, but the pigs were goaded by the need to keep foraging and eventually were all dispersed in the undergrowth. Noises could be heard from all over the island, and occasionally, a squealing infant could be seen but now they were on their own.

No one knew what time it was, but at the first sign of the advancing tide they knew they had to get out of there.

"Time to go," said Peder. "Otherwise they might try to get back."

"Tides don't wait fer no man," said Calum. "They jus' keep comin'."

"*Am agus taoide fannan aon fhear,*" said Frank. "Our da taught me that an' I never unlearned it. The sea can be a fearsome place."

A sudden thunderclap rattled the Shehy Mountains out east and the sky turned black.

"Didn't I tell ye?" shouted Tad. "I'm out of here."

"But the sun's still shining," said Calum, "clear as a bell across the bay. Maybe it ain't meant fer us. Them mountains are allus havin' storms, 'tis natural."

"Nevertheless," said Peder, "'tis suppertime. Me belly's grumblin'."

The tide raced in as they hurried back across the causeway, accompanied by further rumbles of thunder. This was no time for talking. They needed shelter from the approaching storm and maybe a bite to eat at the O'Brien's house.

Another flash of lightning – Calum counted off the seconds: "Eight, nine, ten, eleven –" The heavens shook.

"Gettin' closer boys. We're gonna get soaked."

The dogs trembled and the men made tracks across the last remnants of shoreline. It was clear where the army of pigs had burrowed across the strand, grubbing everything in sight.

Young Rees saw something else, a sight he couldn't understand. He stayed rooted to the spot as everyone else dashed for the path up the cliff. Matt didn't notice at first that his son had gone missing. Rees couldn't shout. He stood stock-still, frozen in disbelief.

The first drops of rain began to fall. Matt yelled to his son as the squall arrived, whipping the sea into a maelstrom. The others heard him and instinctively turned back.

Matt rushed back to Rees and picked him bodily off the beach.

"Peder," he yelled. "Get into the sea, get –"

The squall whipped the words away but everyone followed as Matt dashed into the waves, holding tight to young Rees. Even the dogs understood. Calum picked up the sheepdog that was already out of its depth and in danger of drowning.

Rain pelted down from leaden skies. Waist deep in surf and terrified by the sight that confronted them, the men clung together as an almighty army of rats scurried past the place where, moments before, they had been walking. Thousands upon thousands of rats swarmed across the fast disappearing spit, making no sound other than the rush of their passing. Thunder cracked overhead and the squall increased in intensity, yet still they came, endless, an unstoppable flood, a brown torrent of malevolence.

Peder had seen danger before but shock dulls the senses and this left him stunned. The seething, nightmarish mass became a frenzied race for survival. Legions upon legions of rodents with hairless tails, evil teeth and a glint of ten-thousand eyes scurried over the strand, leaping over each other in an attempt to avoid the encroaching sea.

It ended as quickly as it had begun. Despite the wind, the waves and the fear, every man remained motionless. The rain continued, but there was no doubting the smell. The legions of rats had been panicked into moving *en masse* by the unexpected arrival of several tons of pigs tramping over their haven and the sudden storm that had accompanied the landing. Oileán Muc had been reclaimed.

> rats... scurrying-scrabbling-hissing-bruxing
> wave upon wave upon wave upon wave
> of fleet-footed sleek-beamed sea-'scapee rats

Chapter Five

Deliverance

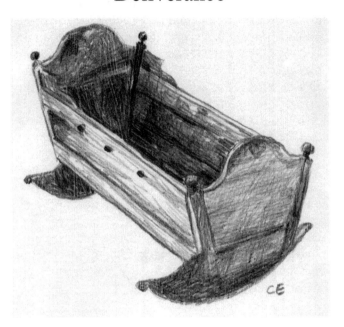

the waiting

they trek back and forth, marram-swift, seashell slow,
past the sand dunes, one way, then the other,
as clouds fly and waves rock the sea and ever
the grass blows and breezes flick-flick from mountains
with sweet meadow scents.

Peder won't linger too long. Paddy waits,
complains with a snort; Chip stays hopeful,
smells hints of soup and stew from the village –
then back again, forth again, trekking each way
as the greensward darkens
and holes in the clouds fill with stars.

Peder had been back and forth between Portleán and the holding twice already today. The third trip would be in darkness, two miles each way. He was thankful for the full moon as the pony objected when asked to work at night.

"And what's with you, Paddy?" said Peder. "Am't I walkin' right beside you?"

The pony whinnied his complaint.

"Tch, tch," said Peder. "You's a proper misery. What say you, Chip?"

The young wolfhound stayed close, wanting to be home.

This track had been well used since the O'Briens took up residence, and a vast meadow had been encouraged ahead of hay harvest. Peder's pigs would normally have stripped the land but they were still being held captive on Muc Island. A heady scent of meadow floated on the breeze off the sea. Despite the late hour, it felt good to be tramping to the village and to have time for thought. Peder had no idea how he would cope with fatherhood.

Jo had gone to Hannah's cottage the previous day, and Peder sent straight up to Lizzie Byrne's cottage to warn her of the imminent confinement. Hannah felt sure the baby was coming, but Lizzie disagreed, and sent Jo back home after a thorough examination.

The next morning Jo felt unmistakable contractions – the real thing this time. She winced, cried out, and before she knew it, Peder had hitched the pony to his sister-in-law's buggy, lifted Jo gently and set her down behind the seat on some jute sacks. No argument. The time was now.

He took hold of the reins, but after some thought clambered back down and led the pony instead along the track. They arrived at Hannah's cottage safely and Peder carried Jo in, too excited to speak.

"Be off with you now," said Hannah. "We don't want you getting in the way."

Peder obeyed without protest, and hurried back home to pick up the cot Griff Sullivan had made. Peder knew precious little of babies and would have to do something about that. Pigs were easy – they looked after themselves – but the newly born were complicated. No wonder Hannah had turfed him out.

Calum was out in the bay, keeping a weather-eye on proceedings. If anything happened, Peder had instructions to burn grass and pitch in the stove as a signal, but the pigman couldn't think straight today and Calum fished on, unaware of the drama.

A third trek came about simply because Peder couldn't feed himself. Jo dictated his meals and without her he was hungry. The soup cauldron had been emptied to provide the dogs with food without considering where his own next meal might be coming from. The breadbin stood empty and he risked excommunication if he opened any of Jo's preserves. He couldn't read labels anyway, and never trespassed inside the pantry. 'Banjaxed' was the word that came to mind during tonight's journey.

As man and dog approached Portleán, they could see the red light on top of the boat shed, guiding boats home. Chip sniffed the air, confident the village would feed him. Peder hitched the pony to an iron rail and walked over to Hannah's door.

"You's not thinkin' of goin' in," said a familiar voice over his shoulder. "Not allowed, Ped – none of us is allowed."

Peder turned.

"It's like this, Griff," he said. "I fergit to give Hannah the blanket. It's still wrapped in brown paper from Dooley's store – oh, and the cradle. Jo will need it after the *leanbh* (baby) is born and –"

"S'that the best excuse yer kin think of, O'Brien? Shame on ye, you ain't allowed to disturb. None of us is. Lizzie an' Hannah is seein' to the babe. Best you leave it to them. There's rabbit stew in the cauldron an' it's kept hot. C'mon Ped, our house is your house, sure enough."

All the houses were built around a central stone fireplace, with black slate tiles on the floor covered with rush mats. The Sullivan's house also had an extension out back where Ronny's brother Griff lived. The smokehouse, where cod, mackerel, sea bass, and occasionally salmon were fumed deep brown, was not in use tonight as the boats were out after the herring.

"Well look who jus' walked in," said Bridey Sullivan. "An' you about to become a father. I'm guessing you ain't seen a bite of food since lil' Jo took off fer a bit of peace an' quiet this mornin'. Am I not right, Peder O'Brien?"

Peder had the look of a man who had been found out, but he always enjoyed Bridey's banter. Living next door to Hannah meant Bridey had seen Jo's arrival and was happy for her. She and Ronny had no children of their own, but she had more than enough to do looking after Ronny and Griff. The brothers built wooden boats and were known as far away as Kenmare and Baltimore for the quality of their work, and the respect and affection in which they were held meant every boat built at Portleán was launched by Bridey herself. The smokehouse had followed naturally because they had materials to hand, and when anyone needed help with building work, they provided custom-designed tools for thatching or wattle fencing.

"Sit yourself down, Peder, you're lookin' fretful, I'm nigh feelin' sorry for you."

She filled a bowl with rabbit stew, new potatoes and a gravy so rich a man could be forgiven if he said out loud it had come from Heaven itself. Two full helpings were gratefully received.

"You must've known," she said. "We allus have meat Saturdays. Six days we have fish, but Saturday is special for us Sullivans."

She excused herself and went round to see if there was news of Jo's baby. Ronny and Griff got out the uillean pipes and squeezebox and Peder was soon asleep in front of the stove, softly snoring.

Lizzie Byrne lived in a small cottage beyond Carravoe, but tended to walk down to Portleán rather than the nearer village, where there were people she did not want to meet. She had her own reasons, and used the rivalry between the fishermen of the two small ports as an excuse. Lizzie was an attractive girl and drew too much attention in Carravoe village for her own peace of mind.

She had been born in *An Daingean* (Dingle) and had been discovered by nuns one stormy night outside the convent's front gate, a few months old and wrapped in a filthy blanket. If it had not been summertime, she likely would not have survived. She was fostered a number of times by desperately poor families before being retrieved by the nuns when she was seven and put to work in the convent laundry. There she lived a pitiable existence, spending twelve hours a day scrubbing clothes. A few years later, a priest requested her transfer to a presbytery in Tralee for all the wrong reasons. Aged eleven or twelve, she fell prey to morning sickness and in her naivety had no idea why.

Scandal had to be avoided without fail. First there was denial, with a nameless voice claiming, "That cannot be – you must be mistaken," but the reply was unequivocal: "If it *is* true, we must act swiftly. There's no time to lose."

Shadowy figures in the night hustled Lizzie into a cart and hid her beneath a blanket. Despite the fear that gripped her, she was determined to survive. As the horses clattered over the cobbles in the dark, she sensed the wagon going uphill. She peeked through the blackness, felt the cool rain and decided to make a break for it. When the horses slowed to a plod, she clambered over the tailgate and dropped onto the road. Murky lights twinkled in the distance. She took off in the opposite direction and headed inland. It was hard going for the barefoot girl, but the sense of relief kept her going until, utterly exhausted, she fell asleep in the rain, sheltered by a stone wall and a thicket of alder.

She woke to dappled sunlight. Sheep were grazing just yards away. She was hungry, but couldn't face eating so began to explore, taking care to stay out of sight. The foothills were easily climbed. Beyond, she could see mountains. Occasionally there were streams and once, a road, which she walked for a time to climb an intimidating gorge. When she sensed people about, she hid in gullies, holding onto her precious liberty.

She had no idea how long she trudged, but eventually she found shelter and stopped as clouds gathered. There were berries to eat and leaves, which made her feel queasy. A tiny spring gave just enough moisture. As darkness fell, she slept again.

By daybreak, she was so cold her teeth chattered uncontrollably and her arms and hands were blue. She headed for the road, leaving the higher ground behind. As the sun rose, she spied a knot of people in the far distance, some on horseback and others on foot, and hid in a gully until they had passed. More people were coming up behind them, so she left the road and headed out across the moor. There were plenty of animal tracks which made the going easy, but on seeing a cluster of cottages and feeling terribly sick, she knew this was it. She could go no further and would have to accept the inevitable punishment.

lizzie

peaks coalesce, thunder rumbles
the hillside, in watery sunlight
she lies, rainwashed, lost fox in the shadows,
moss mocking, as sundew tears

50

trickle, seep out to the sea
meet rocks beneath feet

that slip silent onwards. trees split open,
heedless of bracken, of heather

the summer's beginning, the running
the window, the lies beyond the sky

She collapsed into the bracken just short of the nearest cottage. An elderly couple spotted her and carried her into their simple dwelling. They reasoned that the girl must be a fugitive, but she undoubtedly needed help. No one saw them take her in. They had no children of their own and had saved Lizzie from certain death, so it felt right to keep her.

The tiny village of Brosna lay in a patch of heathland between rain-soaked hills. Few people lived there, and no one questioned Lizzie's presence. *Mháthair* let it be known she was the daughter of a cousin who had passed away. Lizzie had clearly been systemically raped over a long period of time, but Mháthair knew how to deal with the unwanted pregnancy. This involved a knitting needle, a bottle of poteen to deaden the pain and a good neighbour who had bitter experience of such things. There were no prayers offered and no witnesses. The foetus was removed, and Lizzie survived the trauma of violation.

Once she regained her health, her foster mother taught her to read and play the fiddle, but the father died soon after, leaving the women to tend the holding alone. Life became much harder, and when Mháthair died the following year, Lizzie moved on, across the River Blackwater and Bogger Mountains and south to Macroom. Desperately hungry, and having never been inside a shop before, she lifted a big potato and a turnip from an outside stall and was immediately seized. With no money and only a battered violin case and the clothes she stood in, she was sent first to the young offender's court, where the violin was confiscated, and then to another convent.

Lizzie viewed religion as a kind of purgatory, but she resolved to survive. Having tasted freedom at Brosna, she knew there was a better way.

The Abbess interviewed her and was sufficiently impressed to make an offer, which resulted in Lizzie preparing for the novitiate. She had escaped before and felt confident that she could again, but for now she would bide her time. The convent provided a bed and food on the table, and when the Mother Superior produced Lizzie's violin, suddenly she had friends. She stayed five years, patiently waiting for another chance of liberty.

Her caring nature impressed the sisters and it was tempting to stay. Absconding from a convent and denying holy orders was a heinous crime, and a roof over her head and charity had its attractions, but one day a newly promoted Abbess took office and everything changed again. There was to be a celebration in the chancery, and Lizzie would play the violin, in front of the entire assembly and in the presence of his grace the Archbishop of Munster.

"And after that," said Lizzie, under her breath, "I'll be gone, far away."

Fate took a hand in her plans with the advent of the Great War. In December 1915, Lizzie enlisted with the Red Cross as a nurse and took ship from Cobh Harbour. The war years had their own share of traumas, but Lizzie grew swiftly in competence and self-reliance, making herself indispensable. After hostilities ended, she stayed behind in Abbeville for several months nursing the wounded. In 1919 she sought to remain in Picardy, but the authorities, riddled with petty jealousies, scotched the idea and rounded up the last of the volunteer nurses, ordering them home.

On her return to Ireland, Lizzie simply vanished. No one came looking for her. She had no kin and was officially still considered a nun. She shed her Red Cross uniform, took a train to Cork, a bus to Bantry, and continued on foot. In Macroom, she had been Sister Sheelagh, but now she reclaimed her own name, Elizabeth Byrne, and rented a cottage close by Carravoe. She had her skills as a nurse, her freedom and her violin. The rest of the world could do what it wanted.

But then, one day, a message came that the pigman's wife was close to her time, and Lizzie was needed in Portleán.

Bridey Sullivan tried Hannah's door, but was surprised to find it barred. No one in Portleán ever knocked – visitors always let themselves in. She could see a light shining through the curtain, so knocked anyway.

"Now who could that be?" said Hannah. "Travellers lookin' fer shelter, I wonder?"

A second-hand military Dixie was coming to the boil on the driftwood-fuelled stove. Alongside was a tin bath – the only one in the village. It was taking some filling. Childbirth meant lots of washing of bedding and clothing, but Hannah was taking the opportunity to give herself a stand-up bath rather than waste hot water. She wrapped herself quickly in a knitted blanket as Bridey shouted, "S'only me, Bridey, just askin' after the *leanbh* (baby)."

Hannah let her in.

"May you be forgiven, Bridey, am't I in the altogether, scrubbin' meself ahead of the arrival. I thought it wuz the Revenue men lookin' fer whisky."

"This house is fast becomin' an oven," said Bridey, "an' you'll be catchin' the sniffles if you dare go outside. God forgive ye dancin' round naked and if the revenue men did spy you now, you'd be carted off to the colonies without an excuse."

Bridey warmed herself in front of the stove and asked after Jo.

"Lizzie is resting alongside her. No regular contractions yet, but Liz has all the experience, I'm sure. You can peep round the door, 'tis a free country."

Bridey looked in on the candle-lit scene for a moment, whispered a quiet night and closed the door again.

"And where's Calum?" she said.

"Away fishing," said Hannah, "with a lantern. The herring are shoaling, but they don't stay long. Once the sea warms up, they'll be gone to Galway and that'll be that for another year."

"Fishing alone?"

"Ah sure, Peder ought to be with him, but with the baby coming –"

"It would do him good to help Calum, surely. Havin' babies is women's work. Men only get in the way and cry a lot. I'll pop back and rouse Ronny and Griff. It'll do 'em all good to do a bit of netting."

The Sullivan brothers and Peder grumbled and even cursed at being turned out in the dark to go fishing, but no man ever got the better of Bridey Sullivan. She supplied them with bacon *ceapairí* (sandwiches) and tin flasks of tea stored inside blankets for warmth.

"And don't ye come back till ye've a boat full," she said. "We need 'em for the smokin'."

The three men had still been playing tunes and growing ever more morose, especially Peder, who had woken up and sung so out of tune neither musician could carry the melody. Bridey pointed out that their neighbour Calum had already set out on his own so they should cease their moaning and stop wasting the night.

The trio embarked in Ronny's bigger boat having loaded a sizeable net that had been recovered from the sea and could be strung between two boats using cork floats. The net was well oiled and weighed heavy in the prow of *Banphrionsa* (Princess – Ronny's pet name for Bridey).

Griff and Peder rowed in tandem to start, but soon shipped one oar and sat side-by-side with individual oars. Peder was no stranger to rowing having often accompanied Calum, but he was no mariner. They still made good headway under Griff's directions, and with a calm sea and moonlit sky, soon passed Shot Head with Ronny at the tiller. There was no wind, so little point in raising a sail.

"Has to be easterly," said Ronny. "He never turns right."

Lights were visible on Bear Island and across Bantry bay, but there was no sign of Calum. The rowers scanned the shoreline but every so often a cloud passed in front of the moon and it went eerily dark.

"Probably fishin' behind Muc Island," said Ronny. "The tide's still on the ebb. Maybe he's hoping the herring will run between the channel. See those fish boats over by Collack? They're usin' lanterns to attract the shoal."

"Maybe he's crossed the bay and joined with the Bantry boys," said Griff. "He's good mates with those lads."

"Good mates, yes, but I don't like fishin' off Sheep's Head. It's easy to get stranded on an open shore," said Ronny, "and Cal will have to pull against both tide and wind when the moon wanes – guaranteed there'll be a breeze afore he reaches home."

They kept close to the shore, Peder rowing while Ronny steered and Griff prepared the nets. Chip treated it as a game, but as they approached Muc Island, he began a deep-throated growl.

"Whassat?" said Peder. He whistled low, urging the pup to investigate. "C'mon, Chip, what do you see?"

"More like what he can hear," said Griff. "He's but 'prentice boy learning new noises."

Peder shipped the oars. The only sound was the lapping of water against the hull and in the distance, a swish of a breaking wave and the accompanying hiss on the shore.

They sat quietly for a few minutes. Chip remained *en-garde* in the bow with head lowered, ever watchful.

"Maybe them pigs," said Ronny, "or they growd-up hounds on the holding. They 'ear things that humans can't."

Peder replaced the oars in their rowlocks and moved the boat forward, aiming for the island. Suddenly the sea began to heave. Flashes of black and silver broke the surface. The herring were running, desperate to avoid the dolphins and seals that surrounded *Banphrionsa*, stampeding back into the Atlantic, away from Bantry bay.

"Dammit," said Ronny. "They's goin' the wrong way."

A dolphin smacked its enormous bulk on the water, sending spray everywhere; then another, and another, working themselves into a frenzy. Ronny stood at the tiller and bewailed the loss of so many fish. Peder had never seen anything like it. He could only cling onto the gunwale and marvel. Chip stood on the folded net, rooted to the spot.

fishing

horizons blacken to match the rocks,
barnacled hard to stop them drifting.
the fisher sees boulders, half-submerged –
point-turn-pull ropes, stronger than will,
as the wind bears all meaning away.
oh the rhythm of rowing, the silent sweep
of oars, regardless of blisters and burning,

but still the boat drags them close by the ship-fish
that flaunt their fins, their tailspin, their scorn
of these men who sail swift yet stay still;
this current which flows like contumely,
roaring its pain, its indignation
at men and boats and fish-silver shoals

It ended as quickly as it had begun, A seal grasped a stunned, solitary herring off the surface and silence followed, as if nothing had happened.

"Do they bite?" said Peder.

Ronny burst out laughing. "If you kin catch 'em," he said. "Dolphins swim so fast, even the King's Navy can't keep pace. We tried sailin' after some in the boat, fully rigged in a good breeze, an' they were just laughin' at us 'cos we were too slow, so they skidded off some place else, but as to catchin' a fish, well…"

Griff looked over the side and chuckled. "They might be just big fish, but they're the real masters of the sea. We see 'em often in the bay and when –"

Chip barked, then growled, looking directly toward Muc Island.

"The current's easing," said Ronny. "Drop the blades of the oars into the sea to keep her pointing the right way. No need to row – just keep her heading through the channel."

The black boat closed the gap and within minutes Ronny steered through the channel between the shore and Muc Island. Chip was still snarling.

"Stay," said Peder. "What's up Chip – what's with you?"

The boat eased past several wrecked vessels. Another cloud moved across the moon, but they'd already spotted a line of cork floats running between a wooden stake on the shore, and a scuttled boat across the channel.

"Hold it," yelled Ronny. "Hit the beach – now. Go left. LEFT! You're going the wrong way – use your right oar you eejit!"

Griff hung over the gunwale and grabbed the net's top line, steadily working toward the shore. A few seconds more and the boat touched the bottom.

"No harm done," said Griff, "but the net is Calum's surely, so where the hell is he?"

Ronny clambered over the side and secured the anchor. The current was less strong in the channel, but this was slack water and soon the tide

56

would turn. If they wanted to keep the boat buoyant, they would need to anchor her safely, or they would have to wait hours to refloat her.

Chip barked again and wagged his tail.

"Where's Cal?" said Peder. "Go find him!"

Chip leapt off the prow, and followed the shoreline before plunging into the sea and swimming for the island, with Peder and Griff close behind. It wasn't deep. Griff lost his footing once but they only had fifty yards to cross. Neither could swim, but the net gave them all the help they needed. Peder towered over Griff, so kept tight hold of his friend's shirt collar, just in case. The shock of getting soaked reminded him why he preferred a firm sod under his feet.

The wolfhound shook himself dry. Calum's púcán lay safely beached on the mud. Chip had the scent and barked at the wreck of a bigger iron-framed boat. Peder worked himself through a gap in the hull. Chip had already found Calum and was barking excitedly. Peder and Griff assessed the situation, peering through the darkness. Calum must have slipped on the weed-covered deck, and in trying to save himself, fallen heavily. From the angle of his left arm, it was likely broken. The man was incoherent with pain. His arm needed dealing with urgently.

Calum

broken arm,
pointed and ardent with pain
beyond the waves of home

he silent-howls at the ocean
its waves, its spume
and the ocean roars back
with a stench of kelp

he falls through sharp indigo
ocean-deep pain
ever the pain

Griff cut through Calum's clothing. Off came the sleeve of the *bainín* (sweater) along with his shirt. Peder tore up his own shirt into strips for bandages.

"Need to make some splints," said Griff. "See what you can do, Ped. Listen up: there's a bottle of poteen in the boat. Get Ronny to bring it over. The less Cal knows, the easier it'll be to get him back home. Lizzie's been nursing for years, Heaven sent, but we've still got to get Cal back to Portleán. He's sufferin' bad."

Peder clambered down to the shore through the mud while Ronny moved his boat to the middle of the channel, cursing the tide which could leave them stuck fast. There was enough buoyancy for now, but it wouldn't last. Re-floating Calum's boat could be a problem.

"Gae us a hand there, Peder," said Ronny. "If we don't get Cal's boat under tow she'll be wrecked if the weather turns. It'd be wicked to lose such a fine boat. I'll cut the line and drag the net to the shore. That should save the net and the catch, but we'll have to move fast. The herring's been running as the tide's already turned."

Calum's net was weighed down by hundreds of herring. Ronny insisted they salvage every fish but Peder was thinking of Calum. You could catch fish any time.

Ronny leant over the stern and handed the poteen bottle to Peder, who waded back. When he reached the island, he broke off some willow branches and clambered back onto the wreck. Everything seemed to be against him. The wreck listed to port and the darkness meant every step had to be tested before trusting it with any weight.

He crouched down beside Calum. "Are ye still with us?"

There was no response. Griff had laid his coat over Calum's inert form. He took the willow sticks from Peder and fashioned them into a crude splint. The weather remained calm, though the cloud was thickening and this being the Beara, it could change in an instant.

"I'm cutting the line," said Ronny. "Don't fergit to stow it carefully. Cal will need it, sure enough. Anythin' caught in the mesh can be dealt with when we get back to Portleán."

Peder and Griff lashed willow boughs tightly round Calum's arm with cotton strips. They fastened Peder's belt buckle round the whole and finished the job with two lengths of untwisted rope. Griff tried unsuccessfully to get Calum to sip some poteen. He remembered seeing Lizzie using it to sterilize a wound, so sloshed the rest over the broken arm, hoping it would help. Peder filched Griff's belt to make a sling.

Ronny shouted something, but Griff was in no mood. "Will you shut it, Ron. Everythin' comes to they who waits. We's doin' the best we can." He turned to Peder, "He's sayin' if we don't get out of the channel, it'll be too late."

Peder stooped down and lifted Calum.

"Keep tight hold of me, Griff. Watch every step. 'Tis murder walkin' along this deck, but 'tis the only way."

Peder hoisted Calum to his shoulder the way he would a pig and made sure every step was firmly planted.

Griff walked ahead, checking for unexpected obstacles. Every so often, he had to grab tight hold of Peder as they both flailed in the darkness. Finally they scrambled over the stern of the wreck but had to negotiate mud, smooth stones and rotting timbers hidden below the surface. The marine debris made the fifty-yard trek to the boat a nightmare, waist-deep on a slack tide, relying on a single anchor, but eventually Calum was safely stowed in the bow.

"Where's the herring?" said Griff. "Ye didn't just sling it, Ron?"

"Under the net. Hundreds of 'em. We might have to walk both vessels for a time 'cos it's a full load, but if we can get through the channel before the tide changes, we'll make Portleán by sunrise."

Calum had berthed his púcán in a tiny creek so that he could easily re-float it. They dragged it backwards into enough water and fixed a tow-rope using Calum's anchor warp. Peder hated being wet, but he and Griff were obliged to walk beside the black boat for some hundred yards, gripping the gunwale for fear of losing it, and watching out for troughs and debris. Ronny raised the mainsail and sang the praises of an easterly breeze, the least likely wind to blow across the Beara.

"Dammit," said Ronny, "we should have the jib raised, too."

"I'm seein' to it," said Griff. He clambered gingerly over Calum, pushed the bowsprit out to its fullest extent and fixed it in position. From beneath the deck cuddy, he hauled out the jib, threaded it onto its forestay, raised it, and allowed it to fill with wind. Out went the boom, the sail bulging in the breeze as Ronny tied the ropes, but just as they seemed to be free, something graunched on the bottom and the boat shuddered to a stop.

"Bastard!" said Ronny. "She's grounding!"

Ronny leapt over the stern to reduce the weight of the vessel.

"Abandon ship!" he yelled. "Both of you, over the side, and push like you've never pushed before!"

Banphrionsa responded by lifting her head slightly. Calum's unladen púcán followed behind on its tow rope.

"An' again *óige* (boys), keep pushing."

Suddenly Bridey's princess had water beneath her keel. With the breeze still swelling her sails, she began to move forward.

"Get in Ped, and you, Griff. She's flyin', she's a good 'un, sure enough."

Peder didn't need further encouragement. Arms and legs piled into the boat. Chip, who had been trotting along the shoreline, took a flying leap and was hauled over the gunwale by Griff. Ronny regained the helm as Griff adjusted the ropes. Peder cradled Calum, trying to keep him warm. Across Bantry bay, the fishing boats still searched for herring with lanterns, but *Banphrionsa* was galloping for home.

A chill dawn dragged itself across the Shehy Mountains on the easterly wind, with the pungent scent of moorland, hedgerow and meadow. Ronny kept the two boats central in the estuary as they rounded Shot Head. They sailed the final mile close-hauled across the wind.

Damp limbs shook themselves awake and even Calum stirred. On the final stretch, Griff lowered the sails and Ronny turned the boat into the wind. Bridey's princess had delivered.

Nobody was there to greet them. Griff stepped off and moored both vessels to the quayside. It was five o'clock and hardly light, but Peder, with Calum in his arms, spotted a posse of women standing outside Hannah's house, despite the unearthly hour. One of them came down towards him.

"Well who'd a believed?" said Bridey. "What's with you, Peder O'Brien. Isn't it enough that you need to carry a baby of your own?"

The other women moved closer, all talking at once.

"Poor *leanbh*, and him sent out to fish on his own. You miserable *óige*. No wonder there's no fish to be had," said Hannah. "It'll be bread an' scrape for breakfast, dinner an' supper; mark my words."

Just when Peder had begun to think that the world had gone mad, Lizzie appeared in the doorway of Hannah's cottage, holding a bundle of cream swaddling clothes.

The women hushed as she crossed the gravelled roadway.

"I think you've got the wrong babe," she said. "Best you hand Cal over to me. You've another mouth to feed, Peder O'Brien. Born around midnight, I'd say. No problems. You've a beautiful daughter and she's looking far rosier than you or any of us. Jo is resting inside. She's just fine."

the return

seagulls glimpsed through mizzling cloud landscapes:
sky mountains, forests, clouds slumped in purple
as siren songs float through the morning mists
and honeyed scents cling to the moors

the shades of dawn gather:
seabirds with stiff wings gliding
contend with clouds for supremacy.

each flighty black speck, each squawk, each mewl,
each keening cry, each tenacious feather
hints at sweetness unlooked for
                    unknown until Peder's return

Chapter Six

The Petitioners

May was the time for haymaking, but Calum's broken arm meant he was banished from the fields. The heat of the day kept him indoors. He made himself useful watching the comings and goings along the lower track, so was ready and waiting when someone knocked at the door.

"Come in, whoever you are," he said.

Nobody entered so Calum got up to answer despite his bare-chested, stubbly state, his arm still encased in the plaster cast Lizzie had made.

A dark-suited young man in a red choker and tweed cap stood at the door.

"Fine are ye?" said Calum. "We don't get many callers, but you's welcome and the kettle is nigh singing. Come in, 'tis a free country."

The stranger doffed his cap and shoved it in a jacket pocket.

"Issa a warm one," he said. "I just pushed the barrow from Rossdore." He pointed to a quaint contraption outside the house. "I'm a grinder by trade, so if there's folks needing sharp scythes and sickles – anything really – then I'm yer man. I also do whetstones and ash-wood handles."

"If ye've pushed that lot from Rossdore you deserve a wet and some food," said Calum. "Sit yerself down an' I'll be lookin' after ye."

The gorse on the track past Portleán made access difficult, but the villagers were fond of their sheltered place in the sun overlooking the bay. Travellers had struggled a thousand years or more to get over the pass before descending to sea level at Carravoe.

"I was advised to avoid coming this way," said the grinder, "but the track's in fine fettle at the moment as everythin's so dry. 'Tis a bit flinty, but pleasant enough."

"We rarely cross the mountain," said Calum. "Too much like hard work and the weather can change in an instant."

"Fine for those who like the sun, less so in winter, I'm sure. Where is everybody? I've hardly seen a soul."

"The village is haymaking, all of us 'cept me, of course. Broke my arm fishing."

"Maybe I could lend a hand," said the grinder. "Amn't I Jimmy Lamb from Youghal?"

Calum didn't know where Youghal was, not that it mattered as once Jimmy had his feet under the table he was happy to expound on the merits of the town, as well as Cork City, Cobh and anywhere else that Calum hadn't seen. The fisherman's world only extended as far as Bantry and Baltimore, though he had heard of Cobh as his father's schooner had sailed from there to the Newfoundland Banks.

"Is Cobh a grand place?" said Calum.

"'Tis bigger now since the Great War, but most folks are lookin' to get out of Ireland and who can blame 'em with the fightin'. Putting bread on the family's table should be our priority, not civil war."

Calum grimaced. Talk of politics and nationalism went over his head. The streets of Rossdore and Bantry were riddled with revolutionary blarney, despite an awareness of the several thousand sailors on Bear Island, so it was small wonder Calum felt safest in Portleán or out at sea.

He remembered his duties as host and busied himself at the stove. A bit of goose-fat and butter went into a blackened pan, followed by six plump pork sausages.

"Fried-bread doused with porter and a pair of duck eggs?" he said.

"Just so long as you's joining me," said Jimmy, as the sausages spluttered and spat. "I'm only a little fellah."

He took over the stove while Calum searched for eggs.

Cooking done, the two men sat on the bench outside the front door, occasionally burping and enjoying the impromptu repast, their plates piled high with fried onions, bacon, rhubarb chutney, watercress from the stream that trickled by the house and buttered bread. Sated at last, Jimmy Lamb went back indoors to do the washing up.

The fishermen's cottages overlooked the quayside. A crude sundial featuring a mermaid's face and numerals peered out from the thatch of the Sullivans' house, facing south across the bay. A rod served as the mermaid's nose and though rudimentary, it gave a fair approximation of the time if the sun was shining.

"I'm thinking," said Calum as Jimmy returned to the bench, "when the shadow looks straight down, we can walk over to the haymaking and make ourselves known. 'Tis hardly a stone's throw over the bank there."

"I'm with you there," said Jimmy. "S'there anythin' I can tote?"

"Maybe a whetstone or two," said Calum. "That should introduce you to the reapers."

Calum donned a collarless shirt with Jimmy's assistance. The plaster itched, but Lizzie had insisted it remain in place for six weeks. "Otherwise," she'd said, "I'll break the other arm too, just to keep you in order."

Jimmy retied the sling round Calum's neck.

"Whetstones. Let me see now." He grubbed around in his jute sack and pulled out three granite beauties to tempt the Portleán haymakers. "Untouched since I quarried 'em," he said. "The finest in all Ireland."

"I'll carry 'em." said Calum. "You can bring the bottles of *leanna* (stout)."

"Done," said Jimmy. "My God, you live well in this village."

Jimmy joined a score of sweaty harvesters, scything, turning hay for drying, and fixing handles needing repair. One of the girls stitched a shirt-tail to Jimmy's tweed cap to protect his neck. The blazing sun never let up. The labourers had never seen weather like it. They fashioned willow sticks into haycocks to dry the felled hay in the meadows, loading them onto wagons each evening to be built into haystacks in the shelter of a stone wall where the wind wouldn't undo the hard work.

Jimmy

Jimmy grinds sickles and shovels and scythes,
sorts out spades and the *slean*; all manners of blade,
he'll sharpen your chisels, grind knives, every size,
strop your cut-throat razors, hone axes and adzes,
– and Jimmy loves Lizzie (they all love Lizzie).

He sharpens his wits and hones his skills
to woo the fair maid – but who will win her?

Another irregular itinerant was making his way to Portleán just before the end of May, toting a gypsy caravan behind a pair of mules – one for hauling and the other for when a hill had to be climbed. Joshua O'Gara had his name artistically painted on both sides of his caravan, with TINKER beneath in perfect script.

He had reached the summit over the pass at first light, but dropping down to sea-level would take hours. The descent required good brakes made of woodblocks clamped to the wheel rims, which had to be regularly doused with water to keep them operable. The recent sunny weather meant the streams and pools were bone dry and the only solution was to wedge stones ahead of the wheels. Josh had to make frequent stops before reaching level ground halfway down the mountain, where he was relieved to find a trickle of water in a streambed.

"Will you be stealing all the river?" said a woman's voice behind him.

"Damnty, caught in the act," said Joshua. "May I be forgiven, ma'am?"

"I'm no ma'am," said Lizzie Byrne. "When I am, you'll be the first to know."

Josh lowered the two full buckets on the ground and rested his arms.

"Joshua O'Gara at your service – Miss. Tinkerin's my trade. Anythin' needing repair, I'm yer man. Pots an' pans, household renewals, ironwork, solderin', patchin', screws and washers, a bolt or two, leatherwork –"

Lizzie raised her hand. "And lots of talking. I hear you plain enough. Best you call in as there's plenty needing attention, but first give those horses a fill, and if there's grass to be had by the roadside, they're welcome."

Josh made the caravan safe and unhitched the mules.

"'Tis funny weather," he said. "Likely, we'll have to pay for it eventually."

He perched on the doorstep of Lizzie's cottage and examined several items in need of repair. Pennies were scarce on the peninsula, but if you fixed a few things charitably, others would queue for attention. He had missed tinkering because of the Great War and had lost touch with many of his patrons.

"You're a fine looking girl," he said "but I don't recall you at all. Maybe you grew up while I was in France, fighting the Kaiser."

"You weren't the only one," said Lizzie. "Some of us were caring for the wounded. I served as a nurse in Amiens until the Armistice and stayed behind to help the wounded at Abbeville's lunatic asylum. I'd still be there if some fool officer hadn't ordered us home."

"That's 'cos you're a woman. Likely if you'd a moustache and were bald, it would have been a different tale. Girls show men up in this envious world."

"Water under the bridge now. Soldiers I could abide, but officers were troublemakers."

"Spoken as one who knows."

"So, will you wear out my doorstep with your chattering or do the decent thing and mend my pots and pans?"

"Consider it done, Mrs – whatever you call yourself."

"It's Miss, not Mrs, and you're talking to Elizabeth Byrne, but I can't offer you a kettle 'cos it has a hole in the bottom. As soon as it's fixed, I'm sure I'll be able to find a bit of bread and cheese and maybe a mug to accompany the tea you'll be receiving."

Josh began fixing everything needing a fix and several others that didn't, but despite his affable nature his flirting got him nowhere with Lizzie who was immune to such things. She had gone through the Great War dealing with broken men and doctors alike, trying and failing to win her. All men received short shrift, and her cottage, well out of sight of the main road, was her defence against the might of the Catholic Church.

"How much will I be paying?" she asked the tinker.

"Nary a farthing, Miss," said Joshua. "I've enjoyed both your hospitality and the company. My belly is full and if I can cross the river before dark, I'll be a happy man."

"'Tisn't far, barely a mile and it won't be dark for ages. The hardest part is getting round the Mount, but you should reach Portleán tonight. You'll not find many along this road for the tinkering, but if you've a mind, there are cottars in the village who'll welcome you.

Joshua took Lizzie's hand and kissed it. She accepted the gesture with indifference.

"Farewell Lady 'Lizbeth," said Joshua. "I'll return when the meadows turn green again."

"Hopefully before the bottom falls out my saucepan."

Josh

Josh can fix buckets and pails and cans
mend saucepans and kettles, coffee pots, sieves,
the venerable Dixie and baths made of tin
with his snips, his nuts, his bolts, his rivets
his nails, screws and washers, his hammers and pincers,

however, can he fix hearts with a soldering iron?
Stones out of horses' shoes – never a bother –
however, hearts? Especially his own?

Once the hay harvest had been gathered in, Josh turned his hand to fixing various pots, cauldrons, pans, utensils – and even Celia Toomey's silver whistle, discovered under the roof of an abandoned hovel. Celia quickly became proficient on the instrument, to everyone's delight. The tinker worked his way through Portleán and would have moved onto Carravoe had it not been for the arrival of a pedlar with goods to sell when Josh was of a mind to buy.

Billy Bonner hailed from Skibbereen and traded from a four-wheel wagon pulled by a pair of donkeys. He called every season with second-hand clothing, much of it military cast offs of which there was never a shortage. He was known as the Hawker, supplier of apparel to needy folks in Kerry and West Cork. WILLIAM T. BONNER it said on the tailgate and buckboard of his cart: CLOTHES FOR ALL. Billy was always sure of a warm welcome in Portleán.

Jimmy the grinder took to offering haircuts: a penny a trim – children half price, while Josh the tinker spent most of his day repairing horse tack using a rudimentary forge fuelled by driftwood. Bespectacled Billy Bonner set up shop under his wagon's bright red awning and sold haberdashery, fabric and clothing. A line of seamstresses soon appeared, stitching and altering on the steps of Portleán's houses. Summer was just round the corner.

Living in a remote community and unable to hear or speak meant Jo had grown to value Lizzie's friendship greatly, especially as Peder was often away working. She wished Lizzie would leave her hillside cottage and move in with her and Peder, at least temporarily, so she made the suggestion. The more the women discussed this, the more it felt like the right thing to do. From Lizzie's point of view, her isolated cottage might have allowed her to live quietly, but it had brought loneliness – and might be making her conspicuous. Rightly or wrongly, she feared what the Roman Catholic hierarchy would do if they discovered an apostate.

When Jo put the suggestion to Peder, he saw difficulties immediately, arguing that their house didn't have a proper staircase, there was no fireplace upstairs, and they would have to share facilities.

Jo said these were just excuses and easily remedied. She further insisted that she would need the pony and gig next week, because that was when she would be moving Lizzie off the hillside. Reluctantly, Peder agreed – he and Jo were best mates as much as they were man and wife, and the big man always took time to understand her point of view. The solution however could only be temporary, so he set to thinking how Lizzie could best be provided with a permanent home in Portleán.

Calum was itching to have the plaster cast removed, but Lizzie was still refusing. Peder looked on, amused.

"You're in too much of a hurry," said Lizzie. "There'll be all kinds of bits and pieces lodged inside the cast because you won't keep it in the sling. That's why it's itchy."

Cal looked so sorry for himself that eventually Lizzie took pity and plunged the entire arm in a sink of cold water laced with horse liniment and cloves, followed by calamine lotion and talcum powder.

"What are you doing'?" squealed Calum. "Why cloves?"

Lizzie said she had seen this remedy used in France, and he was to mind his own business.

Calum didn't argue. With no affordable doctor in the area, Lizzie was precious – she saved lives – so looking after her was crucial for the village. Besides, wasn't she the finest fiddler in the area? This mattered, with the ceilidh to mark the arrival of Midsummer on everyone's mind.

"Been the best hay harvest ever," said Peder as he filled the kettle.

"Weather's on the change," said Calum. "Wonder what's coming' next?"

Clouds were building on the horizon and the haze had disappeared with the drop in temperature and a westerly wind.

"No change for you," said Peder. "You haven't caught a fish in weeks and if Liz has her way, you'll be eating' sausages till next year."

Peder served the mugs of extraordinarily strong tea to Jo, Lizzie and Calum. Lizzie never complained – she'd been hardened to such brews in Amiens and Abbeville – but Jo wrinkled her nose in disgust.

The two men were still laughing at Peder's efforts to make drinkable tea half an hour later as they walked to the quayside where Billy Bonner was tempting Hannah with an offcut of gingham. Calum had a florin and a threepenny bit in his pocket. Billy was happy to take the florin as payment for the cloth, while the threepenny bit went on a fancy sling for the broken arm.

"Damnty," said Calum. "Caught again. Every time the hawker calls at our house, he picks my pocket."

Hannah was looking after baby Siobhan for the day while Jo and Lizzie decorated the temporary accommodation. The infant's crib stood outside in the sunshine. Billy fussed round the babe as bachelors do, knowing nothing of parental responsibilities.

"Would you like to give me a hand in changing her nappy?" said Hannah, picking up the child.

"I wouldn't have a clue," said Billy. "I'd be scared to drop her. Babies are women's work. I know my place and the nursery aren't one of 'em."

"Pity, pity," said Hannah. "There's a terrible lack of men this side of the bay – the kind that make girls want to marry."

Billy blushed so much he had to take off his horn-rimmed spectacles and mop his brow with a scarlet handkerchief.

Lizzie returned to her hillside cottage later that evening. It was still light, but she didn't enjoy being out late and wished she had taken up Peder's offer of a lift. The next morning she caught sight of a pony and trap making its way along the riverbank. She hoped it was Jo, but ran and hid behind the cottage to watch from its relative safety just in case.

Jo crossed the ford, climbed the gravelled incline and drew up outside the door. She looked around for her friend, puzzled, until Lizzie came out from the side of the cottage smiling and waving.

"Thought you were the revenue man," said Lizzie. The word 'revenue' took some explaining, but Jo loved to learn and was happy to chat. Lizzie had packed everything so they bade farewell to the hillside cottage and loaded the gig with the Gladstone bag from Amiens which accompanied Lizzie everywhere, a white-painted medicine chest from Rossdore Market, a pair of old carpetbags and the precious fiddle.

The move inevitably caught the eye of the trio of itinerant travellers – artisans and gentlemen of the road, James Lamb, Joshua O'Gara and William Bonner. Flaming June had arrived with dreams of romantic attachments, so each of them found an excuse to stay in the village – corn harvest, potato harvest, peat harvest. The cleans and shovels in Portleán were now the sharpest in all Ireland, courtesy of Jimmy; and Josh's ad hoc forge blossomed into the real thing, attached to the Sullivan's boat shed to fashion ironwork such as anchors and pulleys.

Billy Bonner's fancy also turned to Lizzie Byrne, and with Midsummer Day approaching, he grunted and sweated his way over the pass and down the coast road to Castletown where he pitched his wagon on the quayside. Plump Billy worked hard, was scrupulously honest, always had a smile and was renowned for his Irish flannel. By the next morning he had auctioned every bolt and sliver of weave together with shirts, socks and underwear at nonsensical prices on Castletown Quay. Now, lightly laden, he trotted his wagon back to Portleán in the nick of time.

"Made it," he said, "and I took a bath last night."

Along the way, he had gathered a fancy bouquet of dog roses and fuchsias together with bits of greenery and meadow flowers. He put the blooms in the pail he used to water the donkeys, hung from a bracket beneath the wagon.

William

William T Bonner, hawker by trade
carries (wait for it – a take a deep breath):

suits, trousers, jackets; belts and braces;
handkerchiefs, waistcoats, vests and pants;
long Johns; caps, hats, balaclavas;
shoes, boots and laces; shirts, sou'westers;
and let's not forget the ladies of course –
dresses, corsets, thingummies (you know)
lisle stockings, skirts and blouses, cardigans,
buttons and bows, needles and thread,
even string, and the prettiest dancing shoes

– but will Lizzie want to dance with a hawker
or will she choose another?

The Sullivan brothers had worked together to build the staircase just inside Peder's front door, but Griff's own pet project was a box bed with an intricately carved rose on the headboard. Lizzie's arrival had stirred the bachelor's affections and his thoughts had turned to romance. He was grateful for the evening light, as his brother would have complained if he'd used a lantern and candles didn't provide enough light for fine carving.

"That's cosy," said Bridey. "Now who could that be for?"

She had come into the workshop to check that the current boat under construction could be moved out in time for the ceilidh. Griff was so absorbed in his carving, he hadn't heard her come in. He dropped his chisel, and trying to recover it, clouted the headboard and fell to his knees holding a hand to his eye.

Bridey helped him up.

"Will we go into the house, Griff," she said. "There's a bit of pork loin in the larder. Best you slap it on your eye and hope for the best. This new púcán has to be moved out tomorrow and that means using Brendan Tate's shires, so 'tis time for bed. I want you up and about early. Never mind polishing a bed for your secret love."

Griff blushed, stemming the tears that were welling up inside. Bridey had seen straight through him.

There were others.

A young priest had been seconded to Carravoe as curate in charge. The impoverished parish and its school could never support a licensed teacher, but this particular curate had ambitions beyond his calling and was curious about the pretty girl rumoured to be living alone on the hillside. He had visited the cottage twice, but the lady in question always seemed to be out. He had also visited neighbouring Portleán but had found the villagers either hostile or beyond salvation. This made him even more determined to save them from their ignorance. He discovered they were having a ceilidh on Midsummer Eve and diligently prayed for guidance. Celibacy was a requirement for his salvation, but not all the praying in the world would redeem him as he concluded that lust, not the power of prayer, was the only way to cure his melancholy.

A wee poem for Father Cullen

She's never at home
when I call –
never there.
But she's always at home
when I dream.
Mea culpa,
mea maxima culpa.

And her eyes light up
and she beckons me in
and I come, dear Lord, I come!
Holy Mary, Mother of God
pray for us sinners.

But who is the sinner?
The one who calls,
or the one who is never at home
when called?
Surely she sins more greatly than I,
with love in my heart
and lust in my loins –

Lizzie! My Lizzie!
De profundis oro te!

The next morning, at the end of a soaking wet week, which had broken the
earlier heat wave, the clouds finally broke to reveal blue sky from Dursey
Head to Knockboy Mountain. Calum donned boots and an oilskin over his
injured arm while Hannah knotted a string round his middle.

"You's lookin' like a trussed chicken," she said, "ready for the
toastin'."

"Can't expect Lizzie to tramp down here this morning," said Calum.
"Besides, she might say it's still not set enough and would only have to
trek back ag'in. I'll walk to the O'Briens and ask if she'll remove the
plaster."

"You poor mite," said Hannah. "Eight weeks sufferin' and still no
relief. I don't think you oughta go 'cos if you slipped an' broke the other
arm, you'd be pickled an' I'd have to feed you meself an' haven't I got
enough to do as it is?"

"I'm only goin' to Peder's place, Mam. Won't be gone more'n an
hour."

"You an' yer arm," said Hannah. "And don't think you're goin'
dancin' tonight. That arm is stayin' in its sling for the ceilidh an' if I see it
wavin' about, I'll be tyin' it round yer neck."

He slipped and squelched his way over the soggy hill. His arm itched
so badly he couldn't help cursing, and the cuts on his chin made him look
as if he'd been dragged through hawthorns. Calum hated shaving,
especially one-handed, but Lizzie's throwaway quip about standing closer

73

to the razor had got him thinking about love – not that he knew much about it. All thoughts of the opposite sex were based on his experience at market where he'd learnt that girls were a bit peculiar and certainly baffling. They stuck together and talked in whispers, or else they squealed aloud – or completely ignored him. Sometimes he found himself buying things from them with no idea of what they were, and that in turn earned him a ticking off from Hannah for purchases she didn't need. Women were undeniably strange – save for Elizabeth Byrne. He understood Lizzie.

Calum caught a whiff of the baking long before he reached the house. Lizzie and Jo were making sausage rolls, pork pies, bacon tartlets and crackling chips. Peder was away helping a neighbour. Some sheep had drowned, and cottars never wasted an animal. The carcass would be recovered, salted, and distributed freely in the village, with the cottar receiving his reward in kind come winter.

Calum took off his boots in the porch and hung up his oilskin coat after wrestling with the string tied round his waist.

Jo waved flowery white hands at him in greeting. Lizzie had charge of the stove.

"*Fáilte*," (Welcome) said Lizzie too busy to entertain broken-armed visitors.   Calum tried to talk to baby Siobhan but was hopeless in conversing with the newly born. Jo poured a mug of milk and offered Calum a glistening pork pie. She blew on her fingers to signal it was hot.

"You're both looking well – and Siobhan," said Calum, but what he really wanted to know was the latest opinion on the arm. Getting that question out flummoxed him. He couldn't work out how to introduce the subject. He accepted the pie and went through all the questions he could ask, without saying anything at all. The womenfolk got on with the washing-up.

"I'm thinking," said Lizzie, "you're dying to lend a hand, but you being in plaster, you've got the best possible excuse."

"And I suppose you'll be wanting to attend the ceilidh tonight?"

She clicked her tongue and warned that getting the plaster off would hurt ten times worse than the toothache and wasn't it Lizzie who had extracted that wayward molar for him last Christmas? Calum winced. He recalled the pain every time his tongue passed over the gap.

Lizzie went upstairs and brought down the heavy Gladstone bag.

"Be brave," she said. "It's goin' to take time and there's only the two of us."

She winked at Jo, who produced a bottle of Jameson's whisky. Calum was speechless. A bottle of Jameson's in Portleán was a rarity.

"Drink," said Lizzie. "We only have the one bottle."

The binding was tough. Calum stood at the sink while Lizzie reversed the arm to cut through the other side. As the plaster gaped, she drizzled a mixture of paraffin and aloes inside to ease removal, placing a sliver of polished whalebone inside the cast every inch for safety's sake. She'd done this often enough in France, always with worried eyes watching, as Calum was doing now. The more she chiselled and sawed, the more Calum knew he had fallen in love

She had rescued him a few weeks back and now nobody could have been closer. He watched her progress open-mouthed, and finally had to sit down on a stool as he'd been holding his breath for such a long time.

"Be patient," she said quietly. "Halfway there."

Jo passed the Jamieson's again, but Calum shook his head.

"Is it hurting? Tough fellah like you should be able to grin and bear it. Not long now, and if you're brave, there'll be a gingerbread man to eat."

Calum didn't respond. He only had eyes for Lizzie. When Peder came through the door, he received no acknowledgment, not even a nod. "Just in time," said Peder. "Otherwise, likely you'd have emptied the bottle."

Sullivan's boat-shed measured a good seventy feet long and half as wide. It had stayed dry despite the previous night's rain, so the men were able to sweep the floor. The village women commandeered one wall and set up tables piled high with mouth-watering treats. At three o'clock, the village elders gathered for their traditional midsummer get-together around a table specially placed in the centre of the building. The meeting lasted a mere ten minutes.

The boat-shed door had been removed so that villagers could sit outside if they wanted. Some were in the half-finished *Bád Mór* (big boat), some on benches and others on the grass. Musicians had arrived from Carravoe, Rossdore and Bantry, some sailing from the sheltered side of Sheep's Head. One party had come all the way from Baltimore. Colleens were wearing plaited flowers as necklaces and decorating their hair with wild flowers or strips of coloured ribbon. The men were mostly in black, the boys trying to look grown-up in their hand-me-down white shirts under sober waistcoats. A small group was doing some last minute dance practice alongside the colleens who were high-stepping traditional reels. The band had been strengthened with young Celia Toomey on her low silver whistle and Griff on accordion.

Jimmy Lamb, Josh O'Gara and Billy Bonner were sitting as close to the platform as they could. The young priest, Father Cullen from Carravoe, preferred to stand. As soon as the music began, so did the dancing, and all shyness disappeared.

When the band eventually took a break, Lizzie Byrne took the stage to sing *The Wind That Shakes the Barley*. Celia accompanied her and one of the lads from Bantry played the bodhran. Lizzie's voice reached right inside the hearts of listeners; sometimes deep, gravelly on the lower register, before soaring like a skylark. As she ended the song, everyone leapt to their feet.

Calum, painfully shy, ill-at-ease; his mouth so dry, unable to speak; took a single pink rose to the dais, stumbled, recovered his senses and stood in front of Lizzie.

"*A bheidh tú ag pósadh liom?*" he said, and then again in English, just to be sure: "Will you marry me?"

Lizzie was taken aback. A thousand memories crowded into her mind, things that would not go away. She stood motionless, knowing she must give an honest answer to this man whom she had long thought of as her best friend. He was a good man in every way, and she loved him more than she'd thought possible – and now he had asked for her hand in front of the entire village.

Her answer began with a nod, followed by tears. She tried in vain to stem them as she reached down to take his outstretched hand. Taking a deep breath, and putting her whole heart into the song, she sang *Siúil A Rúin* (Walk My Love.)

When she'd finished, Calum gave her the rose, which Lizzie accepted, knowing that the horrors of the past were behind her at last. She had found her true home.

Calum

He knows about fish, and a bit about pigs,
he knows how to stitch frayed canvas, torn nets,
he can sail single-handedly out in the bay,
he knows weather – the signs, the signals, the portents,
the way the tide turns, the times and the seasons,
but women?

What are women?
How do they function at all?

They cackle at market
and tease him and chatter
and one or two even try to flirt
but he blushes and stammers,
his tongue goes all dry and the words fly away
on a stiff offshore breeze
but so what –
it never mattered at all until

Lizzie.
Sweet Lizzie.

He knows about fish, but not about women,
he can fix broken rigging – she sets broken arms,
he can pull shoals of herring from under the seas,
but plucking a rose?

Ah, sweet Lizzie.

Chapter Seven

Tadgh's Shield

black cattle lowing:
herd treks drovers' road
to timeless pasture

Tommy Doyle and Vince Malone leased the Keelbeg holdings on the west side of Portleán, and worked in partnership to milk a herd of black cattle. Their wives, Rose and Lyn Powers were sisters from Carravoe who had met Tommy and Vince at a ceilidh in the village. The joint wedding had been a small affair, the expense of big weddings being out of reach for cottars, so in the tradition of Munster newlyweds, Rose and Lyn began milking Portleán cattle the very same afternoon.

Tadgh Doyle was born to Tommy and Rose a year later, and all was fine until he was eight years old and fell ill with a sore throat which developed into tonsillitis. Such ailments were common enough around hay harvest time. Rose dosed Tadgh with the standard cure of honey, hot water and friar's balsam and nobody worried too much. A week later he was still poorly so Rose sent young Bran from next door – Tadgh's cousin – to stay with Bridey Sullivan as Tadgh was feverish and she worried it could be infectious.

The Keelbeg holdings were quarantined and the cattle moved to higher meadows and tethered as there were no fences or walls. The timing was bad. Just as the cows were giving their best, the milk had to be carried in wooden pails all the way down the hill to the dairy for cheese making. The cottars managed as best they could and their wives took turns looking after Tadgh. At first Rose didn't want her sister to help for fear of spreading the infection, but Lyn tied disinfectant-soaked muslin round her mouth and helped with the nursing anyway.

"You'd be doin' the same fer me," she said. "'Tis what sisters are for."

Neither knew much about infections, but getting a doctor to attend was out of the question. There were few enough doctors on the peninsulas following the Great War and such was the tension between Sinn Féin and the British government, nobody dared ask for medical help, irrespective of the expense.

The community had been decimated by the Great Famine, so the villagers had created a garden of remembrance, sheltered by hazel, alder and blackthorn on the shore of the estuary. As she nursed her son, Rose took to looking through the window across to the memorial garden.

"Don't even think on it," said Lyn. "Tadgh is fighter. He might be small but he has the spirit of a fox. 'Tis just the fever, Rose. If ye can't abide lookin' out the window, then close your eyes."

Just then there was a knock at the door – strong, confident, almost aggressive. Rose went to answer it nervously. A girl in a black cape stood there.

"Bridey Sullivan asked me to see the lad with the fever," said the colleen. "I'm Lizzie Byrne, and I'm a qualified Red Cross nurse, back from France. Will you let me see the boy?"

Rose's eyes filled with tears. Lyn took hold of Lizzie's shoulders and hugged her.

Lizzie pointed to the bedroom. "Is he in there?"

79

She gave Tadgh a full examination speaking only to ask Rose about his symptoms. Inspection complete, she asked for boiled water and clean muslin.

"And if you're able, a good fire in the grate to raise the temperature of the house. Keep the hot water coming as it's essential the lad is kept clean. How long has he had the fever?"

Rose told her about the week of tonsillitis and Tadgh's difficulties in breathing and swallowing. He was lethargic, had a pain in his left side and struggled to pass water. The indicators for polio were adding up and Lizzie knew from encounters with pneumonia and meningitis in French hospitals that the next few days would be critical.

"I'll sleep in the same room," she said, "and if the fever breaks," she looked at Rose and smiled, "it'll be a first step on a long road to recovery. Now – where's that boiled water?"

For six days and nights, Rose and Lyn kept station with Lizzie, alternating auxiliary duties, keeping the hot water flowing, washing linen, disinfecting essentials, and providing a bowl of porridge or a helping of stew for Lizzie when needed.

The fever broke after four days, though Tadgh still needed help with feeding and constant massaging of his arms and legs to keep the blood in circulation. Lizzie's skills had been acquired in nursing injured soldiers from the Belgian trenches, so nursing a young lad was a new experience. She had never faced polio before, and found the encounter frightening. When she eventually returned to her own cottage she slept the clock round.

> when honey cure fails
> war-weary nurse brings sweetness
> to vanquish disease

"Finder's keepers," said Tadgh, "an' I found it fair'n square."

Tommy Doyle didn't argue. When his son had disappeared earlier, he'd guessed the lad had either been exploring the foreshore or hidden in a corner of the house with his nose buried in an encyclopaedia. Tadgh's enthusiasm made a mockery of the handicap which prevented him attending Carravoe's school.

"*Fuair mé amach iad I mo udimh,*" Tadgh said to his mam, who watched as the boy emptied his knapsack. The lad repeated the phrase in English for his father who didn't speak Gaelic: "I found it in my cave."

80

"Tch, tch," said Rose Doyle. "How many times have I told you not to climb into those holes? If you get trapped by an incoming tide, you'll drown, and then we'd have no Tadgh to greet us at the door anymore, you mark my words."

Tommy said nothing. It must have taken the lad a good hour to reach the shore on those feeble limbs.

rune sticks bind writing
with angular striations:
message unfolds

Rose knew exactly where Tadgh had been, but she had no idea what this thing was he'd found. The dark and weathered wooden rod revealed little. Rose peered close and ran her finger along a line of cryptic symbols stretching along both sides. The workman who carved it must have had the greatest patience.

"Runes," said Tadgh. "'Tis a rune stick. Could be hundreds of years old. The Vikings used 'em like a secret alphabet. I must show Bran. They mean something – don't know what – I'll look in my encyclopaedia and find out."

"Not until you've had supper little man. Besides, Bran will be busy with the cheesing."

Calling him her 'little man' was a mark of affection, not a comment on his condition. He might never make a cottar, but he would stand on his own two feet and contribute to the dairy in any way he could.

The boys studied the rune stick for several evenings after essential chores were completed. Bran had a good eye for sketching and drew a picture of each symbol, comparing them with the typescript in Tadgh's encyclopaedia. Soon, every home in the village had learned of the find, and everyone found an excuse to come visiting.

There were eighteen motifs on the stick out of the thirty listed in the encyclopaedia.

81

"Maybe there are more sticks?" said Tadgh, whose facts were restricted to just two-and-a-half inches of notes in the great book of knowledge. "They could be buried under the stones or hidden in a cleft, waiting to be found."

"Not by yourself," said his cousin Bran. "We've already had words off Aunt Rose 'cos you went off by yourself, so this time we'll take a lantern and a rope to be safe."

Calum the fisherman called into Keelbeg that evening, out of curiosity as much as anything. He wanted to know which cave Tadgh had visited, but when the lad tried to explain, Calum said, "No, can't be. I know every inch of that shore. You must be making it up."

"I can show you, sure enough," said Tadgh. "I marked it with a big hazel branch shoved into a rabbit hole."

Rose interrupted at his point. Calum was highly respected for his knowledge of the sea and she valued his opinion. She told the boys they had permission to go, but only if Calum went with them.

They discussed it further. Rose's proposal made sense. Tadgh's discovery looked authentic, and Calum was keen to investigate. He would provide a pair of candle-lanterns and the essential rope, and for sure, who better to ask about the state of the tides than a working fisherman?

The next morning, dank mist blanketed the bay.

"Sea fog," said Calum, who had arrived at Keelbeg with Peder O'Brien. The two men had brought a dray pulled by Paddy, the larger of the pigman's ponies.

"There'll be no harvesting today," said Peder. "It'll take a full day of sunshine to dry the hay out."

As soon as the milking was over at Keelbeg, everyone crowded into Rose's kitchen where they were fed bacon sandwiches and mugs of tea around the scrubbed-oak table. Tadgh was the smallest person there, and he struggled to display Bran's sketches. The torn squares of paper kept slipping from his grasp in his excitement and Bran had to rescue them off the floor.

"Low tide will be midday," said Calum, "so if you're hoping to search that hole, today's your best chance for awhile. If this fog lifts, we'll be too busy in the fields."

Tadgh looked at his mother, then Bran's mother, never daring to look at his father.

"Only if Calum and Peder can spare the time," said Tommy. "And when Calum says you must leave, there's to be no arguing. Peder will take you down to the shore in his dray and Calum can bring two candle-lanterns and a skein of rope. Peder, if ye'll tether the dray on the cliff-top, we'll know the location immediately if anything untoward happens."

entrance long hidden:
whispering willows
yield their secrets

Calum led the pony, keeping a safe distance from the drop. The sea fog still clung to the cliff, so finding Tadgh's marker took some time. They found it eventually, and picked their way down to the raised beach through a seemingly impenetrable thicket where spiny gorse battled with willow and hazel. Neither Peder nor Calum had any idea how Tadgh had managed to clamber down the cliff originally. Below the raised bank of shingle, a tiny stream filtered into the sea. Flotsam lay everywhere.

"Over there, in the bushes," said Tadgh, "where the gorse begins. That willow tree marks the entrance. There's loads of pebbles and stuff, and 'tis a bit smelly at first, but it's dry inside the cave."

"Best I carry you up the bank," said Peder, "and pass you to Calum. Bran can bring your walking-sticks and the lanterns."

Ten-thousand years ago, following the last ice age, the cleft would have been at sea level, but now it was a good scramble up the shingle bank. Shrouded by fog and with the tide at its lowest ebb, the sea could neither be heard nor seen. Peder planted his feet into the pebbles and hoisted Tadgh onto his shoulders and started climbing up through the willow and hazel. Calum followed and Bran brought up the rear.

"By that tree," said Tadgh. "I left my walking sticks by that trunk 'cos I could walk easily enough from there by holding onto the branches."

Through the centuries, succeeding willows had battled against the gorse and won. Peder saw ancient roots lying under new foliage, but no hint of a concealed cave. He put the boy down and Tadgh moved through the undergrowth, holding onto anything that offered support, before vanishing completely.

"Come on!" he called from behind a wall of greenery. "It's in here!"

Peder and Calum stooped under the foliage.

"Well, who'd a believed?" said Calum, looking at the fissure in the rock. "How on earth did Tadgh get through there?"

Peder pushed aside the willow's hanging branches.

"First things, first lads. Get the lanterns lit."

Calum produced a matchbox, and once the flames were steady and burning well, Tadgh wormed his way through the cleft, closely followed by Bran. Calum climbed higher up the cliff face to reach a suitable access point for himself, which Peder, being the bigger of the two, had to grunt and grovel to squeeze through.

Their eyes took time to adjust to the gloom, but then they were astonished by what they saw. The narrow cave measured at least thirty feet in length and most likely had once been a streambed. Peder couldn't quite reach the roof. The floor consisted of pebbles worn smooth by water a long time ago; now it smelled sweet and dry and there were places where a grown man could sit easily.

"What are we actually lookin' for?" said Calum. "Buried treasure?"

Tadgh was on his knees, pushing his lantern ahead of him. Bran searched higher, feeling for hidden crevices and Peder felt at arm's length for anything unusual.

"I'm sure there must be more rune sticks," said Tadgh. "My encyclopaedia shows a load more symbols."

Every sound inside the cave was amplified – dislodged stones pinged and pebbles crunched underfoot, disturbing the silence. No lichens or moss could grow in the dark and a fine layer of dust lay everywhere. Cobwebs crowded the opening, but inside, time was suspended.

Bran swept a handful of dust off a ledge and, to his utter delight, found another rune stick. He tended to feel left out of things when Tadgh had centre stage, but now he had discovered an ancient artefact of his own. There were no toys at Keelbeg. All Bran's worldly goods had to serve a useful purpose. His piebald pony for example, would never have come into his ownership had it not earned its keep.

He handed the stick to Peder for safekeeping.

"Those carvings look like knots," said Peder who couldn't read anyway, as he peered at the rune stick by candlelight.

"Reward for your efforts," said Calum. "You're quite safe here lads. Even on the highest tide, the sea never reaches this level. Those trees guarding the entrance are old. They've never felt the fury of the Atlantic."

The fisherman lifted his lantern as Peder set out to explore further reaches of the cavern.

"Mind your head," said Calum. "The roof is nigh touching it."

"Lend a hand here Cal. 'Tis a bit cramped."

Calum handed his lantern to Tadgh. Peder was gripping a slab of igneous rock which appeared to be firmly embedded in the side of the cave, but he had managed to shift it slightly. As he grunted and heaved harder, little stones dropped in the space behind with a tinkling clatter.

"You take the other end, Cal. I'm too thick to get into that space."

Calum spat on his hands and took hold of the slab. "One, two, three: h-e-a-v-e!"

The rock creaked while smaller stones continued to drop down behind.

"'Tis movin'," said Calum. "Let's rock it to and fro. Get another hold an' try ag'in."

Tadgh shuffled behind the two men, holding tight to handholds as he went. Bran followed with the second lantern. Both boys held their breath as the men wrestled with the huge slab, rocking it with a steady rhythm. Suddenly, without warning, it canted away from the wall and leant at an angle. Tadgh raised his lantern high.

As the thousand-year dust settled, Bran reached over the stone and picked through the powder, hardly able to contain his excitement. His trembling fingers touched an object that made him pull his hand straight back, afraid to take hold of it. Something that might have once been a leather shroud crumbled to reveal a treasure, untouched by the hand of man for a millennium. There in the yellowing light of the lanterns lay a shield, still showing its original ochre colouring, with a metal boss in the centre. Bran felt more confident now he could see what it was. He reached down and brushed the ancient leather away. For a moment, nobody uttered a word.

Calum broke the silence. "All those tales your father told you of buried treasure and the giants of old..." The fisherman stooped over the massive stone, took hold of the shield and raised it to his chest, shedding a cloud of fine dust. "Don't believe I'm seeing this."

Peder reached out to touch the ancient artefact. "Maybe this was the right time for these things to be found. Tell you what lads, I know exactly who to ask about this."

battle-scarred shield:
wrapped with care against the day
when the lost may be found

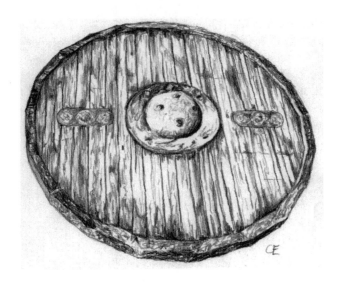

"Are we ready boys?" said Peder as Paddy the Connemara snorted and nodded his head. "To Rossdore then. We're all havin' a day off, an' travellin' in my best wagon. We mustn't fergit to collect Calum on the way as he's comin' too – and there's shoppin' to do, otherwise we'll all be havin' a latherin'."

Peder had a list of things to both buy and sell as well as meat to deliver in town. Market days were always busy and having extra passengers to look after meant he didn't arrive until nine o'clock.

"Thought you'd overslept, Peder," said Fergal Maguire the butcher as he helped Tadgh down from the dray. Walking with crutches on cobbled surfaces required intense concentration from the boy. Bran was also having problems, tripping over kerbstones in his first ever boots.

Peder loaded various essentials onto the wagon as the sun climbed higher. The pony was enjoying the summer flowers and tufts of grass behind Rossdore's few shops. Peder filled a pail from the tap behind the butcher's shop and the Connemara sucked loudly. It took two refills before Peder could unhitch the sated animal from the dray and tether it in the shade of a chestnut tree.

"I'll be back soon," he said, rubbing the pony's nose. "There's a man I have to see in town about a something we found in a cave. He's an elderly gentleman I first met twenty years ago at market. Now then Paddy, I won't be forgettin' you."

Peder lifted the shield with its jute sack wrapping out of the dray and went to join the others.

86

Conor Connolly was a former convenor of Rossdore Market who had retired due to his increasing short-sightedness. Peder had already told him about the shield and Conor longed to see it. He was a Viking history enthusiast, had his own rune stick and had published articles for the West Cork Times and Southern Star on runic markings.

They found him sitting outside his front door on a stool waiting for his visitors, hardly able to keep still.

> he waits in sunlight
> for a boy and his shield:
> the years drop away

"Is it yerself?" said Peder O'Brien. "And no hat to wear to keep the sun out of your eyes?"

"Damnty Peder, with you towering over me, I'd never get sunburned in a month o' Sundays. And here's Calum the fisherman, too. How are ye *buchailli* (boys)?"

"An' there's more of us," said Peder. "I'd like you to meet Bran and Tadgh from Keelbeg."

Conor shook hands with the two young cousins and said he had something truly exciting to show them, and if they went inside, they would find carrot cake and tea provided by his neighbour. Conor whistled to the terraced house next door and a diminutive lady emerged.

"Mrs Small," said Conor. "Small by name and small by nature. She's been looking out fer me since I retired an' I would've a married her if somethin' didn't keep gettin' in the way."

"What's that?" said the naïve Calum.

"Mister Small," said Conor. "C'mon inside lads, yer clutterin' up the roadway."

Mrs Small went inside first to lay an embroidered white cloth on the table. Peder followed, carrying the sack containing the shield, and Bran brought in the two rune sticks. They sat round the table and Conor started to examine their finds. His face lit up when he saw the rune sticks. He opened a drawer in his sideboard and took out a three-foot ruler with runic symbols along its entire length, and handed a big magnifying glass to Tadgh. The lad was in danger of falling off his stool in his excitement and had to be held firmly by Calum.

All hopes of carrot cake and tea were on hold. Even Mrs Small was entranced.

"Well I never did," she said. "Mister Connolly won't be sleepin' a wink tonight, I know."

Peder lifted up the shield and carefully removed the sacking – no easy task as he stood higher than the ceiling and had to sit down so that everyone could admire it.

"This is for you, Conor," said Peder, "an' there's to be no argufying. 'Tis for all the years of good friendship and knowing that Tadgh and Bran will always be welcome in your house. It's the least we can do, and when these lads are grow'd up and learned all that Viking hist'ry stuff, I'm sure they'll be happy to share all those things with their own friends."

"Lord sakes," said Conor, careful not to say the wrong thing in the presence of Mrs Small. "Sure, it belongs in a museum in Dublin, or at least Cork City."

"Never," said Peder. "It's for the people of the foreshore. You look after it, Conor. Keep it safe and when we're dead and gone, these boys will decide its future."

"Are you men just goin' to sit round this here table and jaw-jaw, or can I put something on it?" asked Mrs Small. "The kettle's been singin' for ages."

"Carrot cake, tea and maybe sarsaparilla for the treasure hunters," said Conor. "What say you *buchailli?*"

Mrs Small cleared a thousand years of history from the table and Peder lifted the shield over the dresser and placed it against the whitewashed wall.

"Would you like it hung there?" he said, "or someplace else?"

"That's perfect," said Conor. "They'll be queuing up to see it, sure enough."

The three-foot wide timber disc with its metal boss needed to be balanced on some books for now, but Peder promised it would be fixed in position the following Tuesday.

"Tch tch, more dusting," said Mrs Small with a smile. "As if I didn't have enough to do already."

Chapter Eight

The Incomers

Goose Hill was more a hummock than a hill, but it afforded a fine view of Portleán and there had always been some kind of a house there. Hannah's mother remembered it being called *Gé Noc*. The original was a cob dwelling, turf-roofed with a hole cut to let the smoke out, but a Cornishman had built a stone cottage alongside, leaving the old dwelling as shelter for a cow and a few ewes. The Cornishman became a cottar and leased twenty acres from an absentee landlord before becoming homesick and leaving his cottage overlooking the sea, never to return.

Calum saw the place every time he put out to sea and wondered if one day, when he found a good woman, she might enjoy living there.

Still on the right side of thirty, the fisherman had now found his good woman. It had been a close thing, as several overwrought suitors had signalled their desire to win the hand of the fair maid of Carravoe. Lizzie had spent a few weeks living with the O'Briens, but after the wedding, the couple had set up home in Lizzie's old cottage on the sheltered side of the mountain.

The cottage was three miles from the quay as the crow flies and twice that distance when climbing up and down, negotiating walls and fences, inquisitive animals, over-friendly neighbours and muddy paths. Calum managed for a while, often hurrying home in darkness, without even stopping at Hannah's cottage despite the smell of fresh baking, but most mornings when he sailed past Goose Hill, he imagined what it would be like to live in the old cottage surrounded by meadows rather than halfway up a mountain.

Major Thomas Redmond had bought the Portleán Estate soon after the Great War, and when the newly-weds enquired about leasing the house, he made no objection. The move happened more quickly than Calum would have believed possible. He still had a mile walk to the quay but at least he didn't have to climb halfway up that mountain anymore.

> hummocky cottage
> calls across windblown waters:
> please, make me your home

Lizzie's cottage was put up for sale. The couple who bought it were made welcome by Portleán's villagers. Dai and Sali Roberts were incomers from Tal-y-Bont, Wales, and had lost both sons in the 1914-18 war. They had settled originally on the peninsula to assist in the renovation of a copper mine, but the project was abandoned and the contract cancelled after war when cheap imports from Sweden, Michigan and Chile became available. The cottage above Carravoe felt right for a bereaved couple now fearing insolvency. It wasn't too far to move, was in good order and well-sheltered from the prevailing winds.

On arrival, Dai asked around and within a day had found a decent job building stone walls for the other cottars. Dry stone walling was skilled work, and the Welshman was a master of his craft. The work would be constant as stone walls required running repairs to prevent animals straying. Hedging wasn't an option due to the cost.

Dai and Sali's cottage enjoyed wonderful views across the bay to Sheep's Head, had a sweet-water well, several trees, a sound roof, a porch, and the road – to Castletown or Kenmare – right alongside. Granted, it lay several hundred feet up a mountain, but to the Welsh couple this was nothing, and they were soon in great demand; Sali for her gardening skills, especially with her passion for beekeeping, and Dai with his mastery of building. Sali had been forced to forgo her beehives on moving from Wales as establishing new ones had been impossible next to

90

the windswept mine. At her new home, six hundred feet up the mountain, she soon spotted honeybees when the heather bloomed and the clover was in flower. Griff Sullivan built her three hives within a few months.

Lizzie had first come across the healing properties of honey in Macroon's convent and later in Allied hospitals. The former nurse soon became good friends with Sali and added bee products to her precious medicine cabinet.

Sali brings sweetness:
purple heather hums with life
far from the valleys

Dai needed a pair of apprentices to work for him, mainly to recover and carry suitable stones. Within hours of his enquiry, two Milligan lads were running up the hill to his house. They arrived puffing and blowing, desperate to be first. Tad Milligan couldn't afford to send his children to school and any monetary assistance from his offspring was always welcome. Fourteen and twelve year olds Sean and Flynn started work the next day, grubbing suitable stones for building from streams, scree and wherever weather had exposed them. The stones had to be delivered to the site and placed at ten-yard intervals along a line of marker-pegs. The boys used a flat single-wheeled barrow at first, taking it in turns to push. Within a fortnight, Griff Sullivan had devised a four-wheel cart pulled by an iron drawbar running on wooden wheels, but even this would soon be replaced with a horse-drawn wagon.

Stone walls need solid foundations, so each morning they dug a channel, often through boggy ground, and filled it with reject stone. They compacted this layer with a *whomper* as Dai called it, before laying the base stones. Dai surveyed each line, careful to avoid watercourses and always looked to use places where the underlying rock was exposed. The lads soon became adept at their new trade. Both were safely shod with *brogans*, to prevent injuries from dropped boulders that could render them out of action permanently.

Peder O'Brien often helped. He was not only strong; he was their biggest customer. Besides, he liked Dai, and was keen to learn more about stonemasonry as he was hoping to convert a stone bothy into a privy as a present for Jo. Dai encouraged the idea, and even drew up a plan.

91

One morning in early autumn, Peder attended Rossdore market with several gilts to be slaughtered. Keeping stock through the winter was not good business and he would lose out if he waited to sell until after Christmas. He also had an appointment with the Sullivan brothers. The boat-builders were anxious to get started building portable pigsties for use when the weather turned. These would incorporate skids, enabling easy transit to new pastures. There were few meadows left at this time, so the herd constantly needed moving higher up the mountain. Pigs were scavengers, and could clear the land for re-seeding by quickly eradicated gorse, heather, and bracken, but Peder was pushing boundaries and becoming too successful for his own good. The herd was moving ever nearer to the dangerous scree slopes and urgently needed safe enclosures.

The first portable sty, fashioned out of salvaged timbers, was dragged into service at the end of October. Keeping pigs in movable sties gave them good protection from the weather and predators, and according to market gossip, this was the new way for pigs nationwide. Fergal the butcher reckoned they were already using them on the east coast.

A second sty arrived a week later. The first was already crowded with pigs that refused to leave, and the ones outside couldn't get in as no pig dared go foraging for fear of losing its privileged place. The sounds of porcine chaos grew louder as Griff Sullivan walked across the fields.

"How many sties will we need?" he said.

Peder estimated twenty.

"Jaze, you're a comedian," said Griff. "Come back next year."

Peder puzzled over Griff's answer as he rarely understood a leg-pull – but Griff was already leaving. He had work to do, and portable pigsty construction was proving a useful source of income.

92

taut bristly bodies
snuffle-grunt and clear the way:
progressive chaos

Josephine O'Brien's second child was taking its time coming and was already a few days overdue by Lizzie's calculations when Jo clambered into her gig to go and see her friend. She put Siobhan in her wicker-cot alongside, climbed back down to remove the pony's nosebag and grunted and winced at the sudden tightness across her belly. Back on the padded seat, she whistled to the pony, and set off to visit Lizzie.

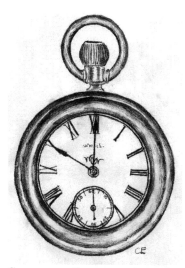

Peder was working with Dai at the bottom of a scree slope. Dai had a silver fob-watch, a legacy of the time he had worked underground. He would tell the time to anyone within hearing distance.

"Just striking the hour of ten," he said. "Time for snap, isn't it. What say you, Peder?"

Dai often tried to explain what life had been like underground but his descriptions were wasted on his fellow worker. The idea that men could tunnel through mountains and find fuel a mile deep under the surface never made sense to Peder. He burned peat. Coal was another country.

Snap over, the men returned to work toting suitable stones from the scree, using the wheeled barrow rather than the horse-drawn cart. A gentle breeze cooled the higher ground where the apprentice boys did the hauling, and Peder lifted the heavier stones.

The rhythm of the work was interrupted when a Milligan youngster arrived, puffing and blowing fit to burst.

"Please – can Mister O'Brien – come – now – right away – the woman's havin' – the baby – Goose Hill – havin' it now – Goose Hill – now – I ran all the way."

The lad lay on his back on the turf gasping.

Peder reached for his shirt, wiped his face and excused himself to Dai. He grabbed the young scamp's hand, pulled him up, and half walked, half carried him over to the pony. They trotted carefully down the hillside, and headed for Goose Hill.

Lizzie was looking out for them and watched them canter across the lower meadows.

"There's no rush, Peder, do hurry-up and take your time," she said, grinning. "You're never here when you're needed and that's good 'cos you'd only get in the way."

"You mean –" Peder tried hard to catch up with himself, "'tis all done?"

"See for yourself. Siobhan has a little sister, Sorcha, born an hour ago. Everything happened very quickly – the journey probably brought it on. I'm in the middle of tidying up here. Give that penny to the Milligan lad, Ped, he's earned it – and he can carry some plaice back to Fran Milligan for tea. Calum brought them in but I've more than enough as it is."

Peder went inside, passing Calum who was busy cleaning ash from the stove.

"*Comhghairdeas,*" (congratulations) said Calum. "It's about time you came. The rest of your family are resting in my bed. Don't mind me, I'll be sleeping in one o' they fancy pigsties on the hill."

Peder winced at the thought, ducked under the lintel, and entered the bedroom.

All the mayhem, the ride to Goose Hill, the ribbing and salty asides were forgotten as Peder knelt beside the bed and kissed his wife. A tiny bundle, hardly an hour old, lay cradled in her arms while Siobhan slept peacefully in her cot.

Now that the days were short and the nights bitterly cold, Dai was insisting his apprentices made their way back home as soon as the sun disappeared behind the mountain. The loss of his own sons at Verdun and Ypres still haunted him, and the chill coming down from the mountain made him more aware of his obligations.

"Time you made your way home, boys bach," he said. "And if it snows or there's rain on the wind, you know the drill. Don't take chances. The wall will still be there, waiting. A better day will come soon, well aye."

He waited for the lads to disappear across the fields before making for his own cottage. The Milligan family was the largest in Portleán but Dai worried for them. Sean and Flynn were already having to help support the family aged just twelve and fourteen. Dai's own sons had been seventeen and nineteen when they had lost their lives. He often shed tears while walking home, and tried to blame the icy wind.

Peder arrived at the site early the next morning. The fresh snow was shining rosehip-orange as the sun lit the mountains beyond the bay. As he climbed higher, Paddy began to slip on the frozen grass. Peder dismounted and led the pony by his bridle, taking his time.

The apprentice boys hadn't arrived yet as they were under strict orders not to set off until daylight. Peder walked the line of the wall, which now measured a good quarter-mile. There was no sign of Dai. Perhaps snow had fallen overnight by his place.

Peder scanned the icy fields for any sign of the boys. He spotted them eventually, about half a mile away, walking in single file.

Leaving Paddy tethered, Peder set off along the path below the mountain. The Carravoe Valley lay spread out beneath him, beautiful in the cold, bright dawn. He paused a while to enjoy the moment, but then something caught his eye – something wrong. He could see an indistinct bundle ahead, just off the path, part hidden by rocks. Whatever it was, he knew it shouldn't be there. He hurried over to investigate. After another hundred yards or so he still couldn't identify the object and was becoming seriously concerned. It looked as though someone had simply dropped a coat, and for a moment he felt a sense of relief, but as he got closer he could see the coat hid a body wearing brogan boots.

Peder was never a man to get over-excited. Some would consider him a bit slow on the uptake, though in reality, he was thinking before he took action.

How long the body had lain there was hard to tell. Experience with pigs had taught Peder to look hard at any animal that appeared to be motionless, as they were full of surprises. An injured hog could suddenly squeal and come back to life. There was no trace of frost on the body. Peder lifted a sleeve and felt the hand. It was still warm. Dai must have lost his footing and slipped off the path judging by the angle at which he was lying. His cloth cap lay a few yards away, but his knapsack, together with the legendary *snap*, was still over his shoulder, bandoleer style.

The gradient was steep. Peder considered whether to leave Dai where he was or risk moving him as the slope was in shadow and would be for several hours. He came to a decision. This man was his friend. He took hold of his coat and hauled him up and onto the path, where he examined him as best he could to determine his condition. The only person nearby with the skills to deal with this sort of thing was Lizzie, but she was two miles away at Goose Hill. Peder thought of using the pony, but that would have caused even more problems, so he hauled the stricken Dai up, balanced him over his shoulder, grunting at the effort, and followed the path down to meet the apprentices.

"Will you bring the pony," he shouted to Sean. "Soon as you reach level ground, ride him to Goose Hill and raise the alarm. Flynn, follow the path to Keelbeg and ask for help. Mister Roberts is hurt bad. Then go to the village and rouse your father – he knows the emergency drill."

Sean led the pony to a safe place. Peder lowered his burden to the ground, and took off his sheepskin gilet, whistling to Sean to put it on.

"Here, take this. I'm sweatin' already and it's cold ridin'. Be careful out there and don't take chances."

He picked Dai up again, balanced him on one shoulder and set out for the village.

For all the desperate efforts to save him, Dai Roberts was already dead. He had no visible injuries so the village accepted the most likely cause as heart failure, and lamented the loss of a welcome incomer and friend, gone far too soon. The stone wall stood silent, unfinished for now, though the village would gather together to complete the first enclosure during the following year.

unfinished stone walls
foreshadow frozen failure:
cloth cap abandoned

Dai's body was interred in the Memorial Garden close by Goose Hill and Sali Roberts moved into a small vacant cottage in Carravoe village overlooking the estuary. And because life goes on, in time there were six beehives in her garden and a further eight dotted along the foreshore.

Chapter Nine

The Great Storm

traction no traction

hissssss
chuff-chuff-chuff-chuff-chuff-chuff
hisssssssss
chuff-chuff-chuff-chuff-chuff-chuff
burrabba-burrabba-burrabba-burrabba-burrabba
rattle-rattle-rattle-rattle-rattle
chuff-chufff-chufff-chufff.......chufff...............chufff
squeeak
chufff....chufff.........chufff....................rattle-rattle-rattle
clank...................................clank

chufff

chuff.........chuffff.............chuffff....................chuffff
hissssssssssssssssssssssssssssssssssssssssssssssssssssssss

split-splat-splot-splat-split-splot-split-splot-split-splat
splot-split-splat-splot-split-splat-splot-split-splat-splot
split-splat-splot-splat-split-splot-split-splot-split-splat
splot-split-splat-splot-split-splat-splot-split-splat-splot
split-splat-splot-splat-split-splot-split-splot-split-splat
splot-split-splat-splot-split-splat-splot-split-splat-splot
split-splat-splot-splat-split-splot-split-splot-split-splat
splot-split-splat-splot-split-splat-splot-split-splat-splot

Pádraig was bringing the last of the ewes down the north side of the mountain when he caught sight of the rumbling mechanical convoy coming through the pass, seeking shelter from the storm. Massive traction engines with spinning flywheels fought to grip the slick road surface. Their efforts were in vain. Even fully laden, they couldn't make much progress due to the hard rain, worn bitumen, ribbed surface and greasy mud.

The shepherd took shelter behind a huge boulder while his two sheepdogs trembled at the thunderous noise. Several well-meaning travellers had telegraphed the coming, but no amount of forewarning would have helped. At least Paddy had managed to secure the leader of the flock – a huge ram – but the clamour of the steam engines meant the rest had scattered. When the first machine crossed the pass, the ram merely expressed disgust and pawed at the ground. Pádraig gripped its halter and hung on in silence, never a man to swear, even when alone.

The mechanical procession's attempt to crawl through the pass came to an abrupt halt when the lead traction engine slid off the bank into a drainage ditch. It lay on its side, half in and half on the single track road, its trailer completely blocking the pass. A troop of gangers huddled under tarpaulins, in cabs, and wherever they could find shelter from the storm. Any thoughts of reaching Carravoe had to be abandoned. Half the labourers were still facing the storm in Kerry on the north side of the pass; the rest were looking across the rainswept bay in County Cork, just yards away.

Paddy shook his head and went home. And it rained, and it rained, and it rained, all night long.

Somewhere in the City of Dublin, anonymous and rarely seen politicians had decided to do something about the diabolical condition of the roads in Munster. With Ireland in a state of flux, Westminster had handed out contracts to all and sundry. Few in County Cork understood the workings of government, Irish or British, but the sudden award of building contracts meant speculators were invited to tender for the work. Unfortunately, nobody had been told about it between Dublin and Cork City. Men drew lines on maps, but in 1921 there were few maps available. The military had been busy fighting the Great War, and although it was now at an end, Ireland was still in the throes of an on-going struggle for independence.

The hastily assembled construction team gathered in Cork City with little idea of what was needed. It took them a week to reach Kenmare and the hotchpotch crew suffered so many breakdowns and mechanical failures, barely half the workers made it. Most had never seen the working-end of a theodolite before or used a measuring-tape, and those operating the steam engines knew little of their maintenance.

Pádraig

loves his dogs
Peg and Roz

knows his sheep
thick-grown fleece

don't need much,
no friends as such

likes complaining
no one blames him

quiet life
no need for wife

chats to dogs
Peg and Roz

Paddy's thing –
shepherding

Pádraig Murphy lived in a stone cottage on the farthest boundary of Portleán and looked after the village's ewes, taking them to the higher ground during summer. This particular flock were the last to come down for wintering. As a long-time bachelor, he preferred being solitary, though to hear him muttering as he worked you would have thought all Portleán should have been out giving him a hand.

The storm was getting more ferocious by the minute. Paddy had no interest in the labourers stuck on the pass – they could deal with their own problems. It was as much as he could do to gather the ewes together. The deluge continued as he herded them across the bridge over the Carravoe River and through the wooden gate, which he secured with a length of sisal. The river boiled below him and he could feel the vibration through his boots.

Seven hundred feet higher up the pass, men huddled beneath tarpaulins and timbers and clung together as the winds continued at storm force. As darkness fell, torrents streamed down the mountain. If a man slipped, he would be swept away in an instant, so any attempt to move to safety would be suicidal. Jeremiah 'Jez' Clancy, the site-manager, had charge of twenty-seven labourers with not a bite to eat between them. It was going to be a long night.

By morning, the eye of the storm had passed over and the howling winds were screaming back from the east. Jez hustled everyone into a line and ordered them to relieve themselves in the nearside draining ditch.

"'Tisn't finished with us yet," he said. "There's plenty more where that came from."

Jez Clancy was a Connaught man who towered over his minions. If he barked "Shut it," they obeyed. His Connaught accent – honed in the streets of Donegal – marked him out as a northerner and men made sure to listen.

The storm rattled by Mizen Head, sucking moisture into an already overloaded atmosphere, and another blitz of lightning and thunder rumbled across the bay.

"Dammit all, God," yelled Clancy. "Yer not fightin' fair. Lave us alone, will ye?"

The tempest took no heed for a further two days. At times it came from another direction, usually in the middle of the night, before turning round and blasting, ferocious and merciless. Winds screamed like banshees and the deluge was so powerful, the men shut their eyes tight, believing this to be the last judgement.

100

On the third morning, Clancy roped his now ravenously hungry men together and led the troop down the mountain. The road was a river. Boulders had dammed ditches and debris was being washed away wholesale by the flood.

The higher river had burst its banks and formed a lake. Where the Carravoe torrent joined it, the road had vanished. The only way to get down was to climb up and across the Carravoe mountain. The troop clawed their way to safety, grabbing anything substantial. After three miles, they reached the Catholic Chapel. The river was running right through the chancel and down the aisle, spilling out through a side door, but it made for temporary shelter.

The ancient bridge linking Portleán to Carravoe had been swept out to sea. From the flooded banks, a few brave souls were watching the muddied waters of the river stretch out into the bay carrying drowned cattle and sheep, clumps of trees, a wrecked curragh, timbers, broken birds, and a sodden book, ripped asunder – words that no one would read again. Inevitably there was a death. A young girl disappeared in the flood and for some time no one realised she was missing.

The peninsular closed its doors for five days. The only man brave enough to face the elements was Paddy Murphy. He was concerned for the flock as they should have been moved to the meadows by now. The ceaseless rain had them trapped behind a stone wall and they needed to feed, but the impoverished beasts, their fleeces sodden, standing in water, had nowhere to go.

The shepherd talked to his dogs constantly. He had constructed a simple stone-built shelter for them on the sunny face of the cottage. It had a tin roof, barley straw on a timbered floor and an open doorway that looked across the bay.

"Sorry, sorry, sorry," he said to the sheep dogs, "but if we don't move 'em, we're goin' to lose 'em."

The pair followed Paddy to where the ewes were resting in the lea of the wall. The hardest part would be persuading them away from shelter and round the mountain to a place where they could feed. One slip on the greasy, rain-sodden surface could be fatal.

The lead ram wore a tinkling bell round his neck. Though too old to breed, he still commanded respect. Paddy took tight hold of his leather collar.

"Time to go," he said.

The only way to move the flock was to get them to follow the leader. Occasionally, the older dog, Roz harried a weaker lamb or a lame ewe. Peg, the younger collie, made up with enthusiasm what she lacked in know-how. Ewes, dogs and shepherd followed the old ram through the low-lying cloud; Paddy at the head of the column and the rest of the flock strung out behind.

Time and again the shepherd slipped and had to grasp the wiry heather to save himself while he searched for his crook. The flock were tramping ancient sheep paths that ran for miles across the mountain and were more sure-footed. The dogs brought up the rear, snarling at any sheep that couldn't keep pace. None could see more than a few feet through the dense mist.

"Damn," said Paddy. "Now where will we be going?"

He was lost, despite having spent all his life on the mountain.

"Keep to the paths," he said, whistling the younger dog to stay behind. "Sheep know where they're goin'. Have faith in the flock."

The shepherd tied a lanyard around Roz's neck for safety. He could hear the ewes bleating clearly enough even if he couldn't see them, and pushed on through the wet heather until he tripped and fell. The whole mountain seemed to be moving beneath him. He heard the rattle of weathered scree and instinctively covered his head. It only lasted a few seconds, but when he tried to move again, more stone rained down on him. Lying on his stomach with his limbs trapped under debris, he was afraid to move for fear of falling further.

A lamb bleated a few feet away, but he didn't dare try to reach her. He moved his head with difficulty and spotted another through the mist, motionless, with blood dripping from a head wound.

Roz, the faithful sheepdog lay nearby with her skull smashed open. Paddy shed hopeless tears as he lay there in shock, terrified of any further movement.

slippy

scree settles
stone against stone against stone

pauses

he hears the trickling of water

then a dancing sound by his ear –
a light-hearted skipping of pebbles
stones shift a little
he waits

piles of scree-shattered pain lie across
his legs
so moving is not an option right now
but that's good –
any movement might pull down the mountain

at least the sheep, its wool red-bloodied,
can't come to any more harm
and the dog, skull smashed
is safe

best not move

in the rain the pouring rain
and the rumbling
distant now
a few flashes
rolling around the bay
distant

in the rain through the mist through the mist and the rain
the bleat of a sheep

skittish
these scree slopes

slippy

The mist swirled round Paddy. His balaclava covered his head but he had lost his cap. He lay quietly, coming to terms with his situation. His legs were hidden, though he could still feel them and wondered if he could risk movement, but he was afraid the stones might give way again. He heard a faint whimpering. Peering through the mist, he called, "Peg – is that you? Good girl, Peg. Can't see, but I'm hearing you."

She scampered across the deadly scree and within moments was licking his hand. Never in his life had he been so pleased to see a dog. Peg worked her way up the scree a little and returned with Paddy's cap. He whispered his gratitude, afraid of triggering another landslide. All around him lay the deadly glistening scree.

Several hundred feet below, Tom Doyle and neighbour Vince Malone were inspecting their cattle when the landslide happened. The two men clambered up the bank and stood at the top of the ridge, listening hard. There was little to see as the mist still blanketed the higher slopes. All they could hear was the constant trickle of water.

"Will we climb higher?" said Vince. "If so, we'll have to skirt the bog-land as it's dangerous enough as it is – and after the rains?"

Tommy grunted, ever cautious. The pair kept close together as they circled round the bog, water dripping constantly from their black oilskins.

"Amt I seein' things?" said Vince. "I swear I saw a sheep. There – see?"

"Red marking," said Tommy. "Must be from Tracashel on the far side."

The ewe stood motionless as the men approached.

"No Tom, she's not a Tracashel ewe; that's blood. Look – her left shoulder has the black mark. 'Tis red blood, and she's one of ours, hurt bad. I'm thinkin' she's dazed and we need to get her back to the village in a hurry."

The ewe didn't flinch when Vince took hold of her fleece. Tom secured her with a length of hemp and was about to lead her down to the village when he spotted another.

"There's more," he said. "This damn fog is a curse."

He clambered across a ridge and found a pair of first-year lambs which seemed-uninjured, but trembling and so weak they could scarcely stumble, let alone walk.

"More Portleáns," said Vince. "They must've fallen down the mountain. We'll need to search the bottom of the scree for survivors."

"Not before we get help," said Tommy. "Best get back to the village and round up the men. A few dogs wouldn't go amiss, too. Thing is, where's Paddy? Surely he didn't go out in the storm?"

Feeble sunshine and a light breeze brought some relief after all that 'unspeakable nonsense' as Bridey Sullivan called it. High on the massif the mists clung on as searchers gathered at the boatshed to plan and allot areas to cover. They formed five groups of half a dozen men, each team equipped with ropes, lanterns, knapsacks of food and animal first aid. The leaders carried whistles for staying in contact with the other searchers. A number of youngsters joined them. The women stood in their doorways, giving kisses to lads who tried to duck away. A damp sun failed to warm the proceedings but in the excitement, no one – not even barefooted lads – noticed the chill.

Peder had charge of the farthest east section known as *Gabhal* (Sugarloaf) and Calum worked the flooded meadows next to him. Matt Hogan searched the middle reach and Brendan Tate's team worked their way across the higher level. Frank O'Connor's men combed the flooded lands in view of Carravoe right down to Goose Hill. Tad Milligan's boys fetched and carried injured sheep down to the village for treatment. At midday, the mountain was still wrapped in mist, the bracken-brown slopes ringing with shouts for Paddy Murphy.

The missing shepherd was eventually spotted an hour before dark. By then, much of the mist had evaporated in a gentle westerly breeze. Brendan Tate had climbed higher up the escarpment to recover a dead sheep, and was puzzled by a shadow two-thirds of the way up a large expanse of scree. He left his son to attend to the sheep and clambered over the larger rocks that had found their way to the bottom of the slope. The sun had already gone down behind the massif and the low light meant poor visibility. He whistled several times up the scree but there was no response, though he was sure he saw some movement. He climbed through the boulders, his heart thumping. A dog's bark echoed through the gully.

"P-a-d-d-y!" he yelled, "P-a-d-d-y!"

He saw the dog at last and watched it scrabble a few feet and pause.

"Paddy! Paddy Murphy! Where are ye?"

Brendan continued climbing but the rattle of wet stones made him hesitate. One man lost is a tragedy, two is a disaster. Up above, the sheepdog was yapping non-stop. It wouldn't move from its spot.

"I'm hearing yer, dog," said Brendan, breathless. "I'm comin', I'm comin'."

He shouted down to his son, asking him to summon the rest of the team and whistle the others to the base of the scree. Each foot needed to be placed carefully before moving higher. At times he had to scrabble on all fours, taking care not to look down for fear of losing his nerve. Beneath him, stones rattled continuously. He stopped for a moment to close his eyes and wipe his face with his báinín, fretting over what he would be able to do for the shepherd in this state.

For a while he couldn't make any progress. He looked around while sweat stung his eyes and vertigo gripped him.

"This'll never do. I'm getting nowhere in a terrible hurry."

The dog was much closer now. Brendan looked up and spotted a black oilskin, stark against the grey of the scree. The dog stopped barking and scuttled the few yards towards him, panting from exertion. Brendan wanted to shout 'Paddy!' but the sheepdog was so excited, she slipped past him and he had to fight hard to save himself from falling. Animal instinct made the dog stay motionless, unnerved by the moving stones. Brendan swallowed hard and moved closer to the shepherd, one limb at a time.

"Are ye hearin' me, Paddy?" he said. "Gie us a shout, will ye?"

No reply.

The scree remained intact for the time being. Brendan cleared a mound of stones, one by one, taking great care. When at last he glimpsed Paddy's hand, partially buried, he gripped it hard. The chill worried him, so he reached higher, feeling for Paddy's collar.

"Holy mother – the man's alive!"

The sheepdog barked in answer.

rescue attempt

slick wet stones, grassy slopes like ice
mist covered hills, brief silence...
then rain, roaring rain, endless rain

candles, lit in copper lanterns
flickering light through the gloom
will-o-the-wisps over scree-littered slopes

a crunch, a twang, someone slips
the silence, the waiting
the distant roar of the torrent

and it rains it rains it rains it rains
heavier pelting, squalls seek out flesh,
wet seeps through, shivers the skin beneath

scattered sheep, bedraggled
wet smell of wet sheep
sodden fleeces, the weight of a wet sheep

teams of wet men, wet sheep, rough breathing,
a hard-bloodied landslip, no hope, but then –
the yelp of a dog, the sight of an oilskin

Dusk had crept up on the rescue party. Frank O'Connor had split the team
into two groups in order to minimise the danger from falling stones. More
rescuers were still arriving, keen to help. Injured and dead ewes were
scattered across the rock-fall but they would have to wait. Paddy had
priority. Candle lanterns bobbed through the gloom. At the shout of "Men
coming!" everyone held their breath.

Brendan had pulled the shepherd's leg and arm clear and managed to
turn him onto his back. It was a tense moment, not helped by the lack of
light, but Brendan knew they wouldn't survive the night out in the open.
They had to move now. He gripped Paddy in a bear hug. The dog would
have to take care of itself.

"Keep tight hold of me, Pad. Try to stay upright. We're goin' down feet first. Men are waiting at the bottom. Trust me, Paddy, I won't let ye down."

After a few seconds when nothing moved, he heard the dreaded rattle and hiss of small stones and the rat-a-tat-tat thump of bigger boulders.

He screwed his eyes shut, gripped Paddy tight, and waited for the inevitable landslide. The ground shifted and there was nothing he could do other than go with it. Once it began the clattering and rumbling rock fall was unstoppable, but then as swiftly as it had begun, there came an unearthly silence.

Aside from some severe bruising, the two men landed at the bottom of the landslide relatively unharmed, still clinging to each other, eyes closed tight.

"Don't move!" said Peder to the rescue party in a hoarse whisper. "You'll bring the whole mountain down round our ears."

Not one lantern moved until the landslip was completely silent, and all that could be heard was the trickling of unseen water.

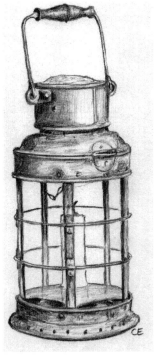

"Right ye are," said Peder. "Frank and Ronny come with me. Everybody else gather round Tad Milligan here and make sure we're all accounted for."

Tad led the way as the two survivors were stretchered down through the foothills, a man at each corner, changing places every hundred yards with other volunteer bearers. A swift check ensured there were no broken bones and little other damage. Brendan claimed he could walk, and even Paddy made the attempt.

"Not so," said Peder. "Do as you're told. When Lizzie says it's fine, then you can hobble."

The limited carrying distance was applied rigorously as bearing stretchers down the lower slopes and across the saturated meadows was fraught with difficulties. Paddy went first, borne by the younger men, accompanied by shouts of "Slippery here!" and "Water ahead!" Brendan followed. His stretcher required a stronger grip as Brendan was a big fellah. Calum remarked it looked like a funeral procession with the only light coming from candle lanterns.

One lad had charge of Peg, Paddy's surviving sheepdog. She was limping slightly but not bleeding from any visible wound, and the lad kept tight hold of her leash. The injured sheep needed medical attention and a team of knowledgeable cottars were setting up camp on the lower slopes to deal with them.

Women took over the nursing duties when the stretcher party arrived. Lizzie had prepared her assistants well and there was plenty of hot water in the recently whitewashed bothy. Paddy arrived first and was immediately divested of all clothing.

"Clothes off – now!" said Lizzie, "and if I hear another squeak from you, Paddy Murphy, I'll shove a sock in your gob, so I will. You don't have anything that I haven't seen before and I've seen bigger shillelaghs in a hen-house, so cease your complaining."

Despite his grumbling, he submitted to a thorough inspection. One volunteer nurse joked that it was likely the first bath that Paddy had ever had.

Brendan's stretcher arrived soon after. The man was beginning to feel sore and remained quiet during Lizzie's methodical scrutiny. Mostly of the bruising wouldn't reveal itself until next morning. He had some facial scratches like Paddy, but the only breakage was his nose, which was to be expected. Lizzie insisted it be left alone. It had stopped bleeding long before the trek to Goose Hill.

Both men were kept warm and relatively comfortable inside the sickroom. Rescuers and temporary nurses said their farewells and melted away to their own houses. Lamps were doused in the bothy other than a few candle lanterns.

"Inevitable there'll be some shock," said Lizzie to Hannah. "It'll show itself come morning and both will ache like the devil, especially Paddy as he was stuck in the same position for such a long time. We'll need to keep them warm and fed, but not too much. Hot tea or soup. I'm sure they'll be back in circulation in a few days."

Lizzie produced a bottle of Jameson's from the bottom of the new medicine chest, where it hid far from inquisitive eyes.

"Just the one for each patient," she said. "Fifty-fifty with hot water."

stripped down and bathed

this never happens
to someone like Paddy.
all this attention – hot water,
tin bath, roaring fire, smell of soap

and that little missy,
that little miss Lizzie,
bossing him about.

He likes being bossed
he notes to his surprise;
young Calum, he's one lucky fellah

Paddy could get to enjoy the craic
the whiskey
the warmth, the whiskey
the craic, the whiskey, the warmth...

until he remembers
Roz

One by one the lights of the village were extinguished. Higher in the foothills, men were still attending to injured ewes and disoriented sheep wandered across the massif. Even with the storm at an end there was floodwater everywhere. The constant trickle of streams was a reminder of the ever present danger of drowning in pools that hadn't existed before. The Carravoe River continued to rage. Both bridges had been swept away and the road up to the pass had collapsed into the torrent. Communication was impossible between Portleán and Carravoe and would remain so until the water levels dropped sufficiently for horses to ford the river. Even at sea-level, the outpouring of flood water made crossing impossible.

Jez Clancy kept his labourers busy assisting families wherever they were needed. Despite the storm and its aftermath, it was a good time for his men. Once the wild weather had abated, families took in the gangers, welcoming them into their homes for as long as they were needed. The Catholic chapel was abandoned because the stream that ran alongside still raged, but everyone had been safely evacuated apart from the one missing

110

child. Much repair work was needed, and the village soon rang with the sounds of hammering and digging, along with the noise of the river in spate.

"When the river puts its slippers on," said Jez, "we'll take a look up the pass and see what's going on up there. 'Tis only when things are at their worst do they start to mend."

Chapter Ten

There's a Thing

Respect for Jez Clancy kept his men together and the goodwill of the villagers meant they were well looked after. The bridge was vitally important to the community, so Jez kept half his labourers in the village and despatched the rest to the pass to rescue equipment. He made mental notes of where repairs were most needed as he led his men back up the mountain road. Below them, the river was still in spate. They got the first machine fired up somehow and the smell and noise of the steam engine made everyone feel hopeful.

Three more machines were rescued that same day and the gangers were able to clear a path alongside the original road using nothing more than elbow grease and shovels. At last they could drive across the peninsular and back through Castletown to Carravoe, though it took three days to reach the village due to the need to clear landslides.

A priest remonstrated with Jez for moving machinery through Castletown just as the bell began tolling to call the faithful to Sunday Mass, but he'd picked a fight with the wrong man. Jez took hold of him and hung him over the parapet by the ankles. The swollen river roared in

112

God's earthly representative's ears as Jez dunked him in the fast-flowing water.

"What wuz you askin'?" yelled Jez. "And stop ringing that blasted bell, 'tis givin' me a terrible headache."

It took another week for the river to settle and the rest of the machinery to steam round the peninsular. Women joined the volunteer army to clean up the village, and aside from the dreadful smell, no one had any complaints. Jez surveyed the remains of the broken buttresses that had been swept away, relishing the task of rebuilding them.

The weather had changed for the better. Every household on the peninsula had heard about the confrontation with the priest, but Jez refrained from passing comment. Today was another Sunday and therefore a day of rest. Tomorrow would signal the start of the planned construction of the road to Rossdore. He had hired nineteen local men to help with the work right on the cusp of winter, which won him many new friends in both villages and no small amount of respect.

brown-stormy river
full-throttle seawards:
debris-shattering

Frank O'Connor and his sons Liam and Dom chanced the river that morning at the point where hours earlier an ebb tide had spread debris all round the estuary. The waters still ran brown. This was the first time in twelve days anyone had braved the crossing from Portleán to Carravoe.

Frank led the way on his black Percheron. Liam and Dom followed, riding their ponies bareback.

"Is good to see you," said Joe Lynch, a Carravoe fisherman. "We've had a bit of wind, I'm thinking. Lost a young girl in the storm and we're still counting livestock. What's with you?"

Frank dismounted and removed his cap as a mark of respect for the missing girl.

"I feared for many more," he said. "All my life, I never seen such a venomous storm. At least Portleán survived unscathed – several sheep, a few cattle and a good dog; a few injuries, nothing broken. I'm sad you suffered such a young loss. It's a miracle there was only the one."

Frank walked to the quay with the fisherman, rivalry between the two villages forgotten in the face of tragedy. The boys tagged along behind to

113

pick wild flowers and lay a posy inside a beached rowing boat that was doing duty as a memorial. No one had recovered the body of the nine-year-old who'd been swept out to sea.

Later that morning the O'Connors walked to the lowly terraced cottage where she had lived. Her mother accepted twenty florins and several pennies as a gift from Portleán's villagers. Both Liam and Dom had attended Carravoe School for a time and had known the girl, but schools cost money and tenant children rarely stayed more than a couple of years.

Building stone bridges was becoming a lost art. Jez didn't have the advantage of an architect or an education – he ploughed his own field and, as was the way with generations of Clancys, directed and organised as both boss and negotiator. The huge man had worked on railways, roads, and bridges, and once, for Harland and Wolff in Belfast, shipbuilding. Now he had to work out how to construct an arched stone bridge over Carravoe River.

There were many standing stones nearby, including a stone circle just below the village, overlooking the estuary. Prehistoric herders, farmers and fishermen had all left their mark here. Children playing in fields or on the foreshore often found ancient artefacts; remnants of the people who had made time to erect standing stones and cromlechs despite the rigours of life. This was how Jez wanted to be remembered. He didn't give a fiddle for religion. His forefathers had, by their own strength and guile, built things that lasted. Jez was going to build a bridge that would last a thousand years.

man tends stones, forms
cromlechs, giants' circles –
river crossings

He stayed up much of the night sketching plans, and rose early the next morning, certain he knew what to do. He rallied his army of labourers on the Carravoe bank and began to delegate. Massive holes would need excavating, to be filled with boulders to create a solid foundation. The diggers had to work waist-deep in freezing cold water, but as the days passed, Jez was relieved to reach bedrock quickly. The men attached chains to huge rocks and dragged them from the fields. A dozen stonemasons chiselled them into shape. One traction engine had a substantial derrick attached, capable of lifting several tons and depositing the rocks in the riverbed. Enthusiastic crowds regularly gathered to watch the bridge and the new road taking shape.

Within a month, the first footing had reached road level. Jez continued with the construction despite no word from the government. He spent much of his time tramping to and from Rossdore, believing Cork or Dublin surveyors would eventually catch up and furnish a made-to-measure blueprint. Irish politics was still very much in flux but so long as the money kept flowing, Jez kept paying wages. He even employed a colleen to keep the ledger and record everything in the neatest script imaginable.

Every Thursday one of his foremen took a pony and trap to Castletown to collect the wages from the Provincial Bank of Ireland. Men were paid just enough for their keep, while promissory notes were held at the bank for disbursement on high days and holidays so that families were never left high and dry. Wives furnished a receipt for monies received, and the ledger was scrutinised to ensure fair play.

A grand white house lay across the river on the Portleán side, hidden behind mature trees. It boasted manicured lawns and exotic blooms under glass. The residence was less imposing than the properties on the south-facing parts of the bay, but still well built and evidently owned by a man who could afford the best. Jez had often looked through the trees and admired it from the gravelled track, but knowing the landed gentry of old, he refrained from visiting for fear of upsetting the owners. The track itself was a public right of way. He had never seen anyone at the house, which belonged to a politician who lived and worked in London. Jez had heard the name 'Walter Jeffries-Boone' in conversation, but it didn't mean anything to him, so on meeting a lady wrapped up tight against the chill on the track to Carravoe, he simply stood aside to let the buggy pass and thought no more of it.

This particular Sunday, Jez was surveying the route of the new road as far as Portleán village. The lady – Mrs Alexandra Jeffries-Boone – appeared to be in a great hurry. Her driver had lost control of the bay horse and was struggling with its reins, one of which dragged beneath the cart. The gelding bolted and the gig veered off the track, clouting the verge and skidding on loose gravel before hitting the far bank and smashing the offside rear wheel. The female driver shot off the buggy and landed in a fuchsia hedge. Her passenger took an almighty tumble as the terrified horse reared. The traces snapped and the cart flipped over, trapping her beneath.

The whole episode lasted no more than a few seconds.

"Well," said Jez quietly. "There's a thing."

Alexandra's life
gravel-crashes around her –
sweet-flowered landing

All went deathly quiet. The horse, still bearing its harness, had galloped off towards the river. Jez couldn't see anyone living or dead until a spluttering buxom female fell out of a fuchsia bush. She spat and cursed in Gaelic, then promptly collapsed.

"Holy Mother," said Jez, "You ain't looking too well, Miss. I dunno where your mate is?"

He took off his tweed overcoat and placed it over the woman's inert form.

A sound of retching emerged from beneath the wrecked buggy. Jez peered under the broken cart and spotted a fur-clad woman lying on the gravel. He grabbed hold of a chassis member and using his vast strength was able to turn the entire contraption over. The fur-coat stirred.

"Hold 'ard," said Jez. "Lie still will ye? Wherever you wuz goin', you ain't goin' no more."

He returned to the driver of the buggy who seemed to have recovered a little. She had blood around her mouth, but was more shocked than anything. She tried to sit up, but Jez pointed a warning finger at her and told her to stay put. He needed help, but the nearest house was some way off. Jez had seen injured men before, but these people were women and he wasn't sure of the rules of touching them.

He returned to the fur-clad female.

"Listen lady, I'm fetchin' help. There's a farmhouse not far from here, the O'Connor's. It'll take a few minutes, but I'll be as quick as I can."

The woman attempted to speak but Jez couldn't understand a word. He helped her sit upright against the buckboard of the buggy, and despite the raw cold, removed his black jersey and wrapped it round her hands, which were bleeding. When Jez took hold of them, she winced at the pain before closing her eyes.

"I'll be back in two shakes," said Jez. "Don't move, will ye now."

Jez was of a time when men walked rather than run, but he didn't dawdle. The plight of the women had him galloping.

The O'Connor girls responded swiftly.

"Frank is repairing a wall," said Karen. "Will I need to fetch him?"

"Nah," said Jez. "Best you look after them women 'cos they're sufferin' bad. I'll round up Frank and the boys. It's a chill morning and those women are in shock. If you wouldn't mind seein' to 'em, I'd be obliged."

Mrs Jeffries-Boone had been suffering excruciating stomach pains and had set out to reach a doctor when the unfortunate mishap took place. Her maid, Minnie, had never handled a horse-drawn buggy before and Mrs

Jeffries-Boone, in her agony, was unable to relay much in the way of instructions. Getting supplies and medical help was a constant problem as motor vehicles were still rare in the peninsula. The reconstruction work on the bridge at Carravoe had only compounded the problem.

The O'Connors didn't know Minnie as she was a Cork City colleen, drafted into the house for domestic duties by Walter Jeffries-Boone. The lady of the house was even more mysterious. Alexandra was the wife of a Liberal MP who harboured unethical ambitions to become a cabinet minister. His constituency lay in North Kent, as far away from Ireland as possible. The Hon Walter Jeffries-Boone was an expensively upholstered bigwig, rolling with money, a serial womaniser and well in with David Lloyd George. He had married in a hurry on Armistice Day, hoping the celebrations would mask public notices in the press. As soon as the honeymoon ended, Alexandra Jeffries-Boone was incarcerated in an expensive remote property in Munster. Her husband excused his behaviour saying Alexandra loved flowers, and as he had invested in several acres on the peninsula, she would have freedom to express herself in anyway she chose. Scandal was averted, though not in the way Walter would have chosen. Alexandra miscarried early in her pregnancy, so he could have saved himself much expense had he waited. Three years on, Walter hadn't been seen in Ireland at all.

"Too busy," he claimed to his fellow Whigs and collaborators. "I'm in government."

Alexandra was no fool. Roedean had been followed by three years at Newnham College, Cambridge, reading botany. That was where she'd had the misfortune to catch the eye of Walter Jeffries-Boone, and the inevitable had followed.

pain explodes –
helpers race, run, hurry,
fates are sealed

Helpers converged quickly on the accident site. The O'Connor girls were despatched to neighbouring properties and a passer-by with some medical knowledge stopped to offer assistance. The morning was bitterly cold with everyone breathing vapour trails through tingling noses. There was hardly time for introductions but the pedestrian turned out to be a naval man returning from shore leave.

118

"Call me Blackie," he said. "I repair the boilers, usually from the inside. The only time I'm white is when I go back to Ballymena to see the family."

Minnie the housemaid had recovered a measure of confidence and was gabbling incomprehensibly while spitting blood, fortunately away from her rescuers. Karen O'Connor and Blackie stood her upright and walked her gently for a time, before depositing her against the gig which lay with the shattered wheel against the bank. Alexandra rested against the buckboard, looking deathly ill. Her eyes were tight shut, and she breathed in short gasps, clutching her stomach with both hands.

"We need to get her to Castletown," said Blackie. "There's a hospital on Bear Island and a clinic at Brandyhall, but that's a dozen miles distant and I fear she'll be lost long before that."

Karen O'Conner heard the sound of a wagon coming along the track and called that her husband was on his way. With the arrival of Frank and his boys and Jez Clancy, the accident site became a roadside workshop. Frank turned the wagon round in the entrance of the white house. Jez barked orders, expecting and getting instant results. Minnie was escorted back to the house to be taken care of by the O'Connor girls. The damaged buggy was dragged into the fuchsia hedge to get it out the way. Frank's boys would repair it later, but first there was an emergency to be dealt with. Alexandra was lifted carefully into the back of the dray and covered with a blanket from the buggy. Blackie attended to her while Jez led the big horse before clambering aboard himself. Frank took the reins.

"Easy, easy; no sense in hurryin'," said Jez. 'Ye'll shake the bones out of the poor woman, I tell ye. We've the river to cross, but after we reach the road proper, then ye kin trot."

The horse steadied its gait and settled into a firm stride. The tide was out, the sun shone and fording the estuary was accomplished without further drama. As the dray climbed the bank leading to the metalled Castletown road, Jez shouted, "Let's be havin' you wagoner, ten miles to Castletown – the lady's dyin'."

It took a full half hour as Jez refused to let Frank's horse break into a gallop.

"Just a steady canter," he said. "You's doin' fine, O'Connor, no sense in racin', the lady will survive, I'm sure."

When they arrived at the clinic, medics transferred the patient inside and swiftly diagnosed appendicitis. A Royal Navy motor-launch crossed the sound from Bear Island, bringing a naval surgeon and attendants. The King's Navy had strict orders to assist locals needing medical help, even on a Sunday. Ireland might be at loggerheads with the British government, but the Navy honoured its promises. Appendicitis would be a death warrant without hospitalization, quite apart from injuries sustained by the accident. By late afternoon, the naval surgeon said she could be moved into a recovery room. The operation had been a success. Jez Clancy and a handful of Portleán villagers had saved Alexandra's life.

In his Kent constituency across the Irish Sea, the Hon Walter Jeffries-Boone knew nothing of the unfolding drama. He hadn't seen Alexandra for three years and fully expected to be in Paris for Christmas. The less he knew of his wife, the better he felt. She had her flowers. He'd even paid for a new conservatory on the east-end wall, at an unholy cost. His eyes were now firmly set on his next dalliance, but an Irish newspaper editor had sniffed out a story that might upset the apple cart. Jeffries-Boone served the constituency of Medway (East) and had asked questions in the House of Commons concerning Armenian refugees still held captive in the Bosphorus. That same week Alexandra Jeffries-Boone had been reported as having undergone an operation after the Royal Navy intervened with a team of surgeons from Bear Island. Walter's headlines made front-page news in the London Times. Alexandra's report made page three of the Cork Examiner. Scandal – or conjecture – stalked the corridors of the *Examiner* on Academy Street, Cork. It was a chance to dish the dirt on a sitting MP.

The following Saturday morning, Jez had his haircut in Rossdore by Willy Toomey and also braved a shave. Several young scamps crowded round the shop-window to watch the operation. Jez was fiery in looks as well as manner with his flaming red hair. The jesting continued despite the risk of igniting Jez's temper. Some ne'er-do-wells pinched locks of red hair as Willy always worked with the door wide open. Others pursed their lips and wore ginger moustaches. Jez couldn't help laughing at the pantomime.

> ruddy locks are shorn,
> fall away with his temper:
> new strength emerges

The site boss was well known in town. He often came surveying and measuring with a pair of cartographers bearing yardsticks, tape-measures, callipers and theodolite. People were fascinated by the idea of going by

120

road from Rossdore to Castletown without the need to climb the mountain. It had been talked of for years and now under the direction of Jez, was actually happening. The man's reputation had soared, not least because people knew he would the job done.

Late Sunday afternoon, the convoy of workers returned to the works site, Jez leading on a mule-drawn wagon, his surveyors following in a steam-powered *Sentinel* lorry. The lorry turned off, having reached its destination, but Jez continued through the ford and onto the Castletown road. He had an assignation, and was guessing the time by the darkness of the sky as the mules splashed through the shallows.

"Damnty," he said. "The nurses in Castletown Clinic will just have to wait on me."

Off came his working boots as he trotted the wagon along the coast road. On went a pair of shiny brown boots and a new jacket that had lain all day under the seat-box.The famous red hair succumbed to a brand-new patterned cloth capand the smell of bay rum and pomade hung in the air. For the first time in his life, Jez was putting on the style, though the boots were too big, the cap too small and the jacket only fitted where it touched. He might have called the whole charade off, but Connaught men are a breed apart and on reaching the clinic, he felt more confident.

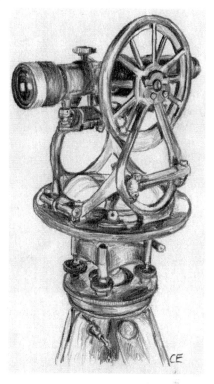

He left the wagon by the roadside, fed the mules an armful of hay from the net that swung behind the cart and pretended to be in no particular hurry as he approached the clinic.

"Mister Clancy, ma'am," said Jez. "I've an appointment to see Mrs Jeffries-Boone. I asked for consideration as I attended the unfortunate accident and transported the lady to hospital."

"'Tis a clinic," said the nurse, "and I'm sorry Mister Clancy, but it's past visiting time. The lady's still recovering."

Seeing Jez look so crestfallen, the nurse took pity.

"If you'd be so kind to wait a moment, I'll ask Matron for permission. You never know, she's a kindly soul. Take a seat, why don't you. I'll be back in a jiffy."

The odour of bay rum and pomade mingled with the more urgent smells of a place of healing. Jez worried if his being here was complicating things. In the past week he had discovered certain truths about the Jeffries-Boones and the more he learned, the more he understood that Alexandra was a jewel left stranded far away from her own country.

"Just a few minutes," said the nurse from a half-open door. "Matron says she'll join you as soon as she can. If you'll be so kind to accompany me to the ward, I'll see you right."

Jez drew himself up to his full height and stowed his too-small cap in a jacket pocket.

"My," said the nurse cheekily as he followed her through the door, "you're a fine looking man, sir." It was entirely the wrong statement to make to a man who didn't understand that physical attraction happens without advance warning, even if a man only lives for his work and has never known romance.

Jez sat down on a creaking wooden bench beside Alexandra's bed. Electric lights glimmered overhead. Alexandra lay under pristine white sheets with a cream cellular blanket on top.

"Five minutes," said the nurse.

She tapped a finger on the side of her nose. On the far wall a resonant wood-cased clock tick-tocked. The nurse stood guard at the foot of the bed. Jez wanted to push his boots out of sight but was worried they might squeak. He whispered to the patient that he had never seen such a clean floor and it was a credit to the staff. Mrs Jeffries-Boone didn't reply, so Jez asked how she was feeling.

Alexandra smiled and gave a tiny wave of her hand.

"'Tis good to see you ag'in," said Jez, "I've been thinkin' on ye. Worryin'."

She made to speak, but whether it was weakness or maybe emotion, the words remained rooted inside her head. Just at that same moment, Matron squeaked across the polished floor.

"Mister Clancy is it? I've heard so many wonderful things about you and now you're here, in person." She turned to the nurse. "We'll be

122

making tea for you before you return to Carravoe, isn't that right, Sister Whelan."

She told Jez about Alexandra's operation, leaving out technical details as she knew from experience that even the biggest men are prone to fainting when made privy to such information.

Alexandra closed her eyes and drifted into a dreamland with thoughts that had never dared enter her head before. A mere seven days ago, she had neither seen nor heard of Mister Clancy. Now she couldn't stop thinking about him.

"A fine man," she thought. "A real gentleman. My champion."

after the drama,
patient and saviour –
spellbound

At first, the visits occupied Thursday evenings and Sunday afternoons only, but then Jez borrowed the gig that had been repaired by the O'Connors, hired a guaranteed placid pony, and added Tuesday evenings to his visits. He ditched the squeaking boots and gradually moved closer to Alexandra.

Newspaper gossip about the Jeffries-Boones faded as both Britain and Ireland drew further apart. The Anglo-Irish treaty was signed on the 6th of December and an Irish Free State established in January 1922. The Hon Walter Jeffries-Boone lost his constituency following the 1922 general election and quietly disappeared from view, together with Lloyd George and his Liberal entourage.

Alexandra, wrapped tightly in woollen blankets from top to toe, escorted by Minnie the housemaid on one side and Jez on the other, finally returned to the white house in the trees on Christmas Eve, five weeks after the accident. They took a gentle pace, crossing the river below Carravoe before clip-clopping over the crunchy gravelled track. The trio arrived at midday in fine fettle, blowing frosty breath.

The men returned to work on New Year's Day. Jez was confident he would have the Carravoe Bridge completed by Easter, the first step in the construction of the new Rossdore road. The entire length of it had now been planned meticulously both in his head and his sketches. It was only a matter of time before Mister Clancy's grand road would be up and running, constructed by and for the common people of Munster.

Chapter Eleven

Bridging the Divide

the bridge

the road across the river grows on –
next year, the shadows won't be so tall
the way will curve less sharply,
while water rushes and laughs and splashes
beneath the slick black road

it's a sweet spot, this bridge, this river, this rock,
but underneath the silt dissolves,
black earth, dark torrent, death and drowning
a gravelling passed out of time

There is something truly pleasurable in watching men at work building something substantial. Add the highly-charged noise, the hum of brightly painted machinery, a brigade of gladiators stripped to the waist – and a crowd of spectators is bound to gather.

The men were constructing a road where none had existed before. Gravelled tracks linked remote holdings, but much of the north foreshore had yet to be tamed and many of its hills ran straight into the sea. For most, Shanks' pony was the only option, clambering over the mountain and clinging to whatever projection offered itself. Many a tenant struggled to make a living as getting to market was a difficult journey, hard to complete in daylight.

Constructing the road was no easier.

"Enough is enough," said Jez Clancy. "If any man wants to quit, he can leave right away as we don't employ fairy folk, tramps or anyone looking to hitch a ride. Are you with me, boys?"

His northern Donegal voice could be heard all the way across the village. Jez had been born in one of the breeziest places in all Ireland and had grown up shouting against the wind.

This morning signalled a special occasion with the opening of the first stage of the Rossdore road. Jeremiah Clancy may have lacked leadership at a political level, but he had forged a team of determined and hardworking followers. He mounted his oversized Connemara pony while Alexandra held the bridle.

"Today," said Jez, "you'll be able to travel all the way to Castletown, westward over the new bridge – though not before ten o'clock please, as that's when the barriers will be removed."

Alexandra curtseyed. For all her exemplary upbringing, she loved a good giggle and now that she had volunteered to sue in a British court for divorce, citing her husband's adultery, her sense of fun knew no bounds. The long-distance divorce had been masterminded by *The Cork Examiner*, which was hoping for a Westminster exclusive now that the Hon Walter had been defeated in the General Election. The *Examiner* had plotted the conspiracy and was happy to underwrite the cost as scoring an exclusive against the Dublin press was an achievement rarely enjoyed by provincial newspapers.

"I'll be there in good time for the opening, sir," said Alexandra. "Would you like me to wear my wedding dress? I still have it in the wardrobe. Only used the once. Minnie could be my bridesmaid, I'm sure she'd like that."

Jez pulled his cap down even further on his head and grinned. Frivolity was not something he had encountered often, but he winced inwardly, knowing Alexandra would be travelling shortly to London's divorce court alone. He admired the way she was able to dismiss thoughts of the petition and the inevitable publicity.

"Listen Lexxie," he said, quietly this time, "I'm not allowed to buy a ring until the judge nods his head and tells the world you're free to marry.

I'm saving my coppers. If I charge travellers a farthing every time they cross the bridge, I might be able to buy a ring in a few years' time."

"Meanie," said Alexandra. "How much longer do I have to wait for my conjugal rights?"

Jez swallowed hard, largely because he didn't know what conjugal rights were. Even kissing in public was taboo, though he had already moved in with his intended. Jez slept in a room above the stables and behaved impeccably. Minnie fed him and even did his laundry, often saying how good it was to have a man around the house.

Lexxie's Song

when we kiss and say goodnight
you don't follow, not yet,
but later
when we're wed...

when you leave, the air closes silent behind you,
branches outside sway and sag in the wind
this, love, this, without lies
this, as you, as I, this

and here, these machines,
sanded air, hot tarmac, the road –
the noise, the fumes

this low wall, we two –
fuchsia blossom

Jez dug his heels into the gelding's ribs but nothing happened. He even tried "Gee-up!"

"He won't move until I tell him," said Alexandra. "Skibbereen ponies don't understand the Donegal lingo."

She led the pony out to the gravelled track and smacked its rump to great effect.

Saturday was the grand opening day. The gangers stood in a squad, ready to jump up and down on the bridge for the benefit of anyone who might doubt its strength – though most locals had crossed it already.

"Jerry-built is it?" shouted one wag. A woman complained that it was too high. "Me bucket won't reach the water!"

At ten o'clock, the NO THROUGH ROAD signs were removed and the oldest resident of Carravoe, ninety-eight year old Miss Meara Powel, cut the bright green ribbon spanning the roadway with a pair of dressmaker's shears.

A king's mile of compacted rocks, gravel and unblemished tar stretched as far as the first smallholding, with plenty of passing places and a few blind corners, but no steep gradients. The spectators sat on stone walls. Some looked seawards and others scanned the mountain, remembering last year's terrible storm damage. It was hard now to imagine the wall of water that had swept the old bridge into the sea. Embankments had been rebuilt, topped with a raised roadway on the Carravoe side, complete with new drains and telegraph poles. Cottages had been whitewashed, doors painted, and flowers and new turf laid on the Portleán bank.

Jez Clancy dismounted and led his pony from the Portleán side, shaking hands with menfolk and kissing the hands of the ladies whatever their age. In the short time he had been working on the road, he'd endeared himself to all.

The festivities continued with cakes and ale, bread and butter pudding, flowers and garlands, home-made toffee and sarsaparilla, hot sausages, a hog-roast and ginger beer in porcelain bottles that made a boy's eyes water with its fizz. No one doubted the afternoon would end with an impromptu ceilidh.

Alexandra watched from the edges until Jez spotted her. She had walked to the bridge by herself and was trying to be inconspicuous among the villagers.

"I'm really proud of you," she said, her cultured accent contrasting with the local brogue. "I brought these white roses to lay in the memorial boat for the young girl who was lost in the flood."

Everyone close by hushed their chatter. Two youngsters with hurriedly scrubbed faces led Alexandra across the bridge to the Carravoe side, where the memorial boat lay on the bank. The other children followed. Alexandra turned to one and asked him to lay the flowers. Everyone applauded, but it was too much for Alexandra. Tears welled up and she couldn't speak. A slightly older colleen felt sorry for her, took her hand and said, "Would you like to see my pictures?"

The English Lady disappeared inside a whitewashed cottage hardly thirty paces from the memorial and met the girl's family. The walls inside were pristine white, colourful curtains hung from polished poles while beautiful hand-crafted furniture lined the rooms. The proud mother made tea while the girl showed Alexandra her drawings.

Horse-drawn wagons, steam-powered tractions engines, twelve motor vehicles and two motorcycles had lined up to head the first convoy across the new bridge. A photographer took pictures with a flashgun that had the entire assembly cowering – such flash-bang picture-taking hadn't been seen in Carravoe before. There followed a mercifully short address by the village's curate-in-charge and a swift sprinkle of holy water as the procession crossed to the Portleán side. The gangers were given the rest of the day off in order to join the villagers in the sunshine and celebrations. Jez remounted his dappled steed, reached down to Alexandra and hauled her up to sit sideways on the ponies' withers.

"One mile done, nine to go," said Jez. "Maybe we should purchase one o' they fancy autocars. A two seater with a canvas on top in case it rains?"

128

The word *we* made Alexandra gasp. It was the first time Jez had used it in that way. She put her arms round him and hugged hard, scandal and gossip thrown to the wind.

The Cork Examiner went to extraordinary lengths to ensure Alexandra's safety during the long passage to The Strand, London. The divorce hearing was now public knowledge and embarrassing for the sitting government. The Honourable Walter Jeffries-Boone became dishonourable and ostracized publicly by his fellow MPs. On the day of the hearing, he applied for the Chiltern Hundreds – under the orders of David Lloyd George – and swiftly disappeared from view.

Alexandra refused to comment other than to answer questions tabled by counsel. She ignored her parents, who had encouraged the marriage in the first place. Free at last, she took the train from Paddington to Fishguard, boarded a ferry to Waterford, and was reunited with Jez at Bantry's quayside railway station. The closer she came to her country retreat in Portleán, the fewer people she encountered. The only staff on the station platform were a porter and the ticket inspector. She was unaware that Michael Collins had been killed the previous day in an ambush at *Béal na mBláth,* north of Clonakilty, and all of Ireland was in mourning.

Republican infantrymen at a roadblock on the edge of Bantry insisted on checking the lights on the four-wheel gig before allowing the couple to continue. At the junction with the Macroom road, another barrier manned by men of the 5th Cork Brigade caused further delay. It was already dark, and the troopers warned that if they continued on to Rossdore, it would be at their own risk. Everything was double-checked including Alexandra's baggage, even though a corporal remembered Jez passing through the checkpoint earlier.

"Trigger-happy," said Jez, "the lot of 'em. Half of Munster is fighting neighbours in the same village."

Alexandra didn't understand the situation, but appreciated the need to remain impartial. She left the talking to Jez.

The twisting road hugged the bay. Mountains loomed ahead, dark silhouettes against the night sky. The blinkered roan wasn't happy working in the dark with compromised vision, but Jez needed no distractions. They made good progress, and were soon negotiating a long bend in a heavily wooded area close to the sea. Jez had to keep brushing biting insects off his face, but Alexandra sat safely behind her hat's veil.

As the stallion eased the pace round the curve, Alexandra screamed, seeing a man directly in their path.

stingers

tortured tree roots fold away from the trunk:
cloud of stingers arises, horse shies and twitches

at bugs' whirring wings, angry thread-angled swarming
flick-slapping tail till they mass-flit away

to find red hair, pink skin, tingle of pinpricks, chattering
itching, red-bump rash rising, fury of scratching –

hiss-strangled yelp of the victim.

Jez had an insect in his eye and couldn't see, but he pulled the reins hard. The horse whinnied and swerved round the man before coming to a halt a few yards on.

Alexandra climbed down the gig's step and onto the road, taking the spare candle-lantern with her.

"Where did he go?" she said.

Jez dismounted and squinted into the dark.

"For sure we missed him otherwise we would have felt a bump or heard a shout. Stay by the wagon, Lexxie – there's another lantern under the seat."

Alexandra found it and passed it to Jez who lit it from her candle.

"Look after the horse," he said. "Give him a peppermint. Talk to him. He was a good lad not to panic. The man can't have gone far. I swear we didn't run over him."

Jez searched the trees on both sides of the road. A silvery moon, almost full, shone between the gaps in the wood, but aside from a rustle in the trees off the sea, nothing stirred.

Alexandra peered through the gloom.

"The horse saw him, I saw him, and I'm sure you must have spotted him from the corner of your eye."

"Well, he ain't here now," said Jez, "and the sooner we get going the better."

Alexandra knelt down on the road to examine some glistening drops; a minuscule trail which led to the embankment. She smoothed the fluid between her fingers and sniffed it.

"I'm sure that's blood." She followed the trail behind the gig. "He must have been walking along the road for some time – he's bleeding badly."

Jez searched the verge, crouched close to the ground and found more traces on the bare roots of a silver birch. He was about to call to Alexandra when a voice cried out, "Don't come any closer! I've got a gun."

There was a stifled groan, the sound of someone falling and finally an Irish curse.

Jez pushed past a huge willow and found a figure collapsed on the ground. He put his lantern down and tried to turn the man onto his back.

"Stay still, will ye," said Jez. "Am't I not tryin' to help ye?"

The man spluttered and gasped, blood and mucus dribbling from his mouth.

Jez propped him up to aid his breathing. "Don't speak," he said. "There's a lady by the wagon lookin' after the horse. I'll park the cart and bring her down to help. We'll get you home somehow."

The man tried to raise a hand but passed out with the effort.

Jez doused the wick in the lantern and hurried back to the wagon.

"Found him," he said. "He's hurt bad – I don't know how – but he's bleeding and we have to get him to a doctor cr someone who knows. The only person I can think of is Lizzie who wed that fisherboy of Portleán."

"Wouldn't it be better to go back to Bantry?"

"No, the place is in uproar. There's been shootings, ambushes, arson and I'm of the opinion this man might be another victim. This damned civil war is raging and didn't I sweat waiting for the train to come. I was there all day wanting word of you. Michael Collins got himself killed yesterday, and the ructions will last a thousand years. I'd rather let this poor man stay right where he is rather than involve you in the troubles, and besides, I'm thinking he won't suffer much longer. He's dying."

"Not if I have anything to do with it. We could reach Rossdore within the hour. Let me see him please Jez."

A week earlier, Alexandra had proved a cool customer in London's High Court, suing for divorce. Tonight, she was running the gauntlet against troopers to help a partisan in his hour of need. Jez had never known anyone like her.

He drove the gig off the road behind a thicket of gorse and extinguished the lanterns. The road remained quiet, thanks to the sentries posted back at the junction.

Alexandra followed him into the wood. It took some time in the dark, but eventually they found the weeping willow, forty yards away. The young man was lying just as Jez had left him.

Alexandra felt for a pulse and spent a long time checking and re-checking, but there was no life left in him. She closed his eyes for the last time.

"I'm so sorry," she said. "I really wanted you to live. You're too young to be wasted by war."

She stared, unflinching, at the bloody wound in the man's side and the shattered arm through which a bullet must have passed, nearly severing the limb above the wrist. A single-cartridge shotgun lay beside him, the breech empty.

"Will you stay with him?' said Jez "I need to fetch a shovel and a blanket to cover the body. I won't be a minute."

Alexandra nodded. She wanted to cry, but now was not the time.

132

forest shadows

willows ride the riverbank
hiding dark shapes among the brambles
the sweetness of deadly nightshade

tree-lined with certainty,
black-greened against the light,
side-washed in silver.

wooded slopes tumble
into the shallows of hidden traps
death stalks the bloodied soil

They worked for an hour, taking it in turns, until they were satisfied they
had dug a decent grave. Jez dragged the man's body to its last resting
place and with Alexandra's help, gently laid him in the ground, covered
with a horse blanket, his shotgun beside him. They shovelled the soil
back, tramped it down and spread any excess around. Alexandra broke off
a branch and used it to camouflage the area. She looked at her watch in
the shielded light of the lantern. It was three o'clock.

"Time for us to be going," said Jez. "Say goodnight and goodbye."

Alexandra couldn't recall any Catholic responses.

"I'll just say farewell," she said. "It's a cruel war and so sad you have to stay here and never return home. May you find peace in this secret place."

As they climbed the bank to the road, Alexandra could no longer stifle her tears. The young man had most likely been a fugitive wanted by the military, but which side? Alexandra and Jez could find themselves accused of being collaborators and tried for treason as enemies of the state.

"My fault," said Jez. "I should have driven on and taken no notice."

Alexandra placed a hand over his mouth.

"Don't talk like that. It was an honourable thing to do."

Jez tried to hush her for she was talking too loud and her voice would carry easily through the windless night. He held her close for a few precious moments, his huge arms around her, rubbing warmth into her shivering body.

The roan suddenly whinnied at being left alone in the dark. They needed to go. Jez disentangled the gig from the gorse bushes and they set off at a gentle pace, there being no need to hurry. Grey dawn broke as they approached Rossdore. A crude, barbed-wire barrier had been dragged to one side and the only man in evidence was a civil police guard, quietly puffing on a Woodbine, happy to let the gig pass without comment.

Alexandra slept, her head laid on Jez's lap, covered with a blanket.

"I'll take no notice of you policeman," said Jez under his breath. "You haven't seen me at all, is that not right, Smoky?"

The roan instinctively turned onto the track to Portleán. As the wagon bumped and creaked over the rough surface, Alexandra stretched into wakefulness. No one could stay asleep on this track.

"Another year," said Jez, "maybe two, and you'll be trotting into town like you own the place, driving one of they fancy motorcars with 'lectric lamps and leather seats. Am't I not good for you, sweetheart? You'll be proud of me when they cut the ribbon to declare the new road open, fit for kings and queens, for workers, their wives and kids alike."

Alexandra smiled sleepily. Jez might not be especially articulate, and he would never lose his Connaught brogue, but she could listen to him forever.

134

Chapter Twelve

Major Tom

Urgent news had come for Peder overnight and Fergal the butcher was impatient to deliver it.

"Your sister-in-law, Mary Anne, needs to see you at once," he said. "Message received first thing this morning. The Major has been taken ill."

Peder set off back home at once to pick up his family. By midday they were all on their way to Kenmare. It was a difficult road, much of it carved out of the mountain, and so steep that at times that Peder had to dismount and walk alongside the pony. There was little traffic on the road that afternoon other than an occasional lorry or an equally rare motorcar, but the journey took hours because of the heat. Dry streambeds meant the brake blocks couldn't be watered, so they had to stop frequently to allow the heat to dissipate. It being May, at least they could complete the journey in daylight.

Arrival

> bump-trundled along a track
> hacked in chunks from hillside rocks
>
> streams slip underground –
> too hot on top to risk a gurgle
> the tiniest splash
> to cool the brake-blocks
>
> Mic braves the descent,
> trusts Peder's firm hand
>
> sundown clip-clopping
> between rustling maples
> heading for warmth and welcome.

The Major's house lay to the east of Killaha, well concealed and sheltered by the woodland overlooking the estuary. The sun finally dipped behind the Knockmoyle hills as the pony clip-clopped up the drive.

"Glory be!" said Peder's mother-in-law Martha. "Didn't expect you until tomorrow."

She lifted both children from their mother's arms. Peder helped Jo down the buggy's step.

"It really is good to see you," Martha said. "We're hardly a mountain away, yet that hill makes hard work of visiting."

Mary Anne came rushing from a different direction and there were tears and greetings before Peder was able to settle the pony for the night in the Major's stables. Mic was led into a stall with straw on the floor, oats in a trough and a manger of last year's hay. It even had a roof. Mary Anne closed the lower half of the stable-door and let the pony explore and get used to the sounds of his equine neighbours. Mic finally slumped down on a bed of straw, exhausted from seven hours between the shafts of the four-wheel cart.

"Peder dear, it's wonderful you came so soon," said Mary Anne. "Major Thomas is not at all well, and the illness is getting right inside his head. I'm afraid he doesn't have much life left in him."

Peder didn't comment as the Major, walking with the aid of a stick, had just come through the paddock gate. Mary Anne told him off for not wearing his coat. Most May evenings were warm and tranquil, but as darkness fell, a cool breeze rustled the maple trees.

Thomas Alan Redmond had served as a captain in the Dragoons during the Great War. A passion for horses and a willingness to travel had served him well in the early part of the campaign, but the Dragoons had been decimated at Ypres and in 1914, the Expeditionary Force managed to create a stalemate by preventing German forces reaching vital channel ports. The Allies held firm but this led to trench warfare and for the next two years soldiers died in their hundreds of thousands. Captain Redmond retrained as an artillery officer and was promoted to Major on the eve of Verdun. He survived only to find himself playing a desperate role in the Battle of the Somme. Knowing the horrific problems in getting guns into position, he pioneered ways of moving artillery using teams of horses, but found the loss of so many fine animals unbearable.

Unremitting artillery bombardment was the root cause of his subsequent problems. He was returned to Epsom, Surrey, at the start of 1918 for treatment before being sent to Seale Hayne Neurological Hospital in Newton Abbot and eventually back to Kenmare, his hometown in Kerry. Shellshock had never been understood by the military, the endless pounding not being considered a problem so long as soldiers survived it. Warfare had changed markedly during the Great War, with men bearing the brunt of constant bombardment and battery, and suffering severe mental problems as a result. Thomas Redmond – decorated with the silver Military Cross and bar – had his condition exacerbated by witnessing the horrific deaths of so many horses.

In the four years following the conflict, he suffered continual nightmares. He couldn't hear due to tinnitus and was half blind. Mary Anne and Martha cared for him with great kindness, but couldn't relieve the torment of anguish and horror that was his constant companion.

"Will we go inside Tom?" said Mary Anne. "The light has faded and Peder hasn't had a bite to eat after his journey."

She placed an arm round Tom's shoulder and led him indoors.

Major Tom

can't forget
the screaming
of horses

Picardy's fields
should be filled with grazing
not screaming

born to sunlight, sweet grasses
not dragging artillery, falling and failing
bones splintered, eyes blinded

the screaming
of horses

they call it tinnitus.
it's not.
it's horses
dying

barrage and battery, breath coming short
flecks of foam, bloody foam on flanks that should be shining
ribs cracked, splintered, shattered

forget
don't forget
never forget
forget

horses in the mud
bloodied and dead

Martha had prepared one of the Major's favourite meals – colcannon –
and was serving it from the biggest baking pan in all of Kerry. The dish
was packed with mashed potatoes, greenery culled from the hedgerows,
onions, shredded ham, salted butter, goat's milk, cream, parsley,
watercress, salt and black peppercorns, topped with grilled bacon. It was
followed by another favourite; treacle pudding served with yet more
cream, and dotted with hidden silver coins wrapped in walnut shells. Jo
struck lucky and found a sixpence.

Jo bedded the children down in an upper room after dinner. They hadn't eaten until eight o'clock, and according to the grandfather clock tick-tocking in the hallway it was now almost ten, very late for young travellers.

Mary Anne and Martha washed the utensils before retiring, leaving Major Tom and Peder sat by the fireplace nursing the log fire, which occasionally crackled and spat. Peder had rarely spoken to anyone beyond his relatives but, faced with an honourably decorated military officer, trained in the ways of law, finance and protocol, he felt obliged. The brandy warmed, the big leather armchair was wonderfully comfortable, the huge hearth pleasurable and dinner had been a memorable occasion. Peder found he approved of how the other side lived. His sister-in-law Mary Anne had been fortunate to find this position for herself and her mother. Looking through the bottom of his brandy glass, Peder started to nod off. His new companion was already snoring, contentment being a rare pleasure in his troubled life.

Evening by the fire

brandy swirling in a glass
warmed by his hand, lit by the embers
glowing in the hearth

Peder rests back, slips slightly
on shiny well-worn leather,
considers the more practical attributes
of a three-legged stool for keeping the sitter
awake and alert

decides there's no need for wakefulness now
sips the brandy

wonders why it skims the side of the glass
in a clear glossy sheen

water doesn't behave like that

brandy doesn't quench a thirst
but it warms, oh it warms
along with the massive logs on the hearth

silence pretends to be mocked by tick-tock, tick-tock
from the grandfather clock;
the spit-crackle-hiss as a log settles down
and the restful snores from the major.

Peder considers his brandy again
takes a sip
enjoys the warmth

Peder awoke at midnight, wondering where the chimes were coming from, having never heard a striking clock before. A few embers still glowed in the hearth. The Major was sound asleep with his feet up on a stool. Soft light glowed from a brass oil lamp on the table. The grandfather clock stopped chiming and the heavy door to the sitting room opened.

Mary Anne came in and whispered, "Sorry Peder, I was dozing upstairs and forgot you men were still down here. I'm so used to clocks chiming, I don't hear them anymore. Tom's deaf, Martha sleeps in the attic and my room's at the back of the house. I suddenly woke up, peeped into Tom's room and remembered you were both downstairs."

Peder roused himself and stretched his aching limbs.

"Where should I be?"

"Top of the stairs and turn left; first door is the bathroom and the second is your room. I'll stay down here and put some peat on the fire. It's the first time the Major's slept soundly in months and that's a miracle. I keep some blankets in the cupboard just in case, but Tom's a stickler for having everything done just right. Military training, you see. You go up to bed and I'll stretch out on the sofa. Thank you for staying with him. I doubt he's much older than you – he'll be forty-one in two weeks – but he's a broken man."

Still a bit dazed, Peder climbed the carpeted stairs and turned left. A soft electric lamp gave enough light at the top of the landing. Inside the bathroom he was obliged to use unfamiliar items. It wasn't the first lavatory he had seen though he wondered about using it. There was a sink with a tap, and even a wooden box of plain paper, but when he pulled the toilet chain something high in the ceiling suddenly erupted and roared into the blue-patterned bowl. Fortunately no one took any notice in the bedroom next door. Neither Jo nor his daughters stirred when Peder finally clambered into bed.

The next morning everyone gathered round the scrubbed beech table in the kitchen. Breakfast was a kedgeree made with smoked halibut, so tasty that both Major Tom and Peder had second helpings to Martha's delight. In the three years she had been employed as cook and housekeeper the Major had never done anything other than accept what was put in front of him and respond with a polite "Thank you."

The women cleared the breakfast things away while the Major enthused about animals, trees, the Kerry landscape and especially the estuary. Mary Anne didn't interrupt. Peder listened closely, aware of the debt his family owed this man. Major Tom had never married and in his current mental state the likelihood of wedlock was remote, yet here, with a mug of coffee in a firm hand, he was able to chatter away with a man he hardly knew other than by reputation. Mary Anne watched closely. Most mornings, Tom kept his mug firmly on the table in case of spillage. Today, he walked confidently to the window and pointed out the Macgillycuddy's Reeks, Mullaghanattin and Mangerton Mountain, and Kenmare with its fine bridge.

"Will we take a stroll down to the shore, Peder?" he said. "There are otter cubs by Dawros Bridge and we could walk the strand back home in time for dinner."

Peder was keen. He turned to Jo and signed with open palms that not only would he do as he was asked, he would enjoy this impromptu ramble.

The Major led Peder round the back to the stables and kitted him out with thick socks, gumboots, a lumberjack shirt and a tweed cap. The shirt was a tad tight but the boots were fine and the socks the first Peder had ever worn. The final flourish was an ash walking stick which made Peder grimace as it was a device he had only used before to keep animals in check. Tom had walked to the stables wholly unaided which had puzzled the pigman at first, but he was beginning to understand the transitional nature of shellshock.

The horses were in the paddock, Peder's Connemara grazing with three immaculate roans. Mary Anne had inspected the pony to see if it had been shod, and tut-tutted on finding it hadn't. She made a note for Mic to see the farrier before returning to Portleán.

Peder had rarely had personal dealings with the military in the past, having always avoided uncouth men full of bravado in numbers. There had been talk of the Black and Tans in Cork not being nice to know, and of a new conflict arising among indigenous people, yet here he was, enjoying the company of a military man who loved his country, kept immaculate horses, and talked of otters and birds.

Now and then Tom paused and leant on his walking stick, but this was to point out something of special interest. When eventually they reached Dawros Bridge, they sat in the shade of the first span and relaxed, dangling their toes in the tingling water of the Dromoghty River. Tom sported a fob-watch hung by a silver chain, but only glanced at it once.

"Halfway Peder, and isn't the estuary in fine fettle. I dreamt of this place during the war. It helped me, knowing that this river would be waiting when I returned. Halfway was never good," said Tom. "Thousands upon thousands of men were slaughtered mercilessly in no-man's land." He stopped, the colour draining away from his face. The sparkling eyes became misty while a drop of spittle formed beneath his chin as he clasped his cap against his chest.

Peder placed a strong arm round Tom's shoulder; not heavy, more as a safeguard. The Dromoghty was a powerful river and Peder was worried. He didn't know whether to speak or not. For several minutes they sat together in silence. In the end, the river said all that needed saying in its endless splashes and gurgles.

Tom turned to look Peder in the face.

"I can't hear," he said, "but I can feel the vibration. This river is alive."

The wan face changed in an instant. Peder, still with an arm round Tom's shoulder, smiled and then grinned. Whatever the terrible memory had been, it had vanished in the flow of the water.

A stroll to the shore

Ceann Mara, head of the sea,
emerald home of otter and deer,
jay, dipper, storm petrel, puffin –
and the river, endlessly fed
from the mists of high *Na Cruacha Dubha*

Tom leans on his stick, eyes bright,
spirit fed, while the man by his side
sees brown birds, green trees,
in a piercing new light,
through the half-blinded eyes of his friend

"Will we find our way home along the shore, the tide has ebbed enough,"
said Tom, "and believe me, Peder, I could eat a horse; figuratively
speaking of course. Not a word to Mary Anne; she is especially fond of
that Connemara of yours – looked round it thoroughly, lifted each foot
and inspected his teeth. I think you're going to receive an offer – and
nothing less than twenty pounds. Promise?"

Peder couldn't stop smiling. Twenty pounds for Mic O'Brien! He
laughed out loud.

In Portleán, the hay harvest had ended. Tad Milligan and Frank O'Connor
had taken over responsibility for Peder's herd while the pigman was away
with the Major. They'd cut down a mountain of blackthorn, hawthorn and
alder and were dragging these into a semblance of hedging. Blackthorn
was one of the few hedges that the pigs respected. The spikes were vicious
and not easily seen, especially by younger pigs with immature skin. This
was only a temporary solution until more permanent stone walls could be
constructed by the villagers.

There had been talk that if Peder went to stay at Kenmare, he might
never come back. The purchase of the Portleán Estate land by an unknown
military man was a mystery and a touchy subject, though Peder himself
was trusted. The name of Rossdore had become synonymous throughout
Munster with the pig breeder, who was now a highly regarded herdsman.
Peder himself had much on his mind. His family came first, but the Major
was clearly enjoying his company despite the social and intellectual gulf,
and another matter needed consideration. Mary Anne occupied a
privileged position as the Major's housekeeper. She had impressed the
military man on his return to civil life and within days, her mother had
been taken on as cook. This had freed her to act as a personal secretary.

Some suggested it was a marriage for the taking, but Mary Anne soon
realised Major Tom was seriously ill. If it were not for her, the property
could well have fallen apart, its goods disbursed by some ne'er-do-well,
but since her arrival, Tom had discovered a reason for living. The war had
left a million men like him in limbo; trembling with every nerve ending,

143

unable to sleep, incontinent and paralysed with fear. Mary Anne had shown him it didn't need to be like that all the time.

She was determined to take advantage of Peder's presence and proposed they should all go to Killarney for a day out, taking the rarely used and extravagant landau. Before Peder could query the idea, Tom was opening the stable door and showing off the burnished carriage. Peder had little idea of how to drive a pair of swanky horses but the Major was highly experienced.

The plans for a day-out were finalized that evening over dinner, served on the terrace overlooking the lawn. Instead of Killarney, the party would head for Muckross Lake, which formed part of Lough Leane. They would go in a couple of days' time to allow the landau to be tried out, as Peder doubted his own abilities and Tom wouldn't be happy until the horses had been attached to the single drawbar for a road test.

After spending all morning checking everything in military fashion, the two men climbed into the driving seat. Tom took the reins and would have turned left at the Beara road, but one of the chestnut bays got spooked by dive-bombing seagulls. The horses veered right and pulled the landau across the bridge towards Kenmare Town.

Tom was visibly upset and embarrassed by the incident, Peder gritted his teeth. Suddenly they were in town surrounded by a cacophony of people, engines, wagons, vehicles, rattling, shaking, bright colours, bicycles, a motor horn, shop bells, traders shouting their wares, excitable women exchanging greetings and more ringing bells. The landau clipped the kerb hard. Two dogs were scrapping playfully and a man called to someone unseen. Above Henry Street, gaudy banners flapped loudly in the breeze and a woman shouted at the driver of the carriage. Tom froze, still with the reins in his hands. The geldings veered to the right, but their way was blocked by a costermonger's barrow. One horse reared and the other slipped, still in harness. Peder took hold of the reins, but couldn't prise Tom's hands away. The young horse reared again and let out a scream. The landau shook, its harness jangling. Women shrieked and a man fell off his bike. Peder threw Tom's jacket over his head. The Major's hands relaxed on the reins at last and the horses began to calm down, sensing Peder in control.

Neither man spoke. Peder gently took the jacket off Tom's head, keeping one hand on the reins. Tom sat flushed and breathing heavily.

"Hold 'ard," said Peder. "I'm goin' to drop down to the road and lead the horses from the front."

He signed the words as well as speaking them. Tom seemed to understand. He whispered the words, "Bell Heights."

Everything returned to normal. Nobody fussed, no one passed comment. It was just a fancy buggy clip-clopping along Henry Street.

At the start of Bell Heights, Peder stayed the horses and remounted.

"Your turn," said Peder. "I dunno where I'm going."

Just for a moment, he thought he detected a slight hesitation, but then the Major took up the reins, breathed in confidently and called, "Jup-jup-jup boys."

The landau turned right towards Killaha and headed for home.

The Drive

a seagull screeches
(and Tom can't forget
the screaming of horses)

the geldings panic, lurch left and right
gallop blindly through marketplace tumult clank-grinding
shout-crying (explosions, destruction, dead bodies, mud flying)
an impenetrable barrier of noise (of barbed wire)
the stink of the market place (stench of the gas)
the creeping fear
the gathering hysteria
the runaway horses, the screams, the terror –

his friend
drags him back from the brink
of churned up mud
and mingled nightmares

Tom can't forget
won't forget

Chapter Thirteen

Intransigence

a thief in the night

blood spatter, spots,
random streaks
a stone, muddied,
here, there, sullied, spoilt
no prints or marks

fox? too cunning –
no tell-tale whiff of reynard
no squealing, grunting in the night
to alert the watchful hounds

something lurks
bloodied
deceitful
near or far

that something
needs to be found

"Foxes," said Matthew Hogan. "Damn foxes. They're back."

"More like bloody wolves," said Tad Milligan, "and a nice fat gilt will only encourage 'em. Blood lust, a divil a one; get the scent, and there's no 'olding 'em."

"Don't think so Tad," said Peder. "If it'd been a fox it would've killed the whole litter and there'd have been a lot of squealing. The hounds would've been on it, quick as lightning. This isn't random slaughter. Foxes spray piss all over, and the dogs aren't sensing that. It would've been a blood bath."

Peder climbed off the ladder and stuffed his hands into his gilet pockets to warm them.

"I'm thinking there's a stranger in our midst," he said. "There's no signs of a fight, just a trail of blood and not much of that either. If Chip had smelled a fox, he'd've been over that wall."

"Will we follow the trail?" said Matt. "If Chip can sniff it out, surely it would be right?"

"Nah," said Peder. "S'pose the culprit is someone we know; what would we do then?"

"There's three of us," said Tad. "Thievin' is ag'in the law. There's two civil guards in Rossdore – they don't have guns, but they do take villains into custody."

"Steady," said Peder. "We're only *saying* it's a thief. Might turn out to be a stray dog with the blood lust, or maybe a cat gone wild, or somethin' innocent."

"But it's still out there," said Matt. "I say we go look before the trail goes cold."

The trio hummed and hawed a while longer, building a case for direct action which didn't cut much ice with Peder, and besides, were they not supposed to be building a stone wall?

"'Tis a fine day," said Peder. "It'd be a pity to waste it lookin' fer a robber who doesn't want to be found and is most likely long gone."

148

He took hold of his heavy wooden wheelbarrow and led the way to the new privy next to the house.

"Everyone's building shithouses these days," said Tad. "Even Matt is thinkin' on one."

"Toilet," said Matt, "not shithouse, and not as good as Peder's here, with a stream running through it and a Belfast sink. Whatever next?"

"A roof," said Peder, trying to lighten the mood. He stopped to show off the new latrine with a proper seat and wooden cover made from a former tar-barrel.

"How does that work then?" said Tad.

"When it's getting full, you lift off the seat, grab hold of the handles and tip it out onto the manure heap. Mix it in with the other stuff – pig's muck, seaweed, fish-heads, whatever. It all helps to fertilize the vegetable patch. Add a scoop of lime every time you use it. Jo even drops a few herbs in the tub to keep it smellin' sweet. I'll empty it first day of the month regular, and my kids will be able to use it under cover all year round."

"I'm thinkin' on it," said Tad. "Seriously. Where'd you get the tar barrels from, Ped?"

"Off Jez Clancy," said Peder. "A florin apiece. I can get one tomorrow if you like, no problem."

"Tad'll need a dozen tubs, so he will. He's got ten kids and another on the way," said Matt. "Dunno where he gets the energy from."

Tad winced at the crude banter and set off with the barrow to fetch another load of stone.

"Poteen," said Peder. "Tad has the biggest potato clamp in the entire village. His kids are just an excuse for growing extra spuddies. The bothy behind his house was his father's place and he was always makin' the stuff."

"You don't say," said Matt. "Is it for selling or for hisself?"

"Someone comes from Rossdore and collects it in a cart. Not a word now Matt; hear much, speak little. Tad is a good friend to all of us."

privy

petals strewn
sweet-scented, loving
allowing a lingering,
a pleasure, enriching
this, the most basic
of functions

That night the pigman tossed and turned. The thought that someone or something had raided an enclosed field and snatched one of his prized Gloucester Old Spots worried him. Around midnight he took a lantern and walked round the holding to satisfy himself that the three hounds were on guard. His biggest fear was for Jo and the children. He opened the outhouse door and sat on the seat with the lantern beside him. Jo had already filled the Belfast sink from the spring that trickled beneath. It made him smile that she was so taken by having her very own privy. He could smell the sweet smelling herbs lying at the bottom of the former tar barrel.

As he replaced the lid, he heard a creak from behind as the door opened.

Jo stood in the entrance and clasped her hands to her face as if to say *Oh!*

I took the lantern for myself, mimed Peder.

He picked it up and offered it to her.

Crowded in here, she signed. She patted the seat then pointed outside. *I want to use it. Go away.*

The naked Peder excused himself and closed the door, wondering if Jo realised the privy was an anniversary present marking four years of being together. He hunted around, found a still-flowering daffodil, opened the door a crack and handed it to her. Suddenly all three wolfhounds leapt from their communal kennel, dived over the wall and hared off into the night. Peder hadn't heard a sound, but something had alerted the dogs.

150

we three

Jack, Chip and Kee;
panting, tongue-lolling
leaping stone walls, streams, rivers,
scree-scattering, heather-jumping
running fleet-footed
sure as the bracken-bound hills
brave as the high-clouded mountains

Jack, Chip and Kee;
inseparable kin
in the quiet of the evening
nuzzling a hand
accepting a treat
standing tall, proud, protecting

Stark naked and barefoot, Peder dashed for the five-bar gate, leapt over it and chased after the hounds. He could hear them baying from the next field where he had installed wooden *arks* (pigsties). He was about to open the gate when two shots shattered the night. The dogs fell silent. Peder dropped behind the wall. Moments later two of the hounds appeared out of the blackness, leapt over the wall and hid behind their master.

The pigman kept still. Chip and Jack huddled close beside him but there was no sign of Kee. He turned back to the house, keeping below the top of the wall, seriously concerned for Jo and the children. He had no protection other than a stone he had wrenched from the wall. Keeping low, he reached the house with the dogs following closely.

Jo was in the kitchen, wondering what all the fuss was about.

Where have you been? she signed. *What happened? Put some clothes on – now!*

Peder ushered her into their ground floor bedroom and got dressed, explaining there was trouble and she must go upstairs and join their daughters in the attic.

Lock the door, he told her. *Use the bar. I'll take a lantern. Don't open up to anyone until you see my light through the window.*

She signed that she wanted him to stay indoors, but Peder needed to find out what had happened. Chip would go with him, but he would leave Jack with her. He tied a length of cord to Chip's leather collar and fixed his Bowie knife round his waist. Jo insisted he wear his sheepskin gilet for extra protection. He put his arms round her and held her close, kissing her forehead. After a few moments he released her and she handed him the candle lantern.

Chip followed him out of the door, and in seconds, they were swallowed by darkness. Peder left the lantern unlit, not wanting to attract further gunfire. Nothing stirred as they walked down to the first gate and across the barren field to the second. Peder's eyes were getting used to the gloom. He easily made out the line of the bay thanks to the broken clouds. Chip grew more confident and pushed ahead, sniffing the air before leaping the stone wall. Whoever had fired that gun was gone.

The pigs had grunted for a time after the shots, but were now fast asleep. The young dog seemed more assured until Peder opened the gate to the next field.

"What are you sniffing?" whispered Peder. Chip refused to go any further. Peder lit the lantern. Its yellow light played across the stone wall. Hardly twenty paces away he spotted Kee at the foot of the wall, covered in blood, her head and chest shattered. The big man cursed and tears filled his eyes.

Chip sniffed the inanimate body, whimpered and lay down beside it.

Two shots meant the first may have missed, but that was small comfort. Firearms indicated ruthlessness. Maybe it was the time for moving away from Portleán altogether. The O'Briens had discussed it occasionally without coming to a decision. Peder's business was

152

successful at the moment thanks to the acres of virgin land, but once they were transformed into grassland, he would have to look elsewhere.

He dug a grave for Kee and laid her in the ground where she had fallen. It was a private farewell, completed before dawn.

Farewell to Kee

Peder clears the rocks away. This
is a sweet spot, sheltered by stone
walls, guarded by beady-eyed
choughs. Kee loved to run here,
back arched, feet silent-pounding
across the green turf. In a month
or so the first blooms of coltsfoot
will break through the ground,
sun-yellow, joyful. Peder digs, weeps
for his faithful friend, gone too soon.
The flowers will bloom unseen
by the hound but each time her
master passes this way he'll
whisper her name in remembrance.

Matt and Tad were the first to hear of the incident. Within the hour, everyone in Portleán knew. Brendan Tate drove across the meadows straight away in his pony and trap, and offered to help to investigate the night-time raid.

"We'll need to raise a posse," he said, "and a few dogs, but I don't know of any guns either here in the village or in Carravoe. Truth is Peder, the longer we wait, the more likely the trail will be lost. Today's a sad day, but tomorrow might be full of rain."

The news had already spilled across the river to Carravoe, and soon a volunteer posse was heading for the bridge. A messenger was sent to the roadworks site from the Rossdore side, and returned with news that no one had passed through last night. Peder thought the thief might have been heading west or possibly northwards, over the pass, but that would have meant going through Carravoe village and crossing the river which was still in flood from winter rains.

Brendan's dog Rooney, would follow a scent for miles. He was nothing to look at, a bit mangy and too low to the ground, but possessed of a priceless pair of ears and legendary nose. Rooney joined the volunteer posse and although there were other dogs in the pack, Brendan's hound walked alone, absorbed by smells the others ignored.

The team split into three groups. Rooney lost interest when he sniffed eastward toward Rossdore, and showed no inclination to climb the mountain northwards. When Brendan led him towards the sea, he cocked his leg on a tree, scratched a bit of turf, and pointed his nose westwards. His master unleashed him. Rooney was off.

Rooney

doesn't look much,
nose low to the ground, ears flapping
not the sleekest coat, breeding
questionable, eyes old and wise,

lives for the scent

and it doesn't matter –
any old scent will do,   .
the thing is the smell,
the subtleties that identify that smell,
and that smell alone

so when
a hint arrives on the breeze
Rooney knows

and when
others give up
that's when Rooney
stops, waits, sniffs, waits, sniffs again
tale-wagging, nose snuffling
off again – Rooney knows.

Peder found the spent shells in the grass at the foot of the wall and Griff Sullivan identified them as shotgun cartridges.

"410 gauge," he said. "Much smaller than regular 12 bore. Some of these shotguns fold to half their size so they can be easily hid inside a coat. Did he fire twice in quick succession or was there a lull, like he was reloading?"

Peder tried to remember, but Griff said it wasn't that important and didn't matter now.

Matt took a dozen men with him, each walking about fifty yards apart across the high ground under the massif. There were few properties up there, but they made discreet enquiries at every homestead before moving on.

Frank O'Connor took ten men and worked across the coastal strip, each man with his own dog. Some locals joined in to search hidden places, the outhouses and sheds, and there was much talk of rebels and partisans.

Brendan and Peder followed the roadway through Carravoe and out the other side where a stream tumbled down from the heights. Rooney abandoned the tarred road at this point and headed upwards.

Several islands emerged from the mist as the sun dispersed the haze. Though cool, it was a grand afternoon and held the promise of spring. Peder, Brendan and the two apprentices, Sean and Flynn Milligan followed behind Rooney. Young Chip obediently stayed at heel while the more experienced dog sniffed every inch.

"Leave him be," said Brendan. "He knows his job."

The dog pawed at a tiny cigarette butt that no one else had noticed and sat on his haunches until Brendan picked it up.

Peder examined the discarded butt.

"Hand made," Brendan said. "See how thin it is. And by the smell, I'd say homegrown baccy. Best we send for help. Frank and his team are nearest. If Flynn keeps Chip behind us on a leash, you'n me can follow Rooney to where they could be hiding and deal with the problem now."

"Nah," said Peder. "No way, Brendan. There's strength in numbers. There must be forty men in the posse now and more are joining us all the time. The more volunteers we have, the less likely there'll be trouble. We'll wait for Matt's men to join us at the top of the massif. We don't know how many of them they are, or even if it's just a loner. If they run, it's only a cold mountain up there, but one or more, they won't want to fight against so many. If we spot 'em, we can stay hid till sundown. By tonight we'll have 'em stopped up tight in a bottle."

Brendan thought on it and conceded.

"Thanks Brendan," said Peder, "and thanks for the loan of Rooney. He's amazing. Right then Flynn; go find Frank and show him where we are. Tell him to join us before dark. Keep to the stream at all times."

Turning to Sean he said, "Get back to Carravoe and take the track to the foothills. When you reach higher ground you should see Matt's men. Round 'em up and tell them to follow the north stream up past the glen, to where the mountain pool is. Matt will know where I mean. Tell him he's to make firebrands and then wait until we fire the bracken."

The apprentices hurried off. Flynn could see Frank's men searching along the distant strand and reckoned he could reach them within the hour. Sean had a more circuitous route, back down to Carravoe, then across the foothills.

"See that?" said Brendan, "Rooney only points his tail horizontally when he's excited."

"Just as I thought," said Peder. "It must be that mountain pool."

The searchers paused to get their breath back.

"Wait – stay!" said Brendan, raising a finger at Rooney. "Stay."

"Worth his weight in gold." said Peder. "Yet he never barks."

"That's 'cos he's shy," said Brendan.

They continued to climb toward a gap between the mountains about fifteen hundred feet up, taking care to scan the area ahead. Four hundred foot peaks towered over them. The terrain was mostly wind-blasted bog, bracken and heather. Aside from the ubiquitous hares, some still in white

156

winter coats; the only wildlife to be seen was a trio of buzzards overhead and a pair of choughs, complaining at the disturbance.

"We're not alone." said Brendan. "Look – fresh footprints – two of 'em walking in single file. I'm betting they're holed up by the water over there."

Brendan pointed to a small lough surrounded by black peat, about a quarter of a mile on. There were signs of movement and the smell of smoke.

"That's where they'll be hiding," said Brendan.

"At least two of 'em," said Peder, "armed with a shotgun. I'm thinking we've a good hour of twilight left. We'll need to wait for Frank's men to catch up."

As if on cue, one of Frank's lurchers arrived and took a drink from the small pond. The rest of the posse came in dribs and drabs, not all as fit as they thought they were. They had been joined by four more volunteer vigilantes.

"You're the pigman," said one. "I've seen you at Rossdore market. *Comas atá tá?* (How are you?)"

Peder now had a platoon at his beck and call.

As the sun set on the western reaches of the peninsula, the group made firebrands, carefully wetted to delay their burning. Peder's plan was to encircle the lake where the rustlers were hidden. Matt's men, approaching from the other side of the mountain, would complete the trap.

As dusk fell it turned chilly. Just as teeth began to chatter, one of Matt's men arrived from the north side platoon, to confer.

"How many is that now?" said Brendan.

"Thirty to forty," said Peder. "Dunno how many dogs but if I were a rustler I'd be quaking in my boots."

The men were all in position and ready to advance.

"Let's go," said Peder. "I'll do the talking, but don't take chances. If they start shooting, lie flat on the ground. They won't have many bullets and we'll have the advantage in the dark."

Peder lit the first flame about fifty yards away from the waters edge. Within a minute, a wall of fire encircled the lake. The men yelled blood-curdling threats, clapped their hands, and trashed the ground like a Viking raiding party. Flames burned higher and higher and the black lake reflected orange light right across the water. The eerie glow must have been visible from Sheep's Head to MacGillycuddy Reeks.

For the moment the dogs remained under control, but as soon as their masters moved, they began baying, enough to strike fear in any would-be rustler. No longer controlled by their leashes, the animals raced forward and as the fires swept right round the lake, one – two – three – four men raised their hands in surrender and dashed into the lough to save themselves. Muddied, reeking of icy-cold bog-water and shivering with fright, the four rustlers refused to leave the water for fear of being savaged by the hounds. It took time to bring the dogs under control as they were too excited to obey their owners.

Eventually the burning bracken was spent and hounds calmed down. The rustlers came dripping from the lough, were bound and sat in a line in the black ooze at the edge of the lake. More fires were lit using silver birch branches and bog myrtle roots. Frank took charge of a single-barrelled shotgun and six cartridges discovered under a blanket in the makeshift shelter where the thieves had been holed up.

Peder, Matt, Frank and Brendan interrogated the rustlers as the villagers crowded around, demanding justice. The air grew heavy with menace. The thieves claimed to be partisans, fighting for freedom by putting an end to British rule. Frank fired all their cartridges into the darkness, signalling for silence. It was time for Peder O'Brien to speak for them all.

"We've heard all this before," he said, "but you need to understand that we struggle to make a living here, and to steal from us is shameful. We won't allow our children to be starved and left begging for politics' sake. We are the children of Ireland, just the same as you."

The rebels sat with heads bowed listening to the big man speak, surrounded by the flickering firebrands of his followers.

"We've no quarrel with you," continued Peder. "We're on the same side, but you've come among us as common thieves, not freedom fighters. You're armed and willing to take innocent lives. There can be no excuses."

Peder's halting delivery of a speech that he had never wanted to make in the first place had upset him, though the villagers had needed to hear it said. As the fires waned, he hauled the first man to his feet, and cut the rope that bound the man's hands with his Bowie knife. He repeated the action with all four rustlers.

"Go away and leave us alone. And if you ever return," he said, taking the shotgun from Frank and hurling it into the middle of the lake, "know this: we will fight you to the death."

158

surrounded

the hills, soft, quiet, protective
surround them – they've lit a small
fire. no one will see it, not here
in the wilds. no one will know.

but when the soft quiet hills
erupt with fire, when the black
smoke billows across the lough
to surround and suffocate, when
rust-coloured bracken
burns bright, when an army
of flame-bearing warriors marches
across the high ground,
their high ground

this is when cowards know fear

a leap into the icy lough
their only escape (no escape)
bedraggled, shivering, shamed
they face the wrath of the warrior chief:
a leader of men, a husband, a father –
the quiet man, who cares.

Chapter Fourteen

Blacksod Migrant

Goodbye to the Bay

Storm howls through Windy Gap,
swirls round Nephin, heads out across
Lough Conn to Blacksod Bay and beyond,

Enough! says Ruari.

He's not the first.
Barnageehy, Birreenacorragh –
the O Lachtnain chiefs left you long ago,
Clann Ricinh Baireid didn't linger either,
the Bourkes, the Barretts, the feisty Lynnots,
forever feuding, sent more on their way.

Ruari's not bothered by tribes or fiefdoms.
Storms, now – there's a thing;
when your boat twists and turns and directions are lost
when the weather mocks and casts you back
into Blacksod Bay, sits in a cloud above Nephin,
weeping with mirth at your plight –
what's a man to do?

So goodbye Barnageehy, Birrenacorragh –
farewell forever you Black-sodding Bay.

Ruari O'Rourke was a *curragh* fisherman and the worst navigator in all Connaught. He fished Blacksod Bay and had never been further than Achill Island because the sodding weather was always against him. He was the last of his clan to leave the Mullet Peninsula in County Mayo, one of the stormiest places on earth. Having sent his kid sister to Boston, Massachusetts, he finally closed the door on his cottage and a life lived in the tiny village of *An Fod Dubh*, known locally as Blacksod.

"If I see the place ag'in," he said, "it'll be too soon," and with that, he walked the fourteen miles to Belmullet through howling wind, only to discover the weekly bus had been cancelled due to the storm. His language wasn't fit to be heard, but he promised faithfully to confess his sins when the storm abated. The only comfort was to have the ear-splitting wind at his back for the next leg of his journey – a hundred miles to the legendary city of Dublin. He reached Killarney four days later, hopelessly lost, saw a sign that said Cork and Dublin, and within the hour was arrested for vagrancy.

Killarney was under curfew and the fledgling Civil Guard – a company of Free State soldiers – was patrolling, rifles cocked, following riotous behaviour. It meant a cell for a night for Ruari, which was still preferable to the hovel he had vacated four days. Killarney being well off, a decent meal was brought in from the café over the road.

The next morning he was arraigned before a stipendiary magistrate and ordered to sweep the streets for the next week while a higher authority decided what to do with him. To Ruari, this was heaven. He had the same cell every night, breakfast and dinner provided, and a navy-blue prison uniform with a pair of second-hand leather boots that fitted a treat.

The following Wednesday, he was roused early and brought before a trio of magistrates.

"Name?" said the court deputy.

"Ruari O'Rourke... Sir."

"Occupation?"

"Fisherman... Sir."

"Address?"

"Blacksod, Mayo... Sir."

"Age?"

"Thirty-one... Sir."

The magistrate took over.

"What were you doing in Killarney?"

"Lookin' fer Dublin... your worship... Sir."

"Has it been moved then?" said the magistrate.

"Dunno sir, I haven't seen it yet... Sir."

"Do you belong to an illegal organisation?"

"Don't think so... Sir?"

"Why the need to travel to Dublin? What are you doing in Killarney?"

"Got lost... Sir. I don't read or see too well... your worship."

The magistrate consulted his deputies before replying.

"There's been insurrection in both Tralee and Killarney so I'm sending you to Kenmare for further investigation. These towns are already full to capacity with rebel republicans. Meantime, I'll give you a note for an optician."

The deputy scrawled on a piece of paper and handed it to Ruari.

"Keep it safe until you reach the Civil Guard Station," he said, "then hand it to the duty officer."

Ruari nodded, not understanding his situation or the unexpected charity. He bowed to the bench several times before two Civil Guard officers led him away.

The optician was nervous at having a desperado handcuffed to an officer in his shop.

"Relax Mister Shaw," said the guard. "He's off to Kenmare soon as you've fitted him with a pair of glasses and if there's any bother, I'll put a hole in 'im with me revolver."

Mister Shaw tried a boxful of lenses and gave his diagnosis.

"You're myopic," he said. "You need to wear glasses at all times."

"What, even in bed?" said Ruari.

"Don't be foolish," said Mister Shaw. "I'll give you a metal case to put them in at night. Your sight is good enough for reading and around the house, but you will see a vast difference outdoors.

162

The optician fitted the lenses into a wire frame and tried them on Ruari, nodding at a job well done.

"I'm attaching a chain to each end so that if they slip off your nose you won't lose them – and please, never touch the lenses. Use this chamois leather to clean them."

He showed Ruari, still handcuffed to the guard's officer, out of the shop to try out his new glasses in Plunkett Street, but the fisherman tripped over the pavement, taking the guard with him.

"Glory be!" said Mister Shaw. "Is he trying to escape?"

The guard fetched up in the gutter and several women shrieked.

"I kin see!" said Ruari. "Praise be – I kin see, I kin see!"

"You'll be seein' stars if I've got anythin' to do with it," said the guard. "Look at me – I'm supposed to be escortin' the culprit to Kenmare; what will I be doin' now?"

Mister Shaw did his best to clean the guard's uniform while his prisoner admired his new profile in the optician's window.

"I can't arrest you twice," said the guard. "You're already in custody."

Two guards came to his aid as a crowd of frightened women gathered in Plunkett Street, crying out for protection against villains, ruffians and hoodlums. The sooner Ruari O'Rourke left Killarney, the better. Their wish was granted, but for Ruari, the twenty miles to Kenmare passed unseen despite his new spectacles as there were no windows in the Black Maria.

the shock of vision

every blade of grass separate, defined,
no longer merged into a neighbourly
green; every leaf curved and angled
with individuality; tree bark marked with flaws,
striations, knot holes like gaping maws,
peels and flakes intent on casting
perfect shadows with intricate detailing.
but skin – marred with hairs and pores
and old remembered scars, long forgotten;
every man's stubble a bristling extrusion
of uncouth growth; the shock of curling hairs
springing from limp trembling ear lobes
the horror of vision! but the joy of the down

on a baby's cheek, dancing fuchsia blooms,
the iridescence of squabbling starlings –
all through a glass, not darkly, but clear.

"All rise," barked the usher. "This court is now in session."

Three magistrates filed into the courtroom. The first cases would be petty sessional as the serious offenders would be dealt with later. Ruari O'Rourke had never been inside a court until this week, yet now he was attending his second hearing. His case was number six. A remote voice announced his name, then another, closer, and finally a guard led him into the defendant's box, closing the door behind him.

There followed a moment of quiet as the sitting magistrate read the charge sheet.

"You're a long way from home Mister O'Rourke," he said. "What are you up to in County Kerry?"

Ruari didn't know if he should speak.

"Well?" asked the magistrate.

"Beggin' yer pardon, Sir, I wuz makin' fer Dublin in a terrible storm an' I got lost. The other magistrate, him from Killarney, gave me the glasses as I wasn't seein' too well, but now, of a truth, I'm seein' everythin' and I'll be on me way to Dublin, so help me God I will, an' won't be no trouble to anyone at all."

"Why Dublin?" said the magistrate. "Is there a problem in Mayo?"

"It's like this, your worship, there's no money to be had in Mayo, 'specially on the Mullet. I've been starvin' for want of food an' when 'tis stormy, I can't fish as I've only me curragh and oftentimes I can't even get off the shore, let alone catch anythin'."

"Dublin is full of shenanigans: whores, porter, fighting, cursing, thieves and hooligans," said the magistrate. "So, what way are you?"

"I'm just lookin' to fill me belly, sir, I won't be fightin' anyone. I'm a peaceful man, sir."

"Republican or a Democrat?"

Ruari didn't speak, for he knew next to nothing of politics and nor did he want to know. His father had been a Fenian many years ago and the thought of him sent shivers down Ruari's spine.

"Catholic or Protestant?" asked the magistrate. "Where are your sympathies?"

"I'm me own man sir," said Ruari. "I don't want no trouble. I wuz just lookin' fer work in order to feed meself. I never hurt no one, ever. Me curragh is smashed to pieces last week in that last storm an' I wuz gettin' desperate sir."

"There's plenty of work to be had in Kenmare," said the magistrate. "I'm sentencing you to be bound over for three months in order that you can find an appropriate job and save your wages against returning to Mayo. You must register with the Civil Guard and present yourself to the station every Monday and Friday at seven o'clock, or you will be hunted down and arrested as a felon to be incarcerated in Tralee Gaol as a guest of the Free State Troopers. Any questions? Right. Next case."

Ruari looked through his spectacles at the man who had just criminalized him.

"But sir?" said Ruari: "I wuz only lookin' fer Dublin."

A massive hand took hold of his shoulder from behind.

"This way," said the guard. "Let's be havin' you, O'Rourke."

"Just a moment," said an assistant magistrate. "Approach the bench please."

The guard propelled the unfortunate toward the bench.

Major Thomas Alan Redmond KC spoke softly so that only Ruari and the guard could hear. A few more words from his fellow magistrates, and Ruari was led away to spend the rest of his day behind bars, beneath the courtroom.

"An' don't be speaking to anyone, or else!" said the guard, drawing a line with his index finger across his throat.

Ruari sat on a bench opposite two other prisoners as the iron bars slammed shut behind him. His fellow inmates were chained to an iron bar on the opposite side of the cell and had obviously been involved in a fight as they were covered with blood and bruises. The smell of blood permeated throughout this lower level, mingling with the stench of urine, vomit, and sweat.

"Welcome to purgatory," said one of his companions. "Would ye have a smokie?"

Ruari didn't dare speak. He closed his eyes.

"Tralee Gaol is where I'm headin'," said one man, "fer the hangin'. Me mate here, is comin' too. That's after they've kicked the shi-"

"Quiet! I told you not to speak and for God's sake, you're still squawking. Shut it O'Rourke or I'll have yer entrails for supper."

"Bollocks," said the second inmate through a mouthful of gore. "Get back in your sentry box, squaddy. It'll take the entire bleedin' army to shut me up. Up the Republic, fight the sick bastards. They're all rejects in the British Army, fit fer nothin'."

Other prisoners began to shout and sing, rattling their chains and spitting at any uniform that dared confront them. Ruari was in a cold sweat. The rebels' din increased as guards stood firm and brandished their rifles from the safe side of the bars.

Calm returned eventually. The partisans were tired and most had lost a great deal of blood. There was no food to be had, no water or sanitation. As the day went on, the prisoners were segregated into ones and twos before being secured inside a Black Maria and despatched to Tralee.

The last to leave, long after dark, was Ruari O'Rourke, citizen of Blacksod, The Mullet, Mayo. He smelled of everything he had always sought to avoid. The flat-bed wagon sent to collect him emerged from the unlit street.

"Phew!" said a female voice. "You stink. Will I be asking you to sit at the back, please."

"Do as you're told," said the escorting guard, "or I'll fetch you such a blow, you won't wake up till you reach the far side of purgatory."

Ruari moved to the back of the carriage and climbed onto the rearmost shelf where the guard manacled him to an iron stave.

"No talking," said the guard, "else I'll bate you senseless."

"Are we ready?" asked the female voice from the front of the carriage.

166

"We are that," said the guard. "The key for unlocking the handcuffs is in your possession, Miss Flynn. Anytime you's passin', just hand it to an officer or the station. Ain't no hurry."

He saluted the unseen lady as the wagon drove into the shadows of the night.

"Holy mother of God," whispered Ruari O'Rourke. "Out of the slough of despond, as they say. Whatever next?"

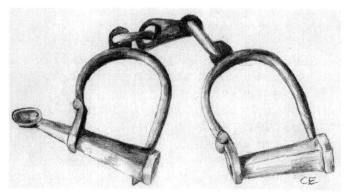

There is a fine line between committing a crime and criminal intent. Major Redmond had understood that Ruari O'Rourke would never make a criminal, no matter how hard he tried. There was also the matter of the less discriminating line often crossed by the military searching for information. Had the Free State Troopers had their way, Ruari would have been incarcerated within Tralee Gaol, beaten to a pulp at best, and dumped in the bay. A man cannot give information if he knows nothing. The Major could see that 'Prisoner 44286' held on remand under emergency powers was an innocent man, in the wrong place at the worst possible time. The Major had seen a million men sacrificed in the Great War for much the same reason.

The carriage drew up outside a front door. Ruari remained mute, glad to have arrived somewhere, but unnerved by this journey into the unknown with nothing to see but the darkness of the tarred road racing by beneath his feet, and sinister trees overhead. Someone jumped down from the carriage and he heard the crunch of feet on gravel and could smell the mysterious Miss Flynn's perfume, a striking contrast to his own stench.

"Will you hold the lantern still please. I'm going to release the bracelets," she said.

"Handcuffs, Milady," said Ruari. "I'm grateful for your kindness, they're awful tight, 'specially on the back of a cart."

She undid both manacles and waved them under Ruari's nose.

"You're a free man Mister O'Rourke, though still under detention. If you abscond, the dogs will hunt you down and if there's anything left of you, you'll be returned to the Civil Guard and I'll wash my hands of you. Follow me, please. You'll be fed twice a day, but first, you stink to high heaven and will be sluiced in the stable until you're fit to eat indoors. There's a bed in the loosebox attached to the stable and that's where you'll lodge for the ninety days of your sentence. Any questions?"

Ruari shook his head, certain that anything would be better than Mayo. He followed the lantern round the corner to where a concrete platform stood in front of the stables.

"Hold your breath, Mister O'Rourke," warned Miss Flynn, "and when it stops, use that bar of carbolic soap to scrub yourself clean."

She took his spectacles, safe inside their case, and put them in her riding jacket.

Ruari stood on the concrete, oblivious of her intentions. He heard a rushing sound, then a *whoosh* as a river of icy water enveloped him. Four times he fell down, gasping for breath, desperate to get up again. Chilled to the bone, he didn't want to cry out as it would have branded him a wimp. At last the stream stopped.

"Now the soap," said Mary Anne Flynn, still gripping the fireman's hose. Ruari scrubbed his clothing but it was never going to be enough.

"Take those filthy clothes off and scrub your body till it's squeaky clean."

He took off his coat and shirt and prison boots happily enough, but she insisted he drop his trousers, and down they went, kicked away against the wall.

"Scrub, Mister O'Rourke. Do it now, please."

Another thunderous sluice followed. Mary Anne threw a big towel at him and when he claimed to be dry, handed him a khaki shirt, a pair of military trousers and a navy-blue gansey.

"Keep to the pathway please, and follow me to the kitchen," she said. "Carry your boots – they're too wet to be worn. You'll be needing slippers."

Ruari couldn't control his shivering. His teeth rattled inside his head, but for sure, he smelled wholesome. When they reached the kitchen she told him to stand beside the big wood-burning stove and get warm. A

168

cook, who Miss Flynn addressed as 'Mother' came into the room with a pair of well-used slippers. They fitted a treat.

Odd

When Ruari stepped out and set his feet
on the road from Blacksod Bay, he'd thought –
no, he doesn't know what he thought, but
thrown into cells and given new eyes and
driven with strangers, these things he can
just about get his head round. No he can't.
He'd thought he could, but no, that must have
been a dream, an odd one, and odder still as
he drops his trousers in front of a lady who
gives him orders and he obeys because logic
and sense don't have any place in this strange
new world and WHAT is she going to do with
that hosepipe. She wouldn't. Would she...?

Major Redmond was working flat out to deal with both republican rebels and defenders of the Free State settlement. Hostility was spilling onto the streets of Kenmare and the only way to bring it under control was to refuse to hand over control to anyone threatening the peace. He gave notice that he would withdraw the Civil Guard and let the troopers arrest anyone committing insurrection, sedition or crimes threatening life and limb. The proclamation was made in front of the courthouse. Within minutes, every Guard officer was withdrawn and businesses closed. Trains and vehicles remained where they stood and the troopers were despatched to all main crossroads.

The Major could now walk in safety along Henry Street in his civilian clothes. He paused every so often to raise his bowler to anyone he passed. People were applauding his firm stand, and many shook hands with him. There were even glasses of spring water, and at one house, a muffin straight from the baking tray. Mrs Riley had just removed them from her oven and on seeing him she brewed a fresh pot of tea, sat on the step of her cottage and shared the pot, chatting as a good neighbour.

"Must be moving," he told her eventually. "'Tis a fine afternoon. I'm grateful for your hospitality, Mrs Riley. Not a word now to Martha about the muffins. She'll bate me round the ear if she catches me nibbling between meals."

Ruari O'Rourke's official job was working for the Major, though he wondered if he was actually labouring for Miss Flynn as she seemed to be in charge. She had delivered the Major to Kenmare's Courthouse earlier that morning and was back at the stables within the hour. It took some time for Ruari to learn that she was just another hired hand, though obviously highly favoured. Just so long as he did as he was told, he realized he had never been so well off. The only problem was his lack of experience with horses. His orders were to take them down to the paddock, close the gate, muck out the stable, tip the highly valued horse-muck onto the manure pile using the wheelbarrow, then fill the hay nets, spread wheat-straw over each loosebox, replenish the water troughs and finally, return to the kitchen for lunch. What could be simpler?

"I'll be back by midday," she told him. "No need to detach Boru from his carriage as I have to go over to Siosta Mill for more oats. Leave him tethered by the sheltered side of the stable. Thank you."

She was always strict in her orders, but never failed to thank him.

The Major owned eight horses, all of which towered over Ruari. Even when they weren't working, someone would be riding them or hauling machinery down the drive. On their return, they would be inspected to ensure they hadn't thrown a shoe or broken a trace. The house didn't function as a farm; rather it served cottars and farmers along the estuary by hiring out agricultural machinery all year round.

He began work that morning in complete ignorance. The working horses didn't recognize his smell. They were creatures of habit and didn't like reversing, yet the hapless Ruari was trying to get them to move

170

backwards. He was standing alongside their back legs when Condo – the biggest shire in the entire stable – let go a terrific kick, which sent him flying as if he were a pup. Condo continued with his hay bag as if nothing had happened, leaving Ruari spread-eagled in the straw.

Fortunately for Ruari, a farmer arrived soon after. There was machinery to be hauled and because the labourer was a regular customer, Condo was soon hitched to a big four-wheel wagon and on his way. Sean, the farm labourer, took the rest of the horses out to loose them in the paddock.

"I owe you," said Ruari. "Me first day with horses and I'm scared."

Sean took a black woolly out of his haversack and handed it to the Mayo man.

"'Tis a bit dirty but wear it anyway as it smells of me and the horse will know you're one of us. Must go, Con's halfway down the drive already, *gártha* (cheers)."

Condo

feathered fetlocks and crafty eye –
meet Condo,
broad of forehead, arching neck,
flickering muscles, deep of chest

and wise;
too clever for Ruari to fathom at first,
too fly, too proud
to condescend to co-operate
with this four-eyed man,
who stands there
scratching his head.

enough of this nonsense. Condo
shakes his head and relents
as Sean's friendly hands
sort out the tack, attend to their task;
Ruari breathes again.

Ruari worked hard all day. Miss Flynn came and went, and around noon, Martha brought him a pork pie and a mug of tea. Being bound over wasn't so bad after all. Given a choice, he would have happily stayed at the

Major's house forever. As Martha collected his mug, she told him to listen for the bell for supper and to remove his working boots before he entered the kitchen as Mary Anne was particular about such things.

It was a grand day. As the sun hovered over Knockmoyle, Miss Flynn came into the yard and told him to accompany her to town to collect Major Redmond from the courthouse, adding: "I'm told there's been further trouble in town and State troopers have closed some streets. There's no danger but the Major isn't as strong as he was and might need assistance."

Ruari clambered onto the bench seat and sat alongside Miss Flynn, and off they went, with Mary Anne's perfume filling his nostrils.

Major Tom was striding through Firgrove, headed for Killaha, sweating a bit as there was hardly a whisper of breeze. He was looking forward to hearing the cattle lowing across the estuary and seeing the sheep grazing the higher ground. It was not a day for being stuck in a courthouse. He would aim for the Dromoghty River and drink from the pool by the bridge, one of his favourite spots. During the Great War the memory of the stream splashing and tinkling down from the heights had helped him blot out the horrors of conflict. He passed several good friends along the way, and acknowledged their best wishes for a peaceful settlement.

A couple of squawking gulls were perched on the parapet of the bridge, while another pair argued over a disembowelled crab. The noise was intrusive, so Tom set off towards the coolness of the maple trees half-a-mile distant, only a mile from home.

"Best I teach you how to handle a carriage in easy stages," said Mary Anne. "Here. Take hold of the reins. Go easy, please. Feel the leather. Don't grab tight hold – a horse will know straight away that someone else is driving. Remember to talk to him."

Ruari pushed his spectacles back on the bridge of his nose and took hold of the black reins, carefully separating each trace. A bead of sweat trickled down behind his left ear and onto his shirt collar. He could sense Miss Flynn's perfume again and because she was so close, couldn't avoid touching her. Every rill, every bump, every stone jiggled the carriage.

When the horse turned onto the tarred road, Mary Anne had to push hard against Ruari in order to prevent tipping them over.

"Well done, O'Rourke." she said. "Just give him a little nudge with the reins and he'll trot now that we're on the main road. Fifteen minutes and we'll be crossing the bridge. He knows the drill, he's been going to Kenmare more times than me."

172

Ruari twitched the reins pointlessly as the stallion trotted along the metalled roadway. The novice waggoner was enjoying himself.

The Major was sweating hard. He had already removed his coat; now he shed his jacket and bowler hat. Damp patches marred his shirt. He desperately needed to relieve himself, and on reaching the thicket of trees, hid behind a huge oak and hung his clothes over a branch before answering the call of nature.

Too much to drink, he told himself. *All that fluid has to be emptied, otherwise?*

It was cool in the trees and he thought he might stay awhile, but there again, if Mary Anne was on her way to collect him, he ought to rest in clear view.

"Made for the job," he said. "Bless you little tree." He felt strange all of a sudden and slumped down to the ground, struggling to breathe. There was a beautiful cluster of fuchsias between the trees. He would have liked to have picked a few, but his arms wouldn't reach. A smear of blood ran down his shirt. He wondered where it had come from.

Boru had always been an enthusiastic trotter and had been to town more often than his mistress. He didn't like being restrained by some novice, but Miss Flynn was ultimately in charge and she was insisting on the steady gait.

Ruari had the reins. He could see the estuary through the trees and the big bend ahead, which is why he was trying, softly-softly, to keep Boru in hand. Miss Flynn was fiddling with her straw hat as it didn't have a ribbon.

The maple trees dissolved into an oak wood as the road straightened again. Ruari wiped his brow. Sitting beside Mary Anne demanded great diligence as the wrong word could lead to reprimand. Miss Flynn took off her hat and pointed to the grass bank about fifty yards ahead. Boru made the faintest whinny. A man was lying on the ground beneath a tree. Mary Anne screamed, and kept on screaming, colour draining from her face. Ruari hauled on the brake, the first time he had ever used it. Mary Anne dropped onto the road, ran across it and sunk to her knees on the verge to cradle Major Tom's inert body. There was blood on his white shirt, and a trickle coming from his mouth.

Her screaming gradually came to a stop. There was no more life left in the Major. She gently closed his eyes.

Ruari tethered Boru to a branch. He didn't want to leave Mary Anne by herself, but didn't know what he should do. A motorcar was approaching, so Ruari put out his hand to hail it. The driver drew to a halt. He recognised the Major at once and set off to summon the Civil Guard.

beneath an oak tree

far from the bloody fields,
from screaming horses,
from churning mud –
here, this haven,
this grove, this oak tree,
this river running –
here is his ending

Shadows lengthened as the news of Major Tom's passing circulated the streets of Kenmare. Mary Anne accompanied the Major's body to the town's hospital, leaving Ruari to pilot Boru home alone. He chose, wisely, to lead the horse by his halter, and the two set off as all Munster mourned the passing of Major Thomas Redmond, a true hero.

Chapter Fifteen

Amen to That

woman in black

she walks
between walls of shocked mourners

her sharp-ironed trousers
an affront to their sensibilities
her heart fair game for gossips

who soon forget their carping
respect recalled
as they doff caps, bowler hats,
bow heads

a woman in black
surrounded by priests, green ribbons, closed shop-fronts,
massed crippled soldiers, burdened with medals –
walks alone with her love

Mary Anne Flynn was dressed in black barathea trousers, uncompromisingly pressed, sharp as a surgeon's knife. No one had seen such a thing at a funeral before.

"The hussy," said someone from the watching crowd of mourners. "Who'd a believed?"

"Granted, she's a grand looker, but fer goodness sake, there's a time an' a place."

The suffragette movement was unpopular with working women, but Mary Anne had remained true to the cause despite the interruptions of civil war. Major Redmond had appreciated her sparky attitude and encouraged her independence.

The cortège set off at ten o'clock, following the pipe and drum band over the bridge and up Bell Heights to Henry Street. Shop windows rattled, and pigeons and seagulls scattered at the sound of the harsh snare drums. Every shop and business had closed its doors. Children bearing flowers stood in front of their parents. The Civil Guard had taken positions on every corner. Republicans wore green ribbons; women, black headscarves or felt hats. Men doffed caps or held black bowlers respectfully to their chest. Those who had survived the horrors of war wore medals won on battlefields far away. Others sported crutches or walking sticks. As the cortège slowed to walking pace and passed between the crowds, even those with missing limbs attempted to stand to attention.

The priest leading the procession bore a brass cross and kept his eyes firmly fixed on the task ahead. He was followed by his black-cassocked brethren. Mary Anne walked alone behind the priests and ahead of the catafalque bearing Major Tom's body. An officer in the military uniform of the 5th Cork Brigade followed, carrying a green cushion bearing Major Tom's military honours.

176

Mourners threw flowers on the road behind the guard of honour and burst into spontaneous applause as the two black stallions hauling the hearse drew close. Two hundred pairs of military boots thundered across the square to the entrance of Holy Cross Catholic Church. The people of Kenmare continued to applaud as the casket was removed from the glass-windowed hearse and borne on the shoulders of six Kerry Civil Guards.

The priest-in-charge intoned: *Benedicat vos omnipotens Deus, Pater et Filius et Spiritus Sanctus*, and the response rippled through the crowd of mourners: *Initum sancti Evangelii secundum Joannem*.

The church was filled to overflowing. Many windows that hadn't been opened in years now let in both light and fresh air. Outside, soldiers stood in solemn knots, having been granted permission to remove their caps until the service had ended. The stallions were watered while a dozen soldiers turned the hearse round, ready for its final departure.

Mary Anne was remembering the peace and quiet of the previous night. Major Tom's body had been kept at his house on the edge of Kenmare, and she had been able to pay her respects privately along with Martha, Jo and Peder. The children had been left in Hannah's care in Portleán. Mary Anne had guessed the Major had known it was time to go, but she grieved

177

at the way he had died alone on the road to Castletown without her by his side. Suffering from shellshock, wracked with tuberculosis, he still wouldn't have chosen to die in that way. Mary Anne knew he had always wished to marry her, but now the question could never be asked.

Réquium aetémam dona eis, Dómine, intoned the priest.
Et lux perpétua lúceat eis, came the response.
The Bishop made the sign of the cross.
Requiescant in pace.
Amen.

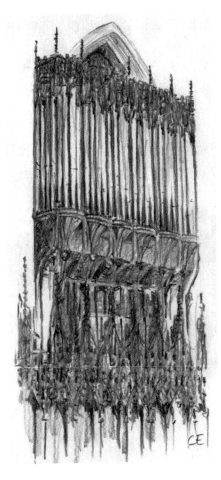

The odour of incense, smoking candles and chrysanthemums mingled with the less favoured smells of tightly packed mourners. Six bearers placed the Major's casket on the catafalque and a lengthy *Dies irae* followed, ending with *Pie Iesu Domine, dona eis requiem* and a hushed *Amen.*

The cycle of prayers ended with the absolution. The Bishop swung the censer above the coffin, filling the air with heady fumes, and sprinkled more Holy water to the accompaniment of the *Libera Me.* The congregation had been sat still and quiet long enough and sang the traditional hymn, *On Eagles Wing,* with great gusto.

"Grant, O Lord, we beseech Thee, this mercy unto Thy servant departed. May his soul and the souls of all the faithful departed, through the mercy of God, rest in peace."

Two pump-men kept the vast organ filled with air as Bach's *Toccata and Fugue in D minor* filled the building with glorious sound. To the congregation, it was as if the Lord of Hosts himself were breathing fire through the organ.

178

inside the church

incense, chrysanthemums
heady flavours of death mixed with promises
Latin responses chanted on clouds of brown smoke
a perfume, sweet to a Saviour's nostrils
sour note of sorrow for those left behind

the organ wheezes:
bellows pump booming vibrations
through reedy pipes, untuned in decades

voices rise on eagles' wings
belting out hymns, relieved
to expand their lungs, let roar their grief
with collective permission

The waiting Guardsmen hoisted the coffin onto their shoulders. It was time for the internment on the hill overlooking the Kenmare estuary, but still the clergy kept everyone waiting. Two priests dealt with the final sprinkling of Holy Water from a polished stoup. *Initium sancti Evangelii secundum Joannem*, intoned a green and white cassocked priest, and then, finally, the oak casket was loaded into the hearse.

The Cork Regiment lined up on each side of the procession and a lone drummer walked ahead. Each soldier carried his cap in his left hand as a mark of respect. The crowd hushed as Bach's magnificent fugue came to an end. The funeral director removed his top hat and bowed respectfully to Mary Anne. She climbed up beside the coachman, and the stallions walked across the Square to the cemetery, followed by the crunch of many feet treading the gravel.

Mary Anne had requested no firing of rifles, only the final prayers as the bearers lowered the casket into the ground. A bugler played the Last Post. Mary Anne's final duty was to sprinkle a measure of Kerry earth onto the coffin, and a single red rose. She had done as Major Tom had asked; she alone knew that his foreknowledge of his own death had been his reason for not proposing marriage.

The rose lay in full view until sundown when Mary Anne returned as arranged with a dozen volunteers to close up the grave. The men raised the casket by its canvas tapes in order to turn the Major round. Catholic tradition required the feet of the occupier to be facing the East, but "No way," the Major had said. "When I'm buried, I wish to be looking over the Kenmare Estuary for all eternity."

Mary Anne had smiled at that. She had never failed to comply with his wishes, so Major Thomas Alan Redmond now lay buried looking westward, across the estuary.

At the graveside

a loving sprinkle
of sweet Kerry soil
a single red rose

a return after dusk
a quiet alteration
a promise fulfilled

Mary Anne had plenty to do and the rest of her life to do it. Her appointed solicitors in Bantry had served the Redmond family for generations. She wanted to travel by train to consult them, but in the final months of the Irish Civil War this was impossible. It would have to be another trek over the Esk Mountain.

Ruari O'Rourke prepared the four-wheeled gig, greasing hubs, replacing lynchpins and checking each section of wheel rim. At eighteen miles, the journey was no great distance, but the road in late autumn was not for the faint-hearted. Mary Anne wanted to go alone, but Peder insisted on accompanying her on the stretch from Rossdore Town to Bantry.

The Major might be dead and buried, but he still gave the orders and had advised Mary Anne to use James Quinn in Bantry rather than a Kenmare solicitor. "Never deal with solicitors in your own neck of the woods," he had said, "no matter how much you admire their scruples; and furthermore, keep away from city lawyers, most of whom are in it for political gain."

Jimmy Quinn employed a legal secretary together with an investigator who did the running around, but otherwise he worked alone in a modest first floor office, and dealt mainly with agricultural business, like his father before him. Today was an exceptional day as Mary Anne

180

Flynn and her brother-in-law would be in his office at midday to study the last will and testament of Major Thomas Alan Redmond. According to her letter, Miss Flynn wished to make significant changes, particularly concerning The Redmond Estate, and these would need to be recorded in the proper form.

The sun sparkled over Esk Mountain and Mary Anne wondered briefly if it would rain but it didn't look threatening so she dismissed the thought.

Peder had walked the seven miles from *Ghabal View* to Rossdore, mulling over the prospect of the journey ahead. He headed straight for the Sunshine Café and sat in the window to wait for Mary Anne, a very different person to her kid sister Jo.

She arrived in good time and gave him a typical frivolous greeting.

"Oi, you – I've done my bit for King and country. It's your turn to drive. I bet you've been in the Sunshine Café since they opened."

"Not so," said Peder. "A lardy cake and a mug of tea is all."

"What's happened to the beard? Did you buy a razor?"

Peder climbed up onto the gig and winced as Mary Anne planted a friendly kiss on his right cheek. This wasn't reciprocated, as he was never physically affectionate outside his immediate family. Mary Anne knew this, and was playing on his shyness. He blushed, seized the reins, and released the brake.

"You're in a big hurry," said Mary Anne. "Careful with this horse. He's young, lacks road sense. He was born at the Major's house and I'd like to keep him a bit longer. Don't forget, I'm staying at your house tonight, with my nieces. Isn't that nice for you?"

Peder grunted. He never knew when she was teasing.

Two hours later they were climbing the stairs to Mister Quinn's office. Jimmy greeted them with a warm handshake. Peder instinctively liked and trusted the man.

Much of the dialogue was boringly legal, though it had to be stated correctly. Time and again Peder asked questions and if he wasn't satisfied with the answer, Jimmy backtracked and started again. The Major had never been especially wealthy, having always managed rather than speculated, but he had inherited a fine house, a few favoured acres, and done well enough on his officer's pension.

Mary Anne and Peder agreed it would be best to retain the house but release any out-lying hill land at auction, keeping the Portleán estate under Peder's stewardship.

When the meeting was over, Peder recovered the four-wheeled buggy from Wolfe Tone Square. The horse was reluctant to move in the murk that had descended, so Peder led it back by its bridle to collect Mary Anne.

Most town houses had some form of electric light in Bantry but by the time they reached the county road, the faint yellow glow of the town was barely visible through the gloom and drizzle. The rain grew heavier, and the euphoria of driving a quick, lightweight cart soon evaporated. The hood was meant to keep the sun off rather than rain and the sides were open to the elements. Peder offered meaningless apologies to Mary Anne and tried in vain to protect her from the worst of the wet. He got a ticking off when he took off his sheepskin gilet to put it over her head, though he insisted on covering her shoulders. She was ill prepared for travelling, and should have known any early morning that sparkled, especially on higher ground, was a guaranteed sign of rain. Peder refrained from saying as much, but wondered what had she been thinking, wearing a scarlet jacket, cotton trousers and a feeble cotton raincoat. Even her riding boots were rapidly filling with water.

There was little traffic. Neither traveller spoke as they reached Rossdore and turned onto the Portleán track. Even Peder was feeling the chill, and the track, still waiting for its tarred surface, was hazardous in the hard rain. Deep rills spooked the young gelding every few yards.

Peder pulled on the handbrake.

"Steady Jack, steady. Hold hard now, I've got you. Easy now."

He kept up a steady stream of words through the endless rain to calm the horse. The wind was becoming particularly vicious, which didn't help. Peder dropped to the ground and patted the gelding. He could hear the sea a hundred feet below and the thunder of waves striking unseen rocks. The road-builders had been constructing a drain beneath the surface at this point and several fir trees had been felled, weakening those that remained. A sharp crack, and a branch fell – Jack reared and kicked at the backboard, screamed and kicked again, dislodging the brake. Peder leapt out of the way, just managing to keep a grip of the reins. Mary Anne would have to look after herself. The blinkered horse could only see forwards and was trying to bolt.

The underground culvert that should have carried the stream beneath the roadway had become blocked with debris, and the water now rushed across the surface. Peder bore the full force of it, and feared he would lose his balance as branches and rumbling stones swept past him in the fast increasing floodwater. He dared not loose his grip of the reins in the dark for fear the lightweight gig would end up in the sea, far below. The trace bit into his arm, but he kept tight hold and grabbed the right-hand shaft. The gig shuddered as Jack tried to break free, but the shackles prevented movement. The gelding kicked back hard and Mary Anne's carpet bag broke away and flew off into darkness. A tree-branch jammed under the offside wheel, a lucky chance – so long as it stayed there, the cart wasn't going anywhere.

Mary Anne clambered down, her drenched coat clinging to her. She took hold of Jack's bridle with both hands and stood in front of the terror-stricken gelding, talking to him continuously. Peder could see the horse's left foreleg was at an angle, with a gash just above the fetlock. No bone was visible in the feeble light, but it needed dealing with urgently. He turned to Mary Anne and relieved her of her silk scarf.

"It's for charity," he shouted against the furious wind. "The Major would want it for Jack. I think he's hurt – he's bleeding."

Mary Anne burst into tears, but Peder was too busy to care. Horses came first. They were only a few miles from home but they wouldn't be going anywhere if they couldn't get out of this flooded culvert. He returned to the gig.

"Where's the hand lantern?" he said. "I need it quick. The horse is bleeding."

Mary Anne shook her head. Her long black tresses had turned into rat-tails. She wanted to do something useful and was determined to remain at her post, just as Major Tom would have done. Peder unhooked the left-hand driving lamp from the gig and took it to examine the horse. The back legs appeared to be sound. Peder felt both fore legs, reaching down to the hooves. He could see the gash clearly now and knew it needed covering. Brendan could do any necessary doctoring tomorrow. Peder wrapped the scarf round the wound as the stricken animal whinnied. Then it calmed a little, lowered its head, and let Mary Anne stroke its muzzle.

Peder loosened his grip. They were still ankle deep in the flooded stream and needed to work out how to reach higher ground. There was no sign of Mary Anne's travel bag. The rogue branch needed to be broken away from beneath the gig. If only the furies would let up a moment, Peder would be able to do something about it. He cut the blinkers away from the bridle so that Jack could see. The gelding remained passive. Peder was relieved to see the foreleg still had its shoe. When he asked the horse to back up, Jack co-operated without a sound. If they chanced moving the outfit forward, it might work.

Peder checked the handbrake; cautiously climbing up to inspect the system. It seemed to be working properly, but when he tried it again, it slipped off. The ratchet was too feeble to hold.

Not to be trusted, he thought. *Let it be a warning and if we ever reach home, it'll be a task for Brendan first thing in the morning.*

Mary Anne continued soothing Jack while Peder disentangled the trapped branch. The sea was raging barely a hundred feet below. They desperately needed to move.

"Get back on the seat," said Peder. "I'll lead Jack by his bridle. When I shout, release the handbrake and keep tight hold of the reins. We're goin' for it!"

The gelding sensed the gig's release and pulled hard. Branches and stones ground against each other, and the wind whipped floodwater everywhere. Peder took a deep breath and gripped Jack's halter. It was now or never. In seconds they were free.

The big man's sheepskin gilet was most likely lost in the Atlantic. He wondered how Mary Anne was doing. The wind had never let up and while the rain had lessened, it was still bitterly cold. A few jute sacks were stored under the box seat. Peder picked out the strongest, cut three holes round the edge for armholes and a neck with his Bowie knife and gave it to Mary Anne. She tied the potato sack round herself with a chord. In the sparse light of the gig's lanterns, she looked as if she'd been saved from drowning.

Peder took hold of Jack's bridle from the left hand side and walked the horse along the newly excavated road. They soon reached the Clancy's work site, which had been abandoned for the time being due to the storm. Peder called a halt. More jute sacks were pressed into service and wrapped round Mary Anne's legs. They still had two miles to go.

"The road is much improved from here on," said Peder. "Maybe another hour and we'll be there."

184

The rest of the journey passed without incident. Peder walked beside the horse, whispering words of encouragement until they could see the lights of home in the distance. They arrived at last, cold and exhausted but safe, each having learned a little more about the other. Peder felt he had finally begun to understand this sister-in-law of his, and for her part, Mary Anne had found a strength in herself she thought she had lost. In the final moments before clambering down from the rain-soaked gig, she whispered her heartfelt thanks to the man lying in a grave overlooking the Kenmare Estuary.

holding tight

he was never so cold
as in this rain, sodding rain, endless rain
which confuses his senses, freezes
heart and limbs
the woman beside him shudders
wraps what little warmth she can
round her shoulders, knows this man
has a strength she never suspected
a good sense she never knew

he *will* get them home – he's promised
he thinks of his family
the warmth of the thought sustains him

the injured pony stumbles on
inured to the rumbling of thunder
confident in the familiar gentleness
the calming voice of its master

the woman gathers coarse sacking
round her thighs, closes her eyes
holds tight to remembrance –
a sunlit view across Kenmare estuary
an old soldier's smile

Chapter Sixteen

Runaway

Vicious weather was sweeping across the bay that spring, but Calum's boat, *John Henry,* struggled in even the lightest winds due to a year's build up of marine growth. Peder and Calum had been planning to scrub the hull, ready for painting, but the March storms were getting in the way. In quieter moments, Calum imagined he could hear his father, the original John Henry Dunn, rebuking him for letting the púcán get into such a state.

sea-weedy growth creeps
barnacle-slow across hull:
spring clean needed

Tomorrow was market day and Peder had ten hogs to deliver in a heavy wagon – the first time he had attempted this feat. Both ponies would be needed. The new Rossdore road was not yet complete, and the first mile worried him with its steep gradients. It was dangerous to walk, let alone drive a fully loaded wagon along the cliff edge.

The sensible move would be to slaughter the hogs and let them bleed out overnight, before loading the carcasses at first light. If the wagon tipped over, he would lose the pigs anyway, along with the ponies.

"Hey, Mister Grumpy," said Calum. "This weather isn't going to go away in a hurry, so I'll be coming with you tomorrow. I'll walk up before dawn and don't try loading 'em by yourself. It's no big task when there's the two of us."

> lumbering wagon
> filled with porcine carcasses:
> ponies snorting

Peder and Calum parked the wagon at the rear of the market where Fergal the butcher made short work of unloading the carcasses, and even hosed out the wagon.

Next stop was the Sunshine Café for a breakfast of kedgeree. The trip to Rossdore had passed without incident and the pairing of Paddy and Mic had worked well. The only people they had seen were Clancy's labourers. Most of the gangers lived in wood shelters or iron-wheeled caravans along the way, and had just been getting up when Peder and Calum passed by.

187

There was shopping to be done and the two men never failed to trade words with girls at market, especially Katy Robins who kept the dairy stall and was the equivalent of the Rossdore Gazette when it came to news.

"Hey Ped," she said. "What's happened to that lad who was arrested for thievin' Tuesday afternoon?"

"Don't know anythin' of any lad," said Peder. "If it was that late, I would be long gone home. Was he local?"

"Don't think so," said Katy. "I'd never seen him before. He pinched a loaf from Corley's bake house and a man from across the road ran after him. It was so quick, you wouldn't believe. The thief tripped over the wall and bang! End of chase. The Civil Guard arrived after a lot of yelling and threw him into a cell, and that's all we know. They won't talk to anyone. I know they're scared of the partisans, but someone should ask questions."

"Why?" said Peder.

"That lad was very young. Boys of that age only steal if they're desperate. Maybe he's a gypsy, but there's none of them about in Rossdore, I swear."

Calum was quizzing another man at the same dairy stall about the theft.

"Black hair," the man said. "Sad looking. Barefoot, no shirt, just a filthy sleeveless pullover and one of those kilt things that my mam used to make us wear when I was but a nipper. No belt. I think that's why he tripped trying to climb over the wall. Mister Corley was straight after 'im but there was no fight left in the lad. He just lay on 'is back splutterin'."

"And the Civil Guard took him away?" said Calum.

"They 'ad to carry 'im, two of 'em. We ain't seen nothin' of 'im since."

Several shoppers had gathered round, wanting Peder to be the one to ask official questions The big man had endeared himself to Rossdore citizens thanks to the infamous fight involving the Auxiliaries, so it wasn't unusual for him to be asked to act as a go-between.

"We'll pop into the Civil Guard station now. Save us a good cheese," he said "A bit of that orange stuff and a slab of the hard white cheese for cooking. We'll be back."

> desperate thieving
> of bread-hungry stripling:
> hopeless endeavour

The station smelled unhealthy, especially out back where three cells were located. Sanitation consisted of bottomless iron buckets, which emptied directly into the stream. Only one man was on duty that morning – a Dubliner, too officious for Peder's liking. He smelled overpoweringly of tobacco.

After an unnecessarily long wait, the officer addressed the two men on the other side of the desk.

"Yes?"

Peder looked over his shoulder, then at Calum, and finally gave a flinty stare to the desk sergeant.

"We're concerned about someone," he said.

The officer shifted his stance and stood to attention. He'd seen Peder in town on market days. He wasn't known as the big fellah for nothing, and Calum was certainly no lightweight.

"Is there a problem?"

"Possibly."

The officer decided against any ridicule. The men didn't smell beery. Perhaps he should show some respect.

"You're holding a lad for stealing a loaf last Tuesday," said Peder. "So, what's the story?"

"Are you a relative, sir?"

"No, I'm Peder O'Brien, factor of the Portleán Estate, and I'm concerned for the lad's welfare."

"Begging your pardon sir, the youth is being held on remand to await the magistrate. As there's no courthouse here, likely it'll be heard in Bantry. The boy won't speak to anyone. We asked Father O'Halloran to help, but the lad has an aversion to uniforms, even a priest's garb, so we chose to leave him be for now."

"Has he been formally charged?" said Peder. "Folk in town saw the arrest and the manner of his capture. Some felt it was needlessly brutal."

"He's a minor, sir, remanded in custody pending the magistrate's decision. We tried to give him breakfast and supper and a medical inspection but he screams if anyone gets close."

"Has Mister Corley the baker pressed charges?"

"No sir. It became a Civil Guard matter when we arrested the boy."

"So he's being criminalized for the sake of two pennies?"

The sergeant was fast appreciating that Peder had the measure of the situation. Calum whispered in Peder's ear just loud enough for the officer to hear that it would be better to pay for the loaf and have done with it. He even took two pennies out of his gilet pocket and pushed them across the counter.

There was an awkward pause.

"No need for that," said the officer. "I don't know the connection you have with the accused, but as I see it, I'd be pleased for the lad to be taken into your custody, sir. He's so frail he could fall down dead right here in his cell. The problem is this civil war – we're right in the thick of it."

He opened the desk-top flap.

"Follow me. It's awfully smelly out back. We'll hose it down soon as you've gone. I'll see to the paper work and I'm sure Mister Corley will cooperate."

> big man makes demands:
> wary desk sergeant weighs odds
> chooses wisely

The lad was too ill to do a runner so Peder left him in Calum's charge while he went back to the market to buy a Naval-issue blanket and collect his own shopping.

"Bless you, Peder O'Brien," said Katy Robbins, handing him a brown paper bag of cheeses. "Let us know how you get on. We'll be thinking of the lad all week, so we will."

Calum had carried the boy through an alley, well away from the market. Moments later, Peder joined him and they loaded the wagon, settling the lad down as comfortably as they could.

By the time they reached the road-works site, the boy was sound asleep, despite the roughness of the ride across the moor. They stopped to deliver the bread, cheeses and vegetables ordered by Clancy's labourers, and Peder took the opportunity to examine the youngster. He hadn't moved at all, and now looked seriously ill. Peder took up the reins, ready to move on.

> sleeping the sleep
> of the grievously weak:
> ragged breaths

"According to that copper he hasn't eaten anythin'," said Calum, "not that I blame him – I've seen better pigsties. He wouldn't have lasted another week in there."

190

They quickened their pace as they approached the higher ground where there was barely a path, let alone a track. The massif was snow covered and the air bitterly cold. The lad stirred, wheezed and gave out a terrible cough so deep-rooted the fisherman lifted him off the wagon's floor and held him close. He was sure they were too late and the boy was dying.

Peder stopped the wagon. Calum's face said it all. They were about a mile from Peder's house and some three miles from Goose Hill. There was a chance that Lizzie might be out visiting a patient, but it was worth the risk.

"You thinking what I'm thinking?" said Peder.

"Goose Hill?"

"Hold tight, Cal. We'll get there."

The ancient moorland path was barely wide enough and whenever a stream crossed it, pools of blackness obscured everything, but the ponies sensed the urgency and responded well. Calum held on tight, and they arrived at Goose Hill within half an hour.

Lizzie had been about to empty her tin bath when the wagon clattered to a halt out in the lane. Calum carried the delirious patient indoors. Lizzie sized up the situation immediately. She stripped off the youngster's clothes and lowered him into the bath, relieved to see no serious injuries. The sudden immersion caused a coughing fit, which Lizzie considered a positive sign, but his emaciated state upset her. The boy looked like a famine victim.

skin-thinned and bony:
fragile boy bathes
between coughing fits

The two men busied themselves in and around the house, while Lizzie warmed and tried to feed the lad.

"Consumption, most likely," she said at last, having put him to bed. "He's far too young to be a war veteran. I doubt he's even twelve and the war ended three years ago. Must be a runaway. I'm not seeing any wounds or infection and the light bruising will be down to trying to jump the wall. The soup I gave him made him choke because he couldn't get it down fast enough. A doctor from the Naval Base should come out and take a look. They said if we needed help they'd visit and, you being Portleán's factor, I know you'll do the right thing for him."

"Now?" said Peder.

191

"Maybe in the morning. By then, I'll have the measure of him. Best you get home to Jo – she'll be wondering where you are. Be off with you now."

Peder never argued with Lizzie, but he didn't fancy asking for help from the Navy. Trading meat was fine, but the base was off limits because of the civil war and he worried about jeopardising his standing with the villagers.

He drove back to Goose Hill the next morning and was informed that the patient had slept well and been ticked off by Lizzie for wolfing down his breakfast of hot kippers and crusty bread. The lad certainly smelled sweeter and Lizzie had found him a shirt, navy-blue trousers that had succumbed to shrinkage and a black woolly. Best of all, she had discovered a name: Ed. She had no idea whether this was Edward, Edwin, Edgar or Edmund, but it didn't matter as the name 'Ed' suited him fine. The hardest task was getting him to say anything. He must have been raised in a place where talking wasn't allowed, maybe a workhouse or orphanage. She had no doubt he was on the run from the way he fought hard for every crust. He was thin, possibly rickety. She listened through her treasured stethoscope to his wheezing and decided to wait another day to see how he progressed.

An hour later Lizzie heard choughs outside making a racket, a sure sign someone was approaching. She looked through the kitchen window and saw Hannah coming up the path. Ed dashed upstairs. If Lizzie hadn't seen him go, she wouldn't have believed it. His footsteps made no sound at all.

"Only me, Lizzie," called Hannah as she pushed open the door. "I heard talk of a newcomer from the lads, but they didn't make much sense to me, so I gave 'em a *boxtie* apiece and came over to see for meself. There's a couple of *builíní* (loaves) for now and there's shepherd's pie in the slow oven which'll be ready for the eatin' by tonight. They boys can bring it over when they've finished scrubbin' that so important fishin' boat."

Lizzie had the kettle singing in minutes and the smell of newly baked bread was everywhere.

"The new arrival," she whispered, pointing upwards, "is upstairs, probably wonderin' what the smell is. He's a bit shy, but I doubt he'll stay up there much longer. Mmm! I fancy a crust myself, with maybe some of that dripping Peder brought down yesterday."

192

Before she could say any more, a pair of bare feet descended the stairs. Hannah's bread could undermine the strongest resolve.

"This is Ed," said Lizzie. "He doesn't say much for himself, but I think he could be made to speak over a slice of bread and dripping."

"Looks like he needs a good feed," said Hannah, "and I thought the famine was long gone."

"Sit yourself down at the table, Ed," said Lizzie, "and this time, break off a piece of bread first and then chew it thoroughly before you take another."

shepherd's pie
and singing kettle:
music to Ed's ears

The following Tuesday Peder made further enquiries about Ed among the market traders, but learnt nothing new. Donal the drover shared his thoughts with Peder over bacon and eggs in the Sunshine Café.

"Now don't be settin' too much blame on others," said Donal. "These things happen and likely will go on happening. Thing is, Peder, there's many a woman out there unable to feed their kin, often at death's door themselves."

Peder knew Donal had four lads of his own, all adopted, possibly from abandoned mothers.

"There's also another source you should consider, Ped, and that's boys desperate to get away from say the workhouse, or mebbe a violent father. I'm not going to point any fingers but I've seen boys turned out of a fine house, sometimes an allegedly holy house, a presbytery, and left to fend for themselves. It happens, Ped. Religion and young boys are poor bedfellows for all the wrong reasons."

Peder was still thinking on it when he got home. Lizzie's lightweight gig was outside – she must have brought the lad to meet Jo.

"Don't be dithering," said Lizzie as Peder walked through the door. "Calum needs a hand to turn the boat over so's he can scrub the other side. Tad Milligan's down there already. We expected you hours ago. Too much drinking tea in the Sunshine Café, I reckon. Best take the boy with you before he eats everything in Jo's pantry. No reason why he shouldn't help with the scrubbing. Go on, get that cart turned round, it'll be dark in a couple of hours."

Ed had a bit of colour in his cheeks now and Liz was confident he was on the mend. He was wearing a pair of Hannah's wood-soled *sabots*

193

and a cloth cap that was too tight for Calum. There were the beginnings of a grin about him and he looked keen. Lizzie was adamant, so Peder was happy to oblige. He took Ed outside and hauled him up onto the seat.

The track to Portleán village needed repairs after the harsh winter, and Mic's spirited dash had Ed gripping tightly onto anything he could hold. Stones rattled beneath the gig and whenever a puddle appeared, Peder whooped and hollered. Ed's face was soon splattered with mud-spots as the pony splashed through the standing water. Peder shouted to hold extra tight as they approached the stream that ran into the estuary. Ed saw the splash and instinctively clung to Peder's sheepskin gilet. As they reached the quay, Peder placed a huge arm round his shoulder. A trek that usually lasted fifteen minutes had been completed in half the time.

> wiry lad clinging
> to big man's shirt:
> puddle-bump and splosh

"Good, eh?" said the pigman. "Mic deserves his oats. Here, hand me that nosebag and you'n me can affix it to his harness."

194

Peder clambered down and lifted Ed to the ground.

"Now watch where you're treadin'. Mic here is a big lad and isn't past standing on your toes if he's kept waiting for his dinner."

Ed was still panting and at times coughing as Peder explained how to attach the nosebag. Just touching a horse was new to the boy.

"There's a pail tied to the back of the wagon," said Peder. "If you can untie it, we'll give Mic a drink of water from the stream."

Ed struggled to untie the rope. He was all fingers and thumbs and still feeble, but managed with help.

March was cloaked in sea mist that year, grey and listless. The scrubbing gang took advantage of the poor weather and got on with cleaning and painting the hull. When Tad asked what else was needed, Calum started them off on a second coat. *John Henry* had never looked smarter. She had bitumen up to the waterline and her topsides glistened with glossy black paint supplied by the Royal Navy.

Ed helped with varnishing the mast and spars. It was hard work, but the more he did, the more he wanted to do. He had graduated from tea-boy to boatman in a matter of days. Goose Hill was now his home, and Hannah had become 'Nan'. Calum was his guardian and Lizzie – who read him like a book – his foster mother.

One Tuesday towards the end of the month, Peder and Calum took Ed to Rossdore market for supplies. Peder had hogs for Fergal, and while carcasses were being offloaded and hung in the cold store out back, Donal joined them in the Sunshine Café. The drover had been making further discreet enquiries about Ed, but there was no news and Peder conceded that likely Donal had been right all along. Donal felt sure he was a child of Munster as he could detect certain inflections in his speech. There was also a more disturbing reflex as if he expected a beating at any time. Usually he hid behind Calum or Uncle Peder.

"You live with a person and soon, you take 'em for granted," said Calum. "Donal sees the lad just once and instantly detects his character."

Ed said nothing as he was busy demolishing a too-hot sausage roll.

"He's looking more laddish now," said Donal. "Got some colour in him. I'll keep asking round but I reckon wherever he was, he ain't goin' back."

> apprentice boy's
> destiny pulled seaward:
> salt-spray calling

A couple of Brendan's shires had dragged *John Henry* into the estuary to await the returning tide. She looked impressive under all that new paint, but Calum was more pleased by Ed's keenness to sail in her.

"We'll need to be up before dawn," he told the boy, "so as we can be in the bay and hunting the herring by first light."

They towed the púcán to the stone quayside, being careful not to slip on the mud bank.

"Take the end of the warp up onto the landing," said Calum, "and pass the end over that mooring post. Wrap it round a couple of times and I'll come up the steps and take it from there."

The tide was coming in fast. *John Henry* sat quiet on the water. Out west, a setting sun broke through the greyness of the Atlantic sky. Calum climbed the stone steps, having fastened the stern with a sliding rope so the púcán would always have water under her keel as she rose and fell.

"Tomorrow then," he said. "Your first time on the ocean. Lots of things to learn but don't be fretting some. I'll be lookin' after you." He put his arm round the lad's shoulder. "Thanks for all the scrubbing and the varnishing you did. I'm proud of you."

They walked the half-mile to Goose Hill through a glowing sunset full of promise.

Hannah waved from the bank the next morning as *John Henry* eased away from the quay on a soft westerly, the wake spreading behind her.

Ed sat next to Calum, taking it all in, listening to the sounds of the sea and feeling the breeze. Over his head, the red sails reached up the mast. He listened to the creaks and groans, the rattle and zip of ropes, breathed the smells, and wondered at the strange contraptions lying in the bottom of the boat. So long as Calum was sat beside him, he felt secure and unafraid, but when Calum asked him to sit on the other side he fell and landed in the bottom of the boat, spread-eagled over the lobster pots. Calum winced, and wished he had explained better how to move about in an open boat.

> red sails and ropes:
> mysteries of seafaring
> end with a ducking

"Stay still," he said. "Take your shoes off. You won't need them until we get back. Bare feet are best in a boat. We'll be stopping soon, probably in the lee of Muc Island. Climb over the fishing gear and get safe in the front

196

of the boat. Keep tight hold with one hand. When I shout, drop the anchor over the side and we'll try for a few flounders. The anchor's heavy, so be extra careful, but when I say 'drop', just let go."

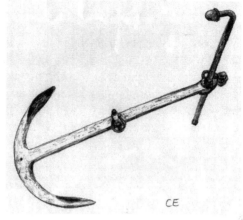

CE

Ed didn't know what a lee was, and had only the vaguest idea about anchors, but Calum was already lowering the sails so he was on his own. The water was gentle and he was getting used to the slap of wavelets and the wind in his ears. He grasped the gunwale with one hand and what he hoped was the anchor in the other, but when Calum shouted "Drop it – now!" Ed still had hold of the rope and didn't understand he had to let go.

Down went the anchor, down went the warp, and down went Ed. The sea engulfed him, shot up his nose and into his eyes and ears. He tried to shout, and took in a huge mouthful of water. Down, down he went, and because it was hardly five feet deep, he touched the bottom still clutching the hook.

Calum saw the sudden baptism by immersion and leapt over the side. He took hold of the panic-stricken youngster and hauled him to safety. Ed's mouth was full of brine, his nose stung and his ears roared. He couldn't stop spluttering, his entire body shivered and his teeth chattered uncontrollably.

"Sorry Ed. No harm done. Stay still a moment, I'll sort you out."

Calum hunted beneath the tangle of gear for the one life-jacket he carried. Ed sat still in the bottom of the boat as Calum tied the clumsy kapok contraption around him – something Calum never wore as he didn't like the way it restricted movement. He preferred to tie a stout line round his waist, hitching it to a seat or the mast when working in rough seas.

"You look like a baby walrus," he said. "One day you'll grow into it. Wave your arms about to keep warm. Sit back on the seat, hold on and keep my jacket over your legs."

The incident was soon forgotten. The sun shone, the breeze was imperceptible and the flask of tea was piping hot. Calum rowed through Muc Sound to the nearest lobster pot, and while there were no lobsters, Ed spotted a huge crab. It was the first undersea creature he had ever seen and it captivated him. The second pot yielded another crab, and after rowing to the next pot, Ed hung over the bow, keen to make amends for his involuntary ducking. Pot three was empty, and the fourth contained an undersized crab that Calum threw back. When Ed hauled the ninth pot to the surface, he couldn't contain his excitement and shouted out loud on finding his first lobster.

marine encounter:
excited baby walrus hauls up
snap-angry crustacean

John Henry moved out of the sound on an ebbing tide which would turn to their advantage eventually. The young sailor had recovered his confidence. Calum had streamed baited lines in the hope of catching bass or anything sizeable, so they tacked across the bay with the foresail raised to reach deeper water. The púcán picked up speed, frisky as a pony as she dashed through the waves, occasionally burying her bowsprit. Ed felt the power of her – she seemed alive, he sensed her, tasted the spray, heard the crack of her sails. When Calum shouted, "Ready about," he did exactly as asked, pushing hard against the tiller. Ropes were eased as they changed seats. Ed took hold of the mainsheet and Calum adjusted the foresail. Off they went, heading for Portleán. Calum was keeping an eye out for something very special – and there they were – porpoises – just under the surface, dashing through the waves exactly on cue. These were Calum's regular companions, though he'd never shared them with anyone else before today.

"Clamber over those lobster pots, Ed. Get safe in the bow, keep tight hold and look over."

John Henry was some two miles out in the middle of the bay and the púcán was flying. Ed peered over the prow. Hardly a dozen yards ahead, five porpoises swam with ease, keeping perfect station ahead of the púcán. The astonished lad didn't know what they were and had no idea such creatures even existed. They more than made up for his unwitting submersion and the fact that they had caught no fish other than a massive six pound plaice.

> five glistening porpoises
> keep pace with púcán:
> fisher-boy entranced

By the time they reached the estuary mouth, Ed had dried out, which was just as well as a pair of anxious fishwives – Lizzie and Hannah – were on the quayside complaining that the poor mite wrapped inside a hill of kapok was far too young to be out on the Atlantic. *John Henry* docked and Ed struggled to lift the plaice, which he was sure was nearly as big as he was.

Calum's world had acquired a son, possibly by default, but it didn't matter. He would be loved as if he'd come about by natural means. Lizzie would take care of him and Hannah would soon build up his puny form and fortify him. He had been to sea, one of the hardest places in which to survive, and he wanted more.

"Are you goin' to sit all evenin' long and admire this whale you caught or can we do the decent thing and turn it into a fish-pie?" said Hannah.

"Coming Mam and there's a grand lobster in the pot. It can stay there overnight. C'mon Ed, and not a word about your first swimming lesson, else we'll never be hearing the end of it."

Chapter Seventeen

Drovers' Road

to market

big fat pigs go to market
and 'opinionated'
don't come close

to describing
the grunting snurgling slobbery fun
of boars, bent on disruption

on charging, fat, fast and furious;
cannonballs, stopping as suddenly
wheezing and huffing

you'd swear they was winking –

with a lick of a tongue, a whispery wet smile
black eyes glinting

munching, strutting,
yawning, snoring –
big fat pigs go to market

Transporting pigs to market is never easy as a man might think. Swine have minds of their own and don't like being hurried or harried as their snouts embrace every bouquet imaginable, smells being uppermost in a pig's mind. Donal O'Dwyer would sooner have led a hundred cattle or a thousand ewes across the hills to Waterford than take a score of hogs down the road to Bantry, but these belonged to Peder O'Brien, and that made a difference.

Pigs were never displayed in the bidding ring as they were uncontrollable, but once the auctioneer's gavel smacked the desk at Rossdore market, Donal's tasks began. First he had to redeem the hand-written bill of sale; next, move the pigs to the wagoners' compound with all the patience, brute strength and guile he could muster. This job usually went to Donal's four sons, but today only one was available to assist. The mature boars didn't like being told what to do – they weighed two hundred pounds at six months and could run at thirty miles an hour, though they would be out of breath after two minutes.

"Forty?" said Donal. "Forty castrated boars to Cobh?"

"Goin' to London, wherever that is," said Peder. "They have to be delivered on the hoof in case they get held up at the docks and need extra feeding. The buyer says they've to be on the ferry tonight and in England within three days."

Donal screwed up his nose.

"Trucks and trains are killing my trade," he said. "Everybody wants to have 'em tomorrow or even sooner. It's a sad day for honest traders, Peder; all they talk about now is horsepower and how soon can it be delivered."

"There's a war on," said Peder, "and that's not helping."

"'Tis that same cruel wind that blows nobody any good," said Donal

Peder sucked cold wind through his lips, careful to be impartial as he never knew from day to day where other people's loyalties lay.

"Better listenin' rather than blatherin'," said Donal, as Peder mounted his pony. "Three of my boys are helping with the lambin' for the Earl at

201

Glandore. Tain't what you know Peder, 'tis who you know. I kept Matthew back in case we had stock to move in a hurry. All this political argufying ain't doin' us no favours."

"Sorry Donal," said Peder, "but they were sold in a minute, the whole bunch. Made top price and goin' to some smithy, I believe."

"Smithfield," said Donal. "Smithfield Market, London. Your reputation as a pigman is leading you to new fields. Don't be minding them boars, any custom is appreciated."

Peder handed five guineas to the drover and added a florin for Matthew, who was busy marking each hog with a blue crayon.

"Bin good to see you ag'in, Peder. Stay in touch." Donal spat on his own hand and clasped the pigman's in time-honoured fashion. "*Gártha* (Cheers). You's a good man, O'Brien."

With the responsibility of managing the Portleán Estate now in his hands, Peder was relying more than ever on the licensed drover for toting stock. The coming of motor and rail transport had paradoxically compounded a need for livestock movement, largely due to the ongoing failure of transport machinery and a lack of roads. English markets were still comparatively rich despite the depression. Even taking into account the costs involved, a seller could get thirty per cent over the domestic rate.

Donal preferred walking to riding, and could go all day dealing with strays, bringing them into line. A herd of cattle might stretch over a quarter of a mile, but sticks were never needed. Whistles, a shout or two, a friendly smack on the rump – or the most effective method, the O'Dwyer stare.

"Use your eyes," he would tell his boys. "Stare 'em out. They won't argue."

His sons were the offspring of prostitutes, handed over to Catholic authorities at birth. When they reached working age, Donal had

202

volunteered to take care of them. From the boys' point of view, it was better to have a law-abiding single parent than endless foster homes – or worse, the workhouse. He had named each lad after one of the apostles: Matthew, Mark, Luke and John, and their ages were respectively, sixteen, fifteen, twelve and ten.

The civil war was dragging on despite the best endeavours of Eamon de Valera, who was in and out of prison – but there were many in Ireland who couldn't abide him, and desperate men do desperate things.

Donal and Matt set off for the harbour, taking Peder's hogs in two open wagons, but were soon forced to stop at a barbed-wire barrier patrolled by a platoon of troopers. The unmade track to Coomhola Bridge was clear, so Donal was ordered to use that instead. As the wagons rattled round a wooded bend, four shots rang out and uniformed soldiers appeared out of nowhere. Both drovers hauled on the handbrake. Donal realised the troops were regulars and meant business. Republicans would have recognized him, but these men were professionals under the command of warranted officers and there was no sense arguing with them.

Donal was arrested and ordered to continue to Coomhola under armed escort. The band of Free State Troopers seized the entire herd on the grounds that they were needed for the war effort. It was the first time Donal had suffered a loss in his own country.

Matthew was left to find his own way home. Donal had always made it clear to the lad that in confrontations with the military, he was never to complain; he should do exactly as directed and never try to hide from view or behave in an aggressive manner. Matt obeyed his father's instructions to the letter, and promptly made for Peder's house.

desperate men

roads that should be safe
men who should be allies
pigs that should be profit
bridge across the river
track of ruts and ridges
argument unspoken

gunshots in the silence
soldiers slick with stealth

Peder was at home when Matt arrived. The lad was in some distress, and all he could say was that his father had been arrested for resisting a military order, but he didn't understand any of it.

"Best you make yourself at home for the night," said Peder. "We'll be up early come morning to go straight to Bantry to get to the bottom of this, though I'm sure Donal is quite capable of looking after himself. He won't be in any danger."

An exhausted Matt bedded down in front of the stove after Jo had fed him, and was soon asleep.

Rossdore was hardly awake as Peder and Matt trotted through the chilly dawn to Bantry. The road was still barricaded, so they took the track to Coomhola past the ambush site. They saw no one until they reached the village, which was swarming with Free State Troopers. The pair were ordered to dismount at rifle point. A corporal waved his revolver in Peder's face, which was entirely the wrong thing to do to a man who weighed twice his poundage and stood six and a half feet tall. Peder remained in control of himself however, and chose to ignore the cretin.

The two stared at each other for anxious moments, the impasse only ending when the corporal engaged his brain. The revolver was quietly holstered and the threat withdrawn.

"Where are you from?" he said.

Peder had considered the possibility of confrontation and what to do if it happened. He hadn't seen or heard anything of Sergeant Jackson for several years, but the big boxer he had felled in Rossdore Market with a swinging blow came to mind. Jacko just might be the man to deal with the situation.

The corporal was facing directly into the sun, and so long as Peder stayed where he was, the man struggled to see him.

"Where's Jacko?" said Peder.

The corporal's jaw dropped. "Staff Sergeant Jackson?"

Peder didn't reply, but the name had clearly rattled the man.

"I'll send a messenger right away."

"No," said Peder. "You fetch him yourself. I'll wait here. And another thing – where's my drover? Who arrested him yesterday? I want answers, trooper and I want 'em now, otherwise Sergeant Jackson is going to be an angry man."

cretin

give a stupid man a gun and you make him
stupider; taking away what dignity, what
commonsense he may once have had; his brain

is channelled away in the hot excitement
of wielding a firearm, brandishing it in somebody's face
who unarmed, is in no state to answer back

except with his wit, his sense, his insight,
his unerring methods of dealing with cretins,
deflecting the stupid away before
anybody
gets
hurt

Peder and Matt led the pony and trap to the sandbags. They found a seat and chatted to a couple of friendly auxiliaries while they waited. All the rifles had disappeared. Several cottages had been commandeered by occupying soldiers and a troop of junior offices still buttoning up tunics soon came hurrying out of one house. Among them was a beefy officer with an eye-patch, instantly recognisable as Staff Sergeant Jackson. Peder got to his feet.

"Ye gods," said the officer as he drew closer. "Mister O'Brien? The big fellah himself? Who'd've believed it!"

The two men hugged each other like Russian bears.

"Well look at yer, O'Brien; and a grand lad, too."

Peder explained the situation as the sergeant led the way to his temporary quarters. When Peder asked about the eye-patch, Jackson said, "No, no, Mister O'Brien, you weren't to blame for that. I got hit by a ricochet in Tipperary after I volunteered to join the Free Staters. If you'd a hit me again, I'd still be on the ground, so help me God."

It turned out that Peder's pigs were not in Bantry or Coomhola but had been taken to Macroom for further transport by rail to Cork. As a non-commissioned officer, Sergeant Jackson had limited influence, but he guaranteed the entire herd would be delivered to the shipping company next day.

The two men supped tea together, with Peder carefully remaining impartial within this stronghold of Munster. Finally they shook hands and Peder remounted. Jacko patted the pony's flank. If it turned out badly, both men would pay the price.

As they left the village and headed towards Bantry, Peder turned to Matt.

"Learn an important lesson," he said. "I haven't seen Jacko for some time but he remembered me sure enough. Friends come from both sides of the road and there are two sides to every road."

Jacko

recollection
of fist against jaw,
crack of the blow – fall

kinship fostered
friendship formed
a memory served well

Bantry Town was in an uproar when they arrived, due to a major disturbance in Wolf Tone Square. Peder left Matt out of sight behind some houses and strode into the mêlée to get answers. He could easily see over the heads of the crowd, and soon spotted a civil guardsman's uniform.

"What's going on?" he said, collaring the man.

"Confrontation between Free Staters and the locals. Most are ag'in the decision to support de Valera."

"I'm not siding with anyone," said Peder. "I'm lookin' for a drover who's been arrested on a trumped-up charge for treason, whatever that means, and –"

"Donal O'Dwyer? He's not here. Been transferred to Bandon. It's to be heard in a civil court, not military. Probably tomorrow."

The guardsman was jumpy. The crowd were looking for an excuse to riot and there had been rumours of firearms and knives.

"It's madness," he said. "Just listen to 'em."

Peder was only concerned with Donal O'Dwyer. "Are you sure of the location?"

"Positive. I watched 'em go. Supposed to be a Black Maria, but it was just a shed on wheels."

Peder thanked him and rejoined Matt. It would be a hard ride to Bandon; thirty miles with the light already fading. Some hours later, they booked into a lodging house – a cottar's holding on the edge of town – and later that evening walked the two miles into Bandon. They soon found where the Donal was being held.

There were two civil guards on duty.

"He's been charged with failing to obey a military summons, sir," said the constable. "The magistrate will be hearing the case tomorrow morning. Are you his legal representative?"

"Hardly," said Peder, who was barely literate despite having lessons from Jo. "I just want to know if he's bein' looked after proper."

"You can see him sir. Not nice for a man who travels the world – being shut in a cell, I mean."

"The lad, too," said Peder, "He's Donal's son. Lead the way officer, thank you kindly."

Donal O'Dwyer was trying his level best to keep his eyes closed against the overpowering walls of a cell that would have been rejected for use as a pigsty. He had a bucket, a single blanket, a candle and a woodworm-riddled door as a bed, plus old copies of the *Cork Examiner* and *Cork Constitution* to use as toilet paper.

"Well, who'd a believed, 'tis Peder O'Brien himself. How are you doin' big man? I'd make you welcome but you'll have to stand as there ain't room for a flea in this 'ere establishment, and who's there with you?" Matt squeezed passed Peder, though the feelings of relief were soon replaced with horror at his father's confinement.

Peder told the civil guard he would stay the night with Donal. "Just so long as you leave the cell door open. For sure, he won't attempt to escape or I'll larrup 'im."

"Begging your pardon, sir," said the guard. "S'not allowed."

"And why not?"

"You 'as to be a prisoner, sir. You 'as to commit an offence an' I 'as to charge you and when the guard's changed tomorrow, I won't be 'ere to 'and over the defendant to the court."

Peder grunted.

"How's 'bout," said Peder, "I truss you to one o' they fancy lampposts and leave you hangin' all night with icicles under yer nose?"

The guard backed away and shouted for someone to bring a revolver because he was being threatened. His request was ignored, but a second guard appeared and agreed that so long as Mister O'Brien promised not to do anything dreadful, he might be allowed to spend the rest of the night inside the guard station.

"One problem," said Peder. "The lad needs an escort back to the lodging house. There are too many trigger-happy troopers in this town at the moment. It's not far, just to the river."

208

He turned to Matt. "I want you up and about early tomorrow. Walk to the civil guard station and be ready to go to the courthouse. I'll be waitin'. No need to be scared – your father hasn't done anythin' wrong."

Matt wanted to stay with Donal rather than be escorted through town like a criminal, but he was used to doing as he was told.

"Will I bring the pony and trap?" he said.

"Yes. I don't know where your dad's horse has ended up," said Peder. "Probably with the troopers by now. Pity I didn't ask Sergeant Jackson, but we can call on passing. Keep the pony and trap at the cottar's place. Be off with you now, do as the guard tells you and I'll see you here tomorrow."

Peder had never spent the night in a house of correction before. The original guard station had been damaged the previous year, the blame being put on the fledgling IRA, but it could equally have been the Free State forces or the hated Black and Tans. He slept fitfully, turning the situation over in his mind before finally falling asleep.

Matt arrived early next morning. Their first port of call was a café for sandwiches and tea. The court session was set for ten o'clock and as it was listed as Petty Sessional, was unlikely to last long.

It was the first time either of them had been inside a courthouse. There were a few observers and a handful of court officials, and the place smelled overpoweringly of carbolic and polish. The sitting magistrate arrived, peered over his pince-nez and substituted a pair of black horn-rims. He started proceedings with an application for an extension of a drinks licence for a hotel, followed by four drunk and disorderlies and a case of salmon fishing by two poachers, which was referred to a higher court as it involved known felons.

"Next!"

"Failure to obey a military order, sir. Donal O'Dwyer of Ardagh, County Cork. Licensed drover. Pleading not guilty to resisting arrest. The case is being heard at Bandon due to circumstances in Bantry causing the courthouse to be out of action.

Peder sat stock still with Matthew on his right-hand side. There were noises from behind as Donal was escorted to the defendant's chair. It would have been a defendant's box normally, but the rebels had been busy and everything was in disorder.

"We've met before, Mister O'Dwyer, several times," said the magistrate. "I've appreciated your service over the years and recognise an honest man when I see one. Not like you to be inside a courthouse."

Donal didn't say a word. He knew landed gentry from all over Ireland and had shaken the hands of many of them. A corporal of the Essex Regiment was introduced as a witness but was told to sit down as this was a civil court and he had no jurisdiction.

"Is that it?" said the magistrate. "No wonder this land is in such dire straights. I'm not going to listen to further fiddlesticks. Case dismissed. I won't have a decent man blamed for the failure of the military. Mister O'Dwyer, your stock will be returned to its rightful owner and as you are a licensed drover, I will ensure redress is made for any animal taken from you, including wagons and tack. Can you recall where your beasts were seized?"

Donal spoke for the first time. "Coomhola sir – the junction. I don't want to be a nuisance."

"Nor will you be. The clerk of the court will deal with this. I sincerely apologize for the trouble you have been caused. Kindly keep me informed."

Donal nodded to His Worship. It was as simple as that. Donal knew landlords, estate owners and traders and took responsibility for thousands of pounds of other people's money, and Peder O'Brien had unexpected friends in the military. Matt sat deep in thought, mulling over the encouraging fact that it didn't matter which side of the road you took – friends were still friends.

along the drovers' road

> failure to obey a military order
> failure to stay a free man
> failure to transport his wagons of pigs
> along the drovers' road

> failure to answer back when charged
> failure to panic and flee
> failure to follow his regular path
> along the drovers' road

> failure to fall out with all his friends
> failure to commit any crime
> failure to falter, to fear, to give up
> along the drovers' road

Chapter Eighteen

Against the Wind

By 1922, the landscape was changing. Those who had survived the war saw it as a wasteland, unloved and good for nothing. The constant battle for food meant half the infants born in winter died. Survivors were trapped in a country reeling from recurring famine. British politicians had turned their backs on the problem, while demanding rents from people with nothing left to give.

bucolic

he rises at five
when cows' breath is scented with yesterday's hay
in the warmth of the byre.

heads toss, all eyes turn
to the young man who yawns and settles to his task,
breathes the sweet-milky air, feels
the murmur and pulse, half asleep
against the flank of cow

Saul Duffy, a herdsman from Ballyerrin, had walked the three miles into Tallow for the regular Saturday night ceilidh. The porter flowed, there were good things to eat and everyone was enjoying the *craic*. Saul had to be up at five o'clock the next morning for the milking, so planned to leave at midnight. He reasoned that by the time he reached Ballyerrin he would be sober, but a pair of armoured trucks arrived just ahead of midnight and as people left the hall, a squad of regular soldiers began arresting any man who could conceivably have been involved in an illegal assembly. Within seconds, Saul was felled, dragged to a wagon and dumped along with half a dozen other suspects; bloody, hardly conscious and soaked in his own urine.

He just was twenty-three years old. His friends were farm labourers. He didn't belong to any illegal organisation and had never understood politics, religion or war. When they arrived at the barracks, his captors tried unsuccessfully to force information out of him. Eventually he was dragged off the stone floor, thrown back into a truck and transported to Spike Island, Cork City for further interrogation.

It took a while for the circumstances of his arrest to become known. During this time, he withdrew mentally and spurned food. After a fortnight of starvation, he was force-fed and when he refused water, had a hose stuffed in his mouth, putting him in danger of drowning. He had become a hunger striker by default and could easily have vanished without trace. Being politically neutral, his protest went unnoticed, and he remained in custody for over a year as Ireland descended further into civil war.

incarceration

hidden
away
from
humanity

no
explanation

only
pain,
mindless
endless

isolation

212

He was finally released, unannounced, following persistent badgering by friends who had been unable to understand his detention. Along with a handful of other internees, all in a poor state, he was dumped on the quayside in Cork City on a cold and foggy night in late November.

During the Troubles, women volunteers were posing as prostitutes in order to gain information and send messages to and from partisans. That night on the Cork quayside, each of the former Spike Island inmates was led away by one of these working girls. No one spoke and the dense fog provided cover. Saul was taken through darkened, grimy streets to a terraced cottage where the girl fed him. Within an hour, he was sound asleep. He woke the next day to find she had already dressed his sores. During the five days he spent in her company, he never saw another soul. On the sixth morning, early, she told him he had to move on.

"When you leave, turn right," she said, "then left across the bridge. Follow the road westward. Likely you'll find friends in Kerry. I won't give you any names or addresses in case you're interrogated again. There's a change of clothes in this rucksack and a bit of money. Follow

213

the signs for Bandon, then take the train to Baltimore and keep moving.
'Tis quieter there. Look for work – you'll not go hungry in Baltimore.
May your god go with you, and be sure to forget all about me."

Saul found it hard walking on the cobbled pavements of the city after
a year in captivity. Hunger strikes alternating with a diet of stale bread and
water had left him anaemic, but he trudged on determinedly, heading
south across the City's two bridges and onto a tarred road with signs to
Macroom and Bandon. It was dark and bitterly cold when he came upon
an apparently empty stone barn where he decided to rest up and wait for
daylight.

unlooked for

the dark of a barn beckons
promises shelter
from November's bitterness.
footsore and frail, he sinks to the floor,
sleeps alone but not alone,
with a friend, not yet a friend

his dreams of warmth
turn nightmarish as memories
crowd him, he shakes in the night
twists and turns, lashes out

the horrors subside at last
he wakes into silence, not silence
hears breathing, not his own

"Who are ye runnin' from?" said a voice in the dark. Saul couldn't see
anything but was in no state to mount a challenge.

"Just waitin' fer daylight sir. On me way to Bandon."

He knew not to trust anyone. At the first hint of trouble, he would
run. He was cross with himself for calling the man 'sir' as it marked him
out as being servile – and after imprisonment he had made up his mind
never to speak that way again.

"I been here two days," said the unseen man, "waitin' fer the weather
to change."

214

"'Tis parky," said Saul, "and will likely stay that way fer several weeks."

"You're from Bandon then?"

Saul hesitated, before saying, "No – takin' a train to Baltimore."

"Are ye lookin' fer work?"

Saul didn't reply. He wanted to leave and not be involved, but was hampered by weakness.

"I wuz thinkin' on Bantry meself," said the stranger, "though I've never seen the place. I'd be pleased to travel with ye – sort of good companions, yer know?"

Saul's eyes had adjusted to the dark and he could make out a little of the man's features. He looked slightly older, unshaven, and a bit battered as if he'd been in a fight or three.

"I just spent two years on Spike Island," said the man, "locked up fer bein' a supporter of the Republicans. They arrested me in Clonmel just ahead of Christmas along with a score of suspects. I ain't seen any of 'em since."

"Then we've got somethin' in common," said Saul. "I was in E-block a year and three weeks. Fifty-five weeks, unbroken; 383 days."

"B-block meself – 'tis why I got no teeth. They put me in the kitchen an' to prevent us thievin' the meat, they kicked me teeth out so's I couldn't chew. Bastards!"

"I've been livin' with a colleen on Eason's Hill for a week," said Saul. "No names, mind. She wuz wonderful, though she turfed me out last night and told me to get out of Cork fast as the Troopers were lookin' fer sympathisers."

"I've been livin' with a lass in Sunday's Well. They must be jumpy 'cos she hooshed me out two nights back. 'Ere, was you one o' they hunger strikers?"

"The same. Maybe there's somethin' goin' on in Dublin 'cos me boat was full of repatriated prisoners and when we landed, this colleen seemed to know I was comin' and started kissin' me like she knew me. So – are ye thinkin' this is the end of it all?"

"Maybe the end of the fighting, not of the war."

"And we only have half a country," said Saul. "The fight will go on, surely?"

"Yer getting' to sound like a rebel. That de Valera man wouldn't like that."

"All these names, I know nothin' of 'em. I'm a stranger in me own country."

"I'm Niall Keane, by the way – 'tis good to know you."

"Saul Duffy, native of Ballyerrin, Tallow, where the sweet waters of the Glenaboy River flow. Not that I'll be returning soon for I don't trust that de Valera or indeed, any of 'em."

The two men shook hands.

They set off at daybreak, hitching a ride for a couple of miles on a farm wagon and walking the rest of the way to Bandon Station, arriving in time to catch the last CB & SCR train to Baltimore. A military unit was guarding the line back to Cork City as the IRA had destroyed a huge viaduct at Chetwynd, three miles from city centre, but Bandon was quiet.

"Usually gets in just after eight," said the railway guard, "but could be late with this fog. The trains are only runnin' from Bandon at the moment."

The train arrived at last and they climbed aboard. Poor visibility meant slow progress so they didn't arrive until eleven that night. They left the station in the biting cold and felt their way from the railway to the quayside through thick fog. The guard had suggested they look for a B'n'B on the quay.

"Not the first, nor the second," whispered Saul. "There – see? That house has a sign up for travellers. Let's try that'n."

"Looks friendly enough," said Niall.

The landlady, a Mrs Kerrigan according to the sign, looked nervous at having travellers arrive at her door so late, but she let them in and fed the pair cod steaks and chips, grateful for any money paid up front.

"Sorry about disturbing you at this hour," said Saul. "We had to feel our way to your house from the station."

"Wet stuff, this fog," she said, shaking her head. "It'll last till the winds return, you mark my words."

Niall enjoyed her cooking as he had no teeth to speak of and her supper scored top marks. The pair were given a tiny room that smelled of lavender, and Mrs Kerrigan let them lie in until eight o'clock the following morning.

"Will I be serving you porridge – or maybe smokies?" she said, as they came down the stairs: "Or the both?"

There was a short and wiry man at the table, tucking into a hearty breakfast.

"Don't mind Calum here, he only comes in when the fog rolls in," said Mrs Kerrigan. "He treats this house like his own. Now then, what's your fancy, boys? And if you're washing, there's two kettles ready on the stove and a sink in the bothy alongside; help yourself now."

"You do as you're told in Nancy's house," said Calum, "or she'll bate you senseless." The fisherman grinned as he shook hands with Saul and Niall. "And don't fergit to make your own beds. I get ticked off because I use Nancy's house as a home from home. I'm from Portleán, Bantry Bay and come in now and then to offload fish."

"We came on the train," said Saul. "The fog meant we didn't get in till late."

"Not surprised," said Calum. "November's the time for easterlies and the chill can make the fog hang around for days."

"I'll take a kettle," said Niall. "I ain't seen soap fer days so I'll go first, right?"

He found Nancy Kerrigan in the kitchen, relieved her of a huge black kettle and disappeared into the bothy. For a man devoid of decency for two years, the past fortnight had been revelatory. The girl who had looked after him in Cork had both shaved him and helped heal his wounds. He had never experienced such kindness before and hadn't expected to find it in Baltimore either.

Back in the dining room, Saul was telling Calum about his sudden release from custody.

"'Tis a terrible shame that people are fighting each other," said Saul, "claiming that they're right and folks in the same village are wrong."

"Much the same in Bantry," said Calum. "I sail round the Mizen to Baltimore if I've a catch to trade, but if they're destroyin' the railway, I'll have no chance selling fish in Cork or Dublin. Better to take it home. It's a good forty miles to Baltimore from my village. I don't mind comin' here; I like the place an' Nancy always looks after me but you don't know the half. It's like with her husband – he fetched a bullet last year in Dublin and was dead before he hit the ground, an' all due to this conflict that none of us understand."

"That's awful," said Saul.

"And that's not the end of it. There's a rumour goin' round of a military landing somewhere close; maybe in Baltimore itself involving Free State forces."

"Aw God, the hurry-up gang would have me back on Spike Island in no time at all. What's the matter with these people?"

"'Tis but a rumour at the moment," said Calum, "probably put around by the partisans, but I wouldn't put it past 'em."

Niall returned from the bothy and the three lads sat down together for breakfast.

"Why the glum faces?" said Nancy. "There's fresh bread, butter and smokies."

She poured tea into tin mugs and disappeared back into the kitchen.

"We came to Baltimore to look for work," said Saul, "though I doubt anyone is goin' to offer it. If Free State soldiers are due, maybe it's better we leave right away."

He said it with some regret, as the smokies were mouth-wateringly good and the juices delicious when mopped up with crusty bread.

"Tell you what," said Calum, "why don't you come with me and make yourselves useful? We're a small village, granted, and you'll never make a fortune, but then again, you'll never go hungry."

"What about the military?" said Niall. "We'd be sittin' ducks, sure enough."

"If they come – and I doubt they'd chance it 'cos the British Navy is in touching distance – there are places we can go. You'd be hidden for as long as it takes."

"How come?" said Saul.

"Because you know nothin'. That's why the Cork colleens told you to get out of the city in a hurry. The troopers can't invade at the moment 'cos of the fog, but that cuts both ways. If they can't see where they're goin', they'll have to stay still."

"But what would happen to Nancy?"

"That's a hard one," said Calum. "I can only offer, but can't make her go. I don't think anythin' bad would happen to her. Even troopers have a conscience where women are involved."

"She's an attractive woman, real pretty," said Niall. "'Tis terrible that her husband got killed."

218

"Ah," said Calum. "You noticed, then."

"Well aye, in a manner of speaking," said Niall. "What exactly happened to him?"

"A Cork man protesting in Dublin. Shot in the back by Regulars in a side street by Smithfield and buried in a pauper's field without ceremony. I don't know the full story as she won't talk on it."

"That's wicked," said Saul. "We fought for independence and just when we're getting somewhere, the country falls apart over things that don't matter."

"Politicians," said Calum: "Collins, de Valera, Griffiths and that Lloyd George. All we asked for was a decent land to live in and see us now – we're behaving like headless chickens afraid of our own shadows."

"You need faith," said Nancy from the kitchen doorway. "Believe in yourselves. You have to believe, else there's no sense to it."

"I'm thinkin' I could be sailin' soon," said Calum. The fog won't be completely gone but that's fine. Get round the Mizen and Sheep's Head, I kin find my way home easy enough."

"Room for one more?" said Saul.

"It'll be cold," said Calum, "and you might have to lend a hand with the oars if the wind drops, but the sea will be calm enough and the rowing will keep you warm."

"I've never been on a boat," said Saul, "aside from goin' to Spike Island in the dark. What's it like, Calum?"

"I'll show you soon enough. This faddy breeze has shifted west so it's time to get going. Say goodbye to Nancy. We'll see her again."

Niall looked through the window at the mist.

"Think I'll stay," he said. "That is, if Nancy will have me. There's things need doing round the house and if I can find a job, I'll give her what I earn. All I need is feeding and I don't eat much 'cos I don't have any teeth."

Saul could understand that after two years in prison, most of it on Spike Island, a friendship with a pretty widow in need had to be tempting.

"I'll take the greatest care of her," said Niall, "you see if I don't."

"Best you ask Nancy first," said Saul. "She might not like you enough to have you under her roof forever and a day. Look at you, toothless, all beat-up, riddled with rheumatism and that terrible cough; you're not actually a handsome beast."

"Early days," said Niall. "I'm gettin' better. Some more of that cookin' from Nancy, you won't recognize me."

Saul pointed to the kitchen door. "Let the lady speak for herself."

Calum left them to it and went outside to smell the wind, taking note of the leaves on the few plants that still had them. The sun hadn't broken through yet, but this run was never easy. Roaringwater Bay was well named, and it would take the rest of the day to reach Portleán.

Niall and Nancy

the pretty widow
doesn't talk much of the past
and Niall doesn't ask

kindness comes
in unexpected places –
a good heart, a plate of smokies
hope when all hope seemed lost

and as for Nancy, well,
Niall might not be much to look at,
not yet, but there's something about him

the others don't notice
a glance here, a half smile there,
eyes meeting, connections forged

The swirling fog was starting to lift and fishermen and harbour workers were already busy when Calum and Saul scrambled aboard the púcán. Calum raised the mainsail; the canvas creaked and cracked as he eased the black boat away from the quayside.

"Stay by the mast," he said. "You kin nestle down on those nets as I'm not fishing till we get back into the bay. Get comfortable in the stern – that's the back of the boat. Don't be frettin' some, I'll be lookin' after ye."

Saul was transfixed by the way Calum handled the ropes, and taken off guard when the fisherman thrust the tiller into his hands. He worried that he wouldn't cope, but his skipper was confident and got on with setting the foresail. The púcán left the harbour by Sherkin Island, passed through Gascanane Sound, keeping Clear Island to port before heading into the Atlantic. For Saul Duffy it was an adventure, with no time to think about seasickness. It took them four hours to get round the Mizen and two more to pass Sheep's Head. By then, a combination of tide, current and a freshening breeze had the black boat dancing.

"Nearly home," said Calum. "With the wind behind us all the way; we'll be at me Mam's table in another hour."

Calum hauled in the foresail as the boat had too much canvas to carry and water was already splashing over her lee rail. The wind increased as they crossed the bay. Saul had complete faith in his skipper, but the motion was making him feel seasick at last, and he sat slumped in a heap at the tiller. The wind howled through the sparse rigging and Calum braced himself, took hold of the stern sheet and pulled hard to centre the mainsail. *John Henry* slowed, though she could broach if Saul the tillerman wasn't up to the job.

"Keep tight hold of her," Calum shouted into the wind. "I'm going to reduce sail or we'll have water coming over the side."

Saul pulled himself up, grateful to have orders and something to cling to at the same time. Calum hauled down the canvas, tying reef-points too fast for Saul to follow the action. The fisherman stowed the foresail and came to sit opposite his apprentice.

"Are ye okay?" he said.

"O' aye." said Saul. "Twas a bit scary at first. It's knowing what to do I s'pose – don't think I'll remember much, but I'd like to. She's a grand boat."

"She was built at Portleán for me dad but he never got to see her finished. He was lost at sea off the Newfoundland Banks, fishin' fer the cod."

"Sorry to hear that," said Saul.

"See that red light next to the house lights? We'll be there soon. The waves lose power as we get deeper into the bay. The Royal Navy have a big base there, on your left, loads of warships comin' and goin' at all times, and –"

Calum stopped abruptly. He had seen a ship approaching and needed to take avoiding action. It came out of the dark so fast he wasn't sure he had time.

"Bastard," was all he said, grabbing the tiller from Saul and pulling it hard to bear away on the port tack. "He's not showing lights, no navigation lights, nothin', but I saw someone in the wheelhouse smokin' a ciggie."

As the vessel squeezed passed they heard the rumble of an engine. The only identification was the name *Helga* on the stern, which they glimpsed before she was swallowed up in the darkness.

"That was so close," said Calum. "I could have reached out and touched her. They're up to no good. Those rumours goin' round about an invasion by Free State regulars could be true."

"I've never been so close to a ship before. I could smell her."

"Don't be frettin'," said Calum. "I'm lookin' out fer you. From now on you're a fisherman. Take the tiller; we've a home to go to and me belly is grumblin'."

"Could she be headed for Baltimore?" said Saul.

Calum thought on it for some time before replying.

"Maybe she's spying. She obviously knows her way around. The Royal Navy would never risk a big ship into Baltimore but there's plenty of landing places in Cork and Kerry."

"I was wonderin' for Niall and Nancy."

"Me too. It's no easy thing for men to wage war, and fewer still who can put an end to it. We were lucky out there and it wasn't our doing. I hope it hasn't put you off sailing."

"Wouldn't have missed it for the world," said Saul. "When can I go again?"

Saul and Calum

Calum sails the wind
while winter rolls fog across Bantry Bay.
Saul knows cows, knows you can't milk fishes,
but when the sea calls...

something in Saul answers,
though the sea is cold, mighty, it swirls, crashes, thunders,
there will be no sweetness of cow's breath here,
just the wet heavy brine, the slapping waves

Calum speaks, half offer, half challenge.
Saul accepts, his life turns on the currents,
the roughness of ropes, the creak of the canvas.

Chapter Nineteen

The Young Man and the Sea

A few weeks later, the women were gathered at the Keelbeg dairy, their gossip good-natured, with the occasional barb thrown in for good measure.

"And where's our two brave fishermen today?" said Bridey.

"*John Henry* is fishing," said Hannah. "Maybe they found a shoal of the herring. No sign of Lizzie either, but I think she's across the river attending a birth in Carravoe village."

The fishwives tended not to say too much when their men were at sea. Unmarked headstones on graves bore witness to the terrible loss of life along Ireland's Atlantic coast. Hannah's own husband had gone missing between Nova Scotia and Newfoundland. Looking across the bay now, she couldn't see any sign of Calum's púcán.

absent fishermen:
windswept graves
look out to sea

"They'll soon be back," said Bridey. "Calum doesn't take chances, 'specially not after that incident with the arm a couple of years back. Will I ask one of Fran Milligan's boys to run over to Goose Hill and see if he's in sight?"

"I'll wait a while longer," said Hannah. "Fran has enough to do, I'm sure."

"Nonsense, it's what boys are for. I'll ask Rees. He's got his pony with him and will deal with it now, if not sooner."

Bridey hurried back to her cottage where Rees listened attentively. "Just an easy trot along the cliff tops as far as Muc Island," said Bridey. "I don't want Hannah fretting. Keep a weather eye open and if you spy Calum's boat, let Hannah know first."

There were three púcáns in total at Portleán, easy enough to tell apart as one had tanned brown sails, another other dark green, while Calum's boat sported red canvas. The other two were back at the quay by noon.

Neither skipper had seen Calum but it wasn't unusual for a púcán to be fishing a remote creek or harvesting shellfish. The two púcáns put to sea again at three o'clock to search for the missing *John Henry*.

Liam O'Connor, Frank's eldest son, rode to Carravoe to ask for a search boat to look round the bay in case the missing fishermen had followed a shoal out into the ocean. Carravoe had a vessel with an engine, which was just then offloading its catch, but her volunteer crew was happy to let go the lines and head back out to sea. A car drove to Castletown to ask for the Royal Navy's assistance in the search.

Just as the fishwives were starting to fear the worst, Rees returned from the far side of Portleán, galloping over the hill to the quay.

"I seen him – I seen Calum!" The lad was out of breath, the pony, too. "He's comin' so he is, just by Muc Island. But I seed him – an' Ed – def'n'ly seed 'em."

"You's a good lad, Rees, well done, I'm grateful, so I am," said Hannah.

Bridey reached up and offloaded the boy from the pony before hurrying to the boatshed's office to unlock the metal locker that contained the flares: red for emergencies, green for signalling the all clear. The rescue boats were out of sight, beyond Bear Island toward the Atlantic, but the signal would be fired as soon as the fishermen were home safe.

hope and despair:
green for heads knocked together
red for utter loss

224

Lizzie arrived from Carravoe at that moment and Hannah filled her in on the developments.

"Him again?" she said. "Why can't it be someone else's turn? He's fast becoming a pain – and Ed follows Calum like a shadow."

She told them the new baby had been a girl, and she had just been enjoying a nice cup of tea when Liam had arrived to tell her about the missing fishermen.

Hannah trundled Lizzie into her kitchen for a fresh and uninterrupted brew.

"Ah, I'd love one," she said. "No sugar, a splash of milk. Not the stuff that Calum drinks. His insides must be made of leather."

Instead of laughing, Hannah burst into tears, which was not like her at all, but Lizzie understood. The two women settled at the table with a fresh brew.

> a nice cup of tea
> to feed desperate tears:
> brittle bone china

"Panic over," said Hannah. "I'll leave you to deal with him when he gets back."

"We'll both be having grey hair at this rate," said Lizzie. "They're so vulnerable out there. I hate it when we lose sight of the boat."

"I reckon it's more to do with they porpoises than anything else," said Hannah. "It's bad enough when Cal gets a seal in his net. If they have pups, he spends an age-shooing them away. He loves sea creatures – loses his bearings completely if a whale appears."

"That's not the only thing he loses," said Lizzie. "When I try to say something about it, he pretends deafness or that old chestnut, he has to run to the toilet. He spends more time in that privvy than any other place in the house – 'cept bed, of course. He loves his bed."

"You'll stay for supper?" said Hannah. "It's shepherd's pie. I've used mutton and pork, a bit of watercress, and gravy so thick you'll need a knife to slice it."

She went into Calum's old room and selected a pan of mushrooms from under the bed.

"And some o' they," she said. "I allus knew that room would prove useful one day."

The day had begun innocently enough for Calum and Ed. The weather was kind, if a little misty, and the surface of the sea hardly rippled. Both master and apprentice now wore life-vests. These had been adapted from an original lifejacket, but redesigned so the wearer's face was now kept above water, enabling them to breathe.

The idea of fishing for lobster had been abandoned, and they had cast several lines of baited tackle from the stern along the foreshore by Muc Island. They were sailing under foresail only and the púcán was hardly moving when they heard and felt a huge splash. Calum instinctively reached out to grab Ed, assuming he had fallen in, but then he spotted the telltale disturbance on the surface and guessed what had happened.

swirling sea surface
glistens with stunned sprats:
hunters prowl below

"We've got company, son," he said. "Don't be afraid, we're not in any danger."

Ed was staring at the hundreds of bubbles on the surface of the sea.

"Fish – there – see? Lots of 'em," said Ed.

"Sprats," said Calum. "Keep watching. There's a whale in the bay."

Calum grinned. Ed had no idea what to expect but he didn't have to wait long. Bantry was one of the deepest inlets along the Munster coast and a whale was a-hunting. At first there was no sound but then, barely fifty yards away, the surface of the sea erupted, followed by an almighty *w-h-o-m-p-h* and an equally enormous *t-h-w-a-c-k*. It was over in seconds, leaving just bubbles and stunned sprats floating on the water. Ed gripped the gunwale tightly with both hands and trembled, his mouth open wide. Calum put an arm round his shoulder.

Minke whales were often seen round the peninsulas, usually in a pod, but this whale was a fin, a different breed altogether. When a second one burst out of the sea, Calum could see the identifying grooves running from mouth to white belly. He pointed out the dorsal fin and the twin blowholes to Ed as both whales cruised along the surface. It was exactly the way they were pictured in his treasured book of whaling. The whales were in danger of stranding in the restricted waters of the bay. It was true that sometimes they beached deliberately, but Calum believed this only happened when they came ashore to die in old age.

He wanted to warn the whales of their danger, but the púcán was no racer. Its only means of propulsion was the wind, which was in short supply today. The tide was still coming in and would be for another hour, so there were no helpful currents. There was a south facing cove, usually full of rotting seaweed and driftwood close by, so Calum raised the mainsail and headed for the gap, stopping the boat about two hundred yards from both headlands.

Ed let the anchor drop, curious to know what they would do next.

> red-sailed púcán:
> frail in the wake of whales
> risking beaching

"Keep the sails raised," said Calum. "As they're bright red, they might just act as a warning. If we need to move fast, we'll be good and ready."

He scanned the bay, but nothing was stirring. He had no real idea if the sight of a red-sailed púcán was enough to deter a whale from beaching. While they waited, Ed munched his honey sandwiches. Calum offered him his own.

"You have 'em," he said. "You're a growing boy."

Sali Roberts had brought a porcelain jar of honey to Hannah's house earlier that week and Ed couldn't get enough of it.

"Think we'll move on," said Calum eventually. "There's no sign of movement and the tide is on the turn. It will be slow going; just an easy zigzag across the bay as the wind is against us. If you spy a whale, shout."

The planned early morning fishing was on hold. While Calum understood that certain animals have to be killed and eaten, he drew the line where sea mammals were concerned. Many years ago, his father had given him an illustrated copy of *Moby Dick*, bought in a bookshop in Halifax, Nova Scotia. It remained on the shelf, unread.

Calum had forgotten he was responsible for a youth who hardly understood the dangers at sea. In his head, he was busy arguing the ethics of whale hunting when *John Henry* set off on another tack across the bay towards Sheep's Head, and Ed spied another whale – at least it looked like a whale. The lad couldn't shout for excitement. This whale was so small he thought at first he had imagined it. Ed knew whales were supposed to be huge, yet here was a tiny whale, hardly half the size of the púcán.

At last he found his voice. "C–C–C–Cal! Look!"

The red sail was stretched tight along its boom and fastened to a cleat, so Calum bent down to peer beneath the spar. He was transfixed by the sight of the baby whale, but knew he had to be wary. The mother would be close by.

The bay was three miles wide at this point with exceptionally deep waters. The fishermen were so engrossed with the baby whale swimming just beneath the surface, neither had spotted the tell-tale signs coming from below. Being on the starboard tack, the red sails hid the view, but they both heard it. *W-h-o-m-p-h*, went the porter-dark sea, swiftly followed by a thunderous *t-h-w-a-c-k*. The púcán shuddered from end to end. Everything was drenched in an instant. Stunned sprats lay on the surface amid thousands of bubbles, but nothing remained of the leviathan of the deep.

Ed watched in astonishment, half-afraid, half-reverential, dripping seawater, but keeping his hands tight on the gunwale so that he wouldn't miss a thing.

sea explodes:
man and boy drenched
in briny delight

Calum wiped his face with the sleeve of his *báinín*. The second adult was about thirty yards away heading for the open ocean. He held the púcán steady. The further whale was likely the mother. She moved effortlessly on the surface of the sea, swimming just enough to keep pace with the infant, and blew a spume of water. Another fifty yards on, the male broke the surface.

Within moments, all three had submerged and headed for the Atlantic, twenty miles distant. All that remained was a host of scavengers: kittiwakes, cormorants, seagulls and terns, screaming for the help-yourself food. Calum adjusted the sails and the púcán bore away on the port tack, keeping close to the southern shore. Ed could taste salt. He was soaked, but had seen one of the most powerful events in nature, and couldn't stop talking about it and asking questions.

Ed stayed the night with Hannah, apparently to assist with the early-morning baking. That was how Hannah explained it. Lizzie had been deeply upset by the whole incident, especially the search made by both villages and the involvement of the Royal Navy. Not only was it distressing, it was embarrassing for her as she worked in both villages. Calum needed to get to grips with his responsibilities. Being absent-minded was no excuse.

Lizzie can't bear it:
Calum risks too much
thinks too little

There was no moon and few stars as they travelled back along the well-worn track, the lights of Bantry just visible across the bay. They spoke in whispers and most of the whispering came from Lizzie. Her anger needed an outlet. Difficult childhood memories remained locked inside her head, but were never far away. Ed's arrival had given her an unexpected gift that she treasured, but today she'd seen that gift endangered by irresponsibility.

As they passed the memorial garden, she couldn't control her feelings any longer.

"You stupid, stupid man," she said, no longer whispering, not caring that anyone could hear. This had been building inside her all evening, and she let rip so bitterly that Calum stopped the pony-cart for fear she would fall off.

The fisherman wanted so much to hold her, but now was not the time, so he waited patiently; something all fishermen knew how to do well. He understood he had exposed Ed to danger when he should have been taking the greatest possible care. The lad had the right spirit, he was a trier and Calum believed that in time he would make a good fisherman, but first he needed educating, especially in commonsense. If Ed had fallen in the water close to a mother whale and her calf, no man could have rescued him; the lifejacket would have been no help.

Lizzie had seen the gravestones in the memorial garden and met the widows of men gone missing. Now she thumped her bare fists against Calum's *báinín,* but when at last he wrapped his arms round her, she clung to him without speaking, all fury spent.

Eventually, they both dismounted and walked the track to Goose Hill, one on each side of the pony's halter. The night was still warm with the softest breeze coming across the bay.

On reaching Goose Hill, they lay together in the big box-bed, in darkness, talking of sea creatures, of *John Henry* and of Hannah and of the latest arrival in Portleán, Ed Dunn as he'd become known, before finally falling asleep long after the oil-lamp had been extinguished.

old copper oil-lamp
brings comfort and solace:
lovers sleeping

Chapter Twenty

Honour Bound

Winter

Nights are narrow for Hannah, lonely
since Calum's leaving; she shrinks in the bitter rains
that chill the marrow. Cold creeps
through the house, its name is Winter, she has
known it too well too long,
her company is sleet on the wind,
a knock at the door, a clatter of hail.

Hannah didn't like living alone, especially when life came to a standstill beneath the cold rains and snow blown in on Arctic winds. At least she now had company. She had missed Calum when he'd moved out, so had been delighted to offer lodgings to his new friend, trainee fisherman Saul Duffy.

Saul had taken to his new trade with enthusiasm and he and Calum had forged a strong and trusting friendship – vital, as one slip, one single unguarded moment, could be fatal at sea. The Atlantic Ocean was unforgiving and Bantry Bay one of the deepest inlets in Ireland, virtually a fjord. Saul found it a stark contrast to the green wooded hills of Tallow.

The first time he had seen the sea had been from the bottom of a boat on its way to Spike Island – an inauspicious introduction – yet here he was, afloat again. The morning was bitterly cold, but thanks to Hannah he was wrapped in more wool than he had ever seen: *báinín*, dungarees with a bib and brace, long-sleeved underclothes, oilskins, sou'wester, and rope-soled boots. Calum had tied a rope round his midriff for safety's sake and lashed it to the mast to stop him falling overboard.

Saul was doing his best to memorise the correct terms, but at this moment all he needed, desperately, was to relieve himself.

"Gotta go," he said. "I'm in agony."

"You'll get used to it," said Calum. "Pee over the side before we leave and whenever there's a quiet spell with the fishing. Oh – and don't drink so much."

John Henry cast off and Saul raised the mainsail by himself for the first time, adjusting it as instructed.

"An' no singin'," said Calum. "We don't want no sea shanties when we're fishin'. I can't sing when workin' and nor can you as you'll be too busy earnin' a livin'."

John Henry had the breadth and depth of a more powerful boat and sailing her was a joy. She wasn't fast and would never feature in a race, but she had Saul in thrall – so much so that he even managed to come all the way round the Mizen without encountering the dreaded *mal de mer*.

Cattle had been Saul's lot for years, but incarceration on Spike Island had left him traumatised. Cattle were easy. You could talk to cows; they were living things and you could give them names. As a junior cowhand, he had rarely seen his employer as he had worked with two others and done the Sunday milking single-handed. He'd bedded down in a bunkhouse, been fed by a cook, and had undertaken a thorough ablution each day for sanitary reasons at his boss's insistence. Life had been hard, but good. Perhaps it could be again. He sniffed the air and put all thoughts of Sunday milking behind him as the wind dropped and the sea sparkled.

"Watch for the wildlife," said Calum. "Seals 'specially. And be sure to look up occasionally at those birds. Them black ones are your barometer. If cormorants are perched on the rocks, it means there's no fish to be had, but if they're diving, likely the pilchards or mackerel are feeding close by."

Right on cue, one dived below the surface. Out went the fishing lines and within minutes the pair had a silvery harvest of pilchards.

"It'll be warmer tomorrow," said Calum. "That's why the fish are jumping; coming up to the surface. Loads of food's being churned up from the bottom."

"How do you know?"

Calum touched his nose. "I know everything," he said, and grinned. "Trust me. I should've been a school teacher."

The tide turned as they passed Bear Island. The wind dropped and vast cumulo-nimbus clouds were massing on the horizon.

"Seals," said Calum. "Greys."

Saul couldn't see much at first as he had charge of the helm and the line that controlled the boom. Calum moved across the púcán and settled on the same side to point them out. The seals were hauling themselves out of the sea onto the rocks at the foot of the cliff.

"They're panicking," said Calum. "Something's up."

A pair of bottle-nosed dolphins came out of the water, close to the púcán. Saul jumped out of his skin and pushed the rudder away, causing *John Henry* to broach. With no forward movement, she stopped completely and seawater sloshed over the side. Calum reacted quickly and the critical moment passed. He knew it was his fault – he shouldn't have let himself be distracted when a novice had the tiller.

Saul was still shaken at the sight of the sea monsters, and could have been put off fishing for life had Calum not explained that dolphins were among the friendliest creatures on earth.

"They'll lead us safely wherever we go," he said, "and that cloud coming in proves my point."

He shipped an oar on the port side and the boat picked up speed.

"No harm done," he said. "'Tis all part of learning."

He started gutting pilchards ready for the fish-box, slinging the entrails over the side. Screaming terns followed like aerial kites.

"If dolphins are friendly, why were the seals clambering onto the rocks?" said Saul.

"That's because of what we call the pecking order. Whales are top of the order an' they won't harm you either. Then come dolphins, porpoises and next seals."

Calum carefully refrained from mentioning sharks, killer whales, squid or octopuses.

"It's like bein' in school," said Saul, "not that I ever went. Too busy with the milking."

"My boy Ed goes three times a week," said Calum. "Don't think he's too keen, but Lizzie insists and she's the real boss in our house."

Saul kept quiet. He didn't understand how families worked, having lived for his cows since he was ten. His parents were virtual strangers, and after he had been arrested and sent to Spike Island, no family member had asked after him. Likely none ever would.

At Sea

John Henry's keel courses
through the foam, Saul leans forward
in the bows as they beat along
the sea, against the slam of waves.

For music, they have the cries of gannets, the bark
of a seal, the keening gulls, the thrash of waves
against barren rocks, the ache of the heavy sea swell,
the depths, where the whales range
far beyond Calum's dreaming.

By midwinter's day, unseasonably warm winds had blown into the estuary leaving *John Henry* unable to put to sea. Endless rollers brought forests of weed and timber ashore, to be gratefully received by the villagers. Once the tide ebbed, carts and wagons were filled with green, brown and occasional red *dúlamán* (seaweed) to be dug into vegetable plots before the wind could blow it away.

After midwinter the wind eased, the rolling swell calmed and Calum and Saul put to sea again. They had a clandestine mission to undertake, under the guise of night fishing. It had been put about that they were searching for sturgeon, but in reality they intended to divert round the Mizen and sail into Baltimore to check on Niall and Nancy.

Saul was worried that he had abandoned Niall. Their time on Spike Island had been brutal, and he felt an obligation towards his former fellow inmate. He was relieved that Calum understood.

"Always on my mind," said Saul. "He was takin' a terrible chance stayin' behind. When the warders released us, I knew we had to get away, but I had no idea where. When that girl picked me out of the convicts, I thought she'd made a mistake, but she kissed me like I was family."

Calum listened without comment. Like most inshore fishermen, he rarely got involved when talk involved the civil war.

As it got dark, the fictitious sturgeon sank to the bottom, never to be seen again, though other fish had been caught to use as an alibi if need be.

It was early afternoon by the time *John Henry* slipped through Bear Haven and past the iron hulls of the Royal Navy. The púcán made Fair Head in two hours and laid a course to round the Mizen, fifteen miles distant. As daylight faded, the temperature dropped, and conditions looked set to turn to fog. The last beat would take them the twenty-five miles into Baltimore. If the outlook remained fair, Calum estimated they would reach their destination by midnight. He bedded down beneath the fishing nets leaving Saul to steer alone, though he'd been warned to wake his skipper before rounding the point. For Saul, this was an adventure – for Calum, a crazy idea, and not a word to Lizzie.

Saul roused his skipper just in time as *John Henry* thrashed round under a moonless sky, with spray coming from every direction.

"They don't like visitors in Roaringwater Bay," said Calum. "'Tis only the locals who are made welcome here. Maybe that's why they didn't attempt to land troops in Baltimore."

He told Saul to grab some sleep while he could, buried under a pile of nets with only an inch of African teak between him and the entire Atlantic Ocean.

The púcán passed Clear Island in darkness accompanied by soft curses from Calum. The breeze had turned and was now a bitter easterly, while the tide made progress difficult. They turned south to pass the next island in the chain – Sherkin – and dropped anchor in Horseshoe Harbour to wait for the current to slow. They had arrived too early, but needed to look round and check it was safe before venturing into town. Both men had the look of typical in-shore fishermen and had Cork accents, but there was still a chance they could be arrested.

Baltimore

Baltimore crouches on battered shores
round Roaring Water Bay, plundered by pirates
desecrated, re-built, surviving attacks,
harbouring fugitives, defying the odds
while its beacon stands tall, white, a pillar
of salt, guarding the storm-coast, warning
all-comers to stay clear, stay safe,
for safety in *Dún na Séad* is a rarity.

They waited huddled under the nets, trying to keep warm. When the current slackened, they pushed on into Baltimore and tied up at the fisherman's quay. A clock chimed five. There was no sign of the military, so they left the boat and walked along the quayside, deliberately passing Nancy's house before doubling back to knock on her door. She lived in a terrace with no access from the rear, so there was no choice but to wait in full view. They constantly checked the street for any possible challenge, their only protection being the fish hung on cords round their necks – Calum had mackerel, and Saul the much heavier halibut.

Nothing stirred, no lights or movement.

They were on the verge of knocking again, dreading the attention the sound must be drawing, when a small voice said: "'Tis early are you?"

The pair nearly jumped out of their skins.

"Well indeed, Nancy Kerrigan it is," said Saul.

"You'd be in a pickle if I wasn't," she said. "Will ye hurry inside now!"

She showed them into the scullery, lit a candle and stirred the stove so that they could warm their hands.

"You can't stay here," she said, softly. "The house is full of regulars. They're sleeping on the floor upstairs – Southern Company soldiers in full uniform, tin hats, and rifles. They're not allowed to remove their boots as they have to be ready for action in an instant. There's eleven men billeted up there and I tell you now, they're getting fish for breakfast, thanks to you two wanderers. I don't know what they'd be getting otherwise; probably toast and dripping."

"I can prepare the fish," said Calum. "Maybe fish stew. There's enough to feed 'em all and if we behave as normal, who's to know anythin' different."

"Where's Niall?" said Saul.

"Gone," said Nancy.

"So why the troopers?" said Calum. "Not the sort of guests you'd want, surely?"

"No choice in the matter. They rolled into town Sunday afternoon just like they were on a Sunday School picnic; three lorries and one of those chicken coops – armoured car things. There was a lot of shouting round *The Algiers* but they were banned from there. They asked the priest if they could stay inside St Kieran's, there being so much hostility from townsfolk, so the order was given to hire any lodging house at a florin apiece. I couldn't object – 'tis my living. Niall went over the back wall as they came through the front door. I haven't seen sight nor sound of him since."

Calum hushed her, conscious of the soldiers sleeping just above their heads. Saul was thinking about Niall. Baltimore was surrounded by the sea on three sides. Even with his limited knowledge of geography, he realised the only way out would be to go north, crossing the Ilen River at Skibbereen. With Cork City occupied by Free State troops, Niall was in danger, regardless of his loyalties. Either side would shoot first and ask questions later, and he would inevitably be regarded as a collaborator.

Breakfast came and went without drama. Nancy served, Calum cooked and Saul kept pace with the dishes. The soldiers were required to regroup in front of the slipway on the quay at 08:00 hours. By 08:15, they had commandeered two fishing boats and were searching the twenty or so largely uninhabited islands in Roaringwater Bay for 'irregulars' – men suspected of supporting Republicans.

Nancy meanwhile went shopping for essentials, washed bed linen, swept floors and generally tidied, happy the troopers would not be returning. She had overheard them grumbling about having to spend a night on an island in the bitter cold.

"You can learn a great deal by acting dumb," she told the fishermen. "The next place they're searching is Skull Town, which will be even colder."

When the sun came out unexpectedly, Calum and Saul went in search of Niall. By mid afternoon they had covered Baltimore's hostelries, the few shops, the church, and the quay where *John Henry* lay safely moored. Niall was nowhere. They returned to Nancy's lodging house as the sun set beyond Sherkin Island.

"No luck?" said Nancy.

Saul shook his head. His friendship with Niall seemed to have ended when it had barely begun. They had survived the rigours of Spike Island only to meet up by chance, spending just a few hours in each other's company. It didn't sound much, but in that short time Niall had become an inspiration to the younger man, and Saul needed to know he was safe.

"Niall's head was filled with terrible nightmares," said Nancy, "and it's not right that he should be killed for something he never did. I'm sick of this war, there's no sense to it."

She drew the curtains and went into the scullery to cook an evening meal for the fishermen.

"We can't leave her here," said Saul. "They say the net's closing round Munster and the Republicans are in disarray. I felt sick to my stomach when those regulars were talking about her. If there hadn't been a corporal keeping them in check, I swear they would have seized her and ravished her. They're evil bastards, the lot of 'em."

Calum raised a finger. Saul needed to show restraint.

He went into the kitchen, where he found Nancy in tears.

"Will you go with us tonight, to a safe house?" said Calum. "It might be cold for a time, though the wind is gentle enough and we'll take blankets and stuff. It'll take six or seven hours to reach Portleán but you'll be okay there. My wife Lizzie will be at hand and I already told Niall where we lived when we met before. I'm sure he'll find us. Maybe we could start again, build a new future, nothin' grand, though you'll never lack for anythin'."

"I've paid the rent to the end of the year," said Nancy. "It's due New Year's day, so I suppose I could leave Baltimore with a clear conscience."

"So you will," said Calum. "Tonight Baltimore, tomorrow Portleán."

"What if the soldiers invade your village?"

"We'd hide you on Bear Island, though I don't think they will, not now. Michael Collins is dead and there's definitely a lull in the fighting. I'm no politician, though I do believe de Valera holds the key to peace. If we can hang on a tad longer, Ireland will see a change, I'm sure."

Nancy blew her nose and dried her tears. "Will we be needing food?" she said.

Calum nodded. "Maybe a pillow, your clothes, anything you need to take."

238

"When will we go?"

"Now. There's hardly anyone outside. Soon as you have everything ready, we'll load the púcán."

John Henry was ready to cast off in the early evening darkness, but as Saul raised the mainsail, someone called from one of the sheds on the quay. Calum turned, instantly alert, and peered into the gloom. Chimes rang across the town, muffled by the mist which had returned. The sail hung limp. Calum could see nothing, and swore quietly under his breath, fearing the worst. He whispered to Saul to crouch in the bottom of the púcán and make sure Nancy and her belongings were safely screened from view by nets. He had the mooring line in his hand, ready to cast off when he heard the voice again. It sounded desperate, not the angry cry of a pursuer; more someone in urgent need of help.

"Wait will ye," it said. "Think I broke me foot. I'm comin', I'm comin'."

Calum let out the breath he'd been holding and hauled the mooring bight to the wall, tied it fast and waited as a limping figure dragged an injured leg along the quay.

"Niall!" said Saul, "'tis yerself. We've been searchin' all over town."

"Can ye gi' us a hand? When I went over the wall to avoid them Free Staters, I landed bad. 'Tis all swelled. I've been waitin' on yer behind that shed there, knowin' that as long as *John Henry* was still tied up, I had a chance to get out of Baltimore."

Calum and Saul eased him into the boat, taking care of the damaged leg.

"And Nancy, too! Will you get that?" said Niall.

"Shhhh," said Saul. "Get down under the nets with Nancy and keep yerself quiet, will ye." He couldn't stop grinning despite his stern words.

Nancy and Niall

under the nets, wet, stinking of fish,
cold-shivery, leaving behind
the tramp of soldiers' boots,
leering looks, spite, violence, fear –
and suddenly the stench of fish
feels more like sweet perfume, the race
of the waves a flight into freedom,
and here, beside Nancy, warm, comfortable,
a man called Niall, and somehow they're
holding hands, and Nancy thinks,
fancy that, but she doesn't let go.

Calum unloosed the mooring line and pushed the púcán away from the quay, turning her round to face west. He propelled the boat silently with one oar and the outgoing current took her out to sea where the full force of the tide pushed her deeper, away from Baltimore. A fickle southerly breeze made itself felt as they cleared the promontory.

"We'll get past Sherkin, squeeze through the sound between Clear Island and head for the Mizen," said Calum. "If we can get round the headland, the breeze will be on our side. We might need to row for a time if the current is ag'in us, maybe move out into the Atlantic to clear the Mizen, but if the weather holds, we'll be safe."

"What about the military?" said Saul. "Won't they see us as we pass Clear Island?"

"All they'll see is a couple of simple fishermen. As we close the gap, shake out the for'sail, and if the wind increases, it's southerly; on our side. Have faith in *John Henry.* We'll be home for Christmas. Nancy – pass one o' they cheesy *boxties* will ye, I'm starvin'."

240

Chapter Twenty-One

The Sound of Winter Murmuring

Sweeney

They slip through the net
these lads who aren't quite there
who don't have someone to care
that they're not quite right in the head
with a vacancy that fails to endear.

So no alarms raised when the church steps in:
Now that's how it should be –
nobody worry, the lad's all right,
the people see, washing their hands of humanity.

Christmas Day in Carravoe – and all twelve year old Caitlin Powell had to look forward to was a tough chicken, baked potatoes and a few vegetables for dinner, with junket or maybe a toffee-apple for afters. She was topping the junket with pear-halves in crab-apple jelly when her dad came in with some driftwood. Her mam was working miracles at the stove while little Dani prepared the oysters Dad had already opened.

"Mam," said Caitlín, "what was that boy doing when Mass ended last night; you know, the lad they call Sweeney?"

Mam couldn't say anything just then as she was concentrating on basting the chicken and laying shallots and carrots round her one-and-only deep dish.

Caitlin repeated the question, determined to get an answer.

"Didn't notice," said Mam. "That Sweeney is *aisteach* (strange); a bit vacant at times. You know – round the bend."

She regretted the words at once, as the boy was clearly backward rather than mad.

"He was dressed in a scarlet cassock and white surplice," said Caitlín, "and carryin' the cross during the service, right up to the final blessing."

"Maybe," said Mam, "the priest was trying to involve him in the service, like a special treat, but God knows why. He's a sad case."

Peder had been asked to supply a score of hogs to Cork City for the New Year and needed to get moving early. It was still dark when Tad Milligan, wrapped up in a naval greatcoat down to his ankles, arrived to help take the pigs as far as Rossdore. The early start paid off. The Sunshine Café was quiet as it wasn't a market day. After penning the hogs, the two herdsmen sat down to share a substantial breakfast.

"Are you knowing Liam Powell?" said Tad. "Lives by the bridge at Carravoe."

"The potter?" said Peder. "Well aye, not to speak to, but I know of him. Jo visits at times and I know he makes good stuff. What's on your mind, Tad?"

"Liam would like you to ask after a lad who was there for a time but seems to have vanished."

"What's his name?" said Peder.

"They call him Sweeney. Likely he's a bastard – no known father and according to Liam, no mother. A bit *dúr*, you know, dim. There was an old woman, lived on the shore in a timber shack, who took pity on him and fed him, but she died well before Christmas. Then he showed up at

242

the curate's manse, and according to Liam he was at Christmas Mass but nobody's seen him since."

"Probably being looked after by the priest's housekeeper," said Peder. "I don't know the woman, but these Catholics never go hungry. How old is the lad?"

"I'd guess twelve-ish. Clumsy, always talking to himself. Not loud. He's never spiteful, but few talk to him and he has this terrible cough. He hangs around the quay. Never goes to school according to Liam, and his clothes are pitifully poor. I wondered if you might ask after him, you being head of the village."

Father Cullen had been warned by Liam Powell to expect a visit from the factor of the Redmond Estate.

"Mister O'Brien it is? Will you come into the warmth? I'm Father Nick Cullen, curate in charge and though we haven't met socially, I've seen you going about your business."

The house was warm enough, but had nothing to relieve its plainness other than a wall of books. A fire burned in the hearth, with hissing logs and the ubiquitous peat beneath. A brass carriage clock, a ship in a bottle and a photo of a stern gentleman adorned a timber mantelpiece burnt black by years of use. Peder sat in the vacant armchair. There were no pictures on the walls, nothing to indicate it was a holy house, not even a crucifix.

"May I offer you a drink perhaps – a whiskey? Something to banish the chill?" said the priest.

Peder looked hard into his eyes, like a lion waiting to pounce, then shook his head. "I'm not a drinking man," he said. "It does strange things to me. Thank you anyway."

Father Cullen sat back in his armchair wondering what had caused this huge man to make the trek across the river. Liam hadn't elaborated, but you didn't trifle with the Redmond Estate's factor.

"Ordinarily," said the curate, "My housekeeper comes in and –"

"Mrs Driscoll," said Peder. "Next door to Liam Powell."

"You know her then?"

"By sight," said Peder. "Liam is a friend."

Father Cullen sat upright and clasped his hands. He changed the subject quickly.

"You do realise I'm not actually a priest at the moment?" he said. "I'm a deacon. In former days, we were known as curates-in-charge. I'm allowed to officiate at weddings and funerals, hold services, that sort of thing – but for anything more important I have to request a priest or a bishop. Trouble is, with this civil war, we're desperately short of ordained priests and sad to say, most have emigrated to the United States or the colonies. I'm a Coleraine man myself, Portrush, and everybody in Carravoe recognizes I'm a Northerner."

Peder didn't know where Portrush was and had never heard of Coleraine, but he could tell that Father, or Deacon, Cullen was uncomfortable inside his dog-collar.

"I wonder if I might have a mug of tea?" said Peder.

"Wonderful!" said the Deacon. "Now that's something that I can do."

He excused himself and disappeared into the scullery.

Peder took the opportunity to examine the ranks of books along the wall. Occasionally he spotted a word he understood, and was soon engrossed.

Father Cullen returned with the tea, saw what Peder was doing and inevitably assumed him to be a literary man. In this he was mistaken. Peder and Jo had worked hard with his reading and while the pigman had made progress, he would never make a scholar.

"I've never seen so many books together in one place," said Peder.

"You're welcome to borrow any volume you wish. I believe my predecessor was responsible for the collection, but he fled to Boston in a great hurry and had to leave his entire library behind."

Peder picked up an illustrated copy of *Treasure Island*. He wondered if young Sweeney had read it, attracted by the pictures. Halfway into the book he found a leather marker imprinted with a golden shamrock.

Father Cullen offered the mug of tea to his visitor.

"Will you make yourself comfortable Mister O'Brien, and I'll be putting another log on the fire."

The tea was good, sweetened with honey. Peder cradled *Treasure Island* on his lap. There was an inscription on the flyleaf. He ran his finger along the words carefully and could just make out: *To Sweeney. May you find your own treasure,* along with some words he couldn't understand concerning a Father in Heaven, and finally – *God bless you on your own journey. Father Nicholas Cullen.* Peder stared at the words. This was clear evidence that Sweeney had been here.

The Deacon had spent several years studying for his position in Belfast. He was young and had his wits about him. Peder on the other hand lacked the confidence to question a man of the cloth and soon felt he had to leave. He still needed answers, but as he trekked home he didn't know what to think about it all. Tomorrow was market day. Hopefully Donal the drover would be there to advise him.

Father Nick Cullen

The thing with Father Nick is...he tries.
But he's not from these parts you know.
He tries to explain, to do the right thing
but here he is stuck in this rambling manse
on his own sipping brandy late at night
bedevilled by books that glower down,
accusing, unforgiving.

He's always tried to do his best

but he doesn't feel welcomed.
These people, they're not his people.
Oh, they come to church, they worship,
they say the right things but some of them
are like the Irish giants of old,
they make him feel puny, helpless.

Sometimes he sees a spider, scuttling
into a hole in the wainscot

and he stares long and hard when the spider is gone
and he's left, abandoned again.

"You's a worried man," observed Donal. "You brought no stock and by the look of you, you ain't buyin' either. Tell you what big fellah, 'tis slow for the trading this mornin'. Let's get inside and I'll treat you to a pint. Only the one mind – I don't want no bother with the little woman left at home."

Peder grinned. Jo would know straight off if he had one too many – which was a shame, as the black stuff, now available from the barrel in Flattery's, was tempting.

The bar wasn't busy, it being midwinter. There was precious little livestock at the market other than a score of barren cows and five horses. The only enthusiasm came from ruddy-faced women looking for bargains among the chickens.

"Hardly worth coming," said Peder, "but I'm grateful for the company. I was hoping you'd be here as I'd like your thoughts on a matter."

The barman brought the tankards. They had taken an age to pour but the room had a glowing fire in the grate and the seats were cosy. "There you is, gentlemen. Are we taking the rest of the day off?"

Both customers raised their pewter tankards. "So we are, Mister Flattery; so we are."

Peder was unsure how to introduce his subject but, with a little prompting, he explained the circumstances of Sweeney's disappearance as far as he knew them, along with the inscription on the flyleaf of the book.

"I can only tell you what I've learned from neighbours and a conversation with the man of the cloth I had in his own house," said Peder. "I think it's called a manse; something like that."

"Am I right in thinkin' that this house is on the foreshore by Carravoe?"

"It is that," said Peder. "The man used to be known as a curate-in-charge, but now calls himself a Father. He says that when he's made a priest, he'll probably be moved to a big town or the city."

"He's a deacon," said Donal. "Like an apprentice, learnin' the trade."

Peder sipped his porter.

"They come and they go," said Donal. "They get a few shillings, a house and a housekeeper if they're lucky to feed 'em while they write next Sunday's sermons. It's a racket, Peder. Starts with the Pope, the man at the top of the pile. Then there are cardinals, bishops, priests, deacons, and a few more in between like monsignors and brothers. Cardinals eat venison. Monsignors get beef, bishops have lamb and the priest will have pork. Your man, if he's a deacon, will be dining on rabbit on good days and those brothers will be lucky if they find crumbs under the table."

"I'm not aiming to become a Catholic," said Peder.

"Good man. Best statement you ever made. Drink up, it's your round."

Peder nodded to the barman. "Can you put a whiskey in it for my drover please; he deserves it."

The talk moved to deeper things. Donal had been droving for years and his knowledge of life was invaluable. He assured Peder it was right that the neighbours had sought his help over the disappearance of a lad who couldn't look after himself.

"Thing is, Ped," said Donal, "children don't have a choice. They're brainwashed. Things are accepted without question; mainly, I s'pose, as

246

Catholics are all-powerful in Ireland. It's been like this for a thousand years and those who refuse to accept it are regarded as evil. Their leaders insist it's their divine right and you don't argue."

Peder was uncomfortable talking religion. Donal accepted his unease and wanted to help.

"Listen big fellah: I'll ride over next Saturday. I'd come now but I've a herd of barren cattle to deliver to Bréantrá Quay and you can't hurry 'em. Saturday would be a good day. We'll take a look at the manse and maybe ask questions. I'll start trotting early, and should be in time for a bit of breakfast. Now drink up and get back to that pretty little woman of yours."

Peder and Religion

This is where it gets difficult.
Peder? Church? There's history here:
Lizzie, and too many like her;
Peder's mother, her fate –
no wonder a gulf yawns between
pigman and church.

A priest – or curate, or deacon; Peder
doesn't know, doesn't want to know –
he'll get short shrift; there's
nothing the pigman can do about that.
And now there's Sweeney and somehow
it's all tangled up with the church,
it proves without proof that Peder's right,
or maybe he's wrong, he can't tell, needs wiser heads,
Donal, Jo, Calum.

The church? Peder?
A thousand times *no*.

Thursday was swill collection day; vital for the O'Briens' business. The Royal Navy had its own pier on the mainland but it was little used, and was now hidden behind timber beams, tarpaulins, massive mooring buoys and naval detritus. By the time the Peder reached the jetty, the Navy pinnace carrying the swill was tied up. Greetings were exchanged and metal refuse bins were returned by Peder, scrupulously cleaned, to be replaced with filled ones. Peder's contract to deal with edible refuse meant his wagon would be followed for several miles by screaming seagulls.

"Where's your mate?" said the bosun. "You know, that lad who lives in the shed there. We ain't seen him for awhile. I thought maybe he'd fallen in a bin and got fed to the pigs."

Peder was puzzled. "You can't mean Ed," he said. "No, Ed's in school now. I'm looking for a lad that's gone missing: vacant-looking, tallish, dark hair. The old woman who used to look after him died last October. Folks in the village have tried to befriend him but he's not friendly."

"Has a terrible cough?" said the bosun.

"That's him," said Peder. "Always talking to himself."

"Haven't seen him for a while. That's why I asked."

A dozen bins needed to be loaded in and a dozen out, all by hand. The army of seagulls had arrived on cue so the sailors didn't dawdle. Peder covered Mic's head with an ancient straw hat and Chip the dog sat safely beneath the wagon.

Before heading back, Peder stopped by the decrepit wooden shed. It smelled feisty and the door was on its last hinge, though the single-paned window was still intact. Inside were piles of driftwood, netting, buoys and lobster pots. When Peder's eyes had adjusted to the gloom, he spotted a grey blanket at the farthest end. Someone had spread dry sand to use as a mattress and several copies of the *Cork Examiner* and *Irish Times* had

248

been used as makeshift pillow. He got down on his knees and pulled out a blue cloth-bound book from under several layers of newspaper, held it to the light and ran his finger along the words: *The Adventures of Tom Sawyer.*

Outside, Mic was battling screaming seagulls, but the pony would have to wait. Peder was sure Sweeney had sheltered in the hut. Chip sniffed for a time, but found nothing.

Eventually the pony had had enough.

"Comin' Mic, I'm comin'; so help me I am."

The straw hat had disappeared, most likely filched by squabbling gulls. A few swishes with a whip, and they were gone.

The Shed

not much more than a pile of driftwood
hammered together, a makeshift roof,
window, door

someone's been in here

but already the sand is blowing inside
and the sea is ready to take back its own

outside,
seagulls, raucous, complaining
inside
blurred signs
secrets

On the way back, Peder thought of returning the book. It would be interesting to see the deacon's reaction, but it could turn out to belong to someone else – there was no inscription.

He stopped the cart in full view of the manse and knocked on the door, twice for good measure, but there was no reply. Chip growled. The pigman knocked again. Still no answer. He returned to the wagon. Mic, who usually waited without complaint, shook his mane. Chip sat still and snarled softly. Peder had a feeling they were being watched. He looked back at the house and thought he saw a movement in a window. An upper pane was ajar as if it had a broken sash. The wind was definitely getting up. They needed to be going. Peder put *Tom Sawyer* back under the box seat, gave the reins a twitch, and Chip leapt aboard.

The piggery should have been coal fired, but driftwood, off-cuts and salvaged boats made a cheap and plentiful substitute. Peder still would have struggled without the additional income from pigswill. He didn't need to separate meat and bones as they were retained and burned in the naval base to provide heating, but most of his evenings were taken up trimming root vegetables, the green leaves being poisonous for pigs. Maybe it was time to employ a helper. This could be a good job for Sweeney, if he could be found. The lad might be backward, but Peder was sure he could cope with a simple routine. He relayed his thoughts to Jo at supper.

Don't know him, she signed, *but yes, a boy would be good.*

Lizzie was there early the next morning, doing her rounds. She found Peder busy cooking the swill. He told her how useful help would be, as this chore took up valuable time. Lizzie thought the mixture smelled wholesome enough, but baulked at the suggestion of Sweeney as an assistant.

"Entirely wrong," she said. "Pigs are dangerous and there are too many of them for a simple lad to handle. Sweeney lacks common sense. I know you mean well Ped, but it's a job for a responsible adult, not a greenhorn."

"You know him then?"

"I know he won't let me examine him, and worse, has a brain injury. Some have tried to befriend him but Ped, he's a danger to himself and the only person who ever looked after him has passed away. Sad to say, this world would only incarcerate him and he knows it. It's why he lives rough. We should bite our tongues and walk away."

"Can't do that, Liz,' said Peder. 'It would be a betrayal. We did it for Ed, didn't we?"

"No comparison. Think on it; he's damaged inside his head. It's a nice idea but a wrong one. And another thing – I popped in to see Sali Roberts this morning. Sweeney filched some of the sheepskin off her beehives last Thursday. She knew it was her stuff because she always dyes it yellow. There he was, bold as brass, wearing it like a gilet, tied round with a piece of string. Sali's not a lady for gossip and was clearly upset. I said I was just goin' over the hill to see the O'Briens, and would have a word with the man himself; she was not to be worrying any. That

Sweeney is a puzzle but I don't think he's a thief. Sali worried that if I told you, you wouldn't rest until the problem was dealt with, but I told her no one else would get to hear of it and she could safely leave it with me. The thing is, Ped," she said over her shoulder as she walked away. "I've seen it all before; the failure of well-meaning schemes to make a difference."

"At least we know someone saw him a few days ago," said Peder, but Lizzie had turned the corner and was out of hearing.

After feeding his pigs, Peder hitched Paddy to Jo's gig and headed down the track to Carravoe. As Sali had seen Sweeney just last week, he should still be around. Peder determined to knock on doors and ask questions of anyone who might point him in the direction of the missing youth. Granted, he had filched a sheepskin, but that just showed the lad had a bit of spirit about him.

He left Paddy grazing the bank overlooking the estuary. All three púcáns were offloading their catch, so it was a good time to walk about and ask questions. An hour or so later he had learnt that everyone knew of the lad, recognized he had a problem and were gracious in their replies, but that was it.

One fisherman mentioned Midnight Mass.

"I thought the priest was asking a lot of the boy to be involving him in the service. Some folks said they didn't think it right."

Other villagers hadn't seen Sweeney for some time, but one man confirmed he had used the derelict shed by the naval pier.

"I seed him occasionally," he said, "especially when it rained. The old woman's place has been trashed you know, where he used to spend the night. Now that she's passed over, I s'pose he doesn't have a place to go."

Another villager said she had seen him on the road to Castletown, but as to where he was now, she couldn't say.

"He's a strange one, always talking to himself," she said. "Sorry Mister O'Brien, I'm not bein' spiteful. The boy needs kindness, not neglect."

"I'm workin' on it," said Peder, "that's if I can find him."

He drove the gig along the foreshore road to the manse. If anyone knew where to find Sweeney, it was the deacon. The place looked exactly as it had the day before. Peder got no response despite knocking on both doors, tapping windows and calling out. He peered through the ground floor windows. Nothing had changed.

There was no sign of any occupation at the naval pier and nobody had been inside the musty shed. Chip showed no interest. It was as if Sweeney had been a figment of Peder's imagination.

Donal arrived the next morning, good as his word. Jo provided a knapsack of goodies and the two riders didn't waste time, crossing the Carravoe Bridge, then past the fisherman's quay with a quick check to see if anyone was home at the manse. There was no sign of life at the naval pier either, so they climbed the pass. They separated where the snow hid the ground, but the only tracks were those of hares, foxes and stoats. The lower ground was soggy with melt water and the single-track road where the villagers had their peat beds was covered with brown slurry.

Donal stopped his pony beside a drainage ditch running beside the road.

"What are you seeing?" said Peder.

The drover dismounted. He didn't speak. It was an eerie place, hemmed in by the massif, with a small pool hidden by dead bracken. Something was floating in the water – maybe the bare branches of a small tree. It didn't belong there. Donal's pony whinnied and the sound echoed around.

Fearing his own pony might panic, Peder dropped to the road and took hold of its reins.

Donal clambered down to the edge of the pool. The water was clear at the top, but some brown detritus lay under the surface.

Peder shivered. A thousand feet up, despite the stillness, there was always a presence – the sound of the mountain, of winter murmuring. It was rare for him to climb so high. He made sure both ponies were safely tied before dropping down to the pool.

Donal raised his left hand and Peder stood still, listening to the low, endless tinkle of water. The branch had a yellowed sheepskin trapped beneath it.

"Hello, Sweeney," said Donal. "We've been looking for you for a long time. Sorry Ped. We tried."

There were tears in his eyes. He waded into the water and reached for the lad's body, hauling it to the bank before laying it gently on the wintered grass.

A body has to be reported and an inquest held before burial can be considered. Word soon spread, and Father Jack O'Halloran, a very different kind of priest to Father Cullen, arrived the following morning and was made welcome. Deacon Cullen was conspicuous by his absence.

"The case has been reported to the Civil Guard," said Father Jack, "and I'm happy to arrange the funeral service as soon as the coroner allows. I'm afraid we've been let down by my colleague at Carravoe. I enquired, but civil war is becoming the standard excuse for most things, Mister O'Brien. I'm so sorry, and saddened. Allow me, please, to make the arrangements. You may be sure the funeral will be both appropriate and dignified."

A few days later, the priest conducted a simple, open air service in the memorial garden in Portleán. It was a lovely sunny day with a hint of spring. The Sullivan brothers had made the casket, and Tad and his boys dug the grave. Carravoe folk might have thought Sweeney strange, but

253

they still mourned his loss. Four Royal Navy ratings carried the coffin from the bridge to his last resting place where Father Jack told the parable of the Good Samaritan.

Inquiries were made concerning the still missing Deacon Cullen and the future of Carravoe's chapel, but Father Jack couldn't speak for the absent cleric and the chapel doors remained firmly locked.

The following Friday, half a dozen men arrived before dawn with two flatbed wagons and a car. They stripped the pews, the altar and all the furnishings from the chapel, driving each load round the corner onto the foreshore. All the chapel contents were stowed inside the manse. It didn't take long. Four trips each, and the job was done. The only item taken away was the chapel bell, which was loaded on the back of a wagon. The doors were locked and a notice fixed to the front door saying the building had been condemned, citing water damage and claiming that due to the Troubles it couldn't be repaired. Villagers' attempts to get answers were in vain. Within the hour, the wagons had departed over the pass while the car took the Castletown road along the foreshore. Carravoe's chapel had been abandoned.

In the middle of the night on the first day of March, the wind got up and the residents of Carravoe closed their doors against an Atlantic storm. Liam Powell smelled smoke. It was strong and acrid, not a peat fire. He woke his wife and daughters Caitlin and Dani. Lamps were lit in the surrounding cottages and men emerged. Liam went round the back of the cottage and up the path to investigate.

"My God!" he said. "Somethin' is well and truly alight!"

Sparks were flying on the blustery west wind. Most Carravoe houses had slate or corrugated iron roofs, but some were still thatched with turf, so despite the drizzle, the sparks had to be dealt with.

"The manse!" someone shouted. "The whole place is alight!"

It was agreed there was no sense trying to control it. All that furniture stuffed inside was always going to be a funeral pyre. The roof went up first, then the entire front collapsed. The stench of burning was everywhere, not just close to the manse, so volunteers patrolled the village keeping a close check on the turf-roofed houses. Flames were attacked quickly with sleans, shovels and pails of water, using the ladders that were always parked beside thatched houses just in case.

There was little sleep that night. The rain continued spitting for some time after the blaze finally died down, leaving a smoking, steamy ruin. Rumours of the cause of the blaze abounded and there were whispers on every corner. Tomorrow was Sunday, but the chapel doors would remain shut. The bell had been filched. Enquiries made in Castletown went unanswered. The village had effectively been wiped off the map. Where was the deacon? Nobody knew.

Caitlin and Dani laid posies of snowdrops, crocuses and struggling daffodils on Sweeney's grave, and some village lads brought big pebbles to mark his last resting place. A proper headstone was soon erected, marked *SWEENEY*, paid for by the Redmond Estate. Father Jack O'Halloran held a simple dedication service, attended by five hundred men, women and children, many of whom had cared little about Sweeney while he still lived – but the priest's words about the Good Samaritan now struck home.

Looking the Other Way

Sweeney, we'll never know
precisely how it happened, how your
last days were spent,

what led you, in a stolen sheepskin
up this cold mountain, what caused you
to lie down in icy water.

255

Did you slip? We'll say that you did.
We'll say you had a sad accident –
it could've happened to any of us.

We'll not lay blame. We can't,
or our thoughts will turn inwards, we'll
see what we did, or rather,
what we failed to do.

Instead, we'll remember your finery
as you carried the cross at Christmas.

We'll hold that thought.
We daren't think anything else.

Chapter Twenty-Two

The Driftwood Tree

Siobhan O'Brien, Gabhal View, Portleán, County Cork, wrote the scholar in black ink, keeping her pink tongue firmly between her teeth. At five years old, it took time and several dips in the inkwell, and maybe too much space on precious paper, but it was the first time she had written anything with a nib.

Jo watched her progress with pride, signing her approval that not only could Siobhan write, she also knew her address.

"Well," said the big man, struggling with his emotions. "If I hadn't seen it with me own eyes."

Gravestones

Brambles bind the stones
drawing them earthwards,
toppling reminders of men,
their wives and children,
with names long forgotten.

Gabhal holds its secrets soil-bound.
Kith and kin come and go;
stone outlasts all knowledge

Gabhal had reinvented itself under the O'Briens ownership. The house had likely been abandoned at the time of the great famine in the 1840s, with survivors forced to emigrate. Peder hadn't been able to trace their history, but he had found a neat line of fourteen graves barely fifty yards from the house. The headstones were hidden by undergrowth and only discovered because Peder suspected they might be there. This raised the issue of how to explain such things to his children – he didn't want to frighten them, but neither did he have time for religious dogma. In the end, he simply told them no one lives forever, and was relieved when they didn't ask any thorny questions, but the discovery of yet another grave meant it was time to take professional advice.

Peder had recently struck up an unexpected friendship with Father Jack O'Halloran. The priest had been using his days off to work alongside Jez's labourers, but his Tuesdays were now free following the completion of the road so Peder asked him to take a look. Father Jack was full of enthusiasm and came armed with a shovel to examine the latest find. Satisfied that there was nothing else for it, the two men set about digging. It was a grand morning and conversation was more about the new road than the dead.

"I'm redundant," said Father Jack. "Look at me Ped – thirty-one Tuesdays of digging, not an ounce of fat, and muscles I never knew existed. What will I be doing now?"

The priest laughed and shook his head. He loved the Bible and would happily quote it at any opportunity, but he only wore his black cassock on Sundays. Tuesday was his official day off and for the past two years he had been wearing a working man's shirt along with his fellow gangers.

The newly-found grave lay just inside the boundary of Peder's property. He hadn't found any more headstones, but didn't want to take any chances. They had only dug down a couple of feet when Peder's pick struck something hard. He stood up straight, nodded at the priest, and the two of them began to dig in earnest. Soon they were uncovering bones in all shapes and sizes, and Peder realised they had found an animal burial pit, filled with the remains of livestock. The final tally included no identifiable human bones, just horses, cattle and pigs. By the time Jo signalled lunch, all the remains had been reburied.

Father Jack was repaid for his labours with a hearty meal, and Peder hitched Paddy to the four-wheel gig to deliver the priest to Rossdore. The last stretch of the new road had finally reached the town. Abandoned cottages had been flattened to make way for the new junction, something no one in the town had yet worked out how to use. Rossdore was built on high ground, which meant anyone needing to reach town had to pick up speed as they approached the new intersection. Warning signs and the concept of right of way hadn't been considered and there were as yet no pavements or drains, so nothing separated traffic from pedestrians. It would take a number of wayward wagons and near misses before the problems would be understood and solved, but for now, everyone was too caught up in the excitement to worry much.

hurley

whacked shins and purple knuckles
the jarring agony of badly bound sticks
clacking together, the crunch of determined bodies –

and they love it, the hurtling round the green field,
the shouts and delighted screams from the girls,
the blood curdling cries when victory is sighted

A small patch of greenery lay behind the Catholic Church within touching distance of the square. In winter it was muddied and threadbare, but in spring it burst into life. Father Jack was its custodian and because it was so precious, his parishioners gladly took on the responsibility of keeping it in good fettle. On summer evenings it rang with the shouts of boys playing hurley and the squeals of girls eyeing up the prospects. Rossdore had gone hurley crazy.

That afternoon, priest and pigman had the field to themselves. Peder had never seen a game of hurley, though he knew something of its complex rules.

"Played by men, right?" said Peder. "I hear them on a weekend. The noise!"

"Boys too," said Father Jack, "and they can be just as deafening. They can't afford real sticks so anything goes. Some tramp miles to find the perfect tree. Ash is best. I used to referee matches but got so many cuts and bruises my parishioners had to patch me up before I could celebrate Mass. You should come and watch."

Peder nodded, unsure where this was leading, and hoped the priest was still talking about hurley rather than going to church. He liked Father Jack, but religion was something he avoided. If he closed his eyes, he could still see that terrible place where his mother had been scourged on Garrah quay.

"I have to go Father – promised to call in and see Conor this afternoon. He's likely in the square already, wondering where I am. When does the game start?"

"Midday, every Saturday. They ring the chapel bell for two minutes before the rough and tumble begins. Be brave. No one's going to clobber you."

The two men shook hands.

Peder led the pony through the back street behind the square. Conor was already there and waiting. They left the pony and wagon behind the market and chatted about pigs, hurley and anything else that happened along. Conor asked a stall girl about the fruits on offer.

"Can't hear you," he said.

"That's 'cos I got a sore throat," said the girl.

"What's the difference?"

"We got strawberries and raspberries."

"Have you got laryngitis?"

"No," said the girl, "only strawberries and raspberries."

Peder had known Conor a long time. He'd met him on his first ever visit to market – toting a dozen geese, all those years ago, and it was he who had watched over Peder when he'd bought his first pigs. Conor, always the comedian, enjoyed Peder's company. After trading banter with the stall girls, they left Paddy snuffling his nosebag and headed up Kenmare Street to Conor's cottage for a bite to eat. Mrs Small from next door provided scones and raspberry jam and a freshly brewed pot of tea. They sat outside to enjoy the sunshine. The conversation was muted now that they were away from the market. Peder had things on his mind and they were not easy to talk about, but Conor waited patiently, understanding that the bastard son of Milly O'Brien would only reveal his burden when ready.

tea

raspberry jam, sweet, red and luscious,
a pat of fresh butter, Mrs Small's scones
baked not half an hour before, still warm
to the touch, and the slight melt of butter,
the splash of milk in the tea cup, the scent
of strong tea, the liquor the colour of peat,

and two men, patient, stoic,
knowing the things that must be said
will be said at the last;
waiting to find the right words.

"Must be going," said the pigman eventually. "I want to speak to Father Jack."

Conor nodded. He wasn't a devout Catholic himself, but if Peder needed to talk to a priest, he was undoubtedly going to the right man.

"See you Tuesday," said Conor. "And get there early. I'll be waitin' on ye."

Peder left Paddy grazing on the greenery fronting the field and knocked on the priest's door. He could hear singing inside, and had to knock again to be heard.

"I'm comin', I'm comin'," said Father Jack. "Can't a decent man take a bath on his day off?"

The door opened a crack and a bare arm and leg appeared.

"Peder O'Brien it is," said Father Jack. "We don't do bed and breakfast and if you's beggin', there's not a scrap of food in the pantry."

"Sorry Father; I'd be willing to wait outside but I need to talk to you."

"Even on my day off?"

"I don't have days off. Too precious to waste."

"Spoken by a responsible heart," said the priest. "Best you get inside, big man. It's draughty with the door open and I warn you, I'm not dressed for confessions, christenings, confirmations or funerals as my cassock is in the bath bein' washed."

Peder closed the door and waited for Father Jack to pull on a navy-blue sweater, regulation black trousers and slippers.

"Will you have something to drink?" said the priest. "I have a groaning shelf in my cellar but no one to help empty it, save meself."

"Just the one Father," said Peder. "I'm not really a drinking man. The ponies like a drop in their mash and I tip some into the pig's swill at times, but Mrs O'Brien has signed the pledge and she has elbows like daggers."

"I feel sorry for you, my son. Every man needs his comfort, and a glass of the black stuff now and then reaches parts that other beverages don't. My parishioners frequently leave bottles, so I'm obliged to partake.

I can't rely on my fellow labourers to empty them any more, now this road is finished."

Peder didn't know if this was a leg-pull or not, but he accepted a stone-cold bottle from the cellar.

"What troubles you Mister O'Brien? Not like you to be lookin' fer answers."

"I know nothin' of religion Father, but people say I need faith, so – what am I missing?"

Father Jack didn't reply right away. He had been told about a village on the Kerry side of Munster where, twenty years ago, a priest had drowned following an altercation with Peder. That village had since been abandoned and was now in ruins, but the memory of the dreadful events still lingered.

Peder sipped from his bottle, Father Jack likewise.

"Faith," said Father Jack, "is being certain of what you're hoping for, and proof of what none of us can see."

Peder frowned. The priest was talking in riddles.

"Don't you be worrying, Ped. I've been doing this job twenty years and I still can't understand it. Thing is, it doesn't matter. The way I see it, you display more Christian compassion in the way you go about your life than any crowd of alleged believers. I wish I had the same commitment. On Sundays I read a bit of the Bible and say a few words, but I never preach hell and damnation. I love these people. I give charity to the elderly and those unable to feed themselves when I can. That, to me, is Christianity. Now are ye understanding me? Bishops and Cardinals all decked out in their fancy costumes – what has that got to do with caring for people? I mind Nurse Lizzie – what a wonderful lady. She's seen the worst of humanity yet she's not forever on her knees praying to a God that never answers. She's far too busy saving lives."

Maybe it was partly down to the bottle of the black stuff, but Peder found he was understanding Jack's reasoning after all.

"Another bottle?" said the priest. "One for each leg. You can't hobble round on just the one – you'll fall over. I try to live my life like the Good Samaritan, doing things for people in need, not spouting from a pulpit. My parishioners are a rum lot and Catholicism is riddled with ritual and rules we're unable to keep. Even women are considered a temptation and have to be kept under control in case a man takes it into his head to marry one."

The second bottles were uncapped.

262

"Would you be playing chess?" said Jack, "I rarely get the chance. I've had a set since I was in college, but the only person who knows how to play is the housekeeper and she's twice my age."

Peder didn't have a clue about the game. He had watched men play dominos at market but considered it a waste of time.

Jack was already taking the pieces out of a polished box and arranging them on a black and white chequered table.

"I'll teach you," he said. "Excuse me while I recover another pair of bottles from the cellar. Here, take your boots off, Ped, your feet must be roasting."

"Well aye," said Peder, now into his fourth bottle of Guinness.

Father Jack returned with more of the black stuff. There were several references to beginner's luck, and as the evening progressed, something mumbled about four-leafed clovers.

The priest raised his bottle. "I'm jinxed," he said. "Banjaxed. Even Kitty, my housekeeper, beats me every time. Not a word now to anyone outside this house. I could be excommunicated and spend years in purgatory. What say you, big fellah?"

"'Tis but a game," said Peder. "You must learn my daughters to play."

"Ah, not learn. You has to *teach*," said Jack. "Besides, I couldn't abide losing to someone younger than me. Kitty would fall in the sink for laughing."

With the last bottle empty, Father Jack helped Peder up the step onto the gig, apologising to the pony for keeping him waiting in the dark. He tied a rope round Peder's waist and attached it to a stay to keep him safe. With any luck the coolness of the night would sober him up before he reached Portleán. He led the pony across the hurley field, round the corner, and through Market Square to the new junction.

"I trust you, Paddy, to deliver your master home. Mister O'Brien should be as right as rain by then."

He tied Paddy's rein to the seat, smacked the ponies flank and waved to the fast disappearing wagon.

pawn to king 4

> this game – a chequerboard cast
> of characters making moves
> across the land, fighting battles,
> pawns in the civil unrest that invades
> every turn, captured, killed, protecting

their queens, storming castles,
riding forth in glory... or gathering driftwood
finding the thoughtful way is the best,
the instinct for justice, for seeking
allies in unlooked for places

it's a quirky old game, and those who seek
violent ends will not prevail, will fall
into traps of their own creation, while
the pawns continue their quiet advance
and reach the end of the board – promoted
to whatever their hearts desire.

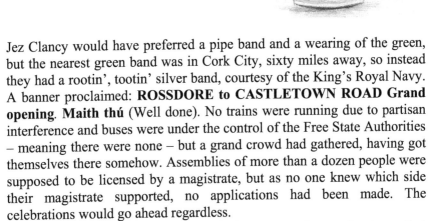

Jez Clancy would have preferred a pipe band and a wearing of the green,
but the nearest green band was in Cork City, sixty miles away, so instead
they had a rootin', tootin' silver band, courtesy of the King's Royal Navy.
A banner proclaimed: **ROSSDORE to CASTLETOWN ROAD Grand
opening**. **Maith thú** (Well done). No trains were running due to partisan
interference and buses were under the control of the Free State Authorities
– meaning there were none – but a grand crowd had gathered, having got
themselves there somehow. Assemblies of more than a dozen people were
supposed to be licensed by a magistrate, but as no one knew which side
their magistrate supported, no applications had been made. The
celebrations would go ahead regardless.

The Royal Navy brass band took the opportunity to play tunes that
hadn't been heard since the armistice – *A Long Way to Tipperary*, *Keep
the Homes Fire Burning* and *If You Were the Only Girl In the World*, and
there wasn't a dry eye anywhere when they played *Danny Boy*.

Traction engines had received a polish, a train whizzed round an endless track under flags and bunting, and there were numerous side shows – Tin-can Alley, Catch-the-Fish, Hoopla, Hook-a-Duck and a Donkey Derby, as well as a steam organ. The biggest crowds were gathered round Punch and Judy and a grunting, desperately fought tug-of-war. A mouth-watering hog roast and a hill of sausages kept townsfolk happy. Bottles of ginger beer, sarsaparilla, dandelion and burdock were provided for youngsters, with porter and home-distilled scrumpy for grown-ups. The celebrations ended with a ceilidh – reels and jigs dancing round a glowing log-fire and *sean-nós* (old-style) songs.

All day long wagons, cars, motorbikes, steam engines and horse-drawn carts passed to and fro on the new road. Inevitably there were accidents as drivers failed to look where they were going, but everyone was full of admiration for the navvies. They had begun on the top of a mountain in the middle of the biggest storm in living memory, and had completed the project on time. The day was a huge success and Jez Clancy was well satisfied, but the following Saturday he would have to prepare himself for an even more important occasion.

Father O'Halloran had taken his pristine white surplice from the middle drawer, cleaned his boots and had a shave. His housekeeper Kitty Donnelly was now polishing his bald pate.

"Vanity," she said. "You's worse than an old woman. 'Ow's about a bit of Mansion Polish to finish off? And don't forget the red carnation. Miss Boone is 'tickly fond of flowers."

Jez and Lexxie were to be married in Rossdore's church today. They were supposed to have requested permission of a bishop, but as neither was a practising Catholic, they had decided that was too big a hill to climb.

Ablutions complete, Father Jack walked across the hurley field and looked into the church to make sure everything was in order. It wasn't, but it would do. Everything smelled of flowers given by well-wishers.

At noon he took up his post at the junction where the traffic was still a pantomime with no one stopping or giving way. Detritus was strewn everywhere – bits of machinery, broken wheels, straw, cow pats, horse droppings, empty sacks, an abandoned rubber tyre, empty bottles, a raffia shopping bag and even a dead pigeon, but that was soon dealt with by mother nature's cleaners.

The priest shaded his eyes. There it was – a white-painted wagon bedecked with streamers and flowers, bringing bride and groom. Instead

265

of taking forever, the journey had been completed in an hour. There was no excuse for not getting to the church on time any more, thanks to Jez's new road – not that the groom had considered that fact when he had started to oversee the construction.

Father Jack had come equipped with his referee's whistle. Several sharp blows on the instrument did the trick. As the white horses came up the incline towards the junction, for the first time ever, the entire town came to a halt.

"Holy Mother," said a man. "Please your Reverend sir, could I be crossin' the road? Tis moider trying to get over at the best of times."

But Father Jack wouldn't let anyone pass, and nobody argued. The way was to be kept clear for the wedding wagon. When it reached the junction, the priest signalled for it to follow him to the front door of the Catholic Church. Bride and groom disembarked and Father Jack addressed them in front of his parishioners.

"Today, before God, I'm asking you, Alexandra and Jeremiah, to face each other and take hold of each other's hands out here in the sunshine, before we enter the place where you are to be joined in Holy Matrimony."

The crowd of watchers whooped and applauded.

"Who gives this beautiful woman to be married to this man?" said the priest, continuing in his customary unorthodox style to everyone's delight.

"That will be me," said Peder from his lofty position on the white-painted wagon.

266

"And are you good people witnesses of this wonderful occasion?"

Everyone was swept along with the sheer joy of it all – especially Siobhan in her bridesmaid's outfit, alongside page boy Tadgh Doyle, minus crutches for the first time. Best man Brendan Tate stood proudly in his best shirt and white tie, looking dapper despite having had to cope with the two shire horses, now being attended by Conor Connolly with nose-bags and a bottle of stout apiece. Jo O'Brien looked resplendent in a straw hat that had survived Queen Victoria's coronation in 1838. The only people missing were the youngest of the children who were being cared for by Fran Milligan, and several boys who shied away from the thought of a wedding, so had been left in Hannah's charge. Calum and Lizzie accompanied Minnie the housemaid from the Boone's house in Lizzie's gig. There was another wedding in the offing – Sean Milligan, eldest of the Milligan brood was now engaged to Minnie. They sat in the back, quietly blushing. Mary Anne Flynn still mourned Major Tom, but was coming to terms with the loss and was happy to sit with her sister Jo and their mother Martha. Celia Toomey played *The May Morning Dew* on the low whistle and Griff Sullivan filled the church with *Caoineadh cu Chulain* on the uilleann pipes.

Father O'Halloran kept looking over his shoulder, nervously expecting the bishop and his henchmen to arrest him and cart him off to gaol for heresy. He had taken a huge risk holding such a service in a Roman Catholic church, but was adamant he had done the right thing. If the bishop didn't like it, the priest would resign his parish and go work for Jez Clancy.

Bless me, Father

sinner or sinned against – lucky
the supplicant meeting a Father Jack
instead of one of the priestly caste
that fling fire and brimstone
at all around them for fear
that their own misdemeanours
may be found out.
the sins of the fathers, the wages
of poverty, the stench of the workhouse –
the undeserving poor
must bear the crosses of all,

hidden as if the sins done unto them
could disappear when hidden behind thick walls.

bless me father
for I have lost my child
and I know not what to do

When it was all over, the guests left the church in high spirits to travel
back to Portleán. Father Jack bowed his head and whispered, "Heavenly
Father, I don't know who I'm talking to, but I'm sure you're on my side."
He hadn't noticed a woman standing nervously a few feet away, and
didn't know she had travelled a long way to reach Rossdore. She had been
waiting all afternoon for the wedding to end so that she could speak to
him.

"Bless me father, for I have sinned," she said, her voice trembling.
"You need to hear my confession. I haven't been inside a church since I
was in the workhouse at Dunmanway, and that was a long time ago."

"You're a long way from home," said the priest, "and it's getting
late."

"Please Father, I'm not there any more – I work in a hotel kitchen in
Kenmare now."

"Pity I didn't know earlier," said Jack. "There was a party from
Kenmare at the wedding today. They would have taken you home if
they'd known."

The woman shook her head and he realised she wasn't asking him for
a lift back – she'd been crying, and really did need a priest.

"I don't normally do confessions," he said, gently. "It's like being
locked inside a dark cabinet – but there's a place beneath the window
here." He pointed it out. "No one else is about, so if you like we can sit
down and I can listen to what you need to say, face to face. How would
that be?"

"Thank you Father."

He took her arm and guided her to the window seat. They sat down,
and he waited for her to speak.

She blew her nose, wiped her eyes, and sat up straight.

"My name is Verity; Verity Driscoll."

"And I'm Father Jack O'Halloran. Welcome to my humble church."

Jack listened without interrupting to a story that could have happened
in any part of Ireland at that time – a terror-stricken girl, beaten by a brutal

268

and drunken father, raped and dumped in the workhouse. Her child, Edward, had been taken from her at four weeks and Verity had been moved to another town. When she had asked after her baby, she had been told he was ill and had been taken to hospital. She never saw him again. There followed a second workhouse, where she might have remained forever had the civil war not happened. Now, twelve years on, she had learned that a drover had been enquiring after a boy who'd gone missing and she was wondering if he could be her son.

Father Jack was in a quandary. 'Edward' wasn't a common Irish name, but he remembered Peder asking after a lad of that name, and Donal O'Dwyer had enquired far and wide. Could Ed really be the same boy? His adoption by Lizzie and Calum had been done with no formal papers but the best intentions. He wondered what he should do.

Verity herself provided the answer.

"It was twelve years back," she said, "and I realize he must be grown by now. I'd never interfere in his life. That would be cruel. All I want to know is if he's safe, healthy and happy. I only had him a few days and I never believed he was really sick. Two nuns took him away while I was scrubbing clothes in the laundry and I never did see the going of him. The manager claimed it was scarlet fever, but I knew that was a lie. They stole my boy."

Verity's words and manner persuaded Father Jack of her honesty. He decided to tell her all he knew. First, there was astonishment, then tears, and finally relief.

Verity asked if it would be possible for her to see Ed from a distance.

"No," said the priest, "I think you should both see him and spend time with him. He's been adopted by a caring nurse and her fisherman husband, goes to school in the village not far from here, and sometimes out in the boat with his adopted father. When he's older, I'm sure he'll want to be close enough to visit. Knowing the lad as I do, I believe he's set to become a fisherman in his own right. How would that be, Miss Driscoll?"

Verity took Jack's hands in silent gratitude.

"You'll stay a couple of days," he said, "in the manse. My housekeeper complains she's too elderly to look after a priest who's incapable of looking after himself, but if you're looking for a fresh start in life, who knows what might come of it? Ed's home is about ten miles from here, but I'll arrange the transport."

As a youth, Peder had gathered sea-washed timber in order to cope with the rigours of life, and the experience would forever retain a deep meaning for him. He had become a pigman, a breeder and stockman. Major Redmond had recognised his talents and invited him to become his factor – and a girl called Jo had seen even more in him, and become his wife. Above all, Peder knew with absolute certainty that *ar scáth a chéile a mhaireen na daoine* – under the shelter of each other, people survive.

Things were moving, and some would say about time too. It had been a long trek for Peder O'Brien and there had been pitfalls along the way, but the big man had survived and prospered. Rossdore had a new road and Portleán was no longer isolated. The foreshore had a certainty about it, a sense of optimism, a belief. Despite civil war and the bitterness it created, the villagers were getting on with their lives and making good. Jo was expecting a baby in the New Year and Peder couldn't help wondering if it might be a boy, but whether it was or not, the newborn would become another treasured branch of the driftwood tree.

The Driftwood Tree

Peder used to walk the white strand,
sand between toes, kittiwakes calling,
bleached wood gatherer working with waves –
but now the wood is safely gathered in,
little daughter Siobhan, has dipped a careful pen
into the ink and written her name;
Jo has found a home and a love
ever-longed for and never expected when
speech and sound left her life long ago;
and Milly... such sorrow, but maybe,
somehow, she knows that her son
has come home at last. Father Jack
says, of course she knows, because
life is full of such mysteries. Behold!
Look at Ed, look at Lizzie – how can it
not be so? And Peder shakes his head
and doubts, but then little Siobhan lisps
into his ear and he laughs and holds her
close to his heart, and all is well,
the branches have spread and nourished
his home, and he asks for nothing more.

~ End ~